PRAISE FOR THE TO'

"*The Towers of Tuscany* is a delightful escape to the Siena we
all love. Carol Cram has crafted a delicious story about
a strong woman torn between her secret past, her love
of painting, and the forbidden charms of her rich patron.
Hard to resist and highly recommended!"
—Anne Fortier, author of *The Lost Sisterhood*
and the *New York Times* bestseller *Juliet*

"Carol Cram's lush descriptions and intriguing characters bring this
dramatic tale of medieval Tuscany to life. If you love Italian art,
a feisty heroine, and a page-turning plot, you will adore this novel."
—Deborah Swift, author of *A Divided Inheritance*

"*The Towers of Tuscany* has all the elements of a wonderful historical
novel—a talented, frustrated heroine; a treacherous, feckless
husband; and a promise to a dying, much-loved father who orders
the heroine on a dangerous mission. Carol is a first-rate storyteller.
The research is well done. Every chapter displays a fine knowledge
of painting techniques of the fourteenth century, and customs and
mores of the age. The details of dress, fabric, and food are flawless.
The clever dialogue and fast pace make the novel zing along."
—Roberta Rich, author of *The Midwife of Venice*
and *The Harem Midwife*

"From the very first page Carol M. Cram captivates with her
writing . . . The twists and turns of the plot and the fast pace of
the writing make it a book that is very hard to put down. I highly
recommend this book as a must read and wish this debut novelist
great success with her career. She is definitely an author to watch
and has earned a firm fan who will be buying her next book."
—Janis Pegrum Smith, *Historical Novel Society Review*

THE TOWERS
OF
TUSCANY

Carol M. Cram

LAKE UNION
PUBLISHING

Published by Lake Union Publishing, Seattle

www.apub.com

Amazon, the Amazon logo, and Lake Union Publishing are trademarks of Amazon.com, Inc., or its affiliates.

ISBN-13: 9781477827215
ISBN-10: 1477827218

Cover design by *the*BookDesigners

Library of Congress Control Number: 2014945026

Printed in the United States of America

For my dad, who is always with me.

PART ONE

San Gimignano, Tuscany
March 1338

CHAPTER ONE

*The occupation known as painting calls for
imagination, and skill of hand . . . presenting to
plain sight what does not actually exist.*
—Cennino d'Andrea Cennini,
Il Libro dell'Arte, Chapter I

ofia did not blame her father for allowing her to marry Giorgio,
but not a day went by when she did not blame herself.

Every night as Giorgio grunted and thrust, she imagined
wrapping her hands around his thick neck and squeezing. His dull
eyes would widen in the moonlight, then bulge as she dug her
thumbs into the swell of his throat and smiled when his lips turned
a pale, pure blue.

But most of the time, Sofia tried not to think about him at all.

A shaft of sunlight fell across the small panel of the Nativity she
was painting. Sofia snuffed out the candle and paused a moment to
watch a curl of smoke spiral to the wooden rafters. She wanted to
be the smoke—light enough to escape through the tower window
and out into the fields, away from her husband, away from San
Gimignano, away from her household with its incessant demands,
away to paint every day in peace. But such thoughts were fancy,

and hadn't her father scolded her often enough for preferring fancy over fact?

Sighing, she loaded one of her smallest miniver brushes with *terre-verte*. Giorgio was out hunting, which meant she had until the next bells to paint. Using tiny, precise strokes, she added touches of the green-tinged pigment under the Virgin's chin and down her neck to suggest a shadow. Delicately, between two fingers, the Holy Mother lifted the fold of a sheet. Sofia added more white lead to the edge of the sheet to give it the illusion of movement, catching Mary at the moment she leaned forward to keep her child warm. Sofia wondered if she would ever lean over her own child, hear its cries, feel her heart swell with the love Caterina was always rattling on about.

She hoped not.

The bells for nones caught her by surprise, as they always did. The only part of her day, her week, worth living was already over. She pushed back from the table and rose to her feet. Massaging a knot in her shoulder with one hand, she stepped to the narrow window. Between the two closest towers, the countryside beyond the town was just visible as a slit of green and gold. The commune of San Gimignano fairly bristled with towers—more than seventy the last time Sofia counted. Day after day, the pounding and clang-ing of endless construction filled the air, along with dust so thick that on windless afternoons citizens squinted across the Piazza della Cisterna.

"Wife!"

Sofia gasped. Giorgio sounded as if he were halfway up the first set of ladders. She looked at her hands. A daub of ocher streaked one finger, a parody of the late afternoon sunlight flooding the tower room. If her husband made it up the ladders, he would destroy the pigments and brushes, destroy the painting even. *No!* He would never be so stupid. The small panel of the Nativity belonged to her father. Even Giorgio knew enough about the painter's trade to respect the rights of a patron. And he would never dare anger her father.

But he could make sure she never painted again.

Sofia picked up a corner of her smock and rubbed at her stained finger. The paint was still wet enough to smear. She spat, rubbed, spat again until finally the yellow lifted. Her hands would pass inspection if Giorgio didn't look too closely. Fortunately, he rarely looked closely at anything.

"What the devil are you doing up there?" Giorgio was barely able to gasp out the words.

For the moment, she was safe. He didn't sound capable of making it to the second level, never mind the third. Giorgio was getting heavier by the day. One night he would fall to sleep on top of her. And then what? If she couldn't rouse Paulina from her pallet at the foot of the bed, she would perish.

"Forgive me, husband!" she called as she ripped off her smock and smoothed her hair. God willing, she didn't have paint on her face. She took a last look at the painting. It was good—maybe even her best work. Would her father agree? He was a harsh critic.

She stepped to the opening in the floor, placed one foot on the first rung, then began to descend. She reached the final rung of the middle set of ladders just as Giorgio was squeezing through the opening in the floor to flop, panting and sweating, onto the landing. She saw at once that he had not spent his day hunting boar or anything else, save a happy turn of the dice. Was that blood on his jaw? Had he been fighting again? How many florins had he gambled away with the sun not even close to the horizon?

"You must ask your father to help us," he said as he rose to his feet, still gulping for breath.

"I wasn't aware we needed help."

Giorgio balled his fists and moved closer. She smelled stale wine and put one hand to her nose. A slight whiff of egg tempera still lingered on her skin. Relief was making her bold. If Giorgio had not yet asked what she'd been doing at the top of the tower, he was unlikely to. He hadn't the wit to concentrate on more than one thing at a time, which was why his saffron-exporting business was falling into ruin. They would be lucky to keep the house with its convenient tower past her twenty-first birthday.

"Go to your father and remind him of his duty to you." Mud streaked the bottom of Giorgio's gown, and a purple bruise bloomed beneath the blood on his chin.

"What duty, husband? You have the keeping of me, not my father." Sofia hoped the wretch on the receiving end of Giorgio's fist would not denounce him. They could ill afford the fine levied by the *podestà* for brawling. She squeezed past him and began to descend the last set of ladders. "Come for supper. Cook's dressed a capon."

"I won't be ignored in my own house!"

"Lower your voice. The servants." At the bottom of the ladder, Sofia descended an outdoor staircase, then crossed the loggia to the bedchamber. She heard Giorgio swear as his boots hit the wooden floor at the base of the staircase.

"When do you next go to your father?" he asked as he lumbered into the room, still huffing.

"My father's been busy for weeks completing a fresco at the house of Messer Delpino. He has no time for visitors, and I've enough to do attending to the affairs of your household."

"I demand you go to your father." Giorgio fixed on his need like a hawk digging its talons into a squirming field mouse.

She remembered how he had once fixed on her with the same persistence. For months he'd worked on his own father to make a bid for her hand. Old Messer Carelli had not considered the daughter of a painter—even one as well respected in the town as Antonio Barducci—a suitable match, but Giorgio had badgered his father until with poor grace he'd consented. Then Maestro Barducci himself made them wait several more months before agreeing to part with his only child.

Sofia looked at Giorgio's boots, thick with the muck of the street. "I saw this morning that the tables in the workroom are empty," she said. "Have you dismissed the clerks? That doesn't seem wise."

"You dare tell me my business?"

"Your business concerns me when you don't have any." She'd pay later for her words, but the sight of the bare workroom had infuriated her. Since her father saw no need to give her money for the panels she painted for his patrons, Sofia had to depend solely on Giorgio to keep her household fed.

"You can't talk to me like this!"

"I'd just as soon not talk to you at all." Sofia turned her back on him and walked through the open door to the loggia. The clamor and stench from the street below reminded her of the industry of the other merchants. None of them spent their afternoons brawling in taverns. How dare Giorgio gamble away their lives? He was no better than a thief and should be taken into the piazza and whipped. She imagined the lash cutting a scarlet trail across his back, heard his screams and the jeering of onlookers a fitting punishment for a common gambler. Then she chided herself. Perhaps God was testing her by sending such wicked thoughts. For penance, she stopped at the top of the stairs that led to the street and waited, head bowed. She thought of the panel she had finished that afternoon, its colors clear and wholesome like the blessed subjects they depicted. Her father's patron had paid well to have a good amount of gold leaf applied—the most she had ever had permission to use on a panel. The haloes would shimmer in the light of the torches at the wedding feast where the finished painting would be displayed.

"Husband." She swung around so fast that Giorgio stepped backward into an open sack of dried crocus bulbs, spilling them across the loggia in a dusty arc. In two months, the bulbs would be planted for harvest in the fall. The bright stamens from the crocus blossoms yielded the saffron upon which their livelihood, and the livelihood of many of San Gimignano's wealthiest citizens, depended. A common joke in San Gimignano was that its many towers were built upon a foundation of purest yellow.

"That's the last of my bulbs!"

"Then you shouldn't leave them here to be stepped on."

"I can leave my bulbs wherever I want!" Giorgio sounded so much like a child that Sofia expected him to stamp his muddy boots and cry. "Now you *must* speak with your father!"

"I won't." She waved away the suggestion. "Tell me. When can we expect an invitation to the marriage celebration of Messer Delpino's daughter?"

Giorgio crouched and began scooping the bulbs back into the sack. Within seconds, light brown streaks mingled with the dried blood on his knuckles. He glanced up at Sofia and scowled. "What do you care about a wedding feast?"

"My father's new fresco will be on display, and I wish to see it."

Giorgio shook his head. "Our kinsmen are at odds with Delpino."

"*Your* kinsmen are at odds. I've no quarrel with Messer Delpino. He's my father's patron."

"Your father! Always your father. You don't belong to your father anymore."

"And yet you expect him to pay your debts."

"You!" Giorgio sputtered. "We will *not* go to the wedding, and you *will* speak with your father."

"You want me to beg for money? Again?"

Giorgio's red face darkened just enough to let Sofia know he was not yet beyond shame. "I have certain, ah, expenses. Your father makes more than he can spend, and you're his only child. He's duty-bound to help me."

"As you are duty-bound to take care of your own household." She swallowed hard and kept her voice low. "I'm sure, husband, that you've no wish to offend my father."

"No wish? What's this? You c-c-cannot . . ."

Sofia felt a stab of satisfaction. Giorgio only stuttered when what he wanted was out of reach.

"If I don't attend the unveiling of his fresco at the wedding feast, my father will be offended. It's very simple."

"Why should your father care if you are there?"

"He cares."

"But I dare not offend my kinsmen." For a moment Giorgio looked almost apologetic, and, to Sofia's surprise, a nub of sympathy stirred within her. Her once handsome, proud husband was unraveling before her eyes. She remembered how she had gone so willingly into his arms as a young bride four years earlier.

Giorgio swayed toward her, then fastened one arm around her waist and scrabbled at her skirts with his free hand. "Let's have no more talk of weddings." His breath flamed across her cheek. She angled her face away from the stench, but she could not in conscience move from his embrace. When first married, she had welcomed his touch, had smiled and laughed with him. They had tumbled into bed every night, oblivious to everything but themselves. But as the months turned to years, Giorgio grew coarse with the frustration of never fathering a son and Sofia mounted the ladders to her tower room.

"We must pray harder to the Virgin," she said. "Perhaps if you gave me money for her shrine?"

Giorgio let go of her so quickly that she stumbled against the wall fronting the loggia. The sun-beaten stones warmed the thick material of her gown.

"I have none. You must speak with your father. He will help if you ask."

"And if I speak with him, you will get us an invitation to the wedding feast?"

"You dare bargain with me?"

"I must attend."

"That's enough. See to my supper."

The wooden floor shuddered under Sofia's feet as Giorgio stamped down the stairs. If only he had brains enough to maintain the goodwill and strong profits his father had left him. Giorgio's younger brother, Ruberto, would have been a much better choice to take over the business. Ruberto could sell eggs to a chicken.

A week later, Maestro Antonio Barducci extracted Sofia's panel from its leather pouch and held it to the light. Behind them in the workshop, an apprentice was knocking nails into a support for a new crucifix. Swirls of sawdust speckled the hem of Sofia's skirts. Usually her father barely glanced at the panels she brought him. Why was he looking at this one for so long? Sofia kept her hands clasped, squeezing them to stop the tingling in her palms. What if he objected to the three angels? But patrons always liked angels. And as for the representation of Delpino's tower that rose to the right of the manger, her father must appreciate the pleasing symmetry of the turret, with its squared-off teeth set against a clear blue sky. Messer Delpino would be delighted at the compliment. But as she waited for her father to speak, Sofia saw her panel through his eyes. The tower distracted from the figures of the blessed Virgin and Child, and the ass and the ox were too prominent. Even the angels showed too much movement. She should have kept the sky blank as her father had requested, or at most filled the space with two or three rows of static angels, leaving no room for a tower.

Barducci exhaled slowly and shook his head as he set the panel gently on the table.

"I'm sorry, Papa," Sofia began, her voice catching. "I thought perhaps you would approve . . ." Of course he would not approve. She had no say in what subjects she painted, and she definitely had no right to add elements that neither the maestro nor the patron had requested. She bowed her head to hide the tears just starting to pool at the edges of her eyes. What if he gave his commissions to someone else? One or two of his apprentices showed some promise, and even Messer Delgrasso, her father's second in the workshop, had enough skill to manage simple subjects if someone else did the drawing. The thought of never again holding a brush brought a sob to her throat. She clamped her teeth together.

"What are you sorry for?"

"The panel. I took liberties."

"Yes, you did." Her father stepped backward and regarded her, his large head cocked to the side. "You had instructions."

"And I followed them. Mostly."

"Mostly."

"I thought perhaps you wouldn't be displeased. The tower, you see, it's very like Messer Delpino's." She swept her hand across the panel, then looked into her father's face. He stared back impassively. "I'm sure he will be gratified to see it included."

"I have no idea what will gratify Messer Delpino," her father said. "I do know that his commission did not specify a tower. And as for the angels, he never mentioned them."

"The three angels support Our Lady. I thought . . ."

"You *thought*? I don't ask you to think, daughter. I ask you to use the skills I taught you to paint what I tell you to paint."

"Yes, Papa. I'm sorry."

"You should be."

Sofia looked again at the panel. It was *not* too crowded. The tower provided a solid support for the Nativity, and the two kneeling shepherds filled out the composition and gave it a pleasing symmetry.

Her father was wrong.

"I regret that my work doesn't please you," she began. He continued to stare at her. "But I am not sorry for my additions."

"You dare say you're in the right?"

"I can't regret the work I've done." The index finger of her right hand hooked the thumbnail of her left. She tugged. As the nail began to tear, she focused on the pain. The throbbing comforted her. It was so much easier to bear pain she caused herself.

Barducci's cheeks, mottled with age and paint, quivered as the lines in his forehead deepened and his eyes narrowed. The hammering coming from the workshop behind them stopped. The silence pressed in on Sofia, startling her with its emptiness. She should not have spoken. Her father never tolerated defiance from anyone—particularly his sharp-witted *cara mia*. She twisted the nail and pulled.

"Papa . . ."

"The panel will do very well," he said. "Now leave me. I don't have all day to waste admiring your work."

Sofia let go of her thumbnail. "Papa?"

"What now? I must get back to Delpino's palazzo while the light's still decent."

"I'm sorry, Papa."

"Yes, so you said, although not sorry enough to paint me the panel our patron actually commissioned."

"I mean I'm sorry to detain you, but Giorgio needs money." She said it quickly, as if speed might dampen the shame.

"I don't doubt it. I hear your husband spends his time in the company of old Ardinghelli's kinsmen, most often gambling in the tavern instead of attending to business. You married a fool."

"You allowed the marriage."

"And I've regretted my permission these four years. Messer Delpino wants peace between the Salvucci and the Ardinghelli. If he hears I'm supporting someone allied with the Ardinghelli family, he might refuse payment. You'll understand when you see the fresco."

"Won't you even give me a hint about it, Papa?" At the mention of her father's fresco, she pushed Giorgio to the back of her mind and stepped forward eagerly. Her father had kept its subject a secret for the past six months. Every time she asked, he just smiled and shook his head, teasing her with shrugs and winks.

"Patience, daughter. I know it's not your strong suit, but you'd do well to cultivate it more—as a wife if not as a painter. Now, no more talk of money for Giorgio. I won't offend my patron."

"Dear Papa, you don't need Delpino's help to get more commissions. You're the famous Maestro Barducci! You have no equal in San Gimignano."

"As always, cara mia, your logic is irrefutable. But you don't understand. Many of the great families have suffered with this famine. Commerce has been affected all over. If the Ardinghelli come back to power, we'll see a return to the fighting that almost laid us to waste not so many years ago. You are too young to remember, but it was a bleak time. People don't want to commission a fresco only to see it crumble in an attack."

"Can I say nothing to move you, Papa?" She knew pouting would only infuriate him, so she looked him squarely in the eye. "The new podestà is said to despise gambling. If he has Giorgio charged, we'll lose everything."

"Then it's your duty to convince Giorgio to leave off his gambling. He can't mean to ruin himself. He should have more respect for the memory of his father." Messer Barducci smiled at his daughter. "This time I can't give in. But do make sure you attend the wedding feast. Your panel will be much admired, even with the additions."

"Maybe because of them?"

Maestro Barducci threw back his head and laughed. "You push me too far, daughter. One of these days your impudence will get you into trouble."

"Giorgio won't give me permission to attend the feast."

"Then he's more of a fool than I took him for. Messer Delpino is a rich man with powerful alliances. He is in a position to do Giorgio some good." Maestro Barducci reached for his cloak and pulled it over his paint-splattered smock. "I'm sorry you'll miss the presentation of the panel, but Giorgio must get himself out of his own mess."

"The panel's for the glory of God. I don't need to see it praised."

Barducci came toward her and clasped her hands between his own. Sofia winced at the pressure on her torn nail, then smiled as she saw a streak of deepest blue on her father's broad thumb. "I'm thinking more that I want *you* to see my fresco." He winked. "It's one of my best, God forgive my pride."

"You've no false pride, Papa." Sofia laughed. "Of course the fresco is good."

Maestro Barducci shrugged, but the warm glow in his cheeks showed that her praise pleased him. "Get off home with you. Your husband's man looks like he's growing impatient." He nodded at Niccolò, who was waiting outside the door to the workshop, shuffling his feet in the dust. Sofia knew better than to argue. She accepted her father's kiss on her cheek, then left, motioning for Niccolò to follow her into the street.

"The master told me to have you home while the light is still good," Niccolò said as they walked down a steep incline toward the Piazza del Duomo. The tops of the cluster of towers lining the piazza glowed golden in the late afternoon sun, and smoke from hundreds of cooking fires choked the air. All along the street, merchants were packing their wares and moving indoors. Sofia and Niccolò crossed the Piazza del Duomo, passed into the Piazza della Cisterna, then skirted the piazza to the Via San Giovanni. Sofia's house was about halfway down the street, which ended at the solid new town walls pierced by the Porta San Giovanni.

Giorgio met her at the front door. "What news from your father?"

"He can do nothing."

Giorgio blocked her from entering the passageway leading to the kitchen at the back of the house. "He refused you?"

"As I said. I'm sorry, husband."

His face contorted with anger in the dim light. "Husband, is it? Ha! Well, your dear father may soon have cause to regret his stinginess. Go in to your supper. I've business in the town."

"But it grows dark. The watch will be out."

"The watch will know better than to interfere with *me*." As he stepped aside to let her pass, she heard his sword scrape the stone wall.

"Husband!"

The heavy wooden door slammed, leaving her alone in the passageway. She put one hand out to steady herself against the wall. What if Giorgio got himself killed?

Then, God forgive her, she wanted to pray for exactly that.

CHAPTER TWO

There are those who pursue [the profession
of painting] because of poverty and domestic need,
for profit . . . [but] above all . . . are to be extolled
the ones who enter the profession through
a sense of enthusiasm and exaltation.
—Cennini, *Il Libro dell'Arte*, Chapter II

Sofia stood quietly in the middle of her bedchamber as Paulina twined a blue ribbon through the thick black braid that circled her head. She was to attend the wedding feast after all, and the prospect made her smile. Not many weeks after she had returned empty-handed from her father's workshop, Giorgio's rage had transformed into an expansive goodwill such as she had not seen since the first months of her marriage. He told her that she need not burden her father, that he had a much better source of funds, and that, above all, she was to ask no questions. The hollow fear in her stomach told Sofia not to trust him, but her desire to take him at his word won out. She made do with thanking God for Giorgio's sudden good humor and resolving to enjoy herself at the wedding feast.

Paulina smoothed Sofia's hair and held up a simple pearl pendant—a wedding gift from her father. Its creaminess perfectly complemented the deep blue of the new gown Giorgio had ordered made for her, his first present in more than three years. Sofia took pleasure in the contrast and knew her father would too. Paulina fastened the chain around her throat, then brought forward a belt made of soft leather in a buttery shade of yellow that shone like burnished gold in the candlelight. She stepped back and motioned for her mistress to turn around. The sound of revelers making their way to the Delpino palazzo floated in through the open door that led from the bedchamber to the loggia fronting the street. As Sofia twirled, the heavy gown spread in a wide arc around her slender frame, a blur of purest blue in the failing light. A giddy joy filled her, reminding her of when she was as young as Paulina, just stepping into life with Giorgio and delirious with the prospect of freedom from her father's rule. She would be mistress of her own house with a husband who adored her, and who didn't harangue her for drawing crooked lines or expect her to waste her beauty in dusty workshops with pigments and brushes as her only companions.

"You're so beautiful, mistress!" Paulina exclaimed.

Sofia laughed and shook her head. "Such nonsense, Paulina. I'm an old married woman. Tell Cook I've given you leave to go to bed early. You don't need to wait for us tonight."

Paulina's young face broke into a wide smile. "Mistress!" she exclaimed. "That's kind of you."

Sofia patted Paulina's hand as she passed. She must be more appreciative of her maid. If it wasn't for Paulina, Sofia would never have her stolen hours in the tower. That evening, she would see her Nativity panel unveiled before half the citizens of San Gimignano. It was too much happiness for one heart to bear. She stepped into the warm air trapped under the eaves of the loggia and marveled at how the light from the torches in the street cast large black shadows across the brick walls. Giorgio was waiting for her at the bottom of the stairs. For a moment, she thought she saw a glint of admiration in his eyes before he turned away and she followed him into the street.

Chattering, laughing voices animated the soft night air. Sofia and Giorgio joined a crowd of richly attired wedding guests streaming up the Via San Giovanni toward the Piazza della Cisterna and the palazzo of Messer Giancarlo Delpino, one of San Gimignano's wealthiest families and kinsman of the powerful Salvucci family. Sofia's cheeks reddened with excitement as she and Giorgio were swept through the open front doors of the palazzo and up a broad staircase to a large hall. Heavy garlands of woven white lilies and gillyflowers dripped from the ceiling, filling the room with a spicy sweetness that almost overpowered the miasma rising from the bodies of a hundred wedding guests. The distinctions of rank were almost obliterated. Sofia needn't have worried about her pearl attracting attention. The *podestà* and his notaries would be too busy collecting a half year's worth of fines from the other guests to bother with her trifling jewel. Many of the women—most of them in fact—were weighed down with splendid displays of gold and silver and gems that elevated them far above their stations. San Gimignano's sumptuary laws were intended to curb excessive shows of wealth at all levels of society, but particularly among the wives of newly prosperous merchants, few of whom had any claim to noble heritage. Sofia knew for certain that Giorgio's own father had been born of a woman married to a baker.

Sofia saw the *podestà* raising a goblet of wine with a man well beneath Giorgio in rank and importance. The man's wife wore a necklace of amethysts and a tippet lined with ermine. San Gimignano, like other communes in the region, purposely appointed a *podestà* who was from another city to guarantee a measure of impartiality in his judgments, but it appeared to Sofia that the new *podestà* had already traded neutrality for the patronage of wealthy men like Messer Delpino. He looked no more ready to read a citation to the offending merchant for his wife's finery than he looked ready to refuse another goblet of Delpino's excellent wine.

"Sister!"

The edges of Sofia's good mood frayed just a little as she watched her sister-in-law, Caterina, bustle across the room toward her. Dressed all in crimson with a headdress that defied even Sofia's skill to depict, Caterina filled the space around her with a cheerful good humor that turned heads. Sofia pasted on a smile.

"Oh! Dear sister! That shade of blue becomes you to perfection. If only I had such a figure. And your hair! What on earth has your maid done to it? I can't get mine to master such intricate braiding. And as for the color! God has not seen fit to bless me. Where is your Giorgio?" Words tumbled out of Caterina's mouth like water from the town pump.

"I believe he has gone to find me something to drink."

"My brother-in-law is so kind!" Caterina's toothy smile didn't slip as she grasped Sofia's arm and pulled her close. "My Ruberto says that some of Giorgio's associations are not what they should be. Giorgio should take care."

"Giorgio's associations can be none of his brother's affair."

"Oh, don't look cross with me! You know I mean no harm. Ruberto's always chiding me for talking too much." Caterina laughed as she drew Sofia even closer. "But Ruberto did say that Giorgio is spending time with the enemies of our kinsmen."

"Giorgio believes them to be friends."

"Yes, well, I'm sure it will all come to nothing. Let's not let it spoil this evening. Isn't this the most beautiful place you've ever seen? Monna Delpino ordered two hundred garlands! I didn't think there were this many flowers in the world!"

Sofia was barely listening. What did Caterina mean when she said it would all come to nothing? What did she know about Giorgio and his associations? As Caterina prattled on, Sofia searched the crowd for a glimpse of her husband's yellow hat. But he was a short man—not much taller than she was. She couldn't see him anywhere.

"I have not set foot out of the house all day," Caterina was saying. "Little Isabetta is teething and Nurse is almost beside herself. And as for little Ruberto, he wants to spend all his time with his papa, which of course he can't. He wails something terrible when Ruberto leaves the house. I so envy you your leisure."

Sofia smiled absently as, in vain, she tried to detach herself from Caterina. When the other woman's grip tightened, she gave up. "The children are well?" she asked.

"Oh yes, of course they are well!" Caterina reached back with her free hand and grasped the arm of her husband, who came forward and bowed to Sofia. "The children are thriving, are they not, Ruberto?"

Ruberto beamed at his wife. "They are the joy of my life!" he boomed. "Children are the joy of life, eh, sister? Where's that brother of mine? Gone off already? He should stay with his wife."

"Good evening, brother." Sofia's head bobbed in the slightest of curtsies. Her brother-in-law was everything his elder brother was not—a loving husband, a shrewd businessman, and a pious, upstanding citizen. All he lacked were the soft looks and flattering tongue that had provoked the fifteen-year-old Sofia to fall in love with the wrong brother. Every time she saw Ruberto, she despised him for her own stupidity.

"Come, sister. The feast is starting and we must be seated."

Sofia followed Caterina to a long table covered with a closely woven linen cloth and piled with platters of roasted quail, pheasant, and partridge, boar pies, prosciutto of pork tongue, pigeons in puff pastry, and plates overflowing with cheeses and fresh fruit. Across the crowded room, she spied her father's distinctive red hat and thick mass of white hair. A circle of admirers surrounded him.

Maestro Barducci courted praise the way a peacock sought applause for its feathers.

"Your father continues well," Caterina was saying. "Ruberto told me of the marvelous picture he completed for Messer Delpino's daughter. It's being talked of as one of the maestro's finest works."

"Yes?" Sofia felt her heart swell with pride that she quickly tried to suppress. Her Nativity was painted for the glory of God and her father. "What else did Ruberto hear?"

"Oh, I can't say. I confess I was occupied with Isabetta at the time and didn't catch one word in ten." Caterina laughed. "Ruberto thinks I hang upon his every word, but it's not true. So often he talks of goings-on in the commune and politics and *vendettas* and such like. I nod and smile while I occupy my mind with more important matters."

"Did you hear anything about my father's fresco?"

"Hmm?" Caterina had just popped a slice of venison into her mouth and was studiously chewing. She shook her head.

Sofia picked up a small knife from the table and speared a slice of boar dripping with thick, fragrant gravy. She bit into the meat and, for a time, forgot about the fresco. Such wondrous tastes! All around her people ate with gusto, stopping at regular intervals to make use of the bowls of water brought by servants for washing their hands. Even for the wealthiest citizens of San Gimignano, such a lavish wedding feast was rare.

After dinner, the master of the house called for music. Tables were cleared and soon the hall heaved with swaying bodies. The good food and cheerful atmosphere filled Sofia with a contentment she rarely felt outside her tower room. She wanted to dance, to let the music of the lute and the drum spirit her feet across the floor. Ruberto led Caterina into the fray. Sofia felt a twinge of jealousy as she watched Caterina tilt her head up and smile into her husband's eyes. Her face radiated the complacency of a woman who knew she was beloved. Sofia searched the room for Giorgio. During a break in the dancing, she asked Ruberto if he had seen his brother but received only a worried frown. As the evening wore on, her contentment dissolved into restless impatience. How dare Giorgio just leave her to sit alone? Even her father did not trouble himself to come speak with her. He was far too busy accepting accolades for *her* work.

Sofia's sole satisfaction was hearing her Nativity panel praised. Messer Delpino had the painting displayed prominently on a table laden with wedding gifts. Snatches of conversation reached her.

"Did you see how the maestro included Delpino's tower? That was well done."

"Do you think the maestro would do such a panel for me? The tower on my palazzo is much finer."

"I liked the ass. It was looking right at the blessed Child."

"Look at the amount of gold in the haloes. Messer Delpino spared no expense."

"Indeed, Barducci's surpassed himself. The panel he did for me five years ago doesn't show half the skill."

"He improves with age."

Sofia smiled at this last comment. Yes, she had improved with age. With God's help—and her father's indulgence—she would continue improving for many more years to come.

When the musicians paused in their strumming and banging, Messer Delpino stepped forward and launched into a long speech praising his new son-in-law, his guests, his kinsmen, his household, his wife, even his poultry, until half the heads in the room lolled against the shoulders of their neighbors. Finally, Delpino gestured at a covered wall and announced the unveiling of Maestro Barducci's latest fresco. As the guests stirred awake, a murmur rustled through the hall. Servants stationed at either side of the curtain pulled ropes, piles of silk slithered to the floor, and every voice in the room was silenced.

Sofia focused all her attention on the story that unfolded across the wall. She looked for haloes and found none. Instead she saw a welter of arms and legs and heads and even buildings that at first glance made no sense. She sucked in her breath and forced herself to start at the beginning—at the far left—and move her eyes along the wall. The silence in the room deepened as every pair of eyes joined Sofia in studying the fresco. Slowly, the fresco's meaning revealed itself to the assembled crowd. The air bristled with whispers—some shocked, some amused. A few chuckles indicated appreciation for Maestro Barducci's boldness.

Sofia almost laughed out loud. The fresco was nothing less than a warning and a celebration of San Gimignano itself! A cluster of towers representing the city marched like jagged teeth across the wall. One scene showed a handful of young men armed with swords attacking well-dressed townspeople—clearly a depiction of the strife that had so often disturbed the city's peace. Another scene showed the bustle of commerce that made San Gimignano one of the richest city-states in Tuscany. And on the side of commerce sat the figure of Messer Delpino himself, in an attitude of peaceful reverence.

The crowd pushed Sofia forward, and she glimpsed her father standing proudly in front of his representation of the Duomo, its doors thrown open, an obvious invitation to choose peace over war. Barducci's face was split in a grin of triumph. New commissions would flow in after this. Sofia could paint for as long as she wished, or for as long as God kept her safe from Giorgio's prying eyes.

"I hope the *podestà* doesn't order it covered up!" a voice to her right whispered to his companion. "He might see it as an invitation to more strife. Old Ardinghelli won't like seeing a kinsman of his enemy so favored."

"The *podestà* might not approve, but I doubt he will hazard more than a rebuke. Messer Delpino's contributions to the council get more generous every year."

"They'll need to be after this!" said another voice.

Finally, Sofia got close enough to her father to get his attention. He was standing next to Messer Delpino. "Ah, dear Sofia," he exclaimed. "My lord, may I present my daughter, Monna Carelli?"

"Monna Carelli!" Messer Delpino bowed stiffly. "You have grown into a beautiful woman."

"My lord?"

"When I came to your father's workshop many years ago, you were playing with the pigments and making a right mess. And now here you are a fine lady. Your husband is nearby?" Messer Delpino looked over Sofia's shoulder, his expression polite and expectant. Sofia smiled and curtsied while inwardly cursing Giorgio. Here she was meeting one of San Gimignano's most prominent citizens, and Giorgio was nowhere to be found.

"I believe my husband has stepped out for some air," she said. "He will be very sorry to have missed the honor of meeting you."

"Ah, well. 'Tis no matter. What do you think of your esteemed father's handiwork?" Messer Delpino flung one arm toward the fresco. "I gave your father leave to interpret my wishes for a fresco that celebrated peace in our city, but I confess I did not expect this!"

"And does it please you, my lord?"

"It does indeed. I've already heard talk from several nobles about commissioning such a fresco for their own palazzi. Mind you, they won't be the first." Messer Delpino beamed. "Oh no, not the first! What say you, Barducci, to more such work? I wager Salvucci would be eager to commission a fresco or two. The walls of his new palazzo are still bare."

Sofia glanced sideways at her father and shared a quick smile of triumph. A commission from the head of the Salvucci family would keep her father's workshop busy for many months, maybe even years. Salvucci had two daughters, one married and another who had just turned fourteen and was already betrothed. Sofia thought a Nativity painting would do nicely to celebrate the married daughter's first child, and then a Birth of the Virgin for the other daughter's wedding, or a panel featuring Saint Fina. Sofia had yet to paint the story of San Gimignano's most favored saint.

"I would like nothing better than to serve you and your kinsmen, my lord," Maestro Barducci said with a slight bow. "You do me great honor."

Messer Delpino opened his mouth to reply, but no sound came out. His eyes stared into Sofia's. They looked startled and seemed to search her face for an answer she could not supply. The ruddiness that had suffused his face with wine and good humor drained suddenly to a sickly white. A single strand of bright red trickled from his mouth. Sofia heard a soft grunt, and then the face of the great Messer Delpino, kinsman to one of the two most powerful families in all of San Gimignano, slipped from her view. Close to her right ear, an arrow thunked into the wall.

"Sofia!" Her father lunged at her and threw her to the ground. She landed on her back and his body fell across her legs, his head coming to rest next to her own. She inhaled the chalky gesso that always dusted the folds of his gown—and another smell—brown and metallic, sharp and thick. When she raised her head, she already knew what she would see and was surprised that her only emotion was curiosity. Her strong father, with his heavy demands and relentless striving, was bleeding just like any man. His eyes looked straight into her own. His mouth moved as he tried to form words, but she heard nothing above the wailing and screaming that filled the hall.

She struggled to one elbow and pulled her legs free. The shaft of an arrow protruded from the deep green of her father's right sleeve.

The blood seeping from the wound was turning the material black. She experienced a moment of relief. The arrow had not pierced his chest. If promptly attended to, he would survive.

"I won't have you stay for me." Maestro Barducci's voice was hoarse with pain but still strong. "Find your husband and get to safety."

A scream ripped from a throat not ten paces from Sofia. She craned her neck around, but all she could see was the thick material of a dozen gowns swishing past her. She smelled burning. Something heavy hit the fresco behind her. She threw her arms over her head to protect herself and her father from shards of falling plaster.

"I don't know where Giorgio is!"

"Then go without him."

"But, Papa!"

"Please, Sofia. You do me no service by staying. I'm safe enough here on the floor until help comes. They will not touch an old man."

"What do they want?"

"*Vendetta*. What else? They want to cause as much trouble as they can. I just hope they don't damage the fresco." He winced as the arrow shifted in his arm.

"But what of Messer Delpino?" Sofia looked over to where Delpino's body was lying in a puddle of blood. His eyes were still open and staring at a fresco panel that showed a circlet of young women dancing.

"His death will mean more strife in San Gimignano. All you can do is stay out of the way."

"There you are! Come away now!" Caterina clamped her fingers around Sofia's arm and dragged her up.

"My father! I can't leave him." She strained against Caterina's grip and tried to twist away, but one foot slipped in the slick dust from the fresco, pulling her off balance.

"Go, daughter!"

"No!"

"We must hurry." Caterina was too strong. Sofia caught one last glimpse of her father slumped onto the floor beneath his fresco before the heaving crowd drew her in.

"Ruberto is furious with me for coming back to find you," Caterina said, using her free elbow to cleave a path through the crowd. "The enemies of the Salvucci have taken the house."

"What of Giorgio? I must find him." Screams and smoke and the curses of fighting men filled the air. A few steps away, a man staggered to his knees. He was staring wide-eyed at a hand resting in the straw. Blood dripped on it from the severed stump of his arm.

"Giorgio is *one of them*," Caterina hissed. Sofia had never heard her warmhearted sister-in-law raise her voice, but now she looked almost wild. Her headdress was askew and soot streaked her face. She kept Sofia's arm clamped in an iron embrace.

"Giorgio? How?"

"Ruberto says Giorgio has allied himself with the Ardinghelli. They paid his debts in exchange for this treachery."

Ruberto appeared at his wife's side. "You found her! Good. Stay close to me." He grabbed Caterina's free hand and pulled her toward the door. The elbow of another fleeing guest jabbed into Sofia's chest. A crush of bodies pressed in on all sides.

Where was Giorgio? Had he gone mad?

CHAPTER THREE

To paint . . . a wound, take straight vermilion
and shade all over . . .
—Cennini, *Il Libro dell'Arte*, Chapter CXLIX

ofia's heel splashed into a pool of blood, black in the dawn light. The groans of the wounded and the buzzing of flies feasting on the dead filled her ears but did not penetrate her mind. She listened only for the low rumble of her father's voice. When grief tried to slip into her heart, she slammed the door.

It was too soon.

In the darkness before the dawn, most of the attackers were either sprawled in the piazza or back in their homes, sleeping off the wine that had fueled their bravado. Any of the guests who had escaped injury were, like Caterina and Ruberto, collapsed onto their beds, thick with rich food and shock. Ruberto had insisted on taking Sofia home with them when Giorgio could not be found. Sofia had waited to hear Ruberto's and Caterina's snores, then crept down the stairs, thrown on an old cloak belonging to Caterina's cook, and hurried through the deserted streets to what was left of the Delpino palazzo.

Fine particles of white dust roiled from the clumps of plaster she kicked in front of her skirts as she stepped around and over bodies. A hand reached for her hem.

"Help me!"

A young man in a purple tunic splashed with blood stared up at her. Sofia knelt and touched his hand. "Someone will come soon," she whispered, then rose quickly, her heart heavy. She had seen the wound; he would not survive the morning.

A voice—too faint to belong to a man. Sofia swung her head around. At first she saw only dust, then heard the voice again—the merest whisper, almost swallowed by the echoes of death all around her. Not her father. Maestro Antonio Barducci had a voice that could cut the air like a hot knife through a cake of sizing.

"Sofia."

Her father rarely called her by her name. It was almost always "daughter" or, if he was pleased, *"cara mia."* Sofia was her mother's name.

Her toe nudged something soft. Another step and she would have tripped over him. She sank to her knees, her new gown pooling around her in a velvet arc of rich blue.

Her father's face was clear of blood. The skin at his neck trembled just enough to let her know she was not too late.

He lived!

Then she saw a slab of wall, still bright with the colors of his fresco, pinning his body from chest to legs. Blood from the arrow wound in his arm had splashed like a shadow across one of the towers.

"Papa!"

Sofia gripped the edge of the shattered wall. The jagged plaster cut into the flesh of her palms. If God spared her father, she would do penance for a month to give thanks.

"Stop!"

The short, sharp sound shocked her more than anything she had seen since entering the palazzo. Her hands fell from the plaster and she sat back on her heels. Her father's face was so pale it looked like the chalky coats of *gesso grosso* she layered over panels before

29

transforming them into objects that glorified God and Maestro Antonio Barducci.

"Don't waste your strength, *cara mia*. It is too late."

"I can run for help. Ruberto—"

"Your brother-in-law will not care to help me. Nor your husband."

"What can I do, Papa? I can't leave you here to die." Fear sharpened her voice. Sharp, like her mother. Sofia gently lifted one of his hands. She focused her attention on the plaster wedged under his nails. His fingers were rolls of dough coated in flour and left to dry in the sun. Her slim fingers curled around his like the sweet young leeks that Cook pulled from the garden each spring. The thick and ropey fingers she cradled in her palm were the fingers of an old man.

Her father would never again hold a brush.

"You must do something for me." His voice was low. She bent closer, felt his breath graze her cheek. The fresco crushing his body was forcing blood to his lips.

"Of course, Papa. Anything." Sofia did not try to pull away her fingers, even when he increased the pressure. She placed her free hand over the hot skin of his brow, twined her fingers in his white hair, smoothed it back from his forehead with one lightly calloused thumb. A smear of paint had seeped into the roots—lapis lazuli, more expensive even than gold. Sofia wondered if she would ever again know the joy of daubing the robes of the Virgin with the deep blue pigment. Her father had taught her never to use the color for anything less exalted.

"The panel." Barducci winced. A trickle of blood bubbled over his lower lip.

"What about it?" Sofia heard the panic in her own voice and tried to gulp it back. Barducci never tolerated emotional outbursts. When she was a girl, he would take away her brushes and order her back to the house if she cried. Tears reminded him how much he had wanted a son, someone capable of taking the Barducci name into a new generation.

"Take the panel."

"It belongs to Messer Delpino!"

"Listen to me!"

His grip tightened and her wedding ring ground into her flesh. Once before, her father had held her hand this hard. She'd cried out for him to let go. But he had paid no attention as he stared through the cold winter rain at her mother's body being lowered into the ground. Sofia remembered the drops seeping beneath the neck of her cloak, trickling down her spine. She knew she should cry for her mother, but she thought only of the pain in her hand.

"Delpino is dead." Barducci licked the blood from his lips. His eyes widened with surprise, as if he just realized the proximity of his own death. He paused a moment, his gaze fixed above Sofia on the ceiling that was already showing cracks in the strengthening light. By nightfall, Delpino's tower would be rubble and the cycle of *vendetta* would resume.

"You have your chance now. Delpino's kinsmen care only about getting revenge on the Ardinghelli."

Barducci coughed again, and a clot of black blood spilled onto his gown. Sofia wanted him to stop talking about panels and kinsmen and revenge. She wanted him to tell her he loved her, that he would miss her, bless her as she went forward without him.

"Look at me!" His voice reminded Sofia of the sound made by pigments when she ground them beneath her pestle—rough, scratchy, coarse. Maestro Barducci prided himself on his ability to talk his way into a commission with a smoothness that was the envy of less successful painters. Sofia had often watched with amusement when her father turned from chiding an apprentice for laziness to greeting a patron with manners as silky as the last layers of *gesso sottile* brushed over the *gesso grosso,* his voice as smooth as a pond on a summer day.

"You have your chance now. Find the panel and take it."

"What should I do with it?" She sounded helpless and hated herself for it, but what did her father expect?

As always, he expected too much.

"Take it to Maestro Manzini."

"But Maestro Manzini lives in Siena!" Sofia prised her hand from her father's grasp. As death neared, the devil must be descending to twist his fine mind. Barducci's raw, ragged gasps sounded obscenely loud. Sofia glanced fearfully around the ruined hall. The young man who had grasped at her earlier saw her move and moaned again for help. Sofia looked away, then dabbed with her sleeve at the blood now flowing in a steady stream from her father's mouth.

His eyes closed.

For a terrible moment, she was sure he was gone—gone before she'd made a promise that she could not keep. She wanted to shake him until he told her how she was to get the panel to Siena.

Maestro Barducci's eyes fluttered open. The blood seeping between his open lips blossomed bright red—the red of the finest vermilion in his workshop. It was the red Sofia had used to tint the flesh of the blessed Child in her last panel. "You must—" he whispered.

"Yes, Papa. I will find a way."

He shuddered, the pain visible in the stiff way he held his head. "Tell Manzini about my fresco."

"Please, Papa, don't speak. You must rest until help comes."

"Help won't come."

He closed his eyes. Green tinged the skin beneath the bright blood—the green of the *terre-verte* she used to show shadows and aging skin. She had used some on the weathered skin of her Joseph in the panel. Would she ever paint another Joseph? Or another Mary with Her eyes cast down, skin clear with just the right combination of red and yellow and white?

"Tell him you can do such a one for him."

His eyes were still closed and his voice so low that she was not sure he had spoken. Her throat tightened. She wanted to follow him, stay with him in his ascent to heaven. They could walk with the angels, kneel at the feet of the Virgin they depicted so often in panels and frescoes. She stroked her fingers along his cheek, the faint stubble scraping under her nails. The pulse at his neck still beat, but erratically now, as if it no longer cared to make the effort. When had he grown so thin? His nose looked as prominent as the beak of one of the dead birds Giorgio sometimes brought home for Cook to dress. The carcasses trailed blood across the floor, and Cook cursed the master when he was not near. Sofia closed her own eyes, weary after a night with no sleep. She rested her head upon her father's chest to better feel his heart. Then at least she would know for certain when the end came.

"Your panel is good, *mia bella*. Show it to Manzini and he'll take you in."

Sofia's head snapped up. "Papa!"

His eyes remained closed. Had he really spoken? Her father had never once said her work was good. She gripped his hand, waited for an answering squeeze, proof he still lived and that after this short sleep he would rise and chastise her for using too much gold in the Virgin's halo. She heard a sound like Giorgio's dice rattling in a bone cup but softer. She bent her ear closer to his open mouth, listened, waited. The sound came again—a whisper—the sound of tree branches brushing against a brick wall on an evening breeze. And then silence. Complete and total. The tips of her father's fingers were cold in her hand.

Sofia thought of stones drying in a winter wind.

The moans of the dying, the reek of blood, the color of her father's skin—all seemed to belong to another place. Sofia existed only to hold her father's hand and remember how that hand had held her up to view his new altarpiece in flickering candlelight, how that same hand had guided her own small fingers in her first attempts to draw with charcoal stubs upon scraps of parchment.

"Papa," she whispered. She waited for the stab of grief. Nothing. She felt nothing. The world contracted to her young body crouched next to his broken one. She should cry out in anguish as her heart broke and the earth burned to ashes. She should—

"Get up!"

Sofia kept her hand on her father's cheek and exhaled slowly. She would not look up. Her husband would have to drag her from the palazzo.

"I said get up!"

A pair of boots appeared behind her father's head. Sofia fixed her eyes on a scuffed patch of leather freckled with dried blood. A glint of metal caught her eye. She looked up and saw the sword held loosely in his hand. Daubs of gore scalloped its edge. With a cry, she struggled to her feet and threw herself at him. Her hand closed over the weapon's hilt, and for a few seconds she was sure it loosened from his grip. She would wield it in a high arc over his head and watch with unholy pleasure as it cleaved his skull.

"Get hold of yourself, wife! You shouldn't have come here." Giorgio's voice held a note of amusement that enraged Sofia even further. How dare he laugh while her father was lying dead at her feet?

"I will stay!"

"Don't be so stupid. Of course you will not stay. This place isn't safe. What's left of Delpino's kinsmen are mustering their forces."

"Not safe for *you*! Ruberto told me you've thrown your lot in with the Ardinghelli. Because of you, my father is dead!"

"It's thanks to the Ardinghelli that I'll have florins enough to keep you and our household fed. You'll come with me now or I'll drag you."

"You wouldn't dare!"

"The streets are empty and I'm not worried that the sight of a man being master of his wife will concern anyone." Giorgio grasped Sofia's wrist.

Sofia twisted from his grip and knelt once more next to her father. She blinked as the first tear slid across her chin. She shook her head, and the drop landed on her father's white forehead.

"Go with God, Papa," she whispered. She felt the anguish escape just for a moment, let it grip her heart, then flex, release, flex.

And then her shoulders slumped and she let Giorgio pull her to her feet.

ᝮ

"Wife!"

Sofia opened her eyes to a shaft of afternoon sun clogged with dust. She stared at the swirling motes and wondered why her chest ached as if crushed beneath the hooves of an unbroken horse. Why was she in bed in the middle of the day? Was she ill?

"You must get up. Messer Ardinghelli's man has just this moment brought us an invitation!" Giorgio's voice was as excited as a boy's. Sofia had never heard him sound so animated, even at the beginning of their marriage when he'd called her beautiful. She pulled the bedcover to her chin.

"No."

"But Messer Ardinghelli has never before asked for me. We *must* go!"

She remained silent. With Giorgio, silence was a far more powerful weapon than tears or shouts. One drew his contempt, the other his rage. Silence bewildered him.

"I *order* you to come with me!"

Sofia rolled her head over to stare up at him. She held his eyes for a few seconds, then rolled away again.

"Wife!"

"Give my excuses," she mumbled into the pillow. "I will not go."

"But every man there will have his wife with him."

"No." She would *not* go and stand in the presence of Messer Ardinghelli and listen to him boast about the toppling of the Delpino tower and the humiliation of the Salvucci. She slid both hands between her bare thighs and gripped at the flesh, then brought her knees to her chin, making herself small and round. As Giorgio's heavy tread circled the bed, she imagined the cloak of the Virgin descending from heaven and enclosing her in its blessed folds. Giorgio nudged the side of the bed. She knew that if she moved even an inch, he'd grab an arm and tumble her to the floor. His rapid breathing filled the room. She closed her eyes and waited.

"Patience, daughter."

"Oh Papa, why must you always say that?"

"Because you need to hear it."

"Why?"

Maestro Barducci laid one large hand on her head. She felt the warmth like one of the thick wool blankets her nurse, Emilia, folded around her on winter nights. His rough palm slid down her chin, patted it fondly.

"You must learn not to ask so many questions, cara. Now go in to Emilia. I'll be along presently."

Sofia let her father's voice wrap itself into her memory, savoring its sound. She searched for some spark of feeling to thaw the frozen nothingness that enveloped her like a shroud. Giorgio's breathing slowed and she felt the air move next to her head as his hand stretched out. Pricks of light exploded behind her closed eyes. Would he dare drag her from the bed? She held her breath, her teeth clenched so hard she felt the muscles in her jaw cramp. She would not bend to his will. He couldn't force her, not if she stayed perfectly, perfectly still.

She heard him suck in his breath, braced herself for the feel of his hand closing over her arm, prayed for oblivion.

"Stay then," Giorgio said finally. "I will say you are unwell."

Slowly, Sofia let her face relax. She listened to him stomp out the door and across the open loggia. His tread on the wooden stairs to the street shook the bed. Moments later the outside door creaked, then slammed shut. Sofia threw off the covers and swung her feet to the floor. The stale air in the bedchamber pressed against her. She could touch it, taste it, feel it, smell Giorgio. A sudden clenching of her stomach flooded her throat with bile. She choked, swallowed, and felt sweat pool beneath her bare breasts. She licked the salt of tears and longed for night.

"Mistress?"

Sofia did not turn at the sound of Paulina's voice. What use was a fourteen-year-old servant girl who could neither read nor write? And yet Paulina was now the most important person in Sofia's world—the only connection to her work. *Her* work. Had her Nativity panel been crushed beneath the ruins of the Delpino palazzo? She slumped onto the bed, her belly collapsing inward, her legs warm beneath her flattened palms. A savage agony forced the breath from her. She let Paulina lift her legs back onto the bed and place a cloth fragrant with lavender over her forehead. Sofia swallowed a wail, held it in like a secret. She would not cry in front of Paulina. She would keep the grief to herself, nurturing it like a cut jewel too precious to share.

The days and months and years stretched ahead with no one left to love and nothing but household cares to fill her days. Paulina murmured something about sleep. Sleep. Yes. If she could not yet die, she could at least escape into a temporary oblivion where nothing could hurt her. Even Giorgio. The pain dulled just a little as she let herself sink into the pillows. Blackness descended, warm and familiar. She was in the workshop, the smooth grain of the brush handle resting in the crook of her thumb, the tiny wisps of her miniver brush shiny with pigment as she dabbed and shaded. When she painted, she soared with the angels. Her eyes closed and her shoulders relaxed. Our Lady would take her and keep her safe.

"Sister? Are you in there? Your maid was not below so I've come up on my own. Here you, step away and let me at her. Oh my! You do look bad."

Sofia just managed to pull the sheet over her breasts before her sister-in-law reached the bed. Caterina filled the room like a bowl overflowing with yeast-risen dough. She flicked the cloth off Sofia's head with one sturdy forefinger and covered her eyes with a palm that stank of cloves and baby vomit.

"There now. You've had a shock. I said to my Ruberto this morning you will be very low today. He told me I shouldn't come to see you and I said that of course I would not. But as soon as he went out, I rounded up Marcello and came straight away." She paused for breath, smiling. "As you see."

Sofia stared at the square of oiled parchment covering the window while Caterina settled herself onto the bed and arranged the voluminous folds of her skirts. "I can see how you suffer. But don't you worry yourself. You lie there and rest and I'll keep you company. Girl! Fetch me something to drink."

Sofia said nothing. The tears she wanted to shed dried behind her eyes. The sobs that burned her throat buried themselves deep in her chest.

"Your father was a good man. Or at least I'm sure he tried to be. Of course he did! It's not right what people are saying about him today. I saw the fresco with my own eyes, as you very well know, and I saw no harm in it. I expected to see more angels—or *any* angels, come to that. Ruberto agreed with me there. I don't think you can ever have too many angels."

Sofia just stared up at Caterina, her mind still fixed on the gray face of her father. She had no will of her own, didn't even care enough to contradict Caterina.

"Of course the fresco's rubble now. Perhaps it's just as well. Ruberto doesn't think it wise to incite more strife in our city. He says the attack probably had something to do with the fresco. I don't know about that—seems unlikely to me, but Ruberto knows so much more about these things than I do. I liked your father's painting of the Nativity and always meant to ask Ruberto to get such a one done for me. I rather fancy something to help with my confinements. Ruberto was sure your father would give him a good price, seeing as we're all related." Caterina let out a noisy sigh. "But I suppose it's too late now." She patted Sofia's bare shoulder, then tucked the sheet around her neck. "At least we can give thanks to God that your father's in heaven. I'll pray for him." She sat back, her hands folded over her stomach. "And now I have some wonderful news, sister. You'll never guess!"

"You're with child," Sofia said dully.

"Oh la! How could you possibly know? I've just learned myself. God willing, you'll soon know my joy! Ruberto is determined this one will be another boy and I'm sure he's right. Oh sister! I am so blessed!"

Sofia closed her eyes but she could not close her ears. The emptiness of her own womb despite Giorgio's efforts to swell it was her secret satisfaction. She wanted nothing to do with mewling and puking offspring. Like Caterina, all the young women of her acquaintance talked of nothing but babies—and all reeked of sour milk or worse. God had kept her barren and she thanked Him for it.

"Sister?"

Wearily, Sofia opened her eyes.

"I said, do you think he'll do such a one for me?"

"Who?"

"Your father's man. His second in the workshop? I don't remember his name, but I'm thinking he might do me a panel for my confinement as well as your father could and probably for much cheaper."

"Delgrasso?"

Caterina waved the name into the air. "If you say so. Will he do?"

"Delgrasso?" Sofia said the name again with a bark of a laugh that startled Caterina.

"What can you find to laugh at? I'm glad you're sounding more cheerful, but I don't see what is amusing about my commissioning this Delgrasso fellow to do a panel like the one at the wedding feast. I know people say your father is—forgive me, was—the great master and all, but that's mostly talk. One panel's much like another."

If Caterina had slapped her in the face, Sofia would not have been more surprised. The very notion that fussy little Messer Delgrasso, who wasn't good for much more than grinding pigments and decorating shields, was indistinguishable from Maestro Barducci was absurd. Infuriating.

Wrong.

Sofia struggled up on her elbows. "My father's workshop will not produce any more panels." She held up a hand to forestall more words. "Another workshop will take in Delgrasso, but I assure you he won't be the one to carry on my father's work."

"Then who will?"

"I don't know." A band of iron circled her chest. Never again would she take a full breath that did not stink of grief.

And guilt.

Would Caterina never leave? And was she right about her father being in heaven? Her father often spoke of things that she knew were not sanctioned by Fra Angelo. Was he at this moment screaming while the devil's hot pokers clawed at his flesh, seared eyes that had seen the world with such vision? He had died unconfessed.

And what of the Nativity panel? How was she to find it in the rubble, much less take it to Siena? She was only a woman. Sofia looked at Caterina and saw her future. She would grow plump and self-satisfied, smothered by children and household cares.

And she would never go to Siena.

CHAPTER FOUR

It is not without the impulse of lofty spirit that some
are moved to enter [the profession of painting]. . . .
—Cennini, *Il Libro dell'Arte*, Chapter II

Y ou cannot be serious, husband. Delgrasso can scarcely hold a
brush."

"What do *you* know about it?" Giorgio sneered, then wiped
his sleeve across his greasy mouth. "I thank you to stay out of my
business."

"It is my father's business. I have a right to know."

"Your father's been dead these three months and you are my
wife. You've no right to anything unless I give it to you."

"But you can't just throw away my father's reputation on such
a man!"

"Delgrasso has promised me he will get enough commissions to
make it worth my while to keep the workshop open."

"Commissions from whom?" Sofia tried without success to
keep the scorn from her voice.

"You do well to moderate your tone, wife. Delgrasso won't be
taking on the fancy frescoes your father did, if that's what you're
thinking. Those frescoes don't pay the bills as reliably as armor and

standards. Delgrasso tells me your father often ran the risk of having payment refused if a patron did not approve his work."

"Not often."

"Often enough. And I'm not willing to take the risk."

Sofia opened her mouth to protest, then closed it and busied herself with her food. She thought of her promise to her father to get the Nativity panel to Siena. The mouthful of cured pork could not mask the tang of grief in the back of her throat. He had been in his grave for three months and she had not even tried to find out if the panel had survived the attack on Delpino's palazzo.

"I'll make a tidy enough income on Delgrasso's work," Giorgio was saying.

"What about my father's reputation?"

"Why should I care? Do I need to remind you that for four years you have been *my* wife and not a grubby apprentice for your father?"

"You never objected to what I did in my father's house before we married."

Giorgio chewed thoughtfully for a moment. "It didn't much interest me. You were pretty enough and your father had money for a good dowry. I knew you would give up your painting nonsense when we married."

"And love?"

"Please, wife, we are far beyond speaking of that. We had our time at the beginning, I'll grant you. Now your only duty is to give me sons. And thanks to God, Messer Ardinghelli, and the income from Delgrasso's workshop, we will have money enough."

"So long as you don't gamble it away."

Giorgio opened his mouth. A morsel of half-chewed meat spilled out onto his chin. Very slowly, he laid his knife upon the table. "You dare chide me? In my own house?"

"When you deserve it, yes!"

She realized her mistake too late. Giorgio flung back his chair so it toppled to the floor. He lunged around the table, grabbed her wrist, and pulled her from her chair. When the blow came, she was so surprised that she crumpled without a sound and lay there unmoving while Giorgio lurched around the room, raving about her shortcomings as a wife, threatening to have her charged as a nag. She saw the rind of a melon, stuck to the heel of one boot, smear the floor a handspan from her eyes. She kept still, refusing even to give him the satisfaction of moving from his path.

Let him walk around her.

Let him walk over her.

She remained still until finally Giorgio blundered from the room, leaving in his wake the reek of his anger. Slowly she raised her head, then curled her legs beneath her heavy skirts, brought her hands to the floor, and grasped the seat of a chair. As her head rose above her shoulders, it bobbed with a dizziness that churned her stomach. She hoped the edge of her jaw, where Giorgio's fist connected, had not bruised. She had no wish to share her shame with the world.

A beam of light sliced through the one window, reminding Sofia that the sun was still high in the sky and she had many more hours to exist before darkness let her sleep. What would her father think to see her brought so low? Giorgio would never have dared strike her while her father still lived. But now that he had made a start . . .

Paulina slipped into the room. "Come, mistress. Let me help you to bed."

For a moment, Sofia wanted to give in to Paulina's ministrations, let her bathe her temples with warm water, then tuck her into bed, never to rise again.

*"You can do better, mia bella. Look at that line. It's crooked. You
are not concentrating."*

"But Papa, my eyes are so tired! We've been working since dawn."

*"And we'll work to sunset if that's what it takes for you to deliver
me straight lines."*

*Antonio Barducci stalked back to his own desk. Sofia scowled after
him. What did he expect her to do—work until she dropped dead of
exhaustion? He was a bully and a tyrant. She felt like putting down her
brush right that second and leaving him to draw his own straight lines.
She was young and she was beautiful—too beautiful to waste away in
a dirty room with its piles of unsanded panels and pots of paints when
outside in the bustling streets of San Gimignano walked plenty of young
men who would flatter her and love her and never expect her to draw
straight lines—or indeed any lines at all.*

"Don't just sit there like a moonfaced cow."

"Yes, Papa." Sighing, she picked up her brush.

Sofia sat up straight and pushed Paulina's hands away. "Fetch
me my cloak, Paulina. I will go to the Duomo."

"Alone? What about the master?"

"I'll worry about the master."

Fear widened Paulina's eyes. "But . . ."

The outside door slammed, and they heard a squeal of pain.

Sofia reached for Paulina's hand. "Come with me. If the master
finds out, we can say we went to visit Caterina." Her voice wavered.
"I need to see my work, Paulina."

Sofia felt Paulina's hand tremble and began to regret demanding
so much. Paulina had already risked everything to help her paint in
the tower while her father lived. If she had been discovered then, her
fate would have been far harsher than Sofia's. *She* would have carried
on being Giorgio's wife; Paulina would have been thrown into the
street to starve. Sofia squeezed Paulina's hand. "You are very brave."

Paulina nodded, then stood up and went to fetch Sofia's cloak. Sofia sighed with relief. Even an illiterate maid with nothing to recommend her but gentle hands and a stout heart was better than no one. For the first time since her father died, Sofia thought that perhaps she was just a little bit less alone.

Paulina returned with a black cloak. She draped it around Sofia's shoulders, then arranged the hood so it hid Sofia's hair and shadowed her face.

When mistress and maid emerged into the Via San Giovanni, Sofia saw what—or rather who—had cried out after Giorgio had banged from the house. A boy was sprawled in the middle of the street, his arm scraped raw. Giorgio must have knocked him over. Sofia helped the child to his feet. He shook her off, stumbled into an alleyway next to the house, then stopped and steadied himself against a wall with one skeletal arm. He turned and faced Sofia. Rage glowered from a pinched face. The long, harsh winter had brought famine to the lower orders of the town and devastation to the countryside. The merchants and nobles of the commune had survived well enough, but many of the poor had starved. Sofia shuddered at the memory of Caterina telling her how a few desperate souls had cut down and devoured an executed body hanging from a gibbet outside the town walls. She considered tossing the child a coin, then thought better of it. He'd be accused of stealing it and condemned to a whipping. She took Paulina's hand and with a stronger step set off toward the Duomo. God must have sent the child to remind her that hope was not yet lost.

She was no wretch starving in a gutter.

She was still the daughter of Maestro Antonio Barducci, and God had not yet taken her eyes.

"Wait here, Paulina," Sofia said when they arrived at the base of the long flight of steps leading up to the Duomo. "And don't look so worried. We'll be back home long before the master returns."

Inside the cool, dimly lit church, Sofia slipped along the south wall to a side chapel containing the altarpiece depicting the life and martyrdom of sweet young Santa Lucia. Sofia bowed her head, whispered a novena, then moved forward. Even in the gloom, she easily picked out the parts of the various panels she had painted. She remembered the trouble she had getting the saint's robe to drape in a way that suggested some movement of her limbs. Her father had been scathing.

"You're attempting too much, daughter. Mix in a half bean of lead to add a few highlights and be done with it. We don't have all day for you to waste."

"But I think I can show something of her movement beneath the gown." Sofia pursed her mouth. The flat panel was at times so unyielding, so unnatural. How was she to show the contours of a body on a surface that could not mimic the depths and shades of life?

The altarpiece consisted of four panels flanking a larger image of Santa Lucia, patron saint of the blind, and one of Sofia's favorites. Born in the time of the Roman emperor Diocletian, Lucia had refused a marriage arranged for her to a local man—a pagan like her parents—and insisted on dedicating her virginity to God. The first panel showed Saint Agatha appearing to Lucia in a vision. Sofia noted that the figures were stiff and unconvincing—a clear sign that Messer Delgrasso had done most of the work.

In the second panel, Lucia was distributing alms to the poor. The saint stood tall and slim in the center of the panel. To her right, Maestro Barducci had clustered a group of figures bowed with sickness, ragged in poverty, some leaning on crutches, some holding hands out for the saint's charity. The panel definitely showed the hand of the master. Fine filaments of gold shot through the draped robe of the saint, and the earnest expressions on the faces of the poor showed a fitting veneration. In the third panel, Barducci showed Lucia being sentenced to life in a brothel because, as a Christian, she had refused to burn a sacrifice to the emperor's image. Sofia shivered as she remembered hearing her father read the words ascribed to the evil Paschasius, governor of Syracuse. "*Call others to you for to defoul her, and labor her so much till she be dead.*" At fourteen—the same age as the saint when she was condemned— Sofia had been horrified. She didn't know what being labored to death meant, but she guessed it had to be a dreadful thing, and all because beautiful Santa Lucia would not renounce God.

Barducci had allowed Sofia to be the principal painter of the fourth panel, which showed a pair of oxen roped to Lucia and attempting to drag her to the brothel. Sofia had painted one of the oxen with its neck extended and snout high in the air, straining to pull the saint off her feet. But the saint would not be moved. Sofia had placed Lucia in the exact middle of the panel, standing upright, dressed in a deep blue cloak lined with gold over a gown of moss green loosely draped over a body at ease—her purity a reproach to the bulging muscles of the oxen pulling her to a life of sin.

Sofia was proud of the expressions on the faces of the men prodding the oxen to make them pull harder. But she was not so satisfied with the depiction of the saint's face. Her father had taken over and painted Lucia as a beautiful young woman who stood serenely apart from the action. Sofia would have given her more expression, showed her resistance to her punishment with more passion.

Sofia smelled incense, pampered flesh, and rotten teeth. She composed her features into a pious mask and turned around.

"Good afternoon, Fra Angelo."

"What business brings you here at this time of day?" Fra Angelo, the sharp-chinned cleric who ran the Duomo like it was his personal property, glanced over her shoulder at the altarpiece. "Admiring your father's work?"

Sofia said nothing.

"Always the sin of pride with you, my child. The death of your father should bring you humility."

"Is it a sin to admire my father's work?"

Fra Angelo moved closer. Sofia looked down at his heavy gold rings set with jewels. Their worth could feed San Gimignano's starving families for months.

"This work was completed before your marriage?" he asked.

"Yes, padre. About two years before."

"And you had a hand in it?"

"Me? Does something about the work displease you?"

Sofia lowered her eyes while her mind scrambled to find a way to avoid lying while also not telling the truth. In the years prior to her marriage, Fra Angelo had often chided her father about Sofia's unmanageable nature, her disobedience, even her lack of piety. When Maestro Barducci took Sofia with him on his journeys—once even to the new papal palace in Avignon—Fra Angelo had made his displeasure well known. Sofia knew he suspected she'd done much more than just accompany her father on his travels—that, in fact, she had been his most promising apprentice.

"I asked you a question and don't expect one in return."

"I don't mean to offend, padre. But all questions about my father's work are for my father and he can no longer answer them. I still grieve and so I came here for comfort." She paused, letting the reproach hang in the thick air.

"Yes, yes, of course, child. We all lament the loss of your father. But you must master this grief. It has been a full three months since God saw fit to take him." He placed one hand upon her brow and mumbled a few words. Sofia tried not to show her disgust as his damp fingers smudged her skin. When he finished, he exhaled and

---

stepped back. "We are glad that your father's man will carry on his work."

"My father's man? Delgrasso? What work?" Giorgio had told her that Delgrasso would not be taking on any large commissions. The Church always ordered altarpieces and frescoes—both far beyond Delgrasso's capacity.

"My child!" The loose skin at Fra Angelo's neck quivered. "This sharp tone is unseemly. A Church commission is no business of yours."

"Forgive me, padre. I am distressed by my father's death." She blinked to force out some tears. "My husband expects me home. I must be gone."

She bent over the damp hand he held for her to kiss. The blue veins snaked under the skin like strips of gnarled cord. As she brushed her lips over the surface of a finely cut ruby, she couldn't help admiring how the light caught and shimmered in its depths. She'd like to mix such a color, perhaps for a cloak, maybe edged in gold and contrasted with a deep blue gown.

"Go with God, child."

He moved closer, and for a moment she wondered if he meant to touch her. But he merely shook his head and sighed before turning away and walking slowly toward the altar.

As she watched him go, she chided herself for coming to the Duomo. Why torment herself? She would never paint again, and the sooner she got used to the idea, the better for her mind and for her soul.

∾

The bells for sext turned the endless morning into afternoon. Sofia's life had become one long succession of nothings. She supervised the servants, suffered through Caterina's visits, and went to the Duomo with Giorgio once a week. Within its cool walls, she kept her eyes averted from the frescoes and the altarpieces. To look upon her work was worse than torture. Only at night, after Giorgio fell off her and into sleep, did she sometimes let herself remember the feel of the brush dipping into pigment made smooth by grinding and water. But only sometimes.

The sole brightness in her long days was that Giorgio ignored her more often than he spoke to her.

On a hot day in July, four months after the death of her father, Sofia lingered in the doorway of her house, hoping to catch a breath of wind. Heat flowed through the streets like melted wax. Merchants lounged in front of their shops, some napping in slices of shade, others murmuring to their neighbors. The usual buzz of commerce had slowed, but every shop except her husband's was still open. The shuttered ground floor workshop infuriated her. Giorgio should be tending the business his father left him instead of wasting his days in the tavern or rushing out on urgent business for kinsmen of the Ardinghelli. Sofia preferred not to imagine what business.

A commotion in the street drew her attention. She caught a glimpse of a dirty yellow hat and heard shouting. Giorgio detached himself from the fray and weaved toward her.

"Get back inside! I won't have my wife standing in the street gawping."

"The house is stifling."

"I want you inside!" he shouted. A few people turned.

"Lower your voice." Sofia edged past him back into the house, then strode through the passageway beyond the deserted workroom that led to the kitchen. He caught up with her and, before she could push him away, crushed her against his chest. She went limp and waited, her cheek throbbing with the beating of his heart through the thick material of his gown. His breath filled the space with fumes of wine that made her gag.

"We were not always like this, Sofia."

"What?" Sofia's knees buckled and for a moment Giorgio's arms supported her.

"You heard me."

"You've had too much wine." She pushed herself away.

Giorgio reached one arm across the passageway, blocking her exit. "I must have a son." A jolt of grinding pain made her gasp as his fingers closed over one breast. She wrenched herself free, ducked under his arm, and darted for the stairs. He lunged forward. "You *must* give me a son. It's your duty."

"It's God's will." She climbed a few steps, then looked back. He was staring up at her, his dull eyes wet. She hesitated. Carefully, she placed one foot on the stair below, kicking the hem of her gown out of the way. With one hand, she braced herself against the wall of the stairwell, ready to retreat if he attacked her, but ready also to talk sense if he would listen. He staggered toward her, caught his heel on the uneven floor, and collapsed backward. His skull cracked against the stone wall. She started forward, her foot dangling in midair above the step. *Is he hurt? I should go to him.* Then she saw his chin drop to his chest and seconds later heard snores.

Abruptly, she turned and continued up the stairs to the loggia. From there, she moved to a second outside staircase and through a small door that led into the first level of the tower. Three sets of ladders rose into the gloom. Her sudden pity for Giorgio had unsettled her. It was worse than rage. It made her weak. She mounted the ladders, her breath coming in ragged gasps. When she emerged into the tiny room at the top of the tower, she could still smell her materials—the whites and yolks of eggs used as binders, pigments from the earth, the chalky gesso, the leaf glue made from bits of goat's hooves. She sat on the stool in front of her table. Regret churned her stomach, an ache both sharp and dull, intermingling like dry pigment dissolving into clear water. What did God want from her? He'd given her a desire to paint, to praise Him with charcoal and colors. Why couldn't she be like Caterina—content with her household, her brood of children, her husband? She must learn to master herself. She was Giorgio's wife. Nothing more.

She stood up and walked over to the window. Five years ago, she had stood with her father upon a hill opposite San Gimignano and admired the skyline of towers.

"It is a noble sight, mia bella. One day you must paint it."

Sofia laughed. "I haven't the skill."

"Perhaps not yet. But you will. The towers will form under your brush and the world will see the glory that is San Gimignano."

"There must be five dozen towers, Papa. How can I capture them all?"

"Close to six dozen at last count. And you will find a way. Now, we must return to the city before the gates are closed. The sun is already starting to set."

"May I make a start on the Saint Christopher panel tomorrow? I have an idea for how to depict the river that Saint Christopher carries Our Lord across."

"You may work on the panel, but only if you promise to go one full day without mentioning Giorgio Carelli."

"Oh Papa! Giorgio's shown you the greatest respect. And I love him. Why do you tease me?"

"I'm sorry, mia bella. I cannot be certain that you'll be happy with this man."

"The marriages of most of my acquaintances have been arranged and none of them have yielded much happiness. If you allow me to make my own choice, then I'll have a much greater chance of happiness than those for whom it is a dream." Sofia looked archly at her father, secure in her logic.

"Perhaps I wish you to choose more wisely. Giorgio is not your equal."

"How can you say that, Papa? Giorgio is tall and handsome and kind and . . . " She faltered, logic forgotten. *"And he loves me. Surely that's enough."*

"For some, cara mia, but not for you. Now, I will have no more talk of Giorgio this evening."

"And tomorrow?"

"You heard my bargain. The Saint Christopher panel in exchange for silence about young Messer Carelli."

"You're a hard man, Papa," Sofia said with a sigh as she let him draw her hand through his arm and lead her along a road that descended from their vantage point to the gates of San Gimignano. Her father could not hold out forever. She was already fifteen. If he waited too long to give his consent, Giorgio might grow impatient and look elsewhere. No, that was impossible. Giorgio loved her.

The only certainty now was that she would never paint the towers of her city—or any city. All she could do was pray to Our Lady for the strength to accept her life with grace. Perhaps if she couldn't give him a son, Giorgio would let her go into a convent. She'd make a good nun. Her years as a painter had taught her how to work with diligence, and what was more pious than her thoughts while she used her paints to breathe life into the saints and the Holy Family? And as for the vows, poverty would be no hardship. In her father's house she'd never known much luxury, and Giorgio was proving himself more adept at draining the family assets than adding to them. And chastity? Sofia would praise God never to have another man slobber over her. Thanks to her father's travels, she had avoided a convent education, but she'd heard other girls talk about the nuns—the harsh rules, the punishments, the nights kneeling on stone floors as cold as death.

And that was the problem. Even Sofia realized that the third vow—obedience—might prove her undoing.

ᐇ

"Ruberto entrusts you to do this?" Sofia couldn't keep the surprise from her voice. She knew of many women in the commune who transacted business alongside their husbands. Several of them—mostly widows—even took charge of their own stalls in the market. But Caterina? Sofia didn't think she had the wit.

"Ruberto's far too busy for such matters. He sent a message to Messer Delgrasso yesterday stating what we want, and now the rest is up to me. He trusts me. Why wouldn't he? There are plenty of merchants in our town who can tell you that I drive a hard bargain." Caterina smiled, showing large yellow teeth. "You just wait, sister. I'll have Delgrasso on his knees by the time I'm through with him. Are you ready? I've only a short time before I must be back. And where is my brother this morning? Will he mind you leaving the house?"

"Giorgio is on business for Messer Ardinghelli. He won't know I've been out."

Or care, Sofia wanted to add. Since his drunken demand for a son, Giorgio had mostly left her alone. Some nights he'd even rolled away from her and gone straight to sleep. She was surprised at the ambivalence of her own feelings. She should be rejoicing—thanking the Virgin for such deliverance. Instead, she felt queerly bereft. It was much easier to be the one who did the despising.

"My Ruberto doesn't approve of his brother's association with the Ardinghelli," Caterina was saying. "He thinks Giorgio should spend more time with his business and that Messer Ardinghelli should look elsewhere for men to do his bidding."

"Ruberto would do well to mind his own business."

Caterina's eyes filled with tears and her white cheeks wobbled. Sofia instantly regretted her sharp tone. Caterina had only been saying what Sofia thought often enough herself.

"Forgive me, sister. I've been distracted. I'm happy to go with you and speak with Delgrasso. I'm somewhat familiar with the painter's craft and may be able to help you settle a good contract."

"I know exactly what I want." Caterina was all smiles again. "A nice panel of Our Lady."

"A *Maestà*?"

"Hmm? Yes, if you say so. And the Child, of course. Can I get one in time for this confinement? The midwife says the babe will be born before the start of winter."

Sofia wanted to laugh. How was it possible that even someone as ignorant of the painting trade as Caterina did not know the length of time required to create a panel worth having? And had she any idea what such a panel would cost? In her father's workshop, many, many months elapsed between the initial preparation of the wood with its numerous layers of *gesso grosso* and *gesso sottile* and the drying of the final coats of varnish. Caterina would be with child again by the time her panel was ready. And it was by no means certain that Delgrasso even possessed enough skill to fashion a decent panel. Without the vision of the maestro (or herself, Sofia thought smugly), any panel he created would be about as lifeless as a scorched stick of wood.

"Let's see what Messer Delgrasso says," Sofia said.

She followed Caterina out the door and then walked by her side up the Via San Giovanni toward her father's workshop. She would never learn to think of it as Delgrasso's. The summer sun had not yet climbed above the tops of the towers, so the walk was a relatively cool one until they reached a flight of stairs that led up to the workshop. It had been built against the highest part of the city walls next to the Fortezza, which commanded panoramic views of the surrounding countryside. By the time they reached the top of the stairs, Caterina's face was brick red and she was breathing so heavily that Sofia feared she would tumble back the way they'd come.

"Monna Carelli! And Monna Carelli! An honor. Oh yes, an honor! Please, come in, come in out of the heat. I have two chairs all ready for you. Here by the door. Some refreshment? A glass of wine and water? Of course, you must have wine. Dear Monna Carelli, you look all in! And Monna Carelli, may I say again how grieved I am?" Messer Delgrasso's wide smile contradicted his words. Sofia suspected that for Messer Delgrasso, life couldn't be much better.

"Thank you, Messer Delgrasso. I know my father would be glad his workshop remains open."

"Yes, yes. As am I. Your husband has done well by me, although I must say the share he demands is high for a poor painter. Perhaps you could speak with him?" Sofia caught a whiff of the urine used to prepare the red lac streaking his hands. Daubs of the same pigment covered his smock and one cheek. He looked like he'd be more at home in the butcher's guild than in a painter's workshop—except that Messer Delgrasso would not last two minutes with slabs of meat bigger than he was.

"I have no influence with my husband," Sofia said. "My sister comes to commission a *Maestà* panel. Can you help her?"

"Yes, yes, of course. That's what we do here, eh? You know that better than anyone." He winked.

"I knew almost nothing about my father's work." Sofia stared at Delgrasso, willing him to keep his mouth shut. Apart from her father and Paulina, Messer Delgrasso was the only living person who knew Sofia had painted many of the panels sold from the workshop. Caterina might be ignorant, but she wasn't deaf.

"Quite right. So, Madonna Carelli, you wish a nice panel of the *Maestà*. Good choice. What are your requirements? Your husband's letter did not specify."

"Something smallish, I think," Caterina said. "Not too much gold, but I would like some of that nice blue color for Our Lady's robes."

"Lapis? Well, yes, it's traditional of course. But I must tell you, Monna Carelli, that it is very expensive." He shook his bald head. "Shocking. But if that is what you want, I'm happy to do it for you. The price will be fifteen florins for the materials. In advance. And then another ten florins upon delivery of the panel."

Sofia stifled a laugh. She knew the price was exorbitant. But she had to give Delgrasso credit. He had learned enough from her father to know that starting high was the only way to get close to a reasonable price.

"I can give you five florins," Caterina said. "And I want the panel by winter."

"Oh no, no." Delgrasso fluttered his hands, sending more whiffs of urine into the air. "Dear me, no! I am sorry, Monna Carelli, but that is just not possible."

"Which part, Messer Delgrasso?" Caterina asked coolly. "The price or the time?"

"Both. Oh yes, dear me, yes. A panel such as this requires many, many weeks—months—of work. Please, Monna Carelli, can you tell her?"

Sofia shook her head. "I think my sister knows what she is about. But perhaps you have something already finished?" She knew very well that he did not. Although some workshops kept small veneration panels for patrons to buy on the spot, her father had always worked to order.

"Goodness me, no. I have nothing. I work when a patron asks me." His eyes tightened and, for a moment, lost their affable expression.

"And you are busy, Messer Delgrasso?" Sofia peered over his shoulder at the large workroom that fronted the house. One apprentice was grinding pigments and another was slumped and snoring in front of a half-finished shield. She couldn't help feeling gratified that the steady profits Giorgio predicted were about as likely to materialize as a new panel for Caterina. "Where are your people?"

"Yes, well, the heat, you know. We're finding it somewhat onerous. But, please, let us think on your sister's request. I can go as low as fifteen florins in total if I use no lapis and a very small bit of gold. Delivery will be in six months. And that, my dear Monna Carelli, is putting me at great risk. But for the sister-in-law of my former master's daughter, anything is possible."

"Except getting what I want at the price I wish to pay," Caterina said calmly.

Sofia wished her father could have been there. He never had a good opinion of her brother-in-law's wife. This proof of her shrewdness would have pleased him.

Messer Delgrasso held out his red-stained hands. "I'm sorry, Monna Carelli. Perhaps if I could speak with your husband in person?"

"My husband is too busy. So you can do nothing for me?"

"Ah, yes, well." Messer Delgrasso looked so miserable that Sofia almost pitied him. She left him to stare dolefully at Caterina while she walked a few steps farther into the workshop. The tang of varnish hung faintly in the air. If the workshop had been operating at full capacity as it was under her father, the smell would have been almost overpowering. Now, it was just enough to bring back memories with a bitterness tempered by distance. She wandered over to a table set into a corner of the workshop—her father's table. Messer Delgrasso had left the table almost in the same state she had seen it the last time she'd entered the workshop to deliver the Nativity panel. Leaning against the wall was the thick ledger holding the records of all her father's commissions, back to the time when he apprenticed under the great Giotto in Florence.

"Well, you know, I do have something that I might be able to let go for that price." Messer Delgrasso's voice drifted over to Sofia. "Come with me, Monna Carelli. I will show you."

Sofia glanced up as Messer Delgrasso pulled a panel from a shelf next to his own worktable.

"It has been damaged, as you see. Quite badly so, I'm afraid. I could have a go at repairing it, but you can see the work is very fine. The maestro himself completed it."

"Why, this is exactly right. Sister! Come look. Messer Delgrasso can let me have the very panel I admired at the wedding. Isn't that wonderful? The damage isn't much, especially if I don't place it too close to a candle." Caterina bustled forward, the Nativity panel clutched in one hand. "It will do perfectly well, don't you think?"

Sofia expected to feel sadness and certainly regret, but she wasn't prepared for the jolt of terror that almost took her breath away. She held out a hand, saw that it was shaking, dropped it, breathed deeply, and then tried again. There—the shaking was less. No one had noticed.

"May I see it?"

"Messer Delgrasso says it's your father's work. It *is* damaged, to be sure." She looked sharply at Messer Delgrasso. "But that will only serve to lower the price. And it's not *exactly* what I wanted. I hadn't counted on a Nativity."

"With Adoration of the Shepherds," Sofia murmured.

"Pardon?"

"The panel—it shows the Nativity with shepherds. See, there are two of them kneeling in front of Our Lord."

"I'm sure I don't care if shepherds are included so long as I get a good price. One florin."

"Monna Carelli! Even if the panel is damaged, I can't let it go for one florin. Eight florins is my lowest price."

Sofia's thumbnail grazed the surface of her tower. Two long scratches already marred the face of one of the angels, and some of the gold in the Madonna's halo had flaked off. She remembered punching the tiny designs into the gold leaf, then burnishing the gold until it shone.

"How did you come by this?" she asked. "My father made it for the Delpino family."

"Yes, yes, of course, but you see, things have changed."

"If you mean the attack on the Delpino palazzo, I am aware of it."

"Oh yes, of course. Forgive me." Messer Delgrasso flushed as his small feet danced across the worn wood floor. He reminded Sofia of one of the rabbits she'd once painted in the corner of a panel of Saint Francis. All he needed was a pair of long white ears. "Messer Delpino, as I'm sure you know, was killed in the attack. Terrible business. And his son has taken his new wife away from our city— to Florence, I believe. Or perhaps Pisa." He paused, shaking his head. "No matter now, I suppose. The panel was found and brought back to this workshop." He looked at her hopefully. "As you see."

Sofia knew very well that Delgrasso had likely been the one who had found the panel. And Delgrasso was well aware that the Delpino family had paid for the panel and that it should be sent to Delpino's son—whether he was in Florence or Pisa or even France. To keep it was little better than theft. Her fingers tightened around the wood. And this was *her* panel. Its return must be a sign from God.

Caterina pried the panel from Sofia's hands, then held it at arm's length and stared, quiet for once. Sofia wanted to snatch the panel back, run into the streets, and keep running until she found Maestro Manzini in Siena and *made* him take her in.

"Three florins." Caterina looked up from the panel, her usually serene expression hard and calculating. "My final offer, Messer

Delgrasso, for a panel that I gather you may not have the right to sell."

"A fair offer," Sofia said. "As I'm sure the guild would agree." She smiled at Delgrasso.

"The guild? Ah, yes, well, of course. They don't have time for such petty matters. And as I said, nothing is too much trouble for the daughter of Maestro Barducci or her honored sister." He bowed at Caterina. "Shall I wrap the panel?"

"Please."

As Sofia watched Delgrasso bustle around the workshop searching for a scrap of leather, she felt the terror ease, replaced by . . . what? A lightness. A weight had lifted that she hadn't even realized she was carrying in her bones in the months since her father's death. She was no closer to Siena, but for the first time since that terrible morning in the Delpino palazzo, she didn't think she was so impossibly far away.

"Come, Caterina," she said almost gaily. "I'll help you find a place for your new panel. I'm sure it will be a great comfort."

"I intend it to be." Caterina took the wrapped panel from Delgrasso and handed over the money. "Thank you, Messer Delgrasso."

"Yes, yes, you're very welcome, I'm sure." He urged them out into the blazing sun, closing the door so quickly that Sofia almost caught her hem. She wanted to laugh out loud.

"Sister!" Caterina bustled across the loggia to meet Sofia. "I'm grieved that this will be my last visit. I will miss our talks. Oh my, the heat out here. Let us go in. I have news."

Sofia ushered Caterina into the room used to receive visitors. Three-year-old Ruberto and his little sister Isabetta followed.

"Paulina, take the children to the kitchen. Cook can find them something sweet."

"Be good, my darlings," Caterina called as the children scampered back across the loggia to the stairwell. She patted her stomach. "I am so blessed, sister. I wish you could know my joy."

"I'm sure I will. One day. Now, what is this news?"

"You'll never guess."

"Since you're already with child, I can't imagine what it could be. Does it concern Ruberto?"

"No, no, gracious me, no. Ruberto has given me leave, of course, but he'll have no part to play in the journey." Caterina laughed. "He'll send Marcello."

"What journey? Your condition surely does not allow travel."

"Heavens! I'm as strong as one of those poor boars your husband likes to kill. And I still have several months before this next confinement. Marcello will not let harm come to me."

"Who?"

"Marcello, my husband's man. Your father sent him to us, oh, I don't know, must be five years ago now. Didn't you know? I thought he lived with you."

"I think he might have worked in the shop, yes," Sofia said with a wave of one hand. "Sweeping floors and such, I don't remember much about him."

"Well, I must say he's proving himself to be a fine young man. Ruberto trusts him to take me all the way to Florence."

"You're going to Florence?"

"Yes, that's what I've been trying to tell you. Ruberto has given me leave to go pray at the Shrine of the Virgin on the road to Florence. He wants another son."

"What is this shrine?"

"It's well known among the other mothers. You'll hear about it when you're with child. I've not been there myself yet, but the journey is said to be easy enough so long as the roads are dry. I'm to leave tomorrow. I'll stay with my sister in Florence and return within the week."

"You have a sister in Florence?"

"Yes, of course. You've met her."

"Ah, yes. Forgive me." Sofia had a vague recollection of a young woman with wispy hair and Caterina's smile.

"I pray you'll soon know my joy, sister. It's beyond describing."

"I'm sure it is. You've been blessed."

"God has been good to us." Caterina helped herself to a piece of the cake Paulina had brought in.

They sat in silence for several long moments, the only sound Caterina's chewing. A few crumbs fell from her mouth to the bodice of her gown, already soiled with drool. Sofia smelled sour milk and shuddered. She couldn't see herself in a life like Caterina's—always so solicitous for the well-being of her children and her beloved Ruberto. Perhaps if she could again love Giorgio?

No. God willing, she would remain barren forever.

"What of your panel, Caterina?" Sofia asked. "Have you found a place for it?"

"Oh yes. I'm vastly pleased with it. Ruberto too."

"Take care how you place it next to the candles. The smoke can damage the surface."

"Hmm?" Caterina took another bite of cake. "If you say so."

"How goes Ruberto's business?"

"What? It does well enough, I suppose. He has his eye on the council."

"I hadn't heard. You must be proud."

"Yes. Ruberto says that after this babe is born, I may help him with the ledgers."

"You read and write?"

Caterina sliced off another generous wedge of cake. "Enough for the purpose. I only need to enter figures."

As Sofia watched Caterina eat, an idea began to form in her head. It was a ridiculous idea—too bold, too dangerous. It would destroy her.

Or be her salvation.

"Caterina. I'm happy you've come to see me today, but I'm feeling unwell. I think I might lie down."

"Oh! Well, of course." Caterina heaved herself up and turned to Paulina. "Bring your mistress a cool cloth. She's faint." She stood aside, kneading her hands. "Are you bilious?"

Sofia tried not to smile at the hopefulness in Caterina's voice. "A little. Do you know a remedy?"

"If it's what I think it is, the only remedy you will need is to see the midwife." Caterina seized Sofia's hand. "Oh sister! Is it?"

"I'm sure it's just the heat. But . . . " She paused as Caterina leaned forward eagerly. "If you should see my husband, perhaps do not mention that I'm feeling unwell. He might, ah, misinterpret. It wouldn't do to get his hopes up."

"Of course," Caterina said, patting Sofia's arm. "Your time will come, sister. When I am at the shrine, I will pray to the Virgin for you."

Sofia inclined her head, feigning exhaustion until finally Caterina swept out. She waited a few minutes, listening while Caterina gathered her children from the kitchen and herded them to the front door.

"Paulina!"

"Mistress?"

"I need to pay another visit to Messer Delgrasso."

"But you're not well."

"I'm fine." Sofia jumped up and paced around the room. "You will come with me. If we leave now, we'll be home long before the master gets back from hunting. Come, help me with my cloak."

"But, mistress, is it safe?"

"It will have to be."

Paulina fetched the cloak and followed Sofia outside into air heavy with heat and silence.

"Quickly," Sofia whispered, leading the way around the corner to a passageway cut between the wall of her house and its neighbor. They emerged into a sunny street that led up to the Fortezza and her father's workshop and avoided the busy piazzas, where Sofia might be seen.

A young man wearing the colors of Caterina's husband stepped out from another passageway, blocking their way.

Paulina slid her slight figure in front of Sofia. "I know him, mistress," she said.

Sofia stepped back into the shadows of a tower, breathing shallowly as her skirts brushed across an open drain. Paulina's head came to the young man's shoulder. She couldn't see his face under his cap, but there was something familiar about the way he held himself. Then, to Sofia's surprise, he placed one hand on Paulina's shoulder with a simple compassion that seemed to comfort her. Paulina turned around, leading him by the hand.

"Marcello will come with us."

"Marcello? You are Caterina's man?"

"Yes, madonna. I have just escorted her home. If you wish, I will escort you, keep watch if you need me to." He smiled and Sofia felt a strange tingle of recognition. Could this tall young man be the ragged boy who had swept sawdust in her father's workshop?

"Why would you help me?" she asked. "Your master and my husband may be brothers, but they are not friends."

"I don't think of your husband, madonna. But your *father* was a great man." He lifted his chin and stared into her eyes.

Sofia gasped, opened her mouth to speak, and then closed it just as quickly. She shook her head and put one hand out to steady herself against the wall. It was not possible. Marcello wore a simple tunic and rough brown hose that bunched around his ankles. Crow-black hair poked out from under his cap. He had a square chin and a nose that reminded her of a bird's beak. It gave his young face distinction and clashed with his round cheeks and full lips.

Sofia shook her head and shakily indicated with one hand that he should lead the way. The long climb up to the Fortezza and from there to the workshop gave her time to think. It wasn't possible. And yet . . . Even when quite a young girl, Sofia had been well aware of her father's appetites—for food, for good wine, for conversation, and for women. She knew that the squeals that sometimes awakened her when they traveled belonged to maids who in the morning cast flirting glances at her father and scowls at her.

It could be true. And if so? Sofia didn't know what to think.

When they arrived at the shop, she directed Paulina and Marcello to wait outside. Messer Delgrasso ushered her into the shop with much less grace than he had shown when she'd come with Caterina. "You honor me again, Monna Carelli. What might I do for you?"

"I don't wish to trouble you, signor, but I need to see my father's ledger."

"Why?"

"Do I need a reason?"

"The guild . . ."

"Doesn't need to know anything about it."

Messer Delgrasso was the same height as Sofia but twice as wide. He swayed on small feet and looked a trifle sick, like he'd eaten something foul that morning. "I don't know, Monna Carelli. Your father never allowed anyone to examine his ledger."

"My father is dead, signor, and I'm sure you must have checked the ledger since."

"Yes, well, perhaps. Your father kept good records."

"My father kept excellent records. Now please, signor. Let me see the ledger." She took a few steps toward the large table where her father had worked. "I will be quick."

Messer Delgrasso darted forward, but he wasn't fast enough to prevent Sofia from taking up the heavy ledger, its calfskin cover stained with pigment. She ignored his squeaks of protest as she ran one hand over the cover. She had seen it a thousand times but had never opened it. Maestro Barducci saw no reason to share with his daughter any information about the flow of funds through his workshop. She looked at Delgrasso. "I need a few moments. Will you be so kind?" He hovered at her elbow, panting. His squashed nose, coarse-veined and mottled, reminded her of a lump of red lac rolled in grit and left too long in the sun. She clasped the ledger to her breast and waited.

"Yes, yes, of course, madonna. I'll be at my bench if you need anything."

"Thank you." She placed the ledger upon the table and opened it. Each entry was dated in her father's precise script. She thanked God for his thoroughness as she turned the heavy pages, pausing at the entries describing the panels she had painted. She smiled at the high prices her father had commanded for her work.

Information about her Nativity panel appeared on the second-to-last page. She glanced over her shoulder. Delgrasso was showing a young apprentice how to grind pigment on the big porphyry slab she'd used so often herself. Delgrasso would find out what she had done, but what of it? He wouldn't dare tell the guild that he had let a woman go through the records. A small knife used to trim parchment had been left on the table. She picked it up and, with one swift movement, sliced the page from its binding.

CHAPTER FIVE

A yellow color known as realgar . . . is really
poisonous. . . It wants to be ground a great deal with
clear water. And look out for yourself.
—Cennini, *Il Libro dell'Arte*, Chapter XLVIII

Sofia sat across the table from Giorgio and tried not to cringe as wine dribbled down his chin. "Did you have pleasant hunting today?" she asked.

"Since when do you care about hunting?"

"I care because you do." Sofia smiled demurely. For a few moments, she thought perhaps she had changed too quickly.

Giorgio opened his mouth wide to reveal teeth furred with half-chewed meat, then let loose a guffaw. "Well it's about time, wife. If you must know, the hunting today was poor. Very poor. I saw not one boar all day."

"You didn't kill?"

"Of course I killed. Never let it be said that Giorgio Carelli goes out hunting and comes home without meat. No, I bagged a couple of birds. But it was a boar I wanted."

"You will have more luck next time," Sofia said and reached across the table to pat her husband's arm.

Giorgio glanced quizzically at her hand, then burped and sig-
naled for Paulina to bring more wine. "I might go again in a few
days if we get cooler weather. I've never seen such a parched time.
Many of the crops we passed today were dry and shriveled."

"We'll have another hard winter?"

"Some will," Giorgio said, with a shrug. "That Delgrasso fellow
promises to bring in new commissions, and I expect a good crocus
crop this fall."

Sofia smiled at how little Giorgio knew about Delgrasso's pros-
pects. The pages in the ledger following the page she'd torn out had
contained just a handful of entries with prices so low her father
would have been mortified. "I am relieved you are content, but if it
pleases you, I'll retire early." She paused. "My lord."

His eyebrows rose. "You've not called me that for some time."

"I am at fault, my lord."

"It's fitting that you remember what is due me." He regarded
her critically, his head tilted, his mouth still chewing. "You're tired
so soon? It's not yet dark."

"I am fatigued, yes. The heat."

"Or something else?"

It was too soon. She must draw him back in so he would be
incapable of denying her anything. She shook her head as she rose
from the table. "Just the heat, my lord. Do I have your leave to
retire?"

"Go on with you." Giorgio waved his dripping knife at the
door. "Take your rest. I'll come later."

Paulina met Sofia in the bedchamber and helped her out
of her blue gown—the one Giorgio had given her for Salvucci's
wedding and that she had been wearing when she watched her
father die. Paulina had scrubbed the blood stains from the hem.
As Sofia waited for Paulina to hang the gown on its pole next to

the bed, she wondered if one day she would have no further need of gowns.

"You'll sleep in the kitchen tonight, Paulina," she said.

The girl looked up, her young face puckering. "Have I displeased you, mistress?"

"Just do as I ask." What Sofia planned was a crime against God and the commune. The penalties were harsh, and Paulina would not be immune from prosecution if Sofia was exposed. It was safest to keep her well away from suspicion. If Paulina did not know what Sofia did over the next weeks and months, she could honestly protest her innocence. Sofia heard her leave the room, not quite stifling a sob. For a moment, she thought of calling her back.

"That was poorly done. I thought better of you, Sofia."

"I'm sorry, Papa."

Maestro Barducci flicked a finger at the face of her Virgin. "More terre-verte. Her nose is too flat."

"I'm trying, Papa."

"Try harder." He snatched the brush from her hand and, with a few quick strokes, added a hint of shadow at the base of the nose, then changed brushes and daubed white lightly tinged with red lac to the bridge. The face of a real woman emerged.

Sofia wanted to weep with frustration. Even if she worked another ten years, until she was an old woman of twenty-three, she would never have such skill. Why did her father persist in making her try?

"You'll soon come to it, daughter."

Sofia looked up, but he was already shuffling across the room to his worktable. Ocher stained the hem of his gown, gesso powdered his hose, even the green hood he wrapped around his head showed streaks of yellow in the dusty light filtering through the open window. She picked up the brush and tried again.

When Giorgio came to her that night, she pleaded her courses and he left her alone. The excuse did not always work, but her submissiveness at supper was already producing results. He grunted and rolled away, leaving her to bind the silence of the night around a heart knotted with fear. When sleep finally came, her mind filled with images of fire and hot pincers and the sound of Fra Angelo's voice promising everlasting torment. When a splinter of morning sun broke through a tear in the oiled square of parchment covering the window, she awoke to the smell of Giorgio brushing her cheek with a kiss. She sat up so quickly that the bedcover fell from her shoulders, exposing her bare breasts. She snatched it up as Giorgio bounded from the bed.

"I'll be in the workroom all morning, wife," he said. "You will help." He stood naked in the middle of the room, smiling broadly.

"What help can I be, my lord?" In the early months of their marriage, Giorgio had never wanted his beautiful new wife engaged in trade. Then, soon enough, neither had any desire to spend more time in each other's company than was strictly necessary. "You have clerks."

"Dolts! No, this morning I want you by my side." His smile widened. "The bulbs need counting."

"Of course, my lord. I'm delighted to help you, but may I have your leave to go first to Chapel?"

Giorgio's smile faded. "Chapel? We attended church yesterday. Why do you need another visit so soon?"

"I'm sure Fra Angelo wouldn't like to hear of you dismissing my chapel-going," Sofia said. "I wish to pray to the Virgin for guidance."

"What guidance? You don't need to be guided. I'm the only guide you need." His white belly quivered as he laughed.

"Of course, my lord." Sofia turned away and rose from her bed, winding herself into a sheet. She sensed his eyes upon her back and for a moment feared he would lunge for her. She turned around. "I'll wait upon you in the workroom, husband, as you wish."

"Good! That's how it should be. Plenty of men employ their wives. Why shouldn't I?" He pulled on his clothes—a pair of muddy hose and a gray gown belted at his waist. "I'll call your maid, shall I?"

Sofia fell back on the bed as he clumped from the room. Giorgio being helpful? Was the world ending?

An hour later, Sofia tied a large apron over her gown and set to work sorting and counting the dusty brown bulbs. The stamens of the crocuses that transformed the fields around San Gimignano into oceans of purple and yellow and white each fall yielded enough saffron to keep them for the winter, so long as Giorgio remained sober enough to get a good price for his crop. At the sound of the bells for terce, Paulina brought in bread and a round of cheese made from ewe's milk. Giorgio fell on the food. Sofia took a few nibbles of bread and ignored the cheese.

More pressing matters than the demands of her stomach preoccupied her. She needed the help of one of San Gimignano's wise women—those who, despite the efforts of the town physicians and the Church, used their herbs and poultices for healing, and sometimes for purposes too dangerous to speak out loud. Paulina's mother, Emilia, was one of them. When Sofia was a child, Emilia had been her nurse, and stayed with her until, at the age of ten, Sofia began traveling with her father to fulfill his many commissions. After Sofia married, Emilia asked Sofia to take her young daughter, Paulina, as her maid. Giorgio was willing to give anything his young bride asked and so Paulina came to them. Sofia had fond memories of her old nurse and had been very glad of Paulina's services. But would Emilia help her now? Sofia knew she still scratched out a living as a midwife and a healer, but what Sofia needed was enough to condemn Emilia to prison—or worse—if the Church found out.

An oath cut through the dusty air of the workroom. Sofia started from her reverie and looked over at Giorgio. He held up a hand dripping with blood.

"Dear God, husband! What have you done?"

"The knife slipped on this blasted cheese. It's as hard as my fist."

"Are you hurt?" Sofia took Giorgio's hand and winced when she saw the depth of the cut across his palm. The blood dripped onto the straw covering the floor, turning it a satisfying crimson. She pulled off her apron and wrapped it tightly around the hand to stop the bleeding.

Giorgio's knees buckled and the color drained from his face. He groaned. "Send for help!"

"A physician?"

"I'll not have one in the house. Send Paulina for one of the women."

"Women? What women?"

"Ach, don't loiter, wife. You know the kind I speak of." He groaned again as the blood began seeping through the layers of cloth. "Find someone, Sofia!"

Sofia wondered if God would forgive the gladness in her heart as she ran from the room in search of Paulina. He must condemn her, yet was not this turn of events proof that He approved her plan?

Paulina had heard Giorgio's yells and was already in the passageway. "What is it, mistress? Such noise!"

"The master's cut himself. Where is your mother?"

"My mother! Why?"

"We need someone skilled at healing. Can you bring her here?"

Paulina bobbed a curtsy. "I need but five minutes." She opened the door to a blast of white heat. "Tell the master he will be well," she called over her shoulder as she stepped into the street.

As Sofia watched Paulina go, the first spark of hope entered her heart. The *mistress* will be well, she reflected, so long as Emilia's skill was equal to the task. She spared a moment to worry about whether she could involve Emilia in her plan without jeopardizing Paulina, and then dismissed the thought. It was in God's hands now.

ᖇᓕ

July melted into August. Airless days and the constant threat of drought kept the whole town on edge. Paulina's mother, Emilia, tended to Giorgio with quiet efficiency. He had lost no fingers, and thanks to her poultices, the wound did not turn putrid. For a few blessed weeks, Sofia had no need of Emilia's poultices for herself, but when Giorgio could complain no longer about his hand, she was ready.

The poultice reeked and made her insides burn with a fire as intense as any she imagined awaited her in hell, but she followed Emilia's instructions. Each night, she squatted over the stinking privy jutting into the lane between her house and its neighbor and, with two shaking fingers, pushed the poultice up into the darkness of her belly. On the nights when Giorgio was not too drunk to take her, she gritted her teeth and prayed to the Virgin for patience.

"Is this what you want, cara mia?" her father asked as he drew her hand through his arm. "It's not too late."

"Oh yes, Papa. I want nothing more." Sofia's eyes brimmed with hope and happiness as she waited to be given in marriage to Giorgio. She loved her father, of course. But he was often so hard on her. Giorgio told her she was beautiful and wouldn't expect anything from her except her love. And she had so much love.

"I pray God that's true," he said, then led her to her new husband.

❦

In the last week of September fresh breezes cut through the streets, bringing the scent of autumn. Sofia knew she could not wait any longer. By late October the rains would flood the road, making the journey impossible. She arranged with Paulina to bring Caterina's man, Marcello, to the house while Giorgio was out preparing for the harvest of his crocus fields.

Marcello stood in the doorway to the room Sofia used to receive guests. The eyes, the wide brow, the thick mass of black hair—so much like her own—were all her father's. *Their father's.* How could she have not seen the resemblance before?

"You wished to see me, mistress?"

"Please sit, Marcello."

He looked at her, surprised. A servant never sat in the presence of a mistress. He didn't move.

"Please. I have something I need to ask of you."

He lowered himself onto a round stool next to the table, his hands hovering on his knees, ready at a moment's notice to push off.

Sofia sat in a chair across from him. "You took your mistress to the shrine on the road to Florence."

"Yes."

"The journey went well?"

"Yes."

Sofia smiled. "You can answer with more words, you know. I won't bite."

"Yes. I mean, I'm sorry."

"May we speak freely, Marcello?" She held up a hand. "Please. Hear me out. I know you are my father's son. He never spoke of you and I won't pretend that it wasn't a surprise to discover your existence, but you favor him and we share his blood."

"Yes. I mean, I know, mistress. Your father—our father—was a good man. He took care of my mother even after he took you away."

"Your mother?" Sofia had not thought about Marcello's mother. She'd assumed his mother had been one of the maids or maybe a whore in the town.

Marcello shifted on the stool. He was a tall man who wore the black-and-yellow livery of her brother-in-law well. "My mother is Emilia," he said, then paused, his black eyes soft. "Your nurse."

"I know who Emilia is!" Sofia snapped, then flushed. "Forgive me. It's a shock." Marcello was a few years older than she, which meant that her father must have lain with Emilia before he married her mother.

"Maestro Barducci's father needed him to marry someone with a good dowry," Marcello said by way of explanation. "My mother was not suitable."

"I'm sorry," Sofia said, realizing suddenly how different Marcello's life would have been if he had been her own mother's child—and the son to carry on the work of Maestro Barducci.

Marcello shrugged. "Your father provided for us and, when I was old enough, he found me a position with your brother-in-law. I am content."

"You're not resentful?"

"To what purpose?" Marcello looked puzzled.

Sofia smiled, sure now that she was making the right choice. Marcello was her father's son. A lesser man would have cursed his fate.

"I need you to do something for me," she said. "It will be dangerous."

For the first time, Marcello smiled. "I'm not afraid, Monna Carelli."

"Take me to Siena." The words hung in the air like a thousand dust motes looking for a place to settle.

Marcello raised one eyebrow and waited.

"I must leave San Gimignano, leave my husband. My father—our father—asked me before he died to take a panel I painted to Maestro Manzini. Your mistress has the panel now, but I will go to Siena anyway. I need you to take me, to protect me. We will tell my husband we are visiting the shrine you took your mistress to and instead take the road to Siena." She paused for breath. Now that she'd described the plan out loud, she saw its absurdity. By asking Marcello to help her, she was condemning him to death if he was caught.

Marcello shook his head, trying to suppress his laughter. "I'm sorry, mistress. But what you propose is so outlandish that . . ." He stopped, shook his head again. "You know what you ask of me?"

"I do. And once we're in Siena, I'll make sure you are rewarded. If you can't find work in Manzini's workshop, any noble family would be glad of your services. Manzini will help."

"You're sure of this?"

"I . . . well . . . ah. Manzini was close to my father. Of course he will help."

"He will take a woman—a woman who has run away from her husband—into his workshop?" Marcello cocked an eyebrow again, looking uncannily like Maestro Barducci during one of the countless times he questioned Sofia and found her wanting.

Sofia felt the life draining from her body. She turned away so Marcello could not see her face sag in defeat.

"Monna Carelli," he said. "Please. Don't distress yourself. I will take you to Siena. Together we will find a way to approach Maestro Manzini."

"You're willing to leave your master?"

"It's not how I'd wish to leave him or my mistress," Marcello said. "They have been good to me. But I confess that your plan is not without merit." He grinned. "And I've never been to Siena."

Sofia rose to her feet and held out her hand. Marcello took it between his two hands and bowed, then looked at her with her father's eyes. "I promise to keep you safe, madonna. You can depend upon it." He dropped her hands and stepped back.

"I'll send a message to you when I'm ready."

He nodded, then turned and left the room. As she heard his footsteps on the stairs leading to the street, she pressed her palms into the thick velvet of her gown to stop their shaking.

Sofia readied herself for bed and, for once, did not use Emilia's poultice. The evening had passed peacefully, soberly. Giorgio had drunk only a few cups of wine and was in an expansive mood. That afternoon he'd bagged a boar. It was a testament to how much the household had changed since summer that he came home to dine with her instead of spending the evening drinking with his Arding-helli cronies. Sofia almost felt regret. Giorgio had responded to her new docility by speaking to her more gently and by penetrating her more slowly at night. Once, he had even stroked her hair and kissed her forehead. Why could she not smile and giggle and pretend to be stupid? Caterina did it every day.

"My lord."

Giorgio was just lowering himself into bed. He looked over his shoulder and smiled. For a few moments, Sofia softened. The candlelight smoothed the coarseness of his features and showed her a glimpse of the man who had taken her from maid to woman. They had loved—passionately and completely. Willingly, she had bound herself to him for life.

And willingly she would sever that bond.

"Yes?" He stretched out one hand to snuff the candle—another concession to Sofia's wishes for light in the evening that he had long denied her.

"Leave the light. I have something I must speak with you about."

"What?"

"I am with child, my lord," she said, her eyes cast down, trusting to the candlelight playing across her smooth cheeks to heighten her beauty and her modesty.

For a moment Giorgio sat completely still, his face blank. Sofia wondered if he had understood her—or worse, suspected that she was lying. Her eyes fluttered open and she raised her chin. "My lord? Is this not good news?"

More silence. Giorgio just stared at her, his eyes wide, his mouth open and slack. And then he lunged toward her and clasped her hands in his.

"You're sure?"

"Yes, husband. Does the news please you?"

"Please me? Please me?" He shook his head, then let go of her hands, leaped out of bed, and began to pace. Sofia remained silent until he stopped at the foot of the bed, his hands on his hips, his legs wide as if he were about to mount a horse. "I'm to be a father?"

"Yes, my lord. You will have a son."

"Ah ha!" He threw back his head and roared so loudly that Sofia was sure he'd wake the whole household. But what of it? They'd know soon enough.

Sofia gazed at her belly, affecting the same serene expression she had seen so often on Caterina's face. "I'm happy, my lord, of course." Then she looked up, her eyes moist and pleading. "But I'm afraid. I hear so many stories. Just last week, Monna Amati died giving birth to her first child."

"Yes, but you're strong," Giorgio said, dropping to his knees next to the bed and stroking her arm. "And you'll have everything you need. I'll send to Florence for a midwife."

"Thank you. But Emilia has the skill. Remember how she tended your wounded hand? And she's attended the birth of all of Caterina's children."

"I'll think on it."

"Emilia will serve us well. But, my lord, would you allow me to visit the shrine of Our Lady to pray for a safe delivery? Caterina made the journey last month."

"What shrine?"

"On the road to Florence—just a few days' journey, I believe. Caterina took her husband's man, Marcello, for protection. Perhaps you could ask Ruberto if he would lend you Marcello for the same purpose? He knows the way. And I wouldn't want to ask you to spare Niccolò." She paused, fearing to push her case too hastily. Giorgio was not able to manage more than one new fact at a time. She studied his face as he thought first about the great news of her condition and second about her request to leave the city.

"I don't know," he said. "The rains will start soon. What about the roads?"

"Ruberto's man won't let me come to harm. Of course, I would ask you, my lord, to accompany me, but . . ."

"I'm much engaged with the harvest," he said absently. "And then there's my business with the Ardinghelli. They may not wish to spare me."

Sofia was very sure the Ardinghelli would be glad to spare Giorgio. "You have grave responsibilities, my lord," she said. "You can't neglect your business for such a trivial woman's matter."

"I don't hold the protection of my son a trivial matter, but maybe you're right. I can send Ruberto's man. He's a strong, hearty fellow. Just last week he ran after a wounded boar and felled it with a stroke of his blade."

"We are fortunate that so able a man has knowledge of the route. Can you trust him?"

"If Ruberto was able to entrust his own dear Caterina to this man, then I'm confident. You'll be gone a few days?"

"I believe a week, my lord. No more. Caterina has a sister in Florence whom I may stay with. It will be arranged, if you so wish."

"I'll consider it. But now, tonight, we must sleep. You can't be taxed." He leaned over and planted a wet kiss upon her forehead.

Later, as the snores of her contented husband filled the bed-chamber, Sofia stared at a ceiling she could not see. Perhaps she should give up. It would be easy enough to tell Giorgio that the baby was lost. If she was more patient, more loving . . . Surely her father never wished her to endanger her life.

"The oxen will not draw themselves, daughter. Are you content to allow Our Lord to lie in His manger without the comfort of beasts? Are you so willing to offend Our Lady?"

"I'm sorry, Papa."

Her father patted her on the head and chuckled, then returned to his own table and took up his brush.

Sofia's throat constricted as her heart filled with something like shame. She knew her reasons for going to Siena had very little to do with the wishes of her father. She longed to bend again over a panel, see the marks she made transform into objects and animals and people, feel the pigments become smooth and liquid beneath her pestle. God forgive her—she wanted to paint panels, frescoes even. She smiled into the dark. Frescoes! The very idea was absurd. Even her father had created no more than a dozen frescoes in his lifetime. When Sofia was just twelve, she had accompanied him to Padua, where he spent a year adorning the walls of one of the new churches. Sofia remembered the smell of the plaster, the dust, the noise of the carpenters constructing the scaffolding. She was allowed to watch and sometimes even to help if no one was nearby to see. Her favorite part was when her father stepped close to the prepared wall and quickly, decisively, laid the paint into the wet plaster, turning the blank white into a riot of color and piety.

Could she one day do the same?

CHAPTER SIX

Let the helm and steersman of this power to see
be the light of the sun, the light of your eye,
and your own hand.
—Cennini, *Il Libro dell'Arte*, Chapter VIII

Sofia was afraid of rupturing into a thousand pieces if she had to keep her smile in place for one more second. Giorgio put one hand on her arm and leaned forward. On the pretext of needing to adjust her cloak, Sofia turned her head just in time to avoid the brush of his lips on her cheek. God willing, she would never again see Giorgio on this earth.

"I must go." As soon as Giorgio moved away, she looked up. His expression was soft, almost fond.

"Take care of my son."

Sofia held his gaze for a few seconds, then turned away without speaking. Marcello led forward the donkey that would take her out of San Gimignano forever. He lifted her onto it and urged it toward the Porta San Giovanni. Sofia looked back just once. Giorgio had already gone into the house, but in his place stood Paulina. She did not wave or show any indication that she knew her mistress would not return. Sofia asked God to keep her young maid safe and then looked forward. She could do no more.

Sofia's nose wrinkled when the donkey ambled past the tanner's vats of hides steeping in stale urine. The pounding of hammers at the site of yet another new tower was the last sound she heard before passing through the gate into the country air. She closed her eyes and let the slow rhythm of the donkey soothe her. The noise and smells of San Gimignano would be replaced soon enough by ten times worse in Siena.

The road from the Porta San Giovanni descended to the main Via Francigena, which led one way to Florence and the other to Siena. Sofia had already established with Marcello that they would start along the road to Florence, pass the Torre di Santa Gabriella on the opposite hill, and then double back along a pathway through the forest. Marcello had been as good as his word. As far as Caterina and Ruberto knew—and Giorgio, for that matter—Marcello would return her safely to San Gimignano within the week and resume his duties as Ruberto's chief manservant.

Sofia looked up at a clear blue sky. The Virgin and her own wits would protect them. Hadn't her father always insisted that she think for herself?

"From where do you take the shape of that hand?" he asked, peering critically at her work.

"I copied it from the new fresco in the Duomo."

"Pfft! That was done by Fantoni. He looks at life through his ass."

"Papa! Maestro Fantoni's workshop does well."

"A healthy sow gives birth to dozens of piglets. That doesn't make the sow any less of a pig herself."

"I don't see what displeases you. All five fingers are present and the wound of Our Lord is artfully done."

"Have you seen blood flow in such a cramped stream? It looks like a stick. I see nothing alive there. And this hand—it's flat."

Messer Barducci flung one arm out, his palm open and facing out as if pinned to an imaginary cross. "Look at my hand, bella. See how it droops, how my thumb falls forward. That is a real hand. Draw that."

"I don't have the skill, Papa."

"You have the skill. What you lack are the eyes." He leaned over and plucked the charcoal from her hand. "For the rest of the day, I don't want you to draw. Look instead at your own hand. Don't think. Look. You are far too prone to believe what you're told. Look at the evidence."

"Mistress?" Marcello came alongside her and caught her donkey's bridle to slow it. "We're coming close to the Torre di Santa Gabriella. The path we must take lies near. Are you ready?"

Sofia looked back at the towers of her city. From her vantage point across the valley, the dozens of gray towers broke the clean air of early autumn with their sharp corners. She shivered. The towers of Siena, she knew, were even more numerous. Would she find what she needed there, what was denied her in the city of her birth? The answer was in God's hands, she thought, then faced forward and nodded to Marcello.

"I'm ready."

The pathway was broad and smooth, shaded by trees arching overhead. Sofia felt enclosed and at peace as the donkey jogged slowly along, the sound of its hooves muffled by the brown leaves littering the path. Marcello walked next to her. She wondered if he really understood the penalty if they were caught. *She* would go back to Giorgio, but Marcello? He'd be lucky to escape the executioner's hot knives before being hanged on a charge of kidnapping.

"I haven't yet thanked you, Marcello."

"So you're thanking me now?"

Sofia laughed. The differences in rank could not hide the similarities. "You remind me of him."

"He was a noble man."

"He could be. He could also be tyrannical, demanding . . ."

"Unyielding?"

"Yes."

"Have you always known?" she asked. The air smelled so pure in the forest—hints of pine and rich earth, drying leaves and air washed clean with rain.

"My mother made sure I knew my father when I was still quite young. She said that even though I could not openly be his son, I should know what blood ran in my veins."

"I can imagine Emilia saying that." Sofia thought about how Emilia's gnarled hands had prepared the poultices that kept her barren. "She was very kind to me when I was a child—and lately."

"My mother was glad when our Paulina went with you to your husband's house."

Sofia wanted to ask something else, but didn't know how.

"You are wondering about Paulina?" Marcello asked.

Sofia nodded, not trusting herself to speak. She was still amazed to be having such a conversation with a man she had known only as a servant. She wondered what her father would have thought had he known—and why he'd never troubled himself to tell her in the first place.

"Paulina's mother was my mother's sister. When her own mother died, Paulina was too young to know better. She always thought of my mother as hers. But we are cousins, not brother and sister."

Like we are, Sofia thought. "Did you wish to paint?"

"Like you did? Yes. But your mother did not wish it." Marcello shrugged. "I wasn't the son your father needed."

"Neither was I."

They looked at each other and, in the twilight gloom of the forest, shared a laugh. For the first time since those far-off days before her marriage, when she had worked side by side with her father in the companionable silence he demanded, Sofia felt cared for. It was a strange feeling—one that made her uncomfortable and elated at the same time. When they got to Siena, she would make sure Marcello found a position. He was a strong young man and would surely be a useful addition to Manzini's workshop. Perhaps the stain of his birth would not matter so much to Manzini if Marcello proved to have something of their father's genius. The vision that rose before Sofia's eyes of the two of them working together in a crowded workshop was almost too wonderful to bear. She smiled. Surely God would not send her such a promise of happiness if He did not mean for her to taste it?

"Sofia!"

She was so startled by Marcello's use of her given name that she pulled on the donkey's bridle and skidded to a halt. "You can't address me thus!" she began. "We may speak freely when alone, but . . ." Marcello clamped his hand over her mouth. She felt his breath against her cheek.

"Go!" he whispered. "Go now and don't look back. If the donkey falters, get off and run. I'll find you." And then he let her go and smacked the donkey on its haunches. Before Sofia could protest, the beast took off along the pathway, its ears flat against its head, its stubby legs churning the leaves. She grabbed the reins and held on. Behind her, she heard a cry and the clash of metal on metal. A moan rose in her throat. She stabbed at the donkey's flanks with her heels. It charged forward. Branches whipped her face. She closed her eyes, hung on with all her strength, and prayed.

Many minutes later the donkey lapsed into a jog, then slowed to a walk. When Sofia jabbed its haunches again, the beast stopped so abruptly she was almost dashed against a tree. Then, with an affronted bray, it bucked. She managed to grab hold of the bundle strapped to its back as she slid to the ground, then cried out when her elbow smashed into a tree stump. She collapsed in a puddle of velvet upon the ground, her chin thrust into the new-fallen leaves, their sweet smell choking her. The donkey crashed into the woods ahead of her. Behind her was silence.

Sofia rolled onto her back and looked up through the leaves hanging low above her head. Streaks of red and gold slashed the sky. She must find Marcello before night fell. The forest that had earlier felt safe and comforting now pressed in on her, the trunks of its trees thick and black. She heard rustlings and imagined wild boars charging out of the undergrowth, spearing her with their yellow tusks. Her stomach churned with fear and hunger. Marcello had promised her that the path led to the home of one of his mother's kinsmen. They'd be given a warm welcome, a bowl of food, a bed.

Marcello would return at any minute to take care of her. He could not abandon her. She scrambled awkwardly to her feet and peered along the pathway snaking into darkness. How far had she come before the donkey threw her off? A half league? Could she walk the distance to where she'd last seen Marcello? Should she? Perhaps Marcello had been injured, was at that moment lying alone under the trees, his tunic slashed open, his blood staining the dead leaves. Or maybe he *was* dead. Unthinkable! She started back along the path. The air was growing colder and the golden light of the setting sun had melted into a dull gray. She must hurry.

The thick layer of leaves beneath her feet caught against her skirts, slowing her progress. Within minutes she was panting and her knees ached. But at least the swish of her skirts drowned all other sounds. Sofia thought of a panel she had worked on for her father not long before her marriage. It had depicted a menagerie of wild beasts, including a boar and a lion. She didn't think lions prowled the Tuscan woods, but she knew that boars were plentiful enough. Her father had assigned Sofia to draw the boar. To help her, he'd ordered a stinking carcass brought into the workshop. Black flies had coated the boar's hide, feasting off the entrails spilling from its ripped belly. She was barely able to make out where the flies ended and the hide began and had to ask one of the apprentices to wave a stick of wood back and forth across the carcass. The tusks had been the only part of the boar not covered in flies. Dirty yellow and razor sharp, each tusk curved upward in a cruel arc. The end of one was tinged pink—the legacy, so her father said, of the poor wretch who went forward after his master speared the boar to finish it off. The beast caught the servant by the arm and tossed him into the air. He died two days later, screaming.

She trudged on through the gloom, each stride deepening her worry. What if Marcello wasn't injured at all, but instead had gone back to San Gimignano? He had their father's sharp wit and might have decided that the risk he took helping Sofia was too grave. He could return to the city, twist the truth of her disappearance, and extort money from Giorgio. Anything was possible. She should never have trusted him. She had let her emotions get in the way of logic. Her father would have been appalled.

How could everything go wrong so quickly? Marcello should never have taken them along such a dangerous path. Sofia scowled as she thought of how she would scold him when she found him. He should have known better. She would allow him to stay with her until he got her to Siena, then she'd find a way to get rid of him. He could be a soldier. Siena sided with the Guelfs and the Pope. His Holiness would have constant need of men to defend his lands. So preoccupied was she by these thoughts that she did not notice she had tripped until she found her face pushed deep into the dirt and felt a dull ache in her ankle. She kept still and listened. Nothing. She pushed herself to her knees and looked around. The light had grown so dim that she saw only black trunks. She squinted into the shadows. With her hands, she scrabbled at the earth behind her, searching for whatever had tripped her up. Her hand brushed something soft and she felt warm stickiness between her fingers. With a cry, she jerked her hand back. She saw a foot shod in a rough boot, a leg bound in cloth and tied with leather straps, and then . . .

She gasped. The leg ended in a ragged clutch of bone and sinew. Sofia let out one short, sharp scream, then tried to propel herself backward, her skirts twisting around her legs. The body that belonged to the leg must be nearby. Was it Marcello? She took a deep breath and forced herself to look again. The thick sole of the boot was made of rough material—coiled rope perhaps. Sofia allowed herself to breathe a bit easier. The leg did not belong to Marcello. Her proud brother-in-law would never allow his man-servant to be so ill shod. Marcello wore leather boots. She forced her gaze upward. The cut was clean. It could only have been made by a sword—and a fine one at that. A common brigand would not possess such a sword.

"Use your logic. What conclusions can you draw? Think! The answer is there if you think."

The sword that lopped this leg must have been wielded by Marcello. Giorgio had given him a good sword before they left. But where was Marcello? Sofia could see nothing in the fading light, not even the body belonging to the leg. Had Marcello killed this fellow and then been taken himself? Taken where?

"Think only on what you see and know. Never waste time on imponderables. What do you know?"

At that moment, Sofia knew that the day was spent, that she was alone in the forest, and that she was likely to remain alone until the sun rose. She must find a way to survive the night. Her stomach rumbled. She took up her bundle and unfastened it, sighing with relief when a fist of bread and a round of fresh cheese wrapped in cloth fell into her lap. The bundle also contained a stone jar of beer. It tasted as good as the finest wine.

Sofia moved as far away from the severed leg as she could and prepared herself for sleep. Her panic slowly began to fade as the bread filled her belly. Her situation was grave, but perhaps it was not yet desperate. The night that would soon hide her was the same that would keep the people who had taken Marcello from returning. She would be in danger from wild animals, but it was a risk she could not prevent. She pulled her cloak around herself, leaned back against a tree, and took out her rosary. The blessed Virgin would protect her.

The first thing Sofia saw when she awoke at dawn was the rest of the body belonging to the leg. The dead man was splayed upon his back just yards from where she had nestled between the roots of a large tree. The vermin that had been the wretch's constant companions had crawled out from clothes stiff with dirt to feast upon his eyes.

She rolled away and vomited into the leaves.

The nausea shook her body with such violence that she wondered if she would leave the forest alive. The pain in her empty belly was at war with the burning in her throat as the meager contents of her meal the night before splashed onto the leaves. God had forsaken her. She would be food for the beasts—a fitting punishment for running away. The sound of her retching drowned out the morning birds, the wind in the trees, the crackling of twigs.

When finally the spasms subsided, Sofia sat back on her heels and smoothed the skirt of her gown with the long, slim fingers her father had often said were the fingers of a true painter. What would he think of her now—reduced to vomiting at the sight and smell of a dead man? He would think her weak if she did not pull herself together and rise. She gathered her skirts and heaved herself up, carefully keeping her eyes averted from the body as she peered along the path in the direction she had come with Marcello. Two choices faced her. She could go back to San Gimignano, tell Giorgio that brigands had attacked them on the road to Florence, and then take to her bed and direct Emilia to tell Giorgio the child was lost. And then what? Giorgio would soon forget he'd ever shown her tenderness. She shuddered at the memory of all the nights spent with Emilia's poultices burning her insides while Giorgio thrust and groaned.

And her other choice? Sofia forced herself to look again at the hacked body of the man who had died by Marcello's hand. Her empty stomach heaved, but she kept her mouth clamped shut. The future spiraled before her, bereft now of all her hopes. With no Marcello to protect her, she had almost no chance of reaching Siena. And if she did? How would she find Manzini? And would he take her in? Whatever debt he owed her father may not be sufficient to combat the risk he took harboring a runaway wife. Her skill with a brush might not be enough. Doubt after doubt roiled through her, weakening her knees. She wanted to fall again to the earth, bury her face in the leaves, and pray for death. To go back meant Giorgio and the end of all painting. To go forward might mean imprisonment, even death.

Sofia picked up her bundle, forced the last piece of bread down her dry throat, then set off in what she hoped was the right direction.

The forest kept her in its embrace for most of the morning. By the time the path ended at the edge of a long slope leading to open countryside dotted with farmhouses, Sofia was cursing her heavy gown and longing for water. But the sight of human habitation at least held a promise of food. She had money in the purse Paulina had sewn inside the waist of her gown. One of the farmhouses was bound to have a mistress glad of a few coins in exchange for a crust of bread and a simple tunic. Siena was still some days off, but if she had food and some knowledge of the route, she might still make it. She could enter the city dressed as a countrywoman going to market. No one would pay her any attention.

She looked critically at the scene. Most of the farmhouses were mean wattle-and-daub dwellings, but in the distance she saw a more substantial house—its walls thick, almost fortresslike. If God was with her, the master would be away in the fields or, even better, off to market, and she could deal only with the woman of the house. But as she walked nearer, she began to feel uneasy. No smoke rose from the roof and she saw no movement in the yard. A crisscross of footprints recently made by large boots creased the mud at her feet. She smelled something acrid. Sofia walked to the open door and peered in. The stench grew stronger, filling her nostrils and making her cough. Hastily, she backed out. Whatever, or whomever, was in the house was dead, very dead. A cow mooed piteously in an enclosure behind her. She turned to see its swollen udder almost dragging in the dirt. At least she could do something to help the poor creature. As mistress of her household, she supervised the care of the cow and the goat they kept in a pen behind Giorgio's workshop. She found a rough wooden pail and squatted on a stool next to the cow. Its warm flank felt good against her cheek as she bent to the work, the rhythmic pulling a soothing relief after her long walk. She had almost filled the pail when she heard the clank of metal. Her back stiffened. She gripped the edge of the pail with both hands. Whomever attacked her would feel the full force of the wood crack his skull.

"Who are you?"

The voice was low and frightened. Sofia relaxed her grip on the pail and twisted around. A boy of maybe thirteen or fourteen—not quite a boy perhaps, but certainly not a man—stood in the middle of the yard. Blood drenched his smock and his hair was matted and wild. He held a heavy scythe in both hands. Tears had carved clean tracks through the dirt on his face.

She dropped the pail and held out her hands. "I'm Sofia. Put that down and tell me what's happened here. I am alone and cannot harm you." He looked frightened almost beyond reason as he stared at her, his hands—large and clumsy with the fast growth of youth—still clutching the scythe. A flash of sun gleamed off the metal. Sofia thought of gold-burnished haloes and prayed silently to the Virgin.

Slowly, very slowly, he lowered the scythe to the ground and walked closer. "What do you want?" he asked.

"I'd be grateful for some bread and perhaps something to drink. Can you help me?"

"They took most of the food."

"Most?"

"I hid some."

"You're very brave."

The boy smiled shyly and then his shoulders slumped. Sofia rose from the stool and hurried forward to wrap her arms around him. Whatever horrors he had witnessed, he had survived, and for that he would be both grateful and grieved. To live when everyone else had perished was a heavy burden.

"Can you tell me what happened?" she asked when his sobs subsided into hiccupping gulps.

He stepped back, smudged a dirty sleeve across his cheeks, and looked away from her, embarrassed now by his tears. "The men came yesterday. My father, he tried to fight them." His voice cracked. "And my mother . . ."

"How did you escape?"

"My father saw them coming. He ordered me to hide until he came for me. I heard the screams. They used fire . . ." He gave in to great racking sobs. Sofia had no words and no idea how to help. She gathered him again into her arms and waited, her heart breaking as she imagined his grief. Compared to the evil faced by this boy, her own plight seemed much less desperate.

When finally his sobs trailed off, he looked down at her with the eyes of a beaten, old man. He was at least six years younger than she but already a good head taller. He gulped. "I only came away from my hiding place this morning." He gestured helplessly toward the house. "But I could do nothing."

Sofia patted his arm awkwardly. "Your father would thank God that you escaped. Do you have somewhere to go?"

He shook his head. "They killed them all—my mother and my father, my sister, my brother. All except Bernardo. They took him."

Sofia looked at the boy's feet and saw the same rough shoes worn by the body in the forest. Marcello had killed not a brigand but the abducted son of this farm. At the thought of Marcello, she wanted to be sick again. Was he at that moment lying dead by the side of the road, his throat slashed? Could God really be so cruel as to give her a brother and then take him away so quickly?

"Come and sit," she said. "We are safe enough, I think. The men have long gone."

"I should bury them . . ."

"Soon," she promised. "And I will help you. But first, tell me your name."

"Francesco. And you are Sofia." He smiled tentatively, proud of himself for remembering. "What's second?"

"Second?"

"Telling you my name was first, so I'm thinking you have more things you want to ask."

"You're a smart boy, Francesco."

His face reddened and her heart clenched with a feeling new to her. She didn't have a name for it, but she knew, even in the midst of the death hanging over the farmhouse so thickly she could almost hear the screams of the dying, that God was bringing her a gift. He had forsaken Francesco's family but perhaps not Francesco.

Or her.

"We must bury them," she said gently. "There is time for what is second. Come, we will do it together." Francesco stared at her, his eyes wide with pain and confusion. She reached out and patted his arm. "It won't take so long with two."

"But you are a lady. You cannot dig."

"I'm not so much a lady," she said with a sad smile. Francesco still looked confused, but he gestured for her to follow him to the house. Sofia sucked in her breath, holding it as the stench of burned flesh grew stronger. She dreaded what she would see inside but knew she could not turn away.

When they reached the threshold of the house, Francesco stopped and barred the way with one arm. "No, it's best I go in alone. You'll soil your gown."

Sofia felt like weeping at his earnest concern—that he could think of her gown in the midst of such anguish. Her voice choked. "As you wish." She gulped, steeling herself to match the courage of this half-grown boy. "I can make a start on the digging. Can you show me where?"

Francesco led her back around the house to a large patch of ground that served as the family kitchen garden. A few rows of herbs still grew in the autumn sun. He handed Sofia a crude shovel, then returned to the house, his steps slow, purposeful. He was so young and yet his bravery almost took her breath away. She felt ashamed of all the times she had cared only for herself.

Within minutes of starting to dig into the cool, dark earth, tiny white blisters erupted all over her palms and between her fingers. Although the autumn air was not warm, sweat soon drenched Sofia's brow and her heavy gown dragged upon her shoulders. She had dug a trench no larger than a foot deep and perhaps three feet wide—not nearly big enough to hold the bodies.

Perhaps God was testing her.

"God doesn't bother Himself with testing us," her father said scornfully. "He has much more pressing concerns than playing tricks."

"Fra Angelo says we must be always vigilant of temptation, that God puts temptation in our path so we can prove ourselves worthy."

"Bah! God does no such thing. Fra Angelo is a fool. And you, daughter, are more a fool for believing him. God has given you a mind and He expects you to use it."

"Yes, and God made me a woman, so I'm not meant to have a mind."

Maestro Barducci waved one hand dismissively. "Of course you can't be the equal of a man, but by God, you can best most of them!"

She wiped her brow with her wide sleeve and kept on digging until she heard a terrible scraping sound. She looked up just as Francesco rounded the corner of the house. He was dragging a bundle of what appeared to be blackened sticks. The stench of burned flesh almost choked her. When Francesco tipped the bodies into the shallow grave, Sofia tried not to look at the streaks of red shining through the charring. She plunged her shovel into the earth with renewed vigor. Neither of them spoke while they shoveled steadily.

When finally all traces of Francesco's family were buried beneath the soil his mother's hands had worked just days before, Sofia dropped her shovel and took his two hands between her own. She whispered a short prayer. Francesco's tears had dried, but the suffering on his face wrenched her heart. She knew he would carry the horror of this day until his own death.

And now he was her responsibility. And, with a start, she realized that she was his. Hours before they had been strangers. Now they had only each other.

Together, they walked back to where Sofia had left the bundle she'd carried since the donkey bucked her off in the forest. She stooped to pick it up, unsure how to speak with Francesco. He should not be rushed, and yet they could not stay in the house. The stink of death was everywhere. And she needed his help.

"Will you tell me what is second now?" he asked when they found a place in the shade.

"You remembered." Sofia smiled.

"So?"

Sofia paused, wishing she had her father's silky way with words. But with young Francesco, the direct route was likely best. "Do you know the way to Siena?"

"Siena? You want to go to Siena? But . . ." He paused, peering at her sharply, realizing for the first time that the appearance of a lady in a farmyard was no ordinary occurrence. "Why are you alone?"

"My man was taken by brigands, likely the same ones who took your brother and murdered your family. We were on our way to Siena."

"You have kinsmen there?"

"Not exactly." How could she explain Giorgio to this illiterate farm boy? Much less Maestro Manzini and the workings of a painter's workshop.

"So you are alone? But surely . . ." The honest confusion on Francesco's face for a moment edged out his blank grief. "I don't understand. You can't go to Siena alone."

"So will you take me?"

Francesco just stared at her.

"You're right," Sofia said, standing up. "I shouldn't have asked such a thing of you. I can see you're still very young." She started to turn away, slowly. Her years with Giorgio had taught her something about young men—and this boy was only a few years away from manhood.

"I'm not so young," he said, jumping up. "And I've been to Siena two times with my father. I know the way."

"It will be dangerous."

Francesco squared his shoulders and drew himself up. "I'm not afraid."

"You must have kinsmen nearby who will take you in."

"Like you, I've none. And I thought you *wanted* me to take you to Siena." He scrunched his face into a confused frown. A hank of thick black hair fell across his forehead, making him look so young that it was all Sofia could do to prevent herself from wrapping her arms around him.

"I don't want you to come with me and then regret your decision when we're not yet in sight of Siena's towers. Where will that leave me?"

"I would never do that!"

"No, Francesco, I don't believe you would." Sofia sat down and motioned for him to join her. "You are sure?"

"I have nothing here now, Sofia. And you've helped me. It's only right that I help you."

Sofia laughed. "You're a good boy, Francesco. Your mother must have been very proud of you."

At the mention of his mother, Francesco gazed out over the farmyard to the mound of black earth. "She called me her monkey because she said I made people smile." He clenched his hands into fists. "I've never seen a monkey."

"I have. And your mother is right. They're curious creatures and they do make people smile. Maybe that's why God has spared you."

"Do you think so?"

"I don't know, Francesco. But I do know that I need your help."

"My mother would want me to help you."

"Do *you* want to?"

"I can't stay here."

"Then we will go together. But first, I need clothes. Can you find me some? And for yourself too." Sofia spoke quickly, knowing that Francesco needed the guidance of a new elder sister as much as she needed him to lead her to Siena.

Francesco looked ruefully at his blood-covered smock and then at Sofia. "We don't have clothes for such as you. My mother was no fine lady."

"Find me something that belonged to one of your brothers. Were they both as big as you?"

"My brothers? But, Sofia, they are . . . they were . . . not maids. And neither am I."

"I can see that. But we'll be safer if we travel as two young men."

Francesco shook his head. "You want to dress as I do? But it's not seemly."

For a moment, Sofia felt like screaming. Seemly? Nothing about her situation was seemly. Her father should not have died. Her husband should not be a brute who made her wish she had not been born a maid. And Marcello—her only friend in a world that had turned against her—should not be lost. And now this boy stood before her and accused her of being unseemly?

She opened her mouth to say as much, then abruptly closed it. Even as pain settled around Francesco's eyes and his full lips quivered with indecision, his broad, honest face really did make people want to smile. For the first time in her life, Sofia experienced an inkling of how a mother might feel when she looked upon a child who needed her.

"You let me worry about what is seemly, Francesco," she said quietly. "Now run and find the clothes. We should go while the sun is still high."

Francesco sprang to his feet and darted back into the house, emerging several minutes later wearing a clean smock and holding out a small pile of clothes, neatly folded. He left her to dress while he released the cow into the fields to make her way to a neighboring farm and the solace of hay and regular milking. Sofia loosened the ties around her waist and let the heavy skirt fall to the ground, then unfastened the stiff bodice and slipped her hands beneath her linen shift to massage breasts slippery with sweat. Her hair cascaded over her naked shoulders and brushed the curve of her buttocks. She stretched her arms above her head and breathed deeply, reveling in the cool air drying her skin. Then, with a sigh, she lowered her arms and stooped to retrieve Giorgio's dagger from the skirts pooling around her feet. She wondered if he'd missed it yet; she'd taken care to steal one of his oldest daggers. Sofia remembered hearing Fra Angelo rail against the vanity of women. She had listened dutifully enough, but in her heart she never could believe that God intended her beauty as a punishment. On the other hand, it had been her beauty that had attracted Giorgio. She placed the sharp edge of his dagger to her hair and began to cut.

By the time Francesco came back, she had bound her breasts with a long strip of cloth ripped from her shift, donned a plain brown smock and leggings wrapped with leather ties, and tucked the chopped ends of her hair beneath a brown cap.

"What should I call you?" Francesco asked, his eyes wide as he took in the pile of cut hair at Sofia's feet. "When we get to Siena, I can't be heard to call you Sofia."

"I haven't thought about it. Do you have an idea?"

Francesco scrunched up his nose, a gesture Sofia would come to know as his habit when thinking. "I had a brother named Alessandro. We called him Sandro. That's close to Sofia."

"And what became of your Sandro?" Sofia hoped he wasn't one of the buried bodies.

"God took him a few years ago. Fever. He was just a year younger than me. Those are his clothes you're wearing." He looked at Sofia, dry-eyed, and then shook his head. "I have no one now."

"Then I will be your little brother."

"But you're the elder!"

"And you're the taller. Be content, Francesco. No one will question us." Sofia picked up Giorgio's dagger and fastened the small purse of florins around her waist under her smock. "Do you have the food?"

Francesco held up a bundle. "A round of cheese and some hard bread. It's not much, but I also have my bow. I can shoot rabbits, maybe even a fox."

Sofia smiled at the thought of eating rabbit and sleeping more nights under the stars. She raised one hand to her head. It felt so light—as if she would drift away with the clouds. Her father would never have expected this. His beautiful *cara mia* was transformed into a dirt-smudged peasant who was blindly entrusting her life to a boy with nothing to recommend him but a bow.

"Ready?" she asked.

Francesco nodded and then, without looking back at the only home he had ever known, led the way out of the yard and across the fields to a rough track leading south.

PART TWO

Siena, Tuscany
October 1338

CHAPTER SEVEN

I will not tell you about the irrational animals,
because you will never discover any system
of proportion in them. Copy them and draw
as much as you can from nature, and you will
achieve a good style in this respect.
—Cennini, *Il Libro dell'Arte*, Chapter LXX

I must speak with Maestro Manzini about a private matter," Sofia said. "Lead me to him."

The man lounging against the open doorway of Manzini's workshop wore the paint-splattered apron of a painter's assistant and was at least a foot taller than Sofia. "Who are you to give me orders?"

Sofia opened her mouth to announce her name and remind the man of his place when her shoulder jerked under Francesco's fingers. "My name is Sandro," she mumbled. "I have a message for the maestro."

"The maestro has no need of any messages *you* may carry. Get on with you. I've work to do."

"The maestro will speak with me," she said as Francesco's hand moved to her arm, his fingers squeezing the soft flesh. She barely had time to wince before another hand the size of a ham shank

swung at her head. A smack exploded in her ear and her body cata-
pulted backward into a mound of fresh horse dung. Her left wrist
slammed into the cobblestones. She just managed to thank the
Virgin for sparing the hand she painted with before the world went
black.

It was the smell that woke her. She let out a cry and struggled
from the steaming pile. "He'll pay for that!" Through the opening
cut into the front of the workshop she could see the oaf raising a
hammer with the very hand he'd used to strike her.

"Sandro!" Francesco grabbed Sofia around the waist and hung
on, lifting her legs from the ground.

"Let me go, Francesco!"

"Remember what you are!"

"I am the daughter of Maestro Antonio Barducci!"

"Hush!" Francesco half carried her around the corner and into
a street no wider than his outstretched arms. She tried to dig in her
heels, but they skittered through the muck.

"I will not be tossed away by that animal." She broke away
from Francesco and started back toward the workshop. Francesco
reached out, ripped her bundle from her back, and clasped it to his
chest. When Sofia swung around, her eyes flashing, he stood firm.

"I won't give it to you until you calm yourself."

"My father wished it."

"Did your father wish this?"

Sofia looked at the globs of dung clinging to her smock. Tears
itched her eyes and made her even angrier. "Manzini must see me!"

"He may see the daughter of Maestro Barducci, but he has no
interest in a dirty street urchin."

Sofia gasped.

"That's what you are," Francesco said. "We need to find a way
into the workshop that won't get you killed."

For a few more moments, Sofia stood rigid before him.

"Do not be content with the surface. Look through the subject and tell me what you see."

"I see a bird."

"No, look again. What do you see?"

The dead bird had been pinned on its side to the worktable. A broken wing was splayed out at an odd angle to expose the intricacy of the feathers, the myriad subtle shades that Sofia could never hope to reproduce.

"The bird once flew."

"Good. What else?"

"It was made by God."

"Of course. And?"

Sofia stared at the two twisted feet and at the soft down of the bird's breast, its color even in death a rich crimson. "It soared among the clouds. It looked down upon us."

"Yes, mia bella. It flew where we cannot go and saw what we can never see. Paint that."

The heat and noise of the street threatened to choke her. So many buildings—all of red brick and many with towers—were clustered too closely together. Children raced after black rats and snarling dogs. The sting of smoke slicked the back of her throat. Pigs snuffled blissfully in the filth, carts rumbled, people shouted, donkeys brayed.

Then she remembered Giorgio's unshaven cheek scratching her bare breasts and shuddered. "Fine," she said. "We'll find an inn. Did you see any when we passed through the city?"

"An inn wouldn't take the likes of us," Francesco said with a laugh. "You forget, Sandro, that you're not a fine lady."

"I don't think I've forgotten," Sofia said sheepishly as she rubbed her bruised hip. "You said you've been to Siena with your father. Where did you stay?"

"With my father's kinsman."

Sofia brightened. "We can go there."

Francesco shook his head. "He died this past spring. You won't like what I'm going to say, but I don't know another way."

"So?" She appreciated Francesco and the company he provided and she had no quarrel with his bravery, but he did take his time coming to the point.

"We wait until darkness and then we find a stable."

"We sleep with the horses?"

"More likely the donkeys, but at least we'll be warm."

Sofia shook her head, laughing now. "Then we must pray the warm donkeys don't trample us in our sleep."

Francesco kept a firm hand to her back and steered her away from the workshop toward a blazing slice of white light at the end of the street. They reached it together and both gasped. The entire piazza looked big enough to fit the whole town of San Gimignano. Since her visit to Siena with her father the year before she married, work had begun on paving the Piazza del Campo with a complicated pattern of brickwork. Fan-shaped swaths of shiny bricks sloped gently upward to a wall of towers, many of them still under construction. The tall and slender Torre del Mangia, at the lowest point of the *campo*, was now completed. With noon approaching, the piazza was emptying rapidly of people returning to their homes for food and rest.

"This is a noble space," Francesco whispered.

"Even in Florence, you'll not see a more pleasing one."

"You've been to Florence?"

"Just once. My father took me with him when he went to help Maestro Giotto decorate the *podestà*'s chapel in the Bargello. The maestro was near the end of his life, but he was still a miracle to watch." Sofia shook her head, smiling. "Maestro Giotto wasn't much taller than I was, even though I was a child. And he was so ugly."

The name meant nothing to Francesco. He was more concerned with finding shade and a kindly shopkeeper to give them food. But Sofia was walking into the piazza, her head thrown back to stare up at the towers. She held her arms out and rotated on one heel.

"Beautiful!"

"Sandro! Stop that. People will stare. We need to find a place to rest out of the sun."

"I don't need to rest. I must study this space. It's a marvel. Go into the shade if you must. I need to walk." And leaving Francesco looking bewildered, she set off around the piazza, measuring its dimensions with her steps. The brickwork was not yet far advanced, but she could see the pattern emerging.

"The Piazza del Campo is what they call it, mia bella. God willing, you may see it when the brickwork is finished. Do you note the shape?"

Sofia turned her attention from the Torre and regarded the piazza. It was not an oval like the Piazza della Cisterna back in San Gimignano or even a square like many of the piazzas she remembered seeing in Florence and other cities.

"The shape is meant to resemble the shell of a scallop."

"A scallop, Papa? I don't know this."

"Pass me a piece of charcoal. I'll show you." Maestro Barducci knelt and, with a few deft strokes, sketched a scallop shell on the smooth surface of one of the new bricks.

"It's a fan!"

"Yes, and the new paving ordered by the Council of Nine will be divided into nine equal segments, each one separated by a narrow band of travertine—white against the red of the brick. It will be something to see when it's done, but I'm afraid it will not be in my lifetime. Maybe in yours, mia bella."

For the first time since arriving in Siena that morning, Sofia allowed herself a quiver of excitement. Manzini *had* to take her into his workshop. He owed as much to the memory of her father. The prospect of working again with brush and paint was bewitching. And to be in Siena! The city's reputation for the quality and quantity of its architecture, paintings, and frescoes rivaled even Florence's. Her father had described the plans for the new cathedral, and she'd seen herself the wondrous frescoes by Lorenzetti adorning the walls of the council chamber in the Palazzo Pubblico. God only knew what other marvels were at that moment being painted in the public rooms of the many palazzos and chapels and churches of Siena.

"Sandro!" Francesco stood in the shadow of a tower and gestured toward the other end of the *campo*. A clutch of armed men was marching toward them, their swords clanking. Francesco caught Sofia's hand and dragged her into a side street. "Come away! The soldiers might wonder why a vagabond boy stands alone in the piazza in the heat of the day."

"Why should they care about me?" Sofia asked, sidestepping a fat hen sitting serenely in the middle of the street.

"It doesn't matter why. What matters is that you don't want such men to get too near. From a distance you look well enough, but up close . . ."

"What?" Sofia looked down at her coarse smock and leather-bound leggings. "I'm dressed like you are."

"Yes, but you don't look the same. You look small and weak." Francesco paused, his young face serious and afraid. "You look like a girl."

"I am a girl!" Sofia grinned, grime cracking her face into rivulets of white. "You worry like an old woman, Francesco. I want to tell the world that I'm the daughter of Maestro Antonio Barducci come to Siena to carry on his work. What does it matter if I'm a boy or a girl?"

"It matters, Sandro. Now, let's find something to eat and a place to rest out of the sun."

At dusk, Sofia and Francesco slipped into a stable a few streets from Manzini's workshop. Two donkeys and a horse scuffled hooves as Sofia spread her cloak in an empty stall.

"Good night, Francesco. You're a good friend to me."

"I'm your only friend," he whispered drowsily, but she could hear the smile in his voice. She grinned into the darkness, then sighed as she thought of Marcello—his deep voice so like their father's. If he had come with her to Siena, she would be with Manzini already, not sleeping in a stable. Did Marcello still live? She pushed the question from her mind and instead reached out and touched the bundle containing the page torn from her father's ledger. If she failed now, the words he wrote about her work would mean nothing. As sleep pulled her deeper into the warm hay, Sofia saw herself dipping a brush into the richest ultramarine blue and daubing at the Virgin's robe. Manzini would admire her skill and maybe even allow her to work on a fresco—perhaps even in the Palazzo Pubblico or the new cathedral.

Siena was bursting with art and Sofia would be a part of it.

"How is it that a maid knows painting?" Francesco asked.

They sat side by side on a low wall alongside a strip of ground where a few weeds blew in a fresh wind. Francesco had chosen the spot. After only one night in the city, he longed for relief from Siena's deep brown bricks and dark alleys. A cloth spread between them held a round of bread and a handful of raisins.

"My father taught me. And I'm hardly a maid."

"Yes, but you were a maid once. Didn't your mother teach you how to run a household? My sister—" His voice broke and he paused. "I'm sorry. My sister was always with our mother. At harvest, she sometimes helped my brothers and me in the fields, but most often she stayed close to the house."

"My mother died when I was six," Sofia said. "I'm my father's only child." She paused a moment, thinking of Marcello. Francesco was looking at her curiously, his broad forehead creased with his own memories. "I loved to be with my father in his workshop. It's as simple as that." Not so simple, she thought, but Francesco had experienced enough heartbreak without needing to share hers.

"But you're not a child now."

"No, but the things I learned haven't left me. I believe God made me see what others can't."

"Like the nuns?"

"What?"

"The nuns. I've heard that some have visions and live in tiny rooms with no light and little food so they can be close to God."

Sofia shook her head. "I speak of how my father taught me to look at the world—at the people, the animals, even the trees and fields. He taught me to look, and God gave me the skill to paint what I see."

"Is it right for you to talk so?"

"What do you mean? I say nothing improper." Sofia palmed a handful of raisins and dropped them one by one into her mouth. They slid into her empty stomach like sweet droplets that were about as effective at staving off hunger as the patter of summer rain on parched crops. She'd wanted to buy fresh bread from one of the baker's ovens in the town, but Francesco had told her they'd look too suspicious in their rough country smocks. They had to get to Manzini today. She had not come all the way to Siena to starve.

"Our priest warned us against the sin of pride."

Sofia almost choked on the last of the raisins as she threw back her head and laughed, then stopped abruptly as she saw the look on

Francesco's face. "I'm sorry, Francesco, but I don't believe I commit any sin when I say the obvious. I have the skill to show others God's world. That's a fact. It's not vanity and it's certainly not pride."

"You talk so fast and say more than I can understand in a week." Francesco shook his head, his black hair ruffling in a sudden gust of wind that held a hint of autumn. "What if you're found out?"

"I won't be found out. My father often called me stubborn— and my husband too." She stopped suddenly, blushed.

"You have a husband?"

She turned to Francesco, placed a hand on his broad wrist. "Please, Francesco. Forget I said anything. I know it doesn't make sense to you, but I can't go back to him. I must work again in the way my father taught me."

"But you can't just leave a husband." Francesco moved his arm away, stared moodily at the brown grass. "It's a sin." He looked up. "Isn't it?"

"Yes, Francesco. It's a sin. But he . . ." She stopped. How could young Francesco possibly understand her life with Giorgio?

"Did he? I mean, was he, ah . . ." Francesco looked miserable as he struggled to find the right word. "Unkind?"

Sofia nodded, not trusting herself to speak. She looked down at her hands, saw they were clenched in the lap of her smock.

"I'm sorry," he said quietly. He lifted his chin, still smooth with youth, and stared out at a patch of waste ground that ended at the city wall. "You don't need to be afraid now. I'll take care of you."

The lump that rose in Sofia's throat brought with it a quiet joy that she never remembered feeling, even when her father lived, or when Giorgio loved her. "Thank you, Francesco. We can take care of each other."

They sat side by side, both staring into a new future. And then with a laugh, Sofia pushed herself off the wall and turned to face

Francesco. "Enough talking! Today, we find a way to get to Maestro Manzini."

"Do you have an idea?"

"Yes." Sofia opened her bundle and took out a square of parchment and a stick of charcoal. She placed the parchment on the rough wall, smoothing it flat with the edge of her hand, then anchored the corners with pebbles. "And you're going to help me."

"Me? I know nothing about drawing."

"Maestro Manzini must leave his workshop at least once during the day. He wasn't there yesterday so it's likely he's working on a fresco in a chapel or a palazzo. We've seen how much building is going on in Siena. When he comes out of his workshop, you need to give him this." As she spoke, Sofia was moving the charcoal across the parchment with short, deft strokes, pausing every few seconds to stare at a bird that had landed in the weeds.

"What are you doing?"

"Drawing. Stay quiet and let me finish. I need to make this sketch good enough to capture Manzini's attention."

Obediently, Francesco stayed silent and watched while the blank piece of parchment filled with life. An oblong shape became the bird's body that soon grew a long neck, a head, and a pointed beak. Two stick legs teetered on the edge of the parchment as if the bird had landed for a few seconds and was trying to decide whether to take flight again.

"It's a wonder!"

"I'm not finished." She sketched in just a hint of feathers with the side of the charcoal, then held the parchment at arm's length. She half closed her eyes, regarded her drawing critically, then added a few more marks around the legs of the bird. "Done. I'll just add a message and we'll see if Messer Manzini dares turn me away." She flipped over the parchment and wrote several words.

"What do you write?"

"Something my father said. Come, we must get back to the workshop before Manzini leaves it. I don't want another night with the beasts."

"At least they kept us warm."

But Sofia was not listening as she led the way into the city. The streets swarmed with people going about the business of making Siena one of the most prosperous towns in Tuscany. Sofia had often heard her father speak of the city with great fondness.

"It's not as large as Florence, to be sure, but it has a beauty that Florence, for all its great size, can't match. The new tower for the Palazzo Pubblico will be taller even than the tallest tower in Florence. There's no telling when the building will end."

The hectic pace of construction she had endured in San Gimignano was nothing compared with the incessant clanging and hammering all around her. It felt like Siena was striving to be the center of the world. *There'll be work for any artist who seeks it,* she thought when they passed a chapel that looked brand-new. Workmen's tools leaned against one wall, and through an open door she glimpsed white walls awaiting the plasterer's trowel and the painter's vision.

When at last they came within yards of Maestro Manzini's workshop, Sofia clutched at Francesco's arm and let him pull her back into the shadows. Several men lounged in front of the opening cut into the building. Sofia recognized the tall assistant from the day before. Some of the other men were of the same type—large and coarse-looking and carrying workmen's tools. Three of the men stood slightly apart. They were all close to her father's age and dressed as prosperous merchants. One wore a scarlet cloak, and all three sported toques trimmed with fur.

"Which one is Maestro Manzini?"

Sofia shook her head. "I didn't pay much attention to him when my father took me to meet him." With a flush of shame, she remembered how she'd barely glanced at her father's friend, preferring instead to spin fantasies of her meeting with Giorgio when they returned home to San Gimignano. She thought Manzini might have had white hair and been older than her father, but he could just as easily have been younger. She remembered them talking about the fresco, but that was all.

"How do we know which one should get your drawing?"

Sofia shushed him with a gesture of her hand and stared at the three men. Her father had taught her to observe the world, to find details that other people miss.

"Don't content yourself with the surface, mia bella. Look deeply. Look fully." Barducci pointed out the open window of his workshop at a man who had paused to study the wares for sale. Like all artists, Maestro Barducci made a portion of his money from the decoration of standards, shields, and armor.

"What does he do?"

"I don't know, Papa. How could I? I've never met him."

"You don't need to meet him to know with a high degree of probability what he must do to feed himself. Tell me what you see."

"I see a man."

"Sofia! Don't insult me. What do you see?"

"He wears a short cloak and his tunic is an uneven shade of brown."

"What else?"

"His hands?"

"Yes?"

"They're stained." She leaned forward. "I see traces of blue on his thumb. And there's a smear of red across the back of the hand he's using to pick up the shield."

"And?"

"He studies the shield not as someone who wants to buy it. See how he holds it to the light and peers at the lines." She looked sharply at her father. "He's not a customer."

"So what is he?"

"I think he must be like you, but maybe not so lucky. The hem of his cloak is tattered. He looks worried. He wants to ask you to take him on. Am I right?"

Maestro Barducci laughed and patted her hand. "Yes, mia bella, you are right. The man's name is Ludovico Delgrasso and he's come from Rome to seek me out. I received a letter a few weeks ago asking if I would meet with him."

"Will you take him?" Sofia was not sure she wanted her father to take another painter into the workshop. Work was not so plentiful that she could afford to share duties with a stranger.

"I may. It depends upon his skill. But why should you care? If you have your way, you'll be married to that Giorgio fellow by the Feast of Saint Geminianus and then what will I do?"

"I can still paint for you after I'm married."

"And how do you plan to manage that with all you will need to do to run your household?"

"Giorgio's rich enough to hire me servants. And I'll have a tower!"

"And you think your husband will approve of you painting?"

"Giorgio will do whatever I ask of him." Sofia raised her brush and dipped it into a pot of rose madder. "He loves me."

"What's this? Has he told you?" Maestro Barducci rose from his table and advanced on Sofia, one hand still holding a dripping brush. "When?"

"Oh! Well, no, not exactly." Sofia blushed and shrank from her father's glare. He would be horrified if he knew of the stolen moments she'd shared with Giorgio. Her father was looking at her gravely, Messer Delgrasso outside the workshop forgotten. "I, ah, well, I think he loves me. In church, he looks at me. And I have spoken with him two times. You were present."

"Yes, yes, I remember. But I heard only pleasantries. I will not allow this talk of love." Barducci put down his brush but did not resume his seat. "I will grant you that Carelli is eligible enough. His father's

business yields good profits, and he might be persuaded to take you with the dowry I can give."

"Of course he will, Papa."

"Hush! These things aren't your concern. I'm not ready to give my consent. Go back to your work. Your paint is drying." Before she had a chance to respond, he was striding into the street to greet the stranger. Sofia looked after him mutinously. When she was married, she'd have her own household to command and the comfort of Giorgio's arms at night. She smiled to herself as she bent over her work. Only yesterday, Giorgio had ridden past the workshop and smiled at her, his eyes mocking, his mouth full of promise.

"Sandro! They're moving off. Which one is Manzini?"

Sofia shook her head and focused her attention on the three men. She could see traces of paint on the hands of two of them. That was not helpful. She looked more closely. One of the men was rubbing the small of his back. He had to be Maestro Manzini. She remembered her father saying that Manzini suffered cruelly from back pains brought on by too many years of working with the wet plaster.

"The one in the green cloak."

"How do we get your picture to him? See how he walks alongside the other men. We can't interrupt him."

"No, but we can follow him. Keep close to the walls." Francesco followed Sofia past shops selling everything from fragrant loaves of fresh brown bread stacked high to rounds of brightly colored cloth to rows of pig carcasses dripping from hooks. Just before the street emptied into Il Campo, Manzini stopped, said a few words, clasped hands with both of his companions, and then strode off in the direction of the Palazzo Pubblico. Banners draped the façade, and around the entrance gathered well-dressed men deep in conversation. Sofia reached back and grabbed Francesco by the wrist.

"Now!" she ordered. "Run and stop him before he gets to that big building. Tell him you have an urgent message and then give him the parchment. I'll wait here."

"What if he won't take it?"

"Do you want us to starve? Maestro Manzini's our only hope. If he goes into the building, we'll need to wait all day for another chance."

With one miserable glance back at Sofia, Francesco entered the broad expanse of the *campo*, the precious parchment gripped in one large hand. He looked to Sofia like an overgrown child. He came alongside Manzini and pulled at his sleeve. The maestro turned impatiently. Seeing a dirty country boy, he raised one hand to strike him. Francesco held up the parchment to block the blow. Manzini lowered his hand, plucked the parchment from Francesco, and squinted at it. Sofia held her breath. A few moments later, Manzini looked up and scowled, then dropped the parchment and ground it into the bricks. He raised his arm again, but this time Francesco was powerless to stop it clipping him against the side of the head and sending him sprawling. With a cry, Sofia darted forward and grabbed Manzini's cloak.

"What? Ho! Get away from me, scamp. I'll have the guards on you."

"Please, Maestro Manzini, you must listen to me!"

"What? You dare use my name? Go away!"

"I come from Maestro Barducci."

"Impossible. Maestro Barducci is dead."

"No! Please. You must listen." She picked up the parchment, waved it in the still air. "Didn't you read the message?"

"*For the Glory of Peace and Commerce?* Nonsense. The drawing, I grant you, is well done, but it means nothing to me."

Sofia took a step backward. "The message didn't strike you?"

"Strike me? What are you talking about? Stop wasting my time. I've work to do."

"The title, his fresco . . . you must remember. You talked of it with him. Here. In Siena. I heard you." She saw herself as Manzini saw her and a cold despair settled over her slender shoulders. "Papa said I could do such a one for you."

Maestro Manzini started to turn away and then paused. "What did you say?"

"My father's fresco of the city at peace. Papa said you'd understand." And then, to her shame, Sofia felt hot tears fill her eyes. She dug her nails into her palms to stop herself crying. Her father never tolerated tears. "Please, maestro. You must listen to me."

"Who are you?" Manzini looked her up and down and then shook his head. "Maestro Barducci had no son that I know of, and if he had, he wouldn't look like you. This must be some trick. And stop blubbering. You should be ashamed of yourself."

"Please listen to her, signor," said Francesco, putting one arm around Sofia's shoulders. "She speaks truth."

"She? What is this?"

"Maestro Barducci was my father." Sofia looked up. "Before he died, he asked me to seek you out."

"But Maestro Barducci had only a daughter. Sofia, after her mother."

"Yes, and I am she."

☙

"What you're asking is impossible." Manzini's gray beard quivered as he set the page from Barducci's ledger on the table. "For one thing, the guild would never allow it. And my own workers would throw down their tools if I allowed a woman to work alongside them. The very notion's absurd."

They had retired from the glare of the *campo* to a rough sort of tavern tucked around the corner in the Via Casato. At such an early hour, its few tables and benches were empty.

"I worked in my father's workshop. There was no trouble there."

"And what of the guild?"

"My father had great influence in San Gimignano. The guild was tolerant."

"You mean he didn't tell them."

"Perhaps. But I did work with my father in his workshop before I was married. After, I helped him fill some of his commissions. Panels mostly."

"You are married?"

Sofia shifted on the hard bench and stared at her hands. The heavy table that separated them bore the marks of a thousand knife points. "I don't wish to speak of it." She looked up, held Manzini's eyes with her own. "You knew my father well, maestro. You know he was a man of honor and that he never lied. If he tells you my skills will be of use to you, then you can believe him." She sat forward. "I know I can serve you."

"Your father would never have approved you coming to Siena dressed as a peasant and in the company of this urchin."

"Francesco has proved himself my best friend. He lost his family and has suffered greatly. He must stay with me."

"Ho! So now I'll have two mouths to feed?"

"Does that mean you'll allow me to stay?"

Maestro Manzini held up one hand. "You move too fast, just like your father. He always wanted to forge ahead without a thought for consequences. The fresco you described—we talked of such a subject and agreed it was too risky. *Vendetta* runs too deep in the streets of San Gimignano. And yet you say your father painted it?" Manzini shook his head. "I would not have believed even your father capable of such boldness."

"It was much admired."

"Yes, I suppose it was." Manzini smiled. "Your father had great skill."

"As do I."

"You think highly of yourself."

"I speak only the truth. If my father were here, he'd confirm it. I don't mean to be immodest, maestro, but I believe you'll find me the equal of any of your apprentices."

"That's as may be, but I can't have a woman in my workshop."

"As you see, I'm dressed as a boy. No one needs to know. My father's panels commanded some of the highest prices in San Gimignano."

Maestro Manzini laughed. "I can believe that. Your father was no stranger to the arts of negotiation."

"His work was much admired."

"You mean *your* work." He shook his head. "You put me in a difficult position, Sofia. If I take you in and you're discovered, I'll be in grave trouble. The fine alone would ruin me and it could mean prison for both of us. How long do you think you'd survive in a Sienese prison?"

"I won't be caught. Francesco will protect me, and we'll make sure your men never find out. Please, maestro, think of my father."

"How do I know that what's written in this ledger is from his hand?" He pushed the page across the table.

For the first time, Sofia laughed as she placed one hand over her father's words. "Do you believe I wrote this?" she asked. "Does it look like a woman's hand?"

Maestro Manzini's stern expression relaxed. "No, it doesn't. And yes, I recognize your father's hand. Often enough he showed me the very ledger you took this page from, usually to brag of a new commission." Manzini smiled. "Your father had an exceedingly good opinion of himself, but of course you know that." He shook his head. "I've never heard him speak so highly of another painter as he does here. I would excuse it as the ravings of a fond father if I didn't know him so well."

"My father wasn't one to lavish praise where it didn't belong."

"I know." Maestro Manzini sat back and tugged at his beard, leaving a faint trace of carmine red that made the gray hairs look dipped in blood. "I *am* shorthanded at present."

Sofia held her breath.

"I can't make any promises. If I let you stay, don't think I can favor you. Keep your head down and concentrate only on your work." He shook his head. "I'm a fool. But for the sake of your father, I can say you're my brother's son come from Florence. And, Francesco, you must stay by Sofia's side and watch out for her."

"Sandro," Francesco said.

"Hey, what's that you say?"

"I call her Sandro. My brother's name before he died."

Maestro Manzini sucked in his full cheeks, then slowly let out the air. "Sandro it is then. Now come back with me to the workshop. You must get out of those appalling clothes. I won't have it be said that Maestro Manzini's apprentices are ill cared for. And have you eaten? You both look half starved."

"I could eat a sow," Francesco exclaimed, then seeing Sofia shake her head, he hung his own. "I'm sorry, maestro. I didn't mean to sound greedy."

"No matter, no matter," Maestro Manzini said affably. "You're a growing boy and need your strength. We can find plenty for you to do. Can you sweep?"

"I'll sweep all night and all day if I can be with Sandro."

"Good lad."

Sofia listened to the exchange with a feeling very close to happiness. She had done it! Her father would be dismayed by the manner of her coming to Siena, but he'd have laughed at her audacity. She hoped Maestro Manzini would let her paint things from the natural world—animals, trees, hills, flowers even. But if Maestro Manzini wished her to do figures, she could show him how adept she was at rendering the folds of a robe, the tilt of a head, the gesture of a hand. He'd never regret taking her in.

Maestro Manzini led the way out of the tavern and back into the *campo*.

"This space is very fair," Sofia said as they walked. "There's so much light and such uniform façades." Each building bore the same series of arched windows that adorned the façade of the Palazzo Pubblico, at the lowest point of the piazza.

"Ah! It's more than fair. The *campo* has no equal. The laws governing its use keep the citizens on their toes, I can tell you. Every week a new stricture is imposed. Even the voiding of a beast within the precincts of the *campo* is prohibited." He laughed. "If you come into the *campo* with a horse, you'd better be sure it has no need of shitting."

"How can you know that?"

"Well, of course you can't. But people are careful. Mostly they keep their animals away. Many other things are prohibited. Just this past week, the Nine passed a law forbidding the eating of figs in the *campo*."

"Figs? How could figs give offense?"

"Perhaps our esteemed council doesn't want the juice dripping upon the bits of new pavement. It's not our place to question their wisdom." But he had a twinkle in his eye as he said it. Sofia was beginning to think that Maestro Manzini, like her own father, was not overly prone to abiding by the rules if he could find a way around them.

When they arrived at his workshop, Manzini led Sofia and Francesco around the side and up the exterior staircase to his living quarters. "You must meet my wife. She'll be uneasy when I tell her what we propose, but we can depend upon her secrecy." He smiled. "My Giuliana's a remarkable woman. Here she comes now."

One of the tallest women Sofia had ever seen sailed forth onto the landing at the top of the stairs. Tufts of gray hair poked from her wimple and bare forearms as muscular as a man's thrust from her sleeves. "Luca! What brings you home at this hour? I'm far too busy to tend to you. The capons are waiting to be trussed, and God and the Virgin only know when I'll get to the brining. That lazy girl you saddled me with is barely able to wash a flagstone without my standing over her and practically wringing out the rag for her." With hands on her wide hips, she paused for breath and peered around her husband, who stood meekly before her. His head just reached her shoulder. "Who are these brats? They're filthy! What are you about bringing them into my house?"

"*Our* house, wife," Manzini said gently. "And I need you to leave off your household cares for a moment and come with me to our chamber. I've something to tell you."

"I've not got all day."

Manzini motioned for Sofia and Francesco to wait, then followed his wife through a spacious dining hall containing a large table and a fine array of silver candlesticks—proof that the painter's trade in Siena was brisk. Sofia willed herself to stand still and wait with patience for Monna Giuliana's verdict, but all she could think of was the dirt crusting her skin and the rustlings and itching along her legs, unwelcome reminders of their night in the stable. She longed for the scented bathwater Paulina brought to her chamber, the touch of her gentle hands when they scrubbed her back and combed her hair. If nothing else, Sofia hoped Monna Giuliana would take pity on her and give her clean clothes. Simple Christian charity could not deny her that comfort.

Sofia couldn't make out any words coming from the bedchamber, only differing tones—rumbling and apologetic from

Maestro Manzini, loud and scornful from Monna Giuliana. Deep within her belly, Sofia felt a hollowness that had nothing to do with hunger. If they were cast out, could they make it back to San Gimignano? The days were growing shorter, and soon the cold along the windswept ridges of the Via Francigena would make travel impossible. And even if they made it, how could she face Giorgio? And what about Francesco?

"Don't look so frightened," Francesco whispered. "Maestro Manzini's a good man. He won't turn us out."

"What about Monna Giuliana? Did you see the look she gave us?"

"She doesn't frighten me," Francesco said. "My mother was the same—all fury and noise, but she had a heart as big as the sun."

"I hope you're right." She didn't believe Monna Giuliana had a heart any bigger than one of the raisins in her belly, but Francesco's attitude made her feel somewhat better. All sound coming from the bedchamber ceased. Had Monna Giuliana cowed the maestro into silence? Was he at that moment accepting defeat?

Finally, the door to the bedchamber crashed open and out strode Monna Giuliana, her wimple half off and her cheeks the color of ripe plums. Sofia almost laughed with relief, but she bit her cheek. With eyes cast down and shoulders hunched, she affected what she hoped was an attitude of humility.

"Look at me. I've heard enough about you from my husband to know full well that humility doesn't suit you."

"I hope I'll always be grateful, madonna."

"Hah! Gratitude is it? I haven't said you can stay. My husband tells me you've a genius with the brush. Is that true? Can your skills help him?"

"I hope so, madonna. My father—"

"Yes, yes, I know about your father. Many years ago I even met him. He was as vain a popinjay as all these painters who style themselves maestros. Even my own Luca." But a slight smile and the flush of her cheek took the sting from her words. Sofia guessed that Monna Giuliana was Maestro Manzini's first and most virulent defender. "What you're asking will endanger all of us."

"I don't wish evil upon you."

"I don't suppose you do. I can see you're not a fool. But the risk my husband takes to keep you is severe. He's worked for thirty years to build his reputation in Siena. I won't have it shattered for anyone—even the daughter of the great Antonio Barducci."

"Yes, madonna. I'll be careful."

"And have you thought what will happen in a year or so when, against nature, you remain a boy? Instead of growing tall and sprouting a beard and a deep voice, your skin remains soft, your wrists slight and delicate. Have you considered that?"

"No, madonna." With a sinking feeling, Sofia realized that Monna Giuliana was right. She could get away with pretending to be a boy for a few years—three or four at most—but eventually someone was bound to notice that the young apprentice in Maestro Manzini's workshop was not growing into a man. Even Francesco, who was at least six years younger, spoke with a voice that cracked when he was upset. A light fuzz was visible along his jawline in certain lights, and his large hands were already the hands of a man twice his age. Sofia looked at her own slim fingers and for the first time saw them as others would—fingers better suited to wear fine rings than to hold brushes.

"I thought as much." Monna Giuliana regarded Sofia critically, her head to one side, her hands once again on her hips. Two large mounds of flesh—as smooth and white as a maid's—strained to escape the laces of her loosened bodice. Sofia blushed and looked away.

"I've nowhere else to go," she said.

"What about your husband? Luca tells me you're married. We should take you right now to the Palazzo Pubblico and have you arrested. A woman's place is with her husband—in God's law and in man's."

"I was not as fortunate as you, madonna. My husband didn't treat me as a good husband should." Sofia raised her chin and looked into Monna Giuliana's eyes. "I can't go back, madonna. Please." She unhitched the bag of money under her smock and held it out. "Here. This will help with our keep."

Giuliana's eyes were damp as she batted away the bag, then caught it up and tucked it into her bodice. "You know the risk if we take you?"

"Yes, madonna."

"And yet you still ask this of us." She cupped Sofia's chin with one hand, held her gaze with flashing black eyes. "You've known much sadness, child. It's against my better judgment, but I'll allow you to stay. My Luca wishes it."

"Thank you, madonna."

"Just make sure you don't make a bigger fool of me than you've made of my husband. Now, you follow me to the kitchens, and Francesco—you go with the maestro. Both of you need to reacquaint yourselves with water." Giuliana swept her wide skirts around and marched toward the staircase. Servants fled before her as she barked orders for buckets of water and a clean smock and leggings for the master's young nephew just arrived from Florence.

"We're fortunate that between Luca's family and my own, kinsmen are always arriving and sometimes staying much longer than we'd wish," Giuliana said between orders. "We've no children of our own, so our kinsmen use us as a convenient place to dump sons and daughters that trouble them. We just got rid of one of my nephews last month. He joined the soldiers, which between you and me, was all he was good for." Monna Giuliana hooked one hand around the arm of a young servant girl who stood against the wall of the passageway leading to the kitchen.

"You! Get the bath filled. Master Sandro needs a good scrub-bing."

Sofia doubted Monna Giuliana's hands would be as soft as Paulina's and she was certain she wouldn't smell lavender. She was right. The soap Monna Giuliana used was of the very roughest sort. Made from beef tallow and lye extracted from wood ash, it was reserved for servants and peasants. Sofia had no doubt Monna Giuliana favored her own skin with imported Spanish soap made from olive oil perfumed with herbs. Giuliana was deliberately reminding Sofia that her days as a lady were well and truly over. She shooed the servants out of the kitchen, ordered Sofia to step into the wooden bath, and then emptied a bucket of icy water over her naked body.

"Scrub yourself. I don't have time to do it for you. I imagine you're used to the attentions of a maid?"

With chattering teeth, Sofia nodded.

"You won't have any such privileges here. You wish to be a boy and so you'll be treated. You'll sleep in the workshop and come to me every morning before lauds to be bound and dressed. I'll make sure none of the servants know you as anything other than my hus-band's nephew. Do you understand?"

"Yes, madonna."

"Keep to yourself and say as little as possible. The men should leave you alone because you're the master's nephew."

"Yes, madonna."

Monna Giuliana handed Sofia a piece of coarse linen to dry herself, then came at her with a long trail of cloth. "Hold your arms in the air."

The cloth felt rough—not like the fine linens she was accus-tomed to wearing next to her skin under her heavy gowns. Sofia inhaled sharply as Monna Giuliana wound the cloth around her breasts and pulled tight. Her breasts flattened into disks that crushed into her ribs. She wanted to cry out, but knew Monna Giuliana would only pull the cloth tighter.

"There," Monna Giuliana grunted as she secured the ends with a hard knot. "You may loosen the cloth at night and remove it to wash. It's fortunate that you're not too large. Don't stand too close to the men and never stand in profile where others may see you. Oh, I'm a fool for doing this. We'll be caught and ruined." Monna Giuliana pulled a smock over Sofia's cropped head. "Don't wear a belt, and for the love of the Virgin, don't take your cap off."

"I promise, madonna."

Monna Giuliana finished helping Sofia pull on leggings and strap them with leather, then stood back to judge her handiwork. "I don't know what you look like," she said finally. "You don't make a convincing boy, but I'm hopeful you'll pass muster so long as you don't call attention to yourself. Now get off to the workshop. The maestro's waiting."

Sofia was grateful to escape. Monna Giuliana spoke truth, but that didn't make it any easier to hear. She must prove to Manzini and his wife that she was worth the risks they took to keep her.

As she approached the workshop, she heard Manzini's booming voice announce to the others the long-awaited arrival of his nephew Sandro from Florence. She paused to listen. "You're to give him the same courtesy as any member of my family. Sandro comes from my brother's workshop in Florence. He has great skill with the brush and will work on the visors and shields. You, Tommaso, will show him what to do. Francesco here has come with my nephew. He'll help with the sweeping and you can ask him to fetch things. Make them both welcome."

Visors? Shields? What was this? From where Sofia stood, just within the shadow of the door, she could see a panel laid upon a table. The image of the Madonna was taking shape, along with the roughed-in shape of the Child in her arms. Surely Manzini would put her to work on the panel. She took a deep breath and stepped into the workshop just as Maestro Manzini held out his hand to welcome her.

"Here he comes now. My nephew Sandro from Florence. Now get back to work, the lot of you. I need you, Renaldo, and you, Bartolo, to come with me to the chapel. The arrival of my nephew has eaten up the better part of the morning. We're behind and will need to work quickly. Monna Giuliana will bring your dinner at the next bells." He swept out the door, followed by Renaldo and Bartolo. Both men swaggered—a not-so-subtle reminder that by accompanying the maestro, they were a cut above the apprentices and workers left behind.

"Come. I'll show you." A boy not much older than Francesco stood before her. "I'm Tommaso."

"Sandro." It came out as a hoarse whisper. Tommaso squinted at her curiously before leading her to a bench piled with unadorned shields.

"We're decorating shields for the Davanzatti clan today. Here's the stencil for the design. You see the holes?"

Sofia's eyes strayed to the unfinished panel. The Virgin's robe needed more definition and the proportions of the lamb at her feet were wrong. She could fix it in a moment. And then she remembered her luck and chided herself for vanity. God had delivered her safely into the care of Manzini and Monna Giuliana. The panels would come in time.

"Place the stencil over the center of the shield, like so." Tommaso was carefully picking up the stencil made from a pliable piece of parchment and incised with tiny holes in the shape of the design. He paused, looked at Sofia. She dragged her eyes back, nodded for him to continue. He draped the stencil across the shield and used circles of gum to hold it in place at each corner. "Make sure the stencil is positioned correctly. The master will check that all the shields are the same. You take this piece of charcoal." He held up a lump. "And lightly rub it across the stencil. The charcoal falls through the holes onto the surface of the shield and you have your design."

Sofia held out her hand for the stencil and charcoal. Tommaso watched while she laid the stencil over another shield, then used the charcoal to render the design. She propped the two shields against the wall and stood back to compare them.

"That's perfect!" Tommaso exclaimed. "You've done this before."

She mumbled something about her father's workshop in Florence. It was enough to satisfy Tommaso. He showed her the pigments used to paint the designs, stayed to watch her complete the painting of one shield, and then retired to a corner of the workshop to stretch out for a nap. Sofia was content to let him go, even as she groaned at the number of bare shields piled upon the floor next to the workbench. She would need weeks to finish them. But at least she was painting again. She steadied her hand and drew the brush smoothly across the surface of the shield. Its simple serpent design, set in red and yellow, was easy to paint. Very little shading was required, which meant she needed just one pot of red, one pot of red tinted with white, and one pot of yellow. For more complex painting, she used three pots of each color—one pot of the pure color, one tinted with white, and a third tinted with black. Painting shields was as far from the fine work she did in her father's workshop as it was possible to get. But she would not complain. If she had time before the sun set, she'd slip out to a nearby chapel and give thanks to the Virgin for her good fortune.

When the sound of the bells for sext wafted through the open door, every man in the shop put down his tools and looked up. Sofia followed their lead. She glanced over at Francesco, who had stopped sweeping. He flashed her a quick grin and rubbed one hand over his belly. A servant girl entered the workshop, followed by Monna Giuliana. Both were laden with trays covered with cloths. The women set out a meal of fresh bread from the baker's oven down the street, several slabs of white cheese, a good supply of apples, and a pitcher of beer. As the rest of the workers fell upon the food, Sofia hung back and allowed Francesco to bring her an apple and a chunk of cheese. Some of the others noticed that she didn't get the food herself. She heard a few mutterings but decided it was all to the good. The workers needed to understand immediately that she was the nephew of the maestro and a cut above the rest of them—even if she was temporarily obliged to decorate shields. She noticed the carpenter who had pushed her into the dung heap the day before. He sat on a stool in the opposite corner of the workshop and tore at the bread with dirty hands. Sofia was about to look away when the man glanced up and caught her eye. He stared at her intently for a few moments. She squirmed on her stool. Would he recognize her and wonder how the maestro's nephew had been a street urchin one day and a cleaned-up, respectable painter of shields the next? Just as she was certain he suspected who she was, he bit down on a nugget of unmilled grain and spent the next ten minutes picking at his yellow teeth. Sofia resolved to stay well clear of him.

For the rest of the day, Sofia bent to her work. She stenciled and painted the same design over and over again, until her back ached and her eyes felt rubbed in sand. In her father's workshop, she was accustomed to working only when she wished. Sometimes she became so absorbed that the hours flew past and her father had to pry the brush from her hand to prevent her ruining her eyes. But on other days she painted for an hour or two, or even not at all. As the daughter of the maestro, she enjoyed complete dominion over her days. And then as Giorgio's wife, she never painted longer than the time between bells during the hottest part of the afternoon—and only when Giorgio was away from the house. In Maestro Manzini's workshop, everyone returned to work almost as soon as they finished eating and toiled without ceasing until sunset. What had been Sofia's heart's desire had suddenly become work of the most mundane sort. By the time she collapsed onto the straw pallet made up for her in a corner of the workshop, she was too exhausted even to indulge in the comfort of tears.

Each morning Sofia rose at dawn to stand shivering while Monna Giuliana's large hands tightened the binding cloth. Then, after prayers, she took her place at a bench in the workshop. Often she was at work by the time the rest of the workers arrived. For the first two months, she saw nothing more than charcoal dots, shields, and the occasional visor. Her dreams were filled with serpents coiling around snails and eagles and crescent moons and the many beasts and symbols that adorned the shields and helmets and banners of the Sienese nobles. She wondered if every citizen in the city brought their armor to Maestro Manzini for decorating. The pile next to her bench never diminished, no matter how hard she worked. One day she asked Tommaso if Maestro Manzini was the only painter in Siena to decorate armor.

"Of course not. Why do you think so?"

"There are so many," she said wearily. "And every day we get orders for more. It never ends."

"But it's all to the good. The more orders the maestro gets, the surer we are to keep employed. I'm glad of it."

"Oh yes, I am too, of course. I'm just wondering if other work-shops have so much of this work."

"Most likely. But you must be used to it. Wasn't your father's workshop in Florence also busy?"

"Yes, of course." Sofia picked up another shield. "We had some trade with shields and suchlike. But the maestro, my father, was much engaged with painting frescoes."

"Were you allowed to work on a fresco? I wish the master would let me."

Sofia was not surprised that the maestro hadn't let Tommaso near a fresco. He was a pleasant enough fellow and meant no harm, but his skills were limited. He could get his lines straight most of the time, but he had no genius for mixing pigments and Sofia doubted he could draw anything more complicated than a full moon without looking at a model.

"I'm sure he'll take you one day," Sofia said, then paused and said casually, "I wish to go as well."

"I've no doubt he'll take *you*," Tommaso said gloomily. "Already he's commented on your skill. He never speaks to me unless it's to curse me for a mistake."

Sofia merely nodded, then returned to her work. She knew Tommaso wanted more sympathy, but she couldn't afford to make friends. Fortunately, she was accustomed to being alone in a busy workshop. At her father's, she had never mixed with the others, and to do so here would be dangerous. She was content with the hour or two a day she spent with Francesco. He had little to offer in the way of conversation, but at least with him she didn't need to keep her head bowed and mumble like she'd eaten a mouthful of cold oats. At first Sofia feared that the stifling city streets, the dirt, and the noise would be too big a change for Francesco from the open fields of his home. But within weeks he knew everyone in the workshop and was a firm favorite—even with surly Pietro, the oafish carpenter who had flung her into the dung heap on her first morning in Siena. One evening Sofia overheard the maestro telling his wife that taking in Sofia and Francesco was proving good for business. She had felt an unfamiliar warmth at the compliment.

Throughout the winter and an exceptionally wet spring, Sofia toiled at her bench. Her only relief came on Sundays, when she went with the rest of the household to church, and on the occasional feast day when all the workers spilled into the street to join the citizens of Siena in celebration. She relished those times, particularly when they involved an opportunity to view the vast amounts of painting and sculpture being done to glorify God and Siena. The walls of every church she entered were either filled with frescoes or criss-crossed with new scaffolding awaiting the brush of one of Siena's many masters.

On a rare sunny day in late February, Monna Giuliana took Sofia to the Duomo to view the altarpiece of the *Maestà* created by the great artist Duccio a generation before. It depicted an enthroned Virgin with the Christ Child and was the most stunning piece of work Sofia had ever seen.

"I wasn't much older than you when I saw it paraded through the streets of Siena," Monna Giuliana said as she stood with Sofia in front of the massive altarpiece. "The Nine themselves led the procession, and all of Siena came out to watch. I was already married to the master and remembered praying that his work would also one day be paraded through the streets."

Sofia looked up at Monna Giuliana with surprise. She usually only spoke to Sofia to scold her for not pushing her hair far enough under her cap or for complaining when her binding was pulled so tight her eyes watered. Sofia could not imagine Monna Giuliana as a young bride jostling for a view of the great altarpiece sweeping through streets thronged with crowds of rejoicing Sienese.

"The master's work is also fine," Sofia said carefully. She didn't want to say too much in the house of God for fear God would see into her heart and know she didn't speak truth. Maestro Manzini's work would never be paraded through the streets of Siena.

The service was over and the Duomo was emptying into the late winter sun. Sofia fixed her attention on the altarpiece that faced out over the cavernous body of the cathedral. The glowing colors, the placement and attitude of the figures, the expression on the Virgin's face gazing upon the blessed Child combined into a work of such extraordinary beauty that Sofia wished she could doff her boyish cap and weep. She squinted at the writing along the edge of the step at the bottom of the Virgin's throne.

"Holy Mother of God, be the cause of repose for Siena," she whispered.

"The Virgin is Siena's protector," Monna Giuliana said complacently.

Sofia glanced up at her. "Doesn't the Virgin protect us all?"

"Shh. Everyone knows that she's blessed Siena with Her special attention. Don't be heard to say otherwise. Now come, we must get home. I've been too fond allowing you to linger."

"Thank you, madonna, for bringing me with you today," Sofia said as they paced the long nave to the door.

"It wasn't my idea. The master wished it."

"Oh?"

"He seems to think you have some skill that should be encouraged."

Sofia paused at the top of the stairs. The clear day smelled wondrously fresh after a morning rain. The piazza in front of the Duomo was swept clean, and the congregation released into the sunshine after the long service was clustered in brightly colored groups. "Does the master have plans for me?" she asked.

"I don't know what the master plans for you," Monna Giuliana said, "but if it was up to me, I wouldn't let you leave your bench." She launched herself down the steps. "We must be off. I see Monna Strozzi. She'll want to talk with me and I don't want to introduce you. She's a sharp one and would see in a minute that my husband's nephew looks more like his niece."

As she followed Monna Giuliana, Sofia kept her cap pulled low over her brow. Since it was Sunday, she wore a simple, unstained tunic of thick brown cloth, dark leggings, and a green cap. From a distance, she looked exactly like what she was supposed to be—the young nephew of a respectable painter—not high-born certainly, but also not a peasant. Sofia kept close to Monna Giuliana's large back as they threaded their way through the crowd and into a side street leading to the workshop. The shops were shuttered for the Sabbath and the usual clanging of hammers had ceased. Sofia tried unsuccessfully to dampen her excitement. The master would soon take her away from painting armor! Why else would he ask Monna Giuliana to show her Duccio's altarpiece? He must wish her to be acquainted with the finest examples of Sienese art before entrusting her with a real painting. She wondered what he'd ask her to do. Should she tell him of the Santa Lucia altarpiece she'd worked on for her father? She could do another one—and this time perhaps she'd be permitted to give the saint's face more expression.

That night, before drifting to sleep, Sofia imagined herself into a new role in the workshop. That the maestro needed her skill was obvious. None of the other apprentices had half her ability. She heard Fra Angelo's voice chiding her for pride, but she knew she had no false pride. God had given her a steady hand and a good eye. How could it be pride to acknowledge His gifts? She heard a rustling and pulled the threadbare blanket up over her head. A rat had gnawed a chunk from her hair just a few nights before, leaving a jagged bald spot that was fortunately covered by her cap. Sometimes she wondered if Siena had more rats than people. They swarmed through the streets and kept her awake at night. She curled onto her side and closed her eyes. It was not wise to get her hopes up. The maestro was very busy with a fresco he was completing in the Church of San Paolo. She needed to exercise a virtue her father had often scolded her for lacking.

"You go too fast, cara mia. God's in no hurry. He'd rather wait for work that does Him justice. Take your time."

Sofia set down the brush and studied the strokes she had just made. Her father was wrong. She had captured an expression of evil glee on the demon's face that would give people more reason to fear than the usual bland renditions of devils that decorated chapels as warnings for people to stay clear of sin. Her demon had spirit.

"Do you not think my demon has life, Papa? See how it hangs just above Saint Nicholas, ready to take him in its claws?"

For several long moments, her father said nothing. She could hear him breathing behind her and wondered if she had gone too far. He never tolerated disobedience from his apprentices, including his precocious daughter.

"Papa," she began, "I'm sorry . . ." And then she stopped. Her father did not look dismayed or irritated or scornful—the expressions he so often wore when he looked upon the work of others.

He looked impressed.

Sofia drifted off to sleep with the image of the black demon floating behind her eyes. Soon, she'd again be entrusted to paint something worthwhile   something that would glorify God instead of a steady stream of pampered Sienese.

CHAPTER EIGHT

Beginning to work on panel, in the name
of the Most Holy Trinity: always invoking that
name and that of the Glorious Virgin Mary.
—Cennini, *Il Libro dell'Arte*, Chapter CIII

Sandro!" The rest of the workers looked up as Maestro Manzini strode over to Sofia's bench and plucked the brush from her hand. "Come."

She hopped off her high stool and followed him to an alcove at the back of the workshop where a table was placed to catch light from a window cut into the wall. She could feel every eye in the workshop upon her. She walked with a slight swagger that she hoped masked the natural sway of her hips. When she passed the oafish carpenter Pietro, she sensed his eyes burning into her back. She heard a crash and whirled around to see Francesco extricating himself from the remains of one of the trestles used to hold wood crucifixes while they were being painted. He flashed her a quick wink and she lowered her head to hide a smile. As usual, Francesco was protecting her. He'd seen how Pietro was looking at her when she crossed the room behind the master and knew a diversion was needed. He'd likely suffer a beating, but for Francesco it was a reasonable price to pay for keeping Sofia safe.

"Ho! You there! What are you about turning my workshop into a shambles? Clean up the mess and come to me after nones. I'll make you sorry for your clumsiness. You, Tommaso, help him. And Pietro, get off with you to the chapel. I'll follow shortly. I need the scaffolding built up another three feet for today's work."

"Yes, master," Pietro and Francesco answered together. Pietro's voice provided a deep counterpoint to the slight squeak in Francesco's voice.

Sofia ducked around the master so she was standing next to his worktable when he turned from the commotion in the workshop.

"Your Francesco should be more careful," he muttered.

"I think, master, that he wanted to draw attention from me. Pietro was watching . . ."

Maestro Manzini shook his head. "That's likely enough, but it was a blundering move nonetheless and Francesco will need to be punished."

"He expects it, master."

"Humph. Well, I didn't summon you to talk about Francesco. He does well enough when he's not going out of his way to protect you. I wish to speak with you about another matter."

Sofia held her fists behind her back to still their shaking. She would not look overeager or betray in any way that she thought herself deserving. She would be humble and meek and grateful.

"I have a commission for a Nativity panel, and you shall do it."

"Oh, master!" Sofia's eyes widened and she clapped her hands to her breast. If anyone had been looking at that moment, they would have had grave doubts about the maestro's nephew from Florence. Fortunately, no one was looking. She lowered her eyes. "I'm honored, master. You won't regret your confidence in me."

"I don't plan to." He laughed. "Although my patrons will have cause to regret when their armor is again being decorated by poor Tommaso. But I haven't time to attend to the panel myself. The fresco for the Contrada della Chiocciola will occupy me for several more months. This commission requires a fine hand."

"I'll do my best."

"Of course you will. Now, let me show you the sketch I made for the patron. He was very specific in his directions. You're to include three angels and two shepherds and no more than four beasts. The patron doesn't mind which beasts you choose, although he did stipulate that one should be an ass. Can you do that?"

"I created a Nativity scene for my father not long before he was killed," Sofia said. "It was much admired."

"Your father approved?"

"In the ledger page I showed you, he said it was my best work." She still blushed at the memory of her father's cramped script, setting out in ink for all to see his high opinion of her work on the Nativity panel commissioned for the Delpino wedding. She looked up at Maestro Manzini. "You knew my father. He rarely praised."

"He certainly never had a kind word to say about *my* work in all the years we knew each other." Maestro Manzini smiled and shook his head. "Your father was a difficult man to please. If he thought your Nativity was good, then I'm satisfied."

"He didn't say it was good," Sofia said. "He said it was my best work." Manzini stared at her, his brow furrowed. "I mean that my father saying it was my best work doesn't logically follow that he thought it good in the general sense."

"He didn't think it good?" Manzini began to place the sketch back on the table.

"No!" Sofia stretched forward her hand. "I mean yes, my father thought the panel was good. And he always had me do the beasts. Your patron won't be disappointed."

"Why didn't you say so? Well, 'tis no matter. I trust your father's judgment as if it were my own. Now, we've not had a commission for a panel for many months, so your first job will be to prepare one. You know how?"

"Of course."

"I'll have four coats of the *gesso grosso* and then four coats of the *gesso sottile*."

"My father insisted on seven coats of each."

"Your father could afford to. I'm content with four. And you're to use gold only on the haloes and in the folds of Our Lady's gown. The patron should have ordered gold for the angels but he didn't." Manzini sighed. "Siena is too full of painters these days. If I don't take the commission, the patron can go elsewhere."

"I'll be careful with the gold, master. My father taught me to be sparing."

"See that you are.'" He picked up a smooth piece of wood. "As you see, the panel's just three handspans wide. The patron pays for no larger."

Sofia stretched out her hand to take the panel. It was made of willow and washed clean. She felt a surge of joy. Under her hand, the thin blank panel would be transformed into an object to glorify God.

"Thank you," she whispered, running her fingertips over the smooth, dry surface.

"You may work here at this table. The light is good and you'll be removed from the others. Tommaso can help you with the gessoes and the pigments."

"May I ask Francesco? I know he's not had the training, but he's quick to learn and surely Tommaso is needed for the armor."

"You mean that Tommaso won't be much help to you," Manzini said with a chuckle. "Yes, I'm well aware of Tommaso's shortcomings, but he is the son of another kinsman and I can't turn him out. It's a good thing not all my kinsmen's sons are so inept."

CAROL M. CRAM

Sofia smiled. "You're very kind, master. I hope you know how grateful I am to you and to Monna Giuliana."

"Yes, and we're fools for it. But if you can make me a panel worthy of the patron, then perhaps it will be worth it. Now get to work." Manzini strode into the main area of the workshop. After shouting orders and cuffing a few heads, he exited into the street, trailed by Bartolo, another of the assistants who accompanied him everywhere and, like the rest of Manzini's workers, had limited skill and no talent. Sofia suspected that he, too, was the son or nephew of a kinsman. It appeared that Maestro Manzini and Monna Giuliana really were the dumping ground for the unwanted children of their many relations.

She took up the panel and held it to the light. It was close to three fingers thick and bore a smooth, even grain. She could not feel any knots or bumps, but knew a great deal of sanding and many coats of the gessoes were needed to make the panel anywhere near ready to receive paint. The long, tedious procedures required to prepare a surface for painting had always bored her. In her father's workshop, she received well-primed panels and never had to concern herself with glues and gessoes. But she knew the techniques well and looked forward to teaching them to Francesco. She gestured for him to leave off his cleaning.

"We have work to do!" she whispered gleefully.

"I have work already."

"Finish it later. See here!" She held up the panel. "I'm to paint a Nativity!"

Francesco did not even smile. "The others will be jealous."

"That's their concern. It's not my fault the master chose me."

"No, Sandro, it's not your fault, but you should refuse."

"Refuse? Are you mad? I've waited six months to get the chance to paint something worthwhile. I'd sooner die than refuse."

146

"I think you're the mad one," Francesco said quietly. He held up one hand to stop her replying. "But we can't be seen to argue. Tell me what you need me to do."

Sofia felt as if Francesco had punched her in the stomach. How could he ruin this moment for her? She had waited so long! And the worst of it was that she suspected he might be right. She should content herself with shields and visors. But if all she wanted was safety, she would never have left San Gimignano.

"I need you to help with the priming. There's much to learn. Can you manage?" She turned away before she could see the hurt expression on Francesco's face.

"Just tell me what you want me to do."

"Find me leaf glue—it's made from the clippings of goats' muzzles, feet, sinews, that sort of thing. In my father's workshop, we made it in January so it would solidify. Ask one of the others if we have any. It looks like slices of jelly. We spread it upon the panel as a base for the *gesso grosso*." She kept her voice neutral, like she was telling Cook what food to get at the market.

"I'll see to it. What else?"

"I need a size to temper the gessoes. We can make sizing from parchment trimmings. You wash the trimmings thoroughly and then soak them a day before boiling them. And then I'll need the gessoes—two kinds." Sofia stopped talking and scanned the workshop. It would be faster for her to investigate the stock of materials herself, but directing Francesco was safer—and perhaps he'd soon be so absorbed by the work that he'd forgive her. She thought about what colors she'd need. The red lac for Joseph's cloak and the poisonous yellow called orpiment for the shepherds' robes were available only from an apothecary. For the Holy Mother's robe, the only choice was ultramarine blue made from lapis lazuli—she would need permission from the maestro to use it.

Francesco listened to her describe the colors and then, without a word, left the workshop. She felt a twinge of guilt as she watched him go. Francesco was only looking out for her welfare, but why couldn't he see how much it meant to her to be painting again—real painting—not dots and stencils and plain colors with no hint of shading. But then, she reflected, how could he understand? Just six months before, he'd been a boy on a farm with nothing more taxing to worry about than keeping the cow milked. She resolved to make it up to him; then she picked up the maestro's sketch, excitement surging through her fingertips. The sketch included no architecture, just the hint of a hill behind the manger. This time, she would not deviate from the maestro's orders. She would reproduce exactly what he wanted and then, just maybe, he'd never again put her to work on shields and visors.

For the rest of the day, she used a silver-tipped stylus to make several sketches on a boxwood panel that had been prepared with a ground of fine white bone. As she settled into the work, a feeling of peace washed over her like a silk veil. Every stroke of the pen delighted her. Of all the arts she learned at her father's side, drawing was her favorite. She loved the immediacy of it, of creating something from nothing.

"You need to draw every day, cara mia. And make sure the light falls upon your left side."

"Why?"

Barducci laughed at the earnest face of the little girl who stood before him, her hand held out for a piece of charcoal, her eyes flashing impatience.

"See for yourself." He picked up her right hand, placed the charcoal in it, and angled her chair so the light from the window shone over her right shoulder. He placed a little boxwood panel that was already washed and ready in front of her, then moved a white flower into her

line of sight. "Here is a lily I wish to include in my panel of the Annunciation. Look upon it and then draw it."

Dutifully, Sofia looked at the lily and then bent to her work. A few minutes later she looked up, frustrated. *"I can't see properly."*

"And so now you know why you must sit so the light falls on your left side when you draw with your right hand. Will you believe me now?"

"I'm sorry, Papa." Her lip quivered and she let the charcoal fall to the panel.

"And if you wish to stay in my workshop, you will not cry." Barducci readjusted the chair, picked up the charcoal, and pushed it back into her hand, then strode to his own table.

Sofia gulped back her tears and bent again to her work.

At sundown, Sofia mounted the outside staircase to receive a generous supper of fragrant chicken broth sprinkled with cheese and a dish of roast pork prepared with asparagus and parsley—good for urination, so Monna Giuliana told them. For the first time since coming to Siena, Sofia took her meal to a corner and ate by herself. She loved Francesco—how could she not? But this night she wanted to be alone to turn the images in her mind over and over, to view them from every angle.

⤫

The next morning, Sofia held the panel up to the window and peered at it. The April sun bathed her in a pleasant warmth.

"See that the surface is perfectly flat and not greasy. Also make sure it's completely dry. If you see any flaw such as a knot or a node, apply boiled leaf glue."

Sofia smiled. The panel was dry and certainly not greasy, but when she looked very closely, she could see a few nodes that, if not flattened, would affect the movement of her brush across the surface. She motioned for Francesco. He left off boiling the parchment trimmings that would be used to make sizing for the gesso.

"I need you to boil up glue."

"I know how. Last month I helped with repairs to that altarpiece. Remember?" He grinned shyly and Sofia knew she was forgiven.

"Thank you, Francesco." She patted his arm. He blushed and shuffled his feet. He was still so much a boy, she thought. Since coming to Siena he'd grown another foot at least and now he towered over her. But he still grinned at her every morning and glowed when she smiled back. "When you're done, get sawdust from the floor and then wet it with the glue."

"What can you do with sticky sawdust?"

Sofia laughed. "Just do as I ask and then I'll show you."

When Francesco brought her a container full of boiled glue and sawdust, Sofia filled the flaws in the panel with the mixture and then showed him how to smooth it with a wooden slice. "We need the surface flat. Keep smoothing until I say to stop. It then needs to dry until tomorrow."

"But tomorrow we're going with the maestro and the other workers to the dinner at the Bellandi palazzo."

"What are you talking about? I know of no such dinner. And keep smoothing."

Francesco drew the wooden slice back and forth across the surface. "You should pay more attention to what goes on around you, Sandro. The maestro has finished the fresco for Bellandi's chapel and the whole workshop is invited to dine with the master. I hear it's a common way for patrons to reward the workers."

"Hmm. Yes. I believe my father often attended such dinners."

"Not you?"

Sofia smiled up at Francesco. "No. My father kept me well away from any notice when I lived with him, and then afterward . . ." She paused. "It's not important now. I won't be going."

"Why not? Messer Bellandi is known for his generosity. Pietro says they'll be a whole kid served and partridges and capons, and if we're lucky, almonds!"

"Almonds? How can I resist?"

"You're laughing at me!"

"Just a little, Francesco. I'm sure the dinner will be very fine, but I'll stay indoors and start laying in the sizing."

"You'd miss a dinner to stay and work?"

"With all my heart." Sofia smiled at the look of wonder on Francesco's face, then frowned when Pietro swaggered past. "I'll be glad to have *him* out of the way."

"Pietro? He's harmless enough."

"He looks at me too much."

"He's just jealous that the master pays more attention to you than to him."

"And why not? Pietro has little enough to offer this workshop."

"Shh, Sandro! You won't make friends with talk like that."

"I'm not interested in friends, Francesco. I care for one thing only."

Francesco's hand stopped moving across the panel. With deliberate care, he put down the slice and rose from his chair. "It's as smooth as I can make it," he mumbled. "I have sweeping to do."

Francesco picked up a broom and swirled sawdust across the floor with such vigor that she had to clutch the panel to her chest and go in search of a cloth to cover it.

Promptly at terce the next morning, the entire workshop emptied into the streets amid much shoving and laughing. Francesco linked arms with Pietro and didn't even look back at Sofia. She watched them all go with mingled regret and relief. To have the workshop to herself was an unspeakable luxury, but she wished her freedom had not come at the expense of Francesco's goodwill. She took up a knife point and scraped the glue until it was even with the surrounding level. Francesco would learn soon enough that there was more to this life than good dinners and joking around with a pack of lunkheads.

"*Your panel can never be too smooth, cara mia.*"

"*Will this do, Papa?*"

"*It's never a question of what will do, daughter,*" her father said sternly. "*You should strive always for perfection. Our Lord deserves nothing less in the panels we paint to praise Him.*"

Sofia scraped for another hour before again taking him the panel. "*Papa?*"

He ran one hand over the panel. "*What do you think?*"

"*I think it's perfect, Papa.*"

"*And so it is.*"

Sofia smiled at the memory as she used a large soft bristle brush to spread across the panel a coat of the sizing Francesco had made from the parchment trimmings.

"*Do you know what the first size with water accomplishes, cara mia?*"

"*No, Papa.*"

"*Think of how it is with you when you have been fasting and then eat a handful of sweetmeats and drink a glass of good wine. You'd be ready for your dinner. Is that not a fair thing to say?*"

"*I suppose so, Papa.*" *Was he giving her sweetmeats? At nine years old, she had not tasted them very often. She looked around her father.*

Perhaps he held a tray behind his back. He sometimes brought her sweet things when her nurse, Emilia, was not present to disapprove.

"Do you have sweetmeats?"

"No, cara mia," he laughed. "I use them only as an example. What I wish to teach you is why we start with a coat of this thin sizing."

Sofia's face fell. "I don't know."

"This first size is like the sweetmeats you eat to prepare your stomach for the dinner to come. You use this size to give your work a taste for receiving the second coat. Come, you may take the brush and put on the second coat. See how it soaks into the first."

As the sizing flowed from her brush onto the panel, Sofia smelled its dense chalkiness and forgot all about sweetmeats.

After she finished with the first two coats of sizing, Sofia took up several old linen cloths she'd gotten from Monna Giuliana the night before. She wished she could use her own binding cloth. It sometimes itched horribly and it was always too tight. She sopped the cloths in the sizing and then spread them over the panel, flattening them with the palms of her hands. The cloths would need two days to dry. A shaft of sunlight slanted in from the window. She caught a whiff of fresh spring air and all of a sudden she wanted to feel earth beneath her feet, the sun on her face.

She hopped off her stool and let herself out of the workshop. She walked quickly, enjoying the freedom her disguise gave her. As a woman in San Gimignano, she was never able to walk so freely through the streets. Soon she came to a break in the buildings and stopped to gaze over a vista of rolling hills and tilled fields stretching beyond the city walls. The day was deliciously warm, with a good wind blowing up from the south. The silver leaves of the olive trees in a grove below shimmered in the afternoon light. She wondered what colors she could mix to capture the exact shades of lights and darks. Impossible! But how she would love to try. She raised her arms, relished the air rushing over and around her, and laughed out loud.

"What are you doing?"

Sofia froze. Pietro! There was a rough edge to his voice that reminded her of Giorgio. If he found out what she was . . . She turned swiftly, hugging her arms to her chest. "Shouldn't you be at the dinner?"

"It's done," Pietro grunted.

"Then I'd better get back." She walked toward him, her heart pounding. He wouldn't dare touch her, not outside where anyone could come by. He moved in front of her, almost blocking her path, swaying slightly. He smelled of roasted meat and wine and dirt.

"Sandro." He said her name tenderly, his rough voice caressing. The sound made her shiver with revulsion. She dodged his outstretched arm and ran.

Sofia decided not to tell Francesco about her encounter with Pietro. Francesco's clumsy efforts to protect her would do more harm than good. And it's not like she was in any real danger since Pietro didn't know she was a woman. If he did, he'd have already announced it to the world and she'd be on her way to prison or worse, back to San Gimignano. She resolved to stay indoors as much as possible and spend every waking moment on her panel. When it was dry, she instructed Francesco to sift the gesso like flour and then grind it vigorously with sizing on a porphyry slab. She scraped the gesso up with a slice and covered the panel with broad, even strokes.

"The master's asked for four coats."

"That seems like a great many!" Beads of sweat stood out on Francesco's forehead as he ground the gesso.

"Be glad we're not in my father's workshop. He always insisted on seven coats. We had one apprentice who did very little except grind gessoes."

"I don't envy him," Francesco said, but he smiled up at Sofia.

"Once we've covered the panel with enough coats of the *gesso grosso*, we'll need to let it dry for two or three days."

"So no more grinding?"

"I didn't say that, Francesco. After the *gesso grosso* comes the *gesso sottile*, which must be ground even finer." Sofia patted his arm. "God will reward you for your dedication."

Francesco just shook his head while he continued to grind the gesso, but Sofia saw that he was pleased. She often wondered how she would have survived without him. Perhaps his presence in her life was a sign from God that she was doing His pleasure.

When she had completed the four coats of *gesso grosso*, Sofia turned her attention to the preparation of the *gesso sottile*. A good *gesso sottile* needed to be purified for a whole month in clear water so it became as soft as silk. Fortunately, the local apothecary sold loaves of *gesso sottile*. She placed one of the loaves into a washbasin of clear water and let it soak up as much water as possible. Francesco ground it on his porphyry slab, and Sofia folded it into a linen cloth and squeezed to remove the water. With a penknife, she cut narrow slices of the sizing and mixed it into the *gesso sottile* with her hands.

"Mix it like it was batter for pancakes."

"I know nothing of batter," Sofia said gaily. *"Emilia doesn't let me near the kitchen."*

"I think it more likely that Emilia would welcome you into the kitchen, but that you won't go."

"I like to be here with you."

When she had mixed the sizing with the *gesso sottile* so that it was the correct consistency, Sofia placed the mixture over a hot kettle.

"Don't let it boil, Francesco."

"Why?"

"If you boil *gesso sottile*, it will be ruined and we'll need to start all over again. Keep it warm so that it's fluid and easy to work with, but not too warm." Sofia took up a bristle brush and laid the first coat of the *gesso sottile* over the panel. She used her fingers and the palm of her hand to smooth it evenly. "The maestro wishes me to apply four coats. We must complete all of them today."

"How is that possible? With so many coats, we'll need many more hours than God sends in a day."

"If necessary, we'll work into the night. I'll get candles from Monna Giuliana."

"What of supper?"

"You'll get your bowl of pasta and time to eat it," she said, laughing. "You think more of your stomach than you do of my panel."

"Your panel is all very well, but it won't keep my stomach from rumbling or keep me warm at night."

"You've no appreciation for this profession, Francesco. And yet you would not eat if it wasn't for the money the master brings in from painting."

"I suppose so." Francesco smiled weakly and rubbed his stomach. "I'm glad of the master's food, but I can't yet see the value of what we produce here."

"So if you can't eat it, wear it, or otherwise use it for your own comfort, it has no value?"

Francesco shook his head, confused. "You talk so fast, Sandro, and say such things. I don't understand."

"It doesn't matter, Francesco. Come, let us see to the gessoing. If we work together, we may not need to go too long past Vespers. And then we have two days to wait while the panel dries in the sun."

"I'll be glad of the break."

"I'm sure the maestro will find plenty to keep you busy." Sofia grinned at Francesco. She couldn't remember a time in her life when she was so content. The work was hard and the hours long and her personal comfort a distant memory, but even in her father's workshop in the days before she married, Sofia had not known so much freedom. Here, she had no demanding father breathing over her shoulder and no need to keep herself hidden away from the other apprentices.

Once the panel was dry, Sofia used a bunch of goose feathers to sweep charcoal dust over the surface, then scraped a straight edge across the gesso. "The charcoal will help me see if any imperfections still remain," she explained to Francesco while she worked. "See here? The charcoal has caught upon a tiny node. I'll need to scrape it off so the panel is perfectly smooth."

Sofia worked for the better part of the day, until she was finally satisfied that the panel was ready to receive the gilding and the colors. The maestro gave her a small measure of thinly beaten gold leaf for the gilding and a florin to buy an ounce of lapis lazuli for the Holy Mother's robe. She placed the prepared panel on the table in front of her and asked the Virgin to bless her work. She then tied a piece of charcoal to the end of a short stick so that the charcoal extended about a hand width from her fingers to the panel. Her father had always stressed the need to keep her hand at some distance above the panel when she was composing. Next to the panel, she placed a feather for erasing any mis-strokes. She took a deep breath and began to draw, using a light touch to add shading for the folds of the robes and the faces.

"When you begin drawing on a panel, cara mia, don't be in too much of a hurry. Do your first drawing and then leave off for a day or more if you can. Then go back with fresh eyes."

The next day was the Sabbath and Sofia was glad of it. She looked forward to leaving the workshop and following Monna

Giuliana to church. Another of Siena's masters was hard at work creating a fresco in the chapel they frequented most often and she wanted to see the progress. Scaffolding covered one wall, but the other wall was finished. The colors of the fresco gleamed in the candlelight, distracting her so much with its beauty that Monna Giuliana had to pinch her arm to force her to her knees in response to the service. While Sofia rubbed her arm, she reflected on the skill of the painter who had completed the fresco. The work was far better than anything she'd seen Maestro Manzini do, although of course she would not share such an observation with Monna Giuliana. Her passionate defense of her Luca sometimes made Sofia laugh. She had never known a woman so fierce and yet so loyal.

When next she approached the panel, Sofia took a feather and rubbed it over the drawing very lightly until her strokes were just barely visible against the ivory white of the gesso. She took a dish half full of fresh water and a few drops of ink and used a pointed miniver brush to cover the whole drawing and set the charcoal lines. With a wash of the ink and a blunt brush, she then shaded in the folds in the gowns and the shadows on the faces. Finally, she took up a needle mounted on a little stick and scratched over the outlines of the figures against the grounds she would be gilding. She whisked the white of an egg into a solid foam that reminded her of the few times in her life when she had seen drifts of snow blanketing the quiet streets of San Gimignano. She poured a glass of clear water over the foam and let it stand overnight.

Sofia spent most of the next morning grinding the egg white tempera with nuggets of Armenian bole—a red claylike substance that, when combined with the tempera, made a smooth solution for covering the areas of the panel that she needed to gild. She took up a sponge, dipped it in good clear water, squeezed it out, dipped it in the bole, then rubbed over the areas to be gilded. When she was finished, she covered the panel with a cloth to protect it from dust and stretched her arms over her head.

"We need to wait now for mild, damp weather," she said to Francesco, who stood at her elbow.

"Why?" he asked.

"Gilding is a painstaking business and best done when the weather's not too hot and dry. The gold flakes in hot weather."

"We've not had any rain for two weeks," Francesco said. "And this heat looks likely to continue."

"The preparation of the panel has taken longer than I expected. I want to be painting."

"You always have armor," Francesco said, indicating with a sweep of one hand the pile of breastplates and shields and visors next to Tommaso's bench.

Sighing, Sofia went over to where Tommaso worked. He looked up at her with red-rimmed eyes and for a moment his expression brightened. "You've come to help?"

"I need to wait for the weather to turn before I can start the gilding." She reached for a breastplate and settled herself at the bench. "Who are we doing today?"

"Eagles for the Aquila clan. Here's the design. I have the colors mixed already." Tommaso beamed at her. "I'm going to pray this hot weather continues."

Sofia didn't reply as she picked up a helmet and, with a barely suppressed sigh, placed the stencil over it and began the tedious process of setting the lines of the design. But at least she was holding a paintbrush in her hand. Even painting straight lines and simple designs on armor was a relief. And poor Tommaso looked so grateful.

"I'll not have Sandro on armor today."

The master's voice right behind Sofia made her jump so she almost dropped the helmet. The master plucked it from her hand and handed it back to Tommaso. "You're coming with me."

Sofia hopped off her stool so quickly that she jostled Tommaso's elbow. The helmet clattered to the floor.

"You do well to smile," he said as he led her away from poor Tommaso, who picked up the helmet and glowered after her. "I've something I want to show you."

"The fresco?"

"Not today, Sandro. All I ask is that you use your eyes." His smile faded. "Your hair escapes your cap! See to it."

Hastily, Sofia pushed the stray curls back under her cap. She must remember to ask Monna Giuliana to cut her hair again. When she was a maid, her hair had cascaded in thick waves that were almost never trimmed. Now, Monna Giuliana seemed to be always hacking ends off hair that grew like wildflowers in unruly black clumps.

Sofia followed the maestro outside, where the early morning sun had yet to reach streets simmering in greasy darkness. After many minutes of weaving around merchants and animals and all manner of industry, Sofia saw a slash of light up ahead. Her excitement mounted. She had been into Il Campo just a handful of times since meeting the maestro eight months earlier. When they emerged into the broad expanse of the piazza, she sighed with pleasure.

"The space is a noble one," Manzini said, "but today I'll show you something even more beautiful."

"I can't imagine anywhere more beautiful than this place!" The *campo* teemed with people, and yet for all their numbers they may as well have been ants on a broad expanse of coarse linen. At the base of the piazza next to the slender Torre del Mangia rose the massive Palazzo Pubblico—a red-bricked fortress with rounded arches and crenellated battlements.

"That's our destination," Manzini said, thrusting his chin toward the palazzo. "I have business to attend to and then I'll show you one of the finest frescoes in all of Siena."

Sofia wondered if it was possible for her heart to burst with happiness as she followed Manzini across the piazza and into the cavernous courtyard of the Palazzo Pubblico, the seat of all power in Siena.

CHAPTER NINE

. . . take pains and pleasure in constantly
copying the best things which you can find
done by the hand of great masters.
—Cennini, *Il Libro dell'Arte*, Chapter XXVII

The great Simone Martini painted it about twenty years ago," Manzini whispered. They were standing in the middle of the largest chamber Sofia had ever seen and looking at a fresco of the *Maestà* that covered one enormous wall. "I was honored to work on portions of it myself a few years back, when the maestro returned to make repairs."

"Repairs?"

"Problems with dampness. Martini supervised the restoration and then painted the wall behind you."

Sofia looked in the direction indicated by Manzini and gasped. The wall opposite the *Maestà* depicted a scene she had never seen in a public place—or any space. "What is it?"

"A portrait of the *condottiere* Guidoriccio da Fogliano. See how he holds his sword? He accepts the surrender of Count Aldobrandeschi. That's the count's castle in the background." Manzini drew her closer to the fresco. Its brilliant colors illuminated the entire chamber. Sofia could not conceive how any mortal man could have created it.

"It is a marvel," Manzini said. "You'll not see anything like it anywhere in Christendom. Even in Florence."

Sofia said nothing while her eyes tried to take in everything at once.

"There's talk of covering it."

"Why would anyone cover such a wonder?"

"Martini's been gone from Siena at least ten years. Some say he went to the Pope in Avignon, which doesn't make him very popular with our bishop. I've heard Lorenzetti is preparing a map piece to set over the fresco."

Sofia stared at the maestro in horror. To obliterate such a glorious piece of work seemed worse than wicked. "Didn't Lorenzetti paint the fresco that my father took me to see?"

"That's him. The fresco's close by, in the council chamber. We can't view it now, but do you remember it?"

"Not much," she admitted and then blushed. "My mind was on other things, but I do remember seeing the maestro himself on the scaffolding."

"He has the hearts and minds of the Nine in his palm," Manzini said bitterly. "Whatever Ambrogio Lorenzetti wants, he gets. And his brother Pietro's just the same."

"I remember the towers," Sofia said thoughtfully. "They were well executed." She nodded at Martini's fresco of Guidoriccio. An imposing series of gray cliffs topped by a church, a fortress, and a hodgepodge of other buildings represented the breached castle of Arcidosso. "The buildings in this fresco are also well done."

"You'll rarely see better. And notice how Martini has executed the folds of the gowns. I'd have you do as well. Stay here and look while I attend to my business. I'll fetch you when I'm ready to leave."

Sofia nodded absently while continuing to peer at the fresco. Guidoriccio's gown was rendered particularly well, and the expression on the face of the vanquished Count Aldobrandeschi captured just the right combination of haughtiness and defeat. One of Guidoriccio's arms was raised in what appeared to be an expression of conciliation, but at the same time Sofia noticed the other hand resting lightly on the hilt of his sword. The famous general left no doubt where the power lay. The figures were real people, not saints or angels. They had flaws and wore the clothes she saw every day in the streets.

She looked again at Martini's *Maestà* at the opposite end of the huge room. His depiction of the Holy Mother flanked by hosts of saints and angels captured the very essence of heaven. The figures seemed to flicker and float in the candlelight. They were real and yet not real. Sofia turned back to the fresco of Guidoriccio. Martini's colors and lines were bold and vigorous. Sofia closed her eyes and saw her home city of San Gimignano as she had viewed it so many times with her father on walks outside the city walls. Could she ever dream of painting it? Smiling, she opened her eyes and shook her head. The notion was absurd. Who would commission it? And besides, she hoped never to see the towers of San Gimignano again.

The maestro completed his business, and together they left the Palazzo Pubblico. In the noon light, the red brick façades of the palazzos fronting the *campo* glowed almost white. Sofia kept pace with the maestro, marveling again at the freedom her disguise afforded her. Sometimes she missed the feel of heavy velvet skirts swirling against her legs and Paulina's hands braiding her hair, but she had not yet learned to miss the confinement.

They had almost crossed the *campo* when a knot of people emerged from a side street. Most were shouting and laughing. Sofia caught a glimpse of a cowed and bleeding young boy in the center of the crowd. Behind him, a large man cracked a whip over the boy's bloodied shoulders. She heard a scream and an answering chorus of whoops and jeers.

"Come, Sandro! This isn't something you should see."

"What's he done, master?" Sofia had no wish to see any of God's creatures tortured, but she couldn't understand why Manzini would worry about shielding her. At home in San Gimignano and in her travels with her father, she had all too often seen terrible punishments inflicted on wretches who may or may not have done much to deserve them.

"Monna Giuliana will be angry if we get home late. Leave the poor girl to her fate."

"Her?" Sofia snapped her head around just as the whip whistled through the air and landed with a splash onto a back now almost stripped to the bone. Sofia saw close-cropped hair and a linen cloth bound across two straining breasts. Anguished eyes shone from a face splattered with blood.

"Sandro!" The maestro grabbed Sofia's arm and steered her into a side street. "Wipe that look off your face. You'll betray yourself."

"I don't understand, master. Why do they torment her?"

"She's being punished for dressing as a boy. Siena's law is very clear about these abominations." He paused, then quoted: *"No woman is to go about the city or suburbs dressed in virile clothing, nor any man in female clothing."*

"Female clothing? What man would want to dress as a woman?" Sofia was so surprised at the notion that for a moment she forgot the girl.

"In my youth, it was quite common."

"Why?"

"For sport. Often during Lent young men looking for novelty borrowed clothing from their female relations and charged about the city playing and cavorting, the richer ones jousting on horseback. Some even whitened their faces. There was so much hilarity and drinking that the council had to put a stop to it. The law that poor girl is suffering under comes from that time."

"She doesn't deserve to be whipped."

"What does she deserve?"

"I . . . well," Sofia stammered. "I don't know. I haven't thought about it."

"No, I know you haven't." Manzini lowered his voice so that she had to strain to hear him. "Which is why you must be doubly careful not to be found out."

Behind her, another roar followed another scream—long and agonized. Sofia focused all her will on imagining the colors and lines of the Martini frescoes. The figure of Mary in the *Maestà* fresco had glowed, her face the most purely rendered Sofia had ever seen. Mary was Mother of them all—the perfect woman, the holiest of protectors. But the image of the Mother of God kept dissolving into the bloodshot eyes and terrified expression of a young woman who wasn't any older than Sofia herself.

Sofia felt the change in the air before she opened her eyes. Thankfully, her dreams had been full of Martini's frescoes and not the girl in the street. She had never seen so many well-executed figures or even imagined that a castle of such proportions could be painted to perch so pleasingly upon a hill. She breathed deeply, smelled rain-damp stone, and smiled.

Then her eyes flew open and she threw back her cover. Before Monna Giuliana was halfway into the room, Sofia was standing with her arms above her head.

"You're the eager one this morning."

"The air has cooled enough for me to begin the gilding!"

"Means nothing to me. Turn."

"Yes, madonna." The air was wonderfully fresh on her skin. She knew Monna Giuliana disapproved of her new position in the workshop, but surely she'd change her opinion when Sofia's panel led to another commission and then another and still another until every noble in Siena was flocking to Maestro Manzini's workshop. Sofia allowed a smile to creep onto her face as she imagined the accolades that would flow and how favorably the master would look upon her. *She* would not be found out and whipped through the streets.

"Leave off your smiling, girl," Monna Giuliana hissed as she pulled the binding cloth so tightly Sofia was sure she felt a rib crack.

"Yes, madonna," Sofia gasped. "Please! It's too tight."

In answer, Monna Giuliana pulled harder. "Pray to Our Lady that the binding holds. Now get to work."

Francesco was already in the workshop removing the stretchers of oiled parchment from the windows. A damp wind swirled into the room, along with the dull gray light of a cloudy dawn. "The weather's cooled!" he said. "Will you work with the gold today?"

His eagerness pleased Sofia. She doubted he had the passion or the skill for painting, but with the right encouragement, he could be an assistant capable of more than sweeping floors and fetching colors. He'd already learned how to make a respectable leaf glue and he understood the composition and purpose of the gessoes.

"Fill me a goblet of clean water and mix in some of the egg white tempera from yesterday," Sofia said. "It should be a little stale." While Francesco set to work, she ran a tiny hook lightly over the flat of the panel, searching for any lumps or grit that might have become lodged in the bole. She then burnished the panel with a piece of linen until she was satisfied it was ready to take the first layer of gilding. The patron hadn't paid for enough gold to make decent haloes, so she'd need to work very carefully. She took up a card in her left hand and, using a small pair of pincers, picked up a leaf of gold and placed it on the card. With her right hand, she wet a brush with the tempera, then brushed it over the area to gild.

"Take care not to let water pool in one area more than another, cara mia. The gold is delicate. Treat it with respect." She smelled warm wine on her father's breath and the tang of boiled parchment.

"Papa! You're blocking the light. And I already know about the water. You've warned me about it often enough."

"Do you listen?"

"Yes, Papa, I always listen to you."

"See that you do."

Sofia took a deep breath and then very slowly brought the card with the gold close to the wet panel. She used her fingernail to extend a single gold leaf beyond the edge of the card so that it slid onto the panel. The moment the gold touched the panel, she drew back her hand, tamped the gold lightly with a bit of clean cotton, and then breathed gently on the leaf to set it. Finally, she ran her brush along the leaf edge to prevent any water from running over it. She worked steadily all morning, oblivious to the sounds of hammering and cursing and rough chatter that filled the workshop. She stopped only when Francesco tugged at her sleeve to tell her food had arrived. He covered the gold with a clean white cloth while Sofia accepted a generous lump of Monna Giuliana's cheese and a slice of fresh bread. She ate quickly, her mind fixed upon the panel resting under the cloth. Her father taught her to always burnish the gold immediately after she laid it. As soon as she swallowed the last morsel of bread, she took up a piece of hematite and held the stone between her hands to warm it. She then began to rub the stone across the gold, first in one direction and then in another. The gold shone brighter and brighter until it seemed to illuminate her entire work area, independent of the afternoon light of a cloudy day filtering through the window.

"It's beautiful!"

The reverence in Francesco's voice made her smile. "Thank you. Now watch me use this stylus to punch tiny holes in the gold of the haloes. I'm making patterns that will sparkle in the candlelight."

"It's the halo of Our Lady?"

"Do you think She will like it?"

Francesco started back and dropped his hand from her shoulder. "You mustn't say such things!"

"Why not? I paint to honor Our Lady and for the glory of God. Of course I hope that She approves it."

Francesco shook his head, confused. "You have so many words, Sandro. I don't know what to think."

"You don't need to think, Francesco. Just look and appreciate. Now, take up a bit of the white lead and grind it with sizing. I'll use it to mark out the figures. And then tomorrow I'll start on the cloak of the Madonna. You can help me with the blue."

Francesco set to work grinding the white lead while Sofia continued punching tiny, intricately twined lines and pinpricks into the diadems for Mary, Joseph, and the blessed Child. She loved working with the gold. The way it shimmered and sparkled when the light touched it made her think of what heaven must be like. When she had completed the diadems, she laid a whisper-thin layer of gold leaf over the shape for the Madonna's cloak. That evening, the maestro glanced at her panel and told her to continue. She was satisfied that he found nothing to criticize.

The following morning, she painted over the gold with the white lead tempered with egg yolk. When the lead was dry, she added sizing and egg yolk to the ultramarine blue to temper it, then laid in two coats of blue over the white lead.

"Why did you put gold on Our Lady's cloak and then cover it with blue?" Francesco asked. "Won't the master be angry?"

Sofia laughed. "You have good eyes, Francesco, and your observation would also be good if it was right."

Francesco drew back, his expression hurt. "I'm sorry, Sandro. I didn't mean to offend."

"Don't be such a boy! I don't mind you asking questions and you shouldn't mind when I sometimes have fun with them."

"I don't understand."

"Look here." She gestured for Francesco to move closer, then picked up her thinnest stylus. It was fashioned from silver and no more than a few hairs thick. She placed the tip of the stylus over the ultramarine blue and then with short, deft strokes, made delicate scratches that penetrated the blue to show fine streaks of gold beneath.

"See, Francesco? I scratch through the blue of Our Lady's gown to reveal the gold. My father used to say I was like a hen in the barnyard scratching through the dirt to find nuggets of grain."

"You don't look much like a hen to me," Francesco said. "More like a bantam rooster."

"Francesco!" Sofia laid down her stylus and looked up at him. "I think that's the kindest thing you've ever said to me."

Again, Francesco's young face clouded with confusion. "I didn't mean it as a compliment."

"I know, but after what I saw some days ago, I'm glad to be thought of as more bantam than hen."

Francesco opened his mouth to ask more questions, but Sofia shooed him away. "I don't have all day for idle talking. Go and grind a nugget or two of red lac. I'll need it later for the shepherds' smocks. And I must finish exposing the gilding before the blue dries."

As her father had taught her, Sofia spent the next several weeks completing all the draperies of the figures. Then, she was ready to start on the faces. By that time, the cool weather had given way to the fierce heat of July.

She started with the old, weathered face of Joseph. She loaded her brush with *terre-verte*, mixed it with well-tempered white lead, and then laid two coats all over Joseph's face, hands, and feet. She then tempered the color with the yolk of a country hen's egg that Monna Giuliana had obtained for her. The brighter yolks produced by country hens were perfect for tempering the color of aging skin. Her Joseph was to look old and careworn, beaten down by the weight of his new responsibilities. She added in a little vermilion to the white lead to make three values, each lighter than the next, then layered the colors onto Joseph's face, working them into each other, fusing and softening. She added more white to the lightest of her flesh colors and picked out the lips, eyes, and nose, then outlined the upper edge of the eyes and the nostrils with black. Finally, she used dark brown and a trace of black to outline all the accents of the nose, eyes, brows, hair, hands, and feet. By the time she completed the face of her Joseph, golden light was pouring through the window and filling the room with a seething, pulsing presence—a living, breathing beast that greedily sucked the air from her lungs and sheathed her body with sweat. Her bindings were soaking wet and chafed each time she moved. The heat seemed to roast her very bones.

She took a moment to fan herself with a scrap of stiffened parchment. The heat might be unbearable, she thought, but her panel would be glorious. The satisfaction she felt when she regarded her work, even as sweat stung her eyes and her breasts burned, was unlike any she had known before, even in her father's workshop.

The heat roiled and crested until all of Siena was fused together in an inferno of airless suffering. Sofia barely noticed it, as each day her panel took shape under her brush. She woke up every morning alive with anticipation and fell asleep every evening longing for the next day. And when she wasn't painting, she sometimes left the workshop with the maestro to view frescoes in palazzos and chapels all over Siena. Once, he even took her to view again the glorious Duccio altarpiece in the Duomo. Sofia never imagined her life could be so full.

By the time summer wilted into fall, the panel was ready for varnishing and then drying. Sofia returned to decorating armor and looked forward to the day when the patron came to collect the finished panel. He would be pleased—and his pleasure was bound to lead to more commissions.

ᕼᕼ

"Sandro!" Every head in the shop flew up and six pairs of eyes stared at Sofia as she scrambled from her high stool and crossed to where Manzini stood. As was her habit, Sofia kept her eyes on the floor, so it was not until she reached Manzini that she looked up and saw the man standing next to him. She gasped so loudly that she feared she'd given herself away. Out of the corner of her eye, she saw Pietro take a step forward, his expression more alarmed than curious. A small part of her brain registered surprise at his reaction, before turning all her attention to the man she had asked God to protect in her prayers every night for more than a year.

He was looking at her like he'd seen a phantom, and she was sure her own eyes held the same astonishment. His mouth began to open and she saw his lips come together to form the sounds of her name. She sprang forward, managed a low bow, then cut him off before his words could betray her.

"A welcome surprise! Maestro Manzini, may I present Marcello? He serves my father in Florence." As she spoke, she used her eyes to silence Marcello. His face suffused with red, but he closed his mouth and returned her bow.

"I've come with news from home," he said.

"And I'll be glad of it," Sofia said formally. "Maestro, may I have leave to speak with this man outside the shop?"

"Of course, of course," Manzini said graciously enough, but Sofia saw that his hands were shaking. What if this young man had come to take away his most promising painter?

As she passed him at the door, she patted his arm and whispered, "Marcello can be trusted, maestro."

"Just keep the workshop out of danger," he hissed back. Without even giving Sofia time to grab a cloak, he ushered her and Marcello out of the shop and into the street. Marcello saw her shivering in the bitter wind. As soon as they rounded the corner into a smaller side street, he stopped and stripped off his own thick cloak. Gratefully, she wrapped it around herself, then gasped again when she saw that it bore the crest of her brother-in-law, Ruberto Carelli.

She was wrong! Marcello had come to take her back to San Gimignano—and Giorgio.

A terror unlike any she had ever known, even in the forest, gripped her so hard that she was afraid she would vomit in the street. She flung off the cloak and ran. Siena was a maze of streets. Marcello would be lost within minutes. She felt the freezing air sear her lungs as her legs pumped beneath her. Not for the first time she blessed her freedom from heavy skirts. Siena would hide her and keep her safe. What a fool she'd been to pray for Marcello's safety. He was no better than a thief—come to steal her away from a life she could finally call her own. She wondered how much money Giorgio had offered Marcello for his loyalty. What price would a man ask to betray a sister?

She heard him running behind her. She begged her legs to go faster, but within seconds he caught her. The ease with which he gathered her squirming body into his arms was like a wolf swiping a lamb with one lazy paw.

"Sofia," he said quietly. "Calm yourself. I'm not here to betray you."

"You serve my husband's brother!"

"Hush! Your husband knows nothing. Find us a place out of the cold and I'll tell you everything."

"This way." Sofia's voice was shaky and she still wanted to run, but Marcello kept a firm grip on her arm as she led the way to a nearby establishment run by a kinsman of Manzini's. The proprietor looked at them sharply, his eyebrows raised. Apprentices did not come into taverns in the middle of the day. "The maestro knows I'm here with my kinsman from Florence," she said with as much authority as she could. "Some wine, please."

The man scowled, then shuffled over with two wooden cups of rough wine. He banged them on the table. The contents slopped out and joined the streaks of red paint on Sofia's smock.

Marcello raised his cup to Sofia. "I'd not expected to see you again in this life," he said. "I thank God you're alive."

Sofia took a sip of wine while measuring her feelings. She still felt wary despite Marcello's assurance that he wasn't going to take her back. Her brother-in-law, Ruberto, had never been her friend.

"What about your master?"

"Don't trouble yourself, madonna," he said, then smiled as the absurdity of the title dawned on him. Instead of the well-dressed wife of a prosperous merchant he'd left in the forest, he was looking across a scarred table at a youth with ragged hair, a smudge of paint on a fine-boned nose, and the drab smock of the painter's apprentice. Only the eyes looked the same—large, black, and sharp with the same intelligence that had shone from the eyes of their common father. "My master's come to Siena to meet with the Nine. There's talk of an alliance between San Gimignano and Florence. Signor Carelli wants to see how the land lies with Siena in case they may counsel another route. He'll be at the Palazzo Pubblico all day."

"My brother-in-law always had political ambitions. You're sure he doesn't know you've come looking for me?"

"As I said, he's much occupied."

"But as his servant, you must have duties."

Marcello laughed, the rich baritone reminding Sofia of her father. She dipped her head and took another quick sip of wine.

"You're not an easy one to convince," Marcello said. "I assure you that all my master's attention is on his mission. Besides, I told him I was going to search for cloth ordered by his wife."

"Caterina? She's well?" An unexpected stab of homesickness darted through her. In San Gimignano, Caterina's endless cheerfulness had often irritated Sofia. But in Siena, with only Monna Giuliana's harsh criticisms for female company, Sofia sometimes longed for Caterina's soft kindness. She reached across the table for Marcello's hand. "Dear Marcello! I thought you were dead." The tears she so rarely indulged flooded her eyes. "How did you find me?"

"By asking at every painter's workshop in Siena," he said. "How else?" He extricated his hand, indicating with a jerk of his head the proprietor at the back of the shop. Two youths holding hands would not be tolerated in Siena.

"Dear God!" She gripped the table with both hands. "You've been saying my name at other workshops?"

"Ah, no, Sofia. Do you think I'm a simpleton? I was discreet. I asked only if someone new had joined the workshop within the past year. I didn't give your name. And the Virgin was with me—Manzini's workshop was only my second stop."

"So you found me."

"Yes." He looked her in the eye—bold and steady, the difference in their ranks obliterated by her new life. "And you're well?"

"As you see."

"Hmm. To be honest, I'm not altogether sure what I see. You're much changed."

"I had no choice. After you left me in the forest, I had to fend for myself."

"I also had no choice, Sofia."

She looked fearfully at the proprietor, who was wiping cups and taking care to place them on a nearby shelf so they would not clink and drown out what appeared to be a very interesting conversation.

"Call me Sandro," she whispered.

"Forgive me. Sandro. My only solace after they took me was that you'd gotten away. I knew God would take care of you."

"Did you?"

"I was right, wasn't I?"

"God and a boy named Francesco who I met along the way," she said. "And I can't say which one gets the most credit."

"You're so like him sometimes. My mother often feared for his soul when he said much the same kind of thing."

"As did mine." They both smiled shyly. Sofia thought again of her dream to have them paint together—side by side in the same workshop, carrying on the work of their father. It was an idle fancy, but at this moment, sitting across from each other in a rough Siena tavern like equals, the dream seemed almost possible.

"Your husband was inconsolable."

The abrupt change of subject caught Sofia off guard. "He cares only for the child he thinks he lost," she said dismissively. "Giorgio hasn't cared about me since we were newly wed."

"I'm not sure that's true, Sandro. When finally I returned to San Gimignano after escaping the brigands, I found your husband beside himself with grief. When you didn't arrive in Florence as planned, he thought you were dead."

"And when you returned?"

"He leaped upon me. I feared for my life."

"And what did you tell him?"

"I told him I was taken by brigands, which was true enough, and that you were dead, which I thank God is not true. I also let him believe I was taken on the road to Florence." Marcello grinned, for a moment looking as young as Francesco. "Your body was never recovered."

"That would be difficult," Sofia said dryly. "Since I'm still in possession of it, even if some days it doesn't feel like mine."

"I speak the truth when I tell you he suffered."

She said nothing, her heart a stone in her breast. She couldn't risk letting it beat with anything close to forgiveness.

"Your husband loves you."

"He loves my womb." But for the first time since leaving San Gimignano, Sofia felt a spasm of shame. She had sinned against God, and Giorgio was suffering for her sins. "Do you think I should go back?"

Marcello raised one eyebrow, again looking uncannily like Maestro Barducci. "I said no such thing. I state the facts."

"So why did you come looking for me?"

"I had to see for myself that you lived. Why else?"

"Thank you, Marcello," she said quietly. "You've done your duty. Now please go and leave me in peace. I can never return to my husband."

If God was merciful, He would help Giorgio find another wife. If she went back, she would be walking into a living death.

"Perhaps *I* want you to return."

"And what relationship could we have?" The exasperation in Sofia's voice raised it an octave. The proprietor looked over. She gulped and lowered her voice. "You're my brother-in-law's servant." She shook her head. "I'll be the kept wife of your master's brother. We could never meet, have no cause to speak. No, Marcello."

"You're sure you want to stay here? The long hours, the poisons in the paint—think what you're doing. It's no life for a woman."

"Our father didn't scorn it."

"He wouldn't wish to see you like this."

"If he could see the work I've done for Manzini, I don't think he'd wish me anywhere else." Sofia smiled. "You have no idea, Marcello. Here in Siena, I'm able to paint in the way our father taught me. I can't turn my back on it. Even for you."

"You're sure? I hate leaving you here."

"Our father's dead, Marcello, and my husband is dead to me. Please go with God, and leave me to the fate I've chosen."

Marcello rose from the table and held out his hand for her. She let him help her to her feet, even though she felt the hot stare of the proprietor on her back. He would have good gossip to share about Manzini's young apprentice, but she could not deny Marcello her hand. He was all she had left of her father. He guided her from the shop and into the frigid air. She smelled sweet wine and the tang of horses.

They walked back to the workshop in silence, their steps slow and measured in spite of the wind whipping up the street and into their faces. Just before they reached the door, Sofia turned to him.

"You could stay," she said.

"You wish that?"

"More than anything." Sofia edged closer to him so they both stood in the shadow of a tower, a pool of frozen waste at their feet glinting yellow in the weak winter sun. "You're so like him. Manzini would welcome you, find a place for you. The workshop's busier than ever."

For a moment, Sofia was sure he'd say yes. She saw him hesitate, his eyes wary. She remembered seeing the same look in the eyes of his mother, Emilia, when she gave Sofia the poultice that kept her barren. She held her breath. He must jump at the chance to join her in carrying on the work of their father.

"I'm sorry," he said finally, shaking his head.

"Why?"

"Because I'm needed in San Gimignano."

"Caterina and Ruberto can find another man. You're not the only servant in the city. Please, Marcello. We're always short-handed, especially now with all the new commissions."

"You think I can break my bond with my master so easily?"

"You were willing to when we left for Siena. Why not again?"

"For many reasons, Sandro," he said, his voice irritated. Her father had sounded the same way when she asked too many questions. "I can't stay in Siena, because I don't want to."

"You'd rather be a servant?" She did not bother keeping the scorn from her voice. To think that a son of Maestro Barducci's—even an illegitimate one—would prefer serving Ruberto Carelli to being with her was unthinkable. "Go, then," she said. "Your master probably waits for you."

"Sofia . . . "

She heard the anguish in his voice and did not let it move her. How dare he leave her again? He didn't deserve all the hours and weeks and months she'd mourned him. Blindly, she wrenched open the workshop door and stumbled into the warmth. The maestro rose, surprised, but she ignored him and took her place next to Tommaso. Her brush had dried. She added clear water to the pot of yellow that Francesco mixed for her and carefully traced the lines of the Contrada del Bruco—the caterpillar—squeezing and opening her eyes while she worked to block the tears.

"You cannot always have your way, cara."

"I know, Papa," Sofia said with a sigh. *"Mama often said the same thing. But why can't we have our way, Papa? All I want is to stay here with you."*

"You belong with your nurse."

"Emilia just scolds me because I won't settle to the needle. I hate the needle."

"And what makes you think you'll like drawing any better? You'll get your new gown dirty."

"I don't care about my gown, Papa. I just want to be here with you." She looked around the busy workshop. *"That boy over there's not much older than me. You let him stay."*

Her father glanced nervously at a young boy sweeping sawdust from under a newly cut crucifix. *"You belong in the house,"* he said. *"Now get along with you. I'll see you at sundown and you can tell me all about your needlework."*

"I hate needlework!"

"So you said." He patted her on the head and turned her in the direction of the door at the back of the workshop that led through a yard to the kitchen.

"Sandro?"

Sofia didn't look up when she felt Francesco at her elbow. "What?"

"Who was that man?"

"Nobody. Mix me another batch of this yellow. I'm almost out."

CHAPTER TEN

If you do your work well . . . you will get such
a reputation that a wealthy person will come to
compensate you for the poor one. . . . As the old
saying goes, good work, good pay. And even if you
were not adequately paid, God and Our Lady
will reward you for it, body and soul.
—Cennini, *Il Libro dell'Arte*, Chapter LIXVI

ofia was decorating a pair of greaves for protecting the shins of
a noble in the Contrada dell'Aquila when the maestro escorted
a patron into the workshop with a fawning deference much at
odds with his usual manner. Her gaze fell first on a back covered in
fine velvet the exact shade of the sky after the sun sets and the world
loiters between light and dark. A matching cap rested on a mass of
black curls flowing over broad shoulders. A gold ring glinted on the
smooth skin of one hand. The patron was a young man—a very rich
young man.

She placed her brush in a dish of water and slid off her stool
to move closer so she could hear his reaction to her painting of the
Nativity. The maestro was holding it up to the light and talking
animatedly. The young man's full lips curved in a slight smile, his
head nodding as he listened.

"You've outdone yourself, maestro," he said. "My father will be delighted."

"I'm honored to be at your father's service, Messer Salvini."

"Of course." The young man kept staring at the panel. Sofia edged closer and saw him peering intently at the figure of Joseph. She held her breath.

"This figure here. This Joseph," he said, pointing with one elegant finger. Sofia had painted Joseph dressed in a welter of ocher-colored robes highlighted with touches of white lead. His head was bent, and his arms were wrapped around a staff, his face serious, dejected even. He didn't look like a man who had just witnessed the birth of his Savior. "What of his attitude?"

"Yes, well, I'm glad you noticed that, my lord. I, ah, well, he's in repose."

"I can see that, but what of his face? His expression?"

"It doesn't please you?"

"I didn't say that. But there is something you've captured in his face that I have not seen before."

"Yes, but it pleases you?"

A sheen of sweat slicked the master's forehead, and Sofia saw that the hand holding the panel shook. She stepped forward.

"Saint Joseph feels the great weight of his responsibilities. The maestro has caught the gravity of his emotions perfectly, don't you think?"

The maestro glared at her but could say nothing as Sofia smiled up at the patron. He looked at her in surprise. Apprentices, even full assistants, never engaged with patrons.

"And who is this?"

"This is Sandro, my lord. He was of some assistance to me on this panel."

"Ho, and is he responsible for Saint Joseph?"

"I regret to say, signor, that I allowed him to work upon the figure. You can assure your father that I will have him turned out."

"Turned out? Why?"

"I thought, signor, that the work displeases you."

"It's not for me to be pleased or displeased. The panel was commissioned by my father. I've merely come to fetch it for him." The young man spoke gravely, his brow furrowed.

Sofia knew Manzini was very far from reassured and regretted her outburst. In her father's workshop, she had never spoken to strangers. But in her father's workshop, she had been kept well out of sight. No patron ever knew that Maestro Barducci's daughter was anything other than a demure maid of San Gimignano.

Her simple tunic and cropped hair were making her reckless. She didn't believe Maestro Manzini would turn her into the streets, but she knew she was on dangerous ground. Apart from Monna Giuliana, Maestro Manzini had just one passion in life and that passion was profit. He could not afford to have his livelihood threatened, no matter what allegiance he might have once owed her father.

She looked at the panel the maestro still held in his hand. The depiction of the Nativity was sober and without innovation. She had followed the maestro's directions faithfully and only in the face of Joseph had she allowed herself to deviate. And yet, God forgive her, she couldn't look upon her work and feel sorry. She was pleased with the way in which she'd arranged the folds of Joseph's robe and positioned him below the manger. And as for the face, the sad expression and heaviness of the skin were perfect. It was the face of her father on the day of his death when he realized the great responsibility he imposed upon his Sofia by leaving her.

The young man nodded solemnly, but Sofia saw, with a start, that a sparkle of wit shone from his eyes.

"I'll take this to my father and you'll hear more in due course. Do not be angry with this young man, Manzini. He shows promise. I'll speak with my father about employing his skills on our next commission."

"Next commission?" Manzini's face relaxed. "Yes, yes, of course. I am at your father's service. Tell him we can be ready anytime he has need of us."

"I don't doubt it. Have the panel wrapped for me. I must be on my way."

As Manzini called for an assistant to help with the wrapping, Sofia turned to go back to her workbench. She was stopped by a hand upon her shoulder and the stirring of moist breath near her cheek. The smell of fine-milled soap and a warm spiciness made her knees feel as flaccid as a brush dipped in thin gesso.

"You show much ability, lad. Next time my father will commission an Annunciation. Can you do one?"

"I follow the maestro's orders," she said, keeping her voice low.

"Not entirely."

She glanced up quickly and, for the first time, looked directly at his face. Skin the color of tanned leather stretched across an aquiline nose and high cheekbones—the face of a man born to wealth and ease. He winked at her and cuffed one of her shoulders. Sofia turned away to hide her smile. An Annunciation! She'd seen a few in her years traveling with her father and had always longed to paint one. Her father had never thought her worthy of the challenge.

"The Annunciation is a somber subject. You must understand the gravity of what has befallen Our Lady."

"Of course I understand. Our Lady receives the news she has been chosen to be the mother of God."

"And how do you think she might feel?"

Sofia stared at her father. "What do you mean? She'd be honored, of course."

Maestro Barducci smiled at the pure, eager face of his young daughter. She had just reached her fourteenth year and had not yet heard of Giorgio Carelli. All her attention and all her love was for him alone and for the panels he allowed her to paint.

"Do you think, perhaps, she might also be afraid?" he asked.

"Of course not, Papa. How can you say that? She is the Holy Mother."

"Yes, daughter, so she becomes. But at the moment of the Annunciation, what is she?"

"A woman, of course."

"I think more like a girl. And you will not paint her at that moment for these many years yet."

"But, Papa!"

"Your colors are drying out. See that you have the robes of Saint Nicholas completed before sundown."

Sofia took up one of the greaves and mechanically began shading the wing of a double-headed black eagle, the symbol of the Contrada dell'Aquila. Behind her, the door of the workshop opened and she heard Manzini ushering young Messer Salvini into the street with many promises of the great work he would do to glorify God and the Salvini family. Her brush moved quickly, but her mind moved faster as she thought about how to arrange the figures of the archangel Gabriel and the Holy Mother in an Annunciation panel. She would make Mary young and beautiful, of course, but she would also show something of her fear, maybe have her turning away slightly from Gabriel. Such thoughts occupied her happily for the rest of the day—so much so that for the first time since Marcello left the month before, she did not think about him nor feel the tightening in her stomach that reproached her for turning from him. Surely God did not wish her to return to San Gimignano and Giorgio, not when He was sending her such an opportunity. Would her father have thought her ready?

Sofia had to endure several more weeks of painting armor and shields before Manzini called her again to his alcove. He looked grave. For a moment she wondered if perhaps Messer Salvini had been displeased after all with her depiction of the Nativity. The master would condemn her to decorating armor until her hands bled and her eyes grew weak.

"You look worried, Sandro."

"I shouldn't have spoken to that young man."

"No, you shouldn't have. Didn't your father teach you to be silent?"

"My father was always very careful to make sure no one knew about my work."

"Well, yes, of course he would be. You're starting to believe your own disguise. You must accept that you can never be master of your own workshop, no matter how great your skill."

"I am aware, master."

"Good. Now, Messer Salvini wants another panel."

"I'm pleased for you."

"Yes, well. The news is even better." Manzini tried unsuccessfully to keep the excitement out of his voice. "I have also been commissioned to paint a fresco at the Salvini palazzo. The house is set right upon Il Campo and is said to be very grand—one of the finest in all of Siena." For a moment, Manzini looked exactly like an overgrown boy, and for the first time since living under his roof, Sofia understood why Monna Giuliana loved him so fiercely. "You shall work upon the panel. The patron has asked for you specifically. It seems that you made an impression upon his son."

"I'm honored."

"You should be. Salvini will pay for more gold and lapis for this panel. Your work on Saint Joseph did not go unnoticed."

Sofia bowed modestly.

"Humility still doesn't sit well on your shoulders, Sandro," Manzini said genially. "But it's no matter. I'll be much engaged these next weeks to finish the fresco at San Paolo before I can make a start on the fresco for Messer Salvini. But you can start the panel right away. Messer Salvini has asked for an Annunciation."

"Thank you."

"Thank God for our good fortune. Now get back to work and don't give me cause to regret my faith in you."

On her way back to her bench, Sofia flashed a grin at Francesco, who was sweeping sawdust into a pile in the middle of the floor. He smiled back, but his eyes were worried.

و~ﻭ

"And what of this flower? Why have you included it?"

Sofia glanced up at Messer Salvini. He was staring intently at her hand as she added strokes of white lead to the petals.

"It's a lily, of course." She smiled and shook her head. "You must know that."

"Yes, yes, of course. A symbol of purity. Forgive me. I should have realized."

"No need for forgiveness from *me*, signor. But your confessor might be somewhat dismayed." She glanced up at him. "It is not my place to teach you the symbols of our faith."

"And you think you know so much more about our faith than I do?"

"It appears so."

"You speak very freely for someone in your position."

Sofia heard the sharpness of his tone and instantly regretted teasing him. She had grown accustomed to his presence in the workshop. Not long after she started work on the Annunciation panel, young Salvini had begun making a habit of popping into Manzini's workshop every few days to watch her progress. Despite the differences in rank, they had discovered a mutual intelligence that made for some lively conversations. Each morning, Sofia was more eager than ever to be up and at her bench.

"I'm sorry, my lord," Sofia said, bending her head to her work. "I didn't mean to offend."

Salvini grinned and slapped her on her left shoulder. "But of course you are right. My confessor would be shocked to discover the depths of my ignorance. Now, explain the significance of this lily and I promise I won't tell Manzini of your insolence."

"You mock me."

"As you do me. But come. Let's be friends. You can talk and paint at the same time. I've seen you do it these many weeks."

"Yes, signor." Sofia glanced up. "The lily represents the beauty and purity of Our Lady. I've placed it close to her so the angel sees it when he looks upon the Madonna."

Salvini bent closer, his shoulder touching hers so Sofia felt his heat. Not for the first time, she thanked God that she was seated. Salvini had no idea what she was, but she was only too aware of what *he* was. With a great effort, she kept her hand steady.

"I like the way you make such small strokes. You have great patience."

"Not according to my father," Sofia laughed. "He used to remind me constantly that this profession is tedious for those who crave quick results."

"So you wish to be finished?"

"At times I confess I wish the work would go more quickly, but mostly I'm content to take the time."

"How so?"

"I suppose, signor, that for me painting is like hunting is for you."

"Explain."

Sofia paused, considering her words. "You enjoy the hunt?"

"Of course. It is a passion for me."

"So you've said. When you hunt, do you wish to leave off?"

"Not readily."

"And why is that?" Sofia had already discovered that Salvini enjoyed the give and take of debate.

"Perhaps because the hunt consumes me." He paused. "Like your painting consumes you. I don't want to stop."

"Exactly, signor." Sofia smiled up at him, hoping her dimple wouldn't appear. "I also don't want to stop."

"Tell me more about the lily."

"Not today, signor. The light's going. You will come tomorrow?"

"If the weather continues dreary."

"And if it's fair?"

Salvini laughed, then stood up and stretched his lean arms above his head. His tunic revealed the muscles of a young man who had not yet succumbed to the pleasures of good food and wine. She remembered how quickly the sharp edges of Giorgio's good looks had blurred and faded, leaving behind a doughy complexion and an expanding girth. She didn't think the same fate could possibly await Salvini.

"If it's fair, I'll seek sport outside the walls of the city."

"And I will continue here."

"Good evening to you, Master Sandro. You're making excellent progress with this panel. I'll tell my father."

"We are at your service, signor."

"Depend upon me, Sandro. I will tell all my acquaintance. Old Manzini won't lack for commissions."

"You'll find us grateful."

"You should be." He flashed a smile that made her shiver. She changed the movement to a shrug. He spun elegantly on one foot and strode across the workshop to the open door. Some of the other workers looked up when he passed. Sofia noticed Pietro scowling at Salvini's retreating back. She knew he resented the special attention she was getting from the son of a patron. But what of it? Pietro was a carpenter fit only to build scaffolding and trestles. If he harbored jealousy for her, he should ask God to grant him patience.

"Will you leave off now, Sandro?"

Sofia smiled at Francesco, who had put away his broom and was coming over to help her clean up the day's work. She knew how he fretted about the attention Salvini paid her. He had no faith in her ability to keep him from penetrating her disguise.

"Thank you, Francesco. I'll be glad of a bowl of Monna Giuliana's stew this evening. The work progresses slowly."

"You would get more done if Messer Salvini did not disturb you so often."

"I enjoy talking with him. He shows great interest in my work."

"So I see," Francesco said glumly. "Just make sure he doesn't start showing interest in *you*."

"Dear Francesco. You worry too much."

"Someone must worry about you, Sandro. You don't realize the danger you put yourself in."

"What danger, Francesco?" She stood up and stretched like Salvini had done, although she took care to extend her arms forward so her shoulders hunched inward. It would not do to let Pietro's sharp eyes see any hint of the body beneath her loose smock.

"You delight in taking risks, and I don't understand why."

"I promise you that I won't encourage his visits. Will that satisfy you?"

"I don't think it matters what satisfies *me*," he said, draping a piece of linen over the panel to keep off the dust, then collecting the dishes and brushes.

Sofia was feeling far too happy to make any reply. She left Francesco to his worries and hurried into the main house. Her stomach tightened at the smell of supper cooking. She thought about her years as a married woman, when she had so few hours to devote to her painting. Now she could paint from dawn until dusk and talk with a man like Salvini who sparred with her like her father had done. God must have forgiven her for leaving Giorgio.

◅♢▻

Sofia gasped as her thin blanket was pulled off. She tried curling into a ball but wasn't fast enough. Her arm was grasped above the elbow and she was lifted to her feet.

"The sun's risen this past hour. Get up!"

Monna Giuliana loomed over her—two heads taller and smelling of Spanish soap and Manzini. She held up a long piece of cloth. "Didn't I tell you to sleep with this on? What if someone came upon you in the night?"

"I'm sorry, madonna. The heat was oppressive."

"It's nothing compared to stones weeping with damp in one of our prisons. You end up there and you'll long for hot nights."

"Yes, madonna." Sofia had learned not to cross Monna Giuliana when she was in full flight.

"You'll be joining the master today."

"What? Ouch!"

"You heard me. Breathe in. If you're to go out into the world, we need to secure these bonds."

"I still need to breathe."

"Use what breath you have to pray no one discovers you. I told Luca it was a bad idea, but he insisted. He says you've earned the right to work with him at the Salvini palazzo."

Sofia gasped again as Monna Giuliana pulled the binding so tight she felt her heart pressed into her back. The Salvini palazzo? What was this? Salvini never mentioned anything about her working on the fresco at his father's house.

"I'll work on the fresco?" Sofia asked between gasps. "The maestro has said I'm to work on the fresco?"

"The master's said no such thing. He probably wants you to mix the mortar and fetch the bread and cheese for lunch."

But Sofia had grown to know Monna Giuliana well during her daily bindings. The tone of her voice did not match the viciousness of the hands pulling the cloth. There would be no question she'd be wasting time mixing mortar. Manzini had plenty of apprentices and assistants good for not much else. She had heard the praise heaped on the maestro for her work. One patron had even said that her latest panel, depicting a *Maestà*, was the maestro's finest work—rivaling even Simone Martini himself. She had barely slept the night after hearing that and only wished her father could have heard it. With each new panel, Sofia was steadily developing her skills and the range of subjects she was able to handle. She particularly liked depicting buildings and honing techniques she had first explored painting the tower in the Nativity panel for the Delpino wedding. She delighted in the clean, smooth lines of the walls and the challenge—frustrating at times—of making the buildings appear in proportion to the figures.

"Don't speak," Monna Giuliana commanded. "If the maestro allows you near the fresco, do your work quickly and then step back."

"Yes, madonna."

Sofia was pulled around so she was face-to-bosom with Monna Giuliana. Strong hands gripped her two arms and held her steady. Sofia waited for another round of commands to wash over her. *Stay quiet. Keep your head down. Get away from the light. Don't draw attention to yourself. Pray to the Virgin to protect us all.* But for once, the air above her was silent. Sofia looked up. Monna Giuliana's eyes were damp and her mouth quivered.

"Stay safe, *cara*. Do your best work to make my husband rich and then come back to me."

Sofia reached one hand up and held it gently against Monna Giuliana's cheek, just as she had done so many years ago when Emilia had held her—and even longer ago when it was her own mother. For a moment, Sofia wished she was a daughter again.

Then Monna Giuliana stepped back abruptly and shooed Sofia out the door. "Make haste. My husband must not be kept waiting."

An hour later, Sofia stepped joyfully into the street. Every nerve ending was on fire with anticipation. Finally, the maestro was rewarding her. And rightly so. Wasn't she far and away the best painter in the workshop? She heard the admonishing voice of Fra Angelo. *"Curb your pride, girl. You are nothing before God. Don't think so highly of yourself."* But surely acknowledging that her skills put her far above the other workers was not pride. Her father had taught her to examine evidence—and the evidence was conclusive. Her lines were the straightest, her color mixing without flaws, and her imagination beyond any of the other dolts who stumbled through their duties, some barely able to prepare a decent ground on a panel.

Sofia walked briskly through the teeming streets in the direction of Il Campo.

"You're not yet ready for fresco, cara mia." Her father smiled indulgently. *"But if you like, you can stay and watch me."*

"But, Papa, you've always said that when I was older you'd let me help you with the frescoes. I'm thirteen! You let Gino help and he's not even twelve. And you know I'm much better at drawing than he is."

"Perhaps, but I can't have you be seen."

"I'll dress like one of the workers. Please, Papa. You know how I've longed to work with the plaster, and you promised!" Sofia wondered why she'd never thought of it before. It was the perfect solution. She

could get a smock and leggings from one of the other apprentices. No one would look twice at her.

"No!" *Barducci's voice thundered through the empty chapel.* "That's enough. You do me great dishonor to even propose such a thing. Now sit quietly and watch me, or I'll get one of the men to take you home."

A man stepped directly in front of her so suddenly that she stumbled into his arms. For a few seconds his large hands held her close to his chest. She breathed the raw scent of him and felt her throat constrict. His arms flexed, pulling her closer so she felt his heart beating. The fine material beneath her fingers belonged to the dress of a nobleman. Gasping, she pushed herself backward and looked up.

"Messer Salvini!"

"Sandro?"

She tried to step back, but it was too late. His hands were already moving down her back to meet the curve of her waist. He tightened his hold on her. Her breath caught. A softness pulsed between her legs and then a quickening.

"What ho, young master, why so fast?" Salvini held her in his arms for a few moments longer—far longer than he was likely to hold the body of a youth. When finally he released her and stepped back, he remained close enough to catch her if she tried to run. Sofia squared her shoulders and assumed her haughtiest air.

"I am on business for Maestro Manzini," she said in what she hoped was her deepest voice. "I must not be late."

The light in the narrow street was dim, but Sofia sensed his eyes regarding her with new interest. "I believe we are going the same way. I'll accompany you."

"No!" Sofia's voice climbed an octave. She gulped more air and willed her voice lower. "I must hurry, signor. Please, don't trouble yourself."

"Ah, it's no trouble," he said, falling into step next to her. "We can continue our conversation from the other day. How goes your latest panel?"

Sofia's head came just to Salvini's shoulder. He matched her gait stride for stride. Perhaps he had not seen through her disguise and they could carry on as before, talking, disputing, laughing even. Sofia suspected that most of Salvini's associates cared more for hunting and fighting and the thrills of the *palio* than for matters of the mind. Salvini was not of the class to learn painting himself, but he had a fascination for the profession that Sofia had never encountered outside a workshop. He seemed to enjoy watching her use her brushes to coax an image to life.

"The panel of the *Maestà* for your kinsman is finished and being varnished. I think he will be satisfied."

"He should be. Your reputation grows."

"I'm grateful, signor."

"Are you?"

He'd never used such a tender, questioning tone with her—the tone a man used when speaking with a woman. Her heart beat faster—with fear, perhaps, or something else. She stared at the rivulet of filth that kept pace with them as they descended toward the *campo*. "Of course, signor. The maestro also. We owe a great deal to your patronage."

"You certainly owe a great deal to *me*."

Sofia's head jerked up. His full lips curved into a mocking smile and he winked at her. She wondered if her legs would hold her. All her months of work, all her happiness, gone in a second. "I hope we are not ungrateful, signor." Why did he toy with her? If he knew what she was, why didn't he just accuse her and be done with it?

"And now you're set to work on the fresco in my father's house."

"Yes, signor. The maestro has asked for me."

"What will you paint today?"

"What the maestro asks."

"I imagine that goes without saying. But I also think it's likely you have some knowledge of what you will be painting. It's not like you to lack curiosity, Sandro."

"No, signor." Why wouldn't he leave her? She was almost running now and yet he kept pace easily—his long legs barely moving beyond a saunter. The June sun bounced off the bricks of the *campo* and burned her face.

"My father's house is to your right." Salvini gestured with a fine-boned hand at one of the tall, handsome palazzos across the piazza from the Palazzo Pubblico. "You will be working in the chapel." He smiled down at her. "You have nothing to fear from me. I won't tell a soul."

Sofia stopped so abruptly that Salvini had gone two paces farther before he realized she was no longer at his side. She stood her ground and stared at him until finally he turned around and walked back.

"Tell *what?*" she demanded. He wouldn't take her without a fight. No one would say that Maestro Barducci's daughter was a coward. She doubled her fists and glared. "Tell *what?*" She could disappear into the crowd, slip into one of the alleyways leading from the *campo*, and double back to the maestro's workshop.

Francesco would go with her and protect her. And with no money and no place to go they would both be dead within days. Why couldn't she have been born a boy?

Salvini's smile widened to a grin. He spread his arms in a gesture of surrender. "Your disguise is good," he said. "Don't trouble yourself that anyone else will find out unless"—he paused and winked—"they have the good fortune to get close enough to feel that God's noble work is unaccountably hidden beneath a dirty smock."

"My smock is not dirty!"

"I hardly think the cleanliness of your smock is the issue. But come, Sandro, you look like you are about to flee and there's no need for that."

"You accuse me of I don't know what and I am to be content?"

"I think you know very well what I accuse you of." He was openly laughing now, but his eyes shone with kindness. A longing in the pit of her belly flamed when she looked down at the fine, strong fingers clasping the hilt of his sword. Pale blue veins were visible below the skin. She wondered what pigments she could mix to capture that exact shade.

"Come, Sandro. Allow me the pleasure of accompanying you into my father's house. I am interested in seeing what you paint today."

"You're taking great pleasure in mocking me."

"I'd never presume to mock *you*."

The situation grew more dangerous by the moment, but not only because he might hand her over to the authorities at the Palazzo Pubblico. More and more, Sofia realized that the true danger was within her. She must distance herself from this man with his kind eyes and shapely hands who talked to her of painting and beauty and made her feel like a woman.

Sofia took a deep breath. "I thank you, Messer Salvini, for your kindness. You perhaps have guessed what I am and yet you choose not to expose me. Is that true?" She looked boldly into his eyes, willing her heart to slow its rapid beating.

"It is." He looked serious now and, Sofia thought, just a touch regretful. Could he be feeling the same way she did? Impossible.

"I must go," she said, but she wasn't able to make her feet move.

He placed one hand upon her arm for just a moment, but it was long enough to feel his warmth. "Will you allow me to view your work?"

"I haven't done any yet."

"As always, Sandro, your logic is irrefutable." He smiled again and then leaned forward to whisper. "Maestro Manzini plays a dangerous game having you in his employ, but I assure you that your secret is safe—on one condition."

"Yes?"

"That you let me accompany you of a morning."

"You're the son of our patron. It's not my place to object to anything you do."

He bowed. "As Sandro, the workman, you are of course right. But as a woman—and I wager a very beautiful one—you have a right shared by all women."

"And what right is that?" Sofia couldn't keep a note of bitterness from her voice.

"The right to refuse my advances."

"Many would argue that we women don't even have that right."

"More of your logic. How come you to speak so?"

"I am the daughter of Maestro Barducci, the painter. You'll have heard of him."

"And does your father know you go around the streets of Siena disguised as a boy in a dirty smock with paint under your nails?"

"My father is dead," Sofia said quietly. "And now, signor, I must beg you to let me go in to work. The maestro will wonder where I've gotten to."

"Yes, of course. Go to work, Sandro. But depend upon it, we will talk again."

Sofia didn't reply. She slipped into the palazzo and hurried along the cool, high hallway toward the sounds of hammering. She had no time to waste on idle thoughts. She was no longer a woman, and no matter what young Messer Salvini said or did, nothing would change that.

"You took your time." The maestro glanced up when Sofia entered the chapel. He was standing in front of a half-finished fresco depicting the birth of the Virgin. "You'll be working on the bed. Get the pattern going in the right direction. If you do well, I may consider letting you work on the gown of Our Lady's mother."

Sofia stepped forward eagerly. The maestro held up one hand before she spoke.

"Go to your colors and mix what you need. I'll call you when the plaster's ready."

"Yes, maestro."

If Manzini found out that her disguise had been penetrated—and by the patron's own son—she would never leave the workshop again.

CHAPTER ELEVEN

. . . another cause . . . can make your hand so
unsteady that it will waver more, and flutter
far more, than leaves do in the wind, and this is
indulging too much in the company of woman.
—Cennini, *Il Libro dell'Arte*, Chapter XXVIV

"My sister's expression is not generally so serene."

Sofia kept her focus on the wall and gripped the brush to prevent it shaking. The other workmen and the maestro had left the chapel for cups of wine at a tavern across the *campo*.

"I paint from a drawing done by the maestro. It's not for me to change your sister's expression."

"I would have you do so."

Sofia started at the quiet intensity in his voice. She felt his body close to hers, smelled his rich maleness. Giorgio had smelled of horses and sweat and stale wine. This man . . . didn't.

"You must talk to the maestro." She daubed the tip of her brush along the folds of the lady's skirts. The daughter of the house was being given the honor of having her face represent Mary's mother in the scene of the birth of the Virgin.

"The maestro takes his orders from my father."

"And I take my orders from the maestro." Sofia was on firm ground again. "So the situation is hopeless. I cannot change your sister's face, and you don't have the authority to ask me."

"You speak boldly for someone in your position."

"And what is that position?"

"You're just a workman," he said, slightly stressing the *man*. "I could have you up on charges for insolence."

"And I could tell the maestro of your dissatisfaction with his work. He's paid by your father, no?" Sofia smiled, just for a moment allowing her face to relax. A dimple creased one cheek.

"Perhaps I act on behalf of my father while he's away from Siena."

"If you were acting in place of your father, you'd never have allowed me into your house. Besides, I had the honor of seeing your father only this morning." She paused a moment. "You don't favor him."

He laughed. "Yes, I suppose that's true, although my sainted mother would have disagreed. Your presence here doesn't harm me, but my father's reputation would suffer if word got out that he employs a woman."

"You must forget what I am."

"That may prove difficult. Now, will you change the expression on my sister's face?"

"I can't."

"You mean you won't."

Sofia turned back to the wall. "The plaster dries quickly and I must finish the folds of this robe before the maestro returns." She dipped her brush in a pot of white lead and leaned forward to add a highlight to indicate the sheen of velvet. She would not let Salvini interfere with the pleasure she took in working on her first fresco. She loved the speed of the process, the exacting care required to make the plaster bend to her will.

His fine-veined hand grasped her wrist. Her fingers opened and the brush dropped to the floor—a trail of white spattering the hem of her smock. He pulled her to him. Before she could cry out, he was pressing his lips against her own. She stiffened. The only other man to have kissed her was Giorgio, and that was so long ago that she barely remembered. In recent years, he'd never bothered to kiss her before taking her. Then she realized that she was being held with gentle firmness that kept her close but not a prisoner. She could step back at any time, push him away at any time. Her body softened and her mouth curved into a smile against the insistent pressure of his lips. He smelled of clean hay and sun-warmed leather. Deep inside her, a languid, liquid heat began to spread. She forgot everything—her life with Giorgio, her escape to Siena, her painting.

She pulled back. If they were discovered, she'd never again hold a brush, study shapes, imagine how to transform a few shallow dishes of color into creatures who breathed life into cold white plaster.

"What's wrong?"

"I must finish my work. Please, don't come here anymore. You're putting me in great danger."

"But I want to be with you!" he exclaimed, reaching for her hands. She clasped them behind her back. Even as her heart raced and sweat pricked her palms, she knew she must hold on to logic.

"You can't."

"I can do whatever I wish. And I wish to take you."

Her eyes widened.

"I'm sorry. I didn't mean that I would take you. I meant that I want to, to . . ." He blushed and, for a few moments, looked as young and vulnerable as Francesco. She wanted to take his head between her two paint-stained hands and kiss his forehead, to tell him all would be well and that she would be his. Then she glanced back at the fresco. Its colors were drying quickly—too quickly. It was a hot day and the plaster was not forgiving.

Silently, she gave thanks to the Virgin for reminding her of her duty. The face painted into the plaster of the fresco may have the look of Salvini's peevish sister, but Sofia knew the Mother of God had protected her this day. She picked up her brush and turned back to the fresco.

"You show your back to me?"

She shook her head, kept her eyes facing forward. The maestro had finished the face that morning. It looked out at her with passive serenity and vacant eyes. That was the problem, she realized. The eyes. They lacked life. They lacked goodness. The woman in the fresco had just given birth to the child who would be mother of Christ, and the maestro had made her look like she cared only for the cut of her gown.

"Please."

She kept her back to him, willing all her attention to the end of her brush, reminding herself that Sofia was dead. Nothing he said could move her. But she tensed as she waited for him to speak again. He didn't even know her real name. But she was resolved. Of course she was resolved. Would he speak again? She would not yield. But what might he say to get her to turn around? The silence was broken only by a light scratching of a rat's claws against wood. That morning, she had stepped on a crushed one just outside the palazzo. Its deep brown fur had contrasted pleasingly with the fresh red of the bricks.

She heard a sigh so slight that it hardly stirred the air.

"I'll have you yet," he whispered and then, with a rustle of velvet and a clink of metal, he was gone. Sofia listened to his footsteps recede across the stone floor. The heavy door shut behind him. She would *not* relent. But she couldn't prevent feeling a shudder of pleasure at the extent of his longing for her.

The plaster was almost dry and she still hadn't finished the folds of the Virgin's gown. Manzini would demand an explanation. She could not tell him that the master's son kept her from her work with ill-judged kisses and idle promises. Sofia shook her head, disgusted with herself for giving in even for a moment to the heat of his embrace.

When the maestro returned to find her still at work on the gown of the Virgin's mother, much of the plaster was dry and the colors were not holding.

"What's this?"

"I'm sorry, master. I will do it again tomorrow."

"You certainly will." Manzini stepped forward and took the brush from her hand. "You disappoint me, Sandro. I expected more."

"Forgive me."

"Humph. Get on with you. Francesco's come to take you back to the workshop. Monna Giuliana thinks you shouldn't be going about Siena on your own."

In the entranceway, Francesco was gazing awestruck at the height and splendor of the palazzo. Sofia guessed he had never seen such wealth.

"What's happened to you?" Francesco asked as soon as they emerged into the dazzling afternoon light that flooded the *campo* and turned the bricks of the buildings ringing it to vermilion.

"What do you mean?" Sofia tried to speed up, but Francesco stepped in front of her.

"You look different."

"Of course I don't."

"You do. You *are* different."

"I'm the same, Francesco. Don't talk nonsense."

"How long will you be coming here?"

"I don't know. Why ask me? It doesn't affect you."

"Since you've been going out of the house every day, you are not the same. And when you come back, you don't talk to me anymore."

"Of course I talk to you." Sofia laughed and patted his broad arm.

"You're not the same," he said stubbornly. "You're softer." He frowned and shook off her hand. "I can't protect you if you insist on acting like a woman."

"I'm not acting like a woman!"

"Hush!"

"Oh, pooh, Francesco. No one's paying any attention to us." She looked around the bustling *campo*. Young apprentices scurried around clutches of finely dressed noblemen and workmen hurried to their homes after a day's toil in the endless construction projects that infested every corner of Siena.

"Maybe not now, but what if Pietro heard you?"

"He wouldn't understand me."

"You look different," he said again. "And I'm afraid."

"I'm the same as I've always been since we came to Siena. You imagine things."

Francesco caught her wrist in one large hand. "Please, Sandro. Take care. You don't know how you look. If I've noticed the change, then others may have too. Pietro already resents you. What do you think he'd do if he found out you're not a boy?"

"Pietro's a fool."

"And that, Sandro, is the point. Haven't you tried often enough to teach me your logic, as you call it?"

"You're a good student."

For a moment, Francesco blushed and looked again like the young boy who stepped away from the ashes of his family to guide her to Siena. "Then listen to me. Pietro's a fool and that makes him even more dangerous."

"How so?"

"He doesn't have the sense to see that exposing you would hurt him just as much. The maestro would throw him out at the same time you were carried off to prison or whipped through the streets or taken back to your husband."

Sofia shuddered. "Don't say such things. Even Pietro's not that stupid."

"People who hate often do very foolish things."

"You're becoming wise in your advancing years," Sofia teased. "Come on, let's get home to our dinner. I haven't eaten a thing since dawn, and Monna Giuliana told me she was planning to kill a chicken."

"Really?"

"A nice plump one. And let's have no more talk of Pietro. I'm who I've always been and I promise I'll stay well out of Pietro's way. Will that satisfy you?"

"No," Francesco said, but he smiled in defeat as he fell into step next to her. "But I have learned one very important thing about you, Sandro."

"And what's that?"

"Once you decide something, you can't be swayed easily."

"Easily?"

"You can't be swayed at all." Francesco grinned. "Are you sure your husband didn't run away from *you*?"

"Walk with me." The voice behind her shoulder sent a thrill to her core. For the first time in many weeks, Sofia was leaving the Salvini palazzo to walk home alone. Francesco had taken ill that morning and Monna Giuliana had insisted he stay in bed and submit to her nursing. Sofia had seen Salvini only a handful of times since the day he kissed her. To her relief, their conversations had not differed from the days in the workshop when he'd known her as Sandro. Sofia had almost convinced herself that Salvini had chosen to forget what she was so that she could continue to paint without fear of discovery. A hand propelled her forward, its warmth smoldering pleasantly through the coarse material of her smock.

"I'm expected back before sundown."

"I won't keep you long."

The pressure on her back increased as he nudged her across the *campo* and into a side street. Blinded by the gloom, she stumbled over something. She looked down. The spindly arm of a very old woman was grabbing at her legs. Salvini paused to press a coin into the woman's hand. Sofia glimpsed the milky white of one blind eye and a toothless mouth. After a few minutes more of walking, Salvini stopped at a doorway set into a brick wall. He unlocked it and stood aside to let Sofia pass.

"Why did you favor that old woman?" she asked when he joined her. Just visible in the light from the open door was a counter. Behind it rose shelves filled with the jars and remedies of an apothecary.

"What woman?"

"The beggar. You gave her a coin."

"Yes? What of it?" He looked at her with frank surprise. "Aren't we taught to give to the poor?"

"Well, yes, but . . ." Sofia paused. "It's just that . . ."

"You didn't expect it from me?"

A blush spread up Sofia's cheeks. "No," she whispered as she let her eyes be held by his. "I didn't expect it."

"You misjudge me."

"Do I?"

Salvini gently pulled off her cap. He placed one finger on her chin and rubbed at a tiny splatter of white paint. She trembled under his touch, raised her eyes to meet his, pleaded mutely for him to stop before she could not stop herself.

Abruptly, he lowered his hand and stepped back. "I'm sorry. You're so beautiful that I forget myself."

Sofia ground her fists against her thighs. "Why did you bring me here?"

"I have a commission. I want you to take the likeness of my betrothed."

Sofia had known many emotions in her life—passion, rage, despair. But she had never known the sharp sting of jealousy. Its green tendrils twisted upward from the pit of her belly and took hold of her heart, squeezing it, constricting her breath. She felt worthless—a castoff, good only to spend her days dressed as an unkempt boy pretending to be a painter while another woman enjoyed Salvini's warm smiles and elegant hands. He was looking at her, his mouth set in a slight smile that seemed to mock her. She wanted to reach up and claw her fingernails across the smooth expanse of his cheek, see tracks of red bloom and spread. How dare he use her? Just weeks ago he'd told her that he wanted her.

"I'm a poor apprentice. It's not generous of you to ask such a thing."

"Aren't you skilled with the brush?"

"You know I am." Sofia stood in the middle of the apothecary's shop and stared at the rows of charms and imitation relics sold when the apothecary's usual remedies did not take effect, or perhaps as insurance.

"It's a scandal. Preying upon the gullible, that's what it is. The Church should do something about it, but of course they won't."

"Why not, Papa?"

"Mother Church has too much invested in the ignorance of its people."

"Fra Angelo says that God put us on this earth to serve Him so we may be saved."

"Yes, and since the Church represents God on earth, it's in a perfect position to receive the fruits of that service." He glared at Sofia. "Don't believe everything Fra Angelo tells you, daughter. You know better."

Sofia reached out and picked up an amulet from the apothecary's counter. "My father didn't approve of such things. He thought they were no better than chimeras. And that, Messer Salvini, is exactly what your offer is to me."

"You think I'm lying?"

"No. I think you don't see what's before you."

"I see the most beautiful woman in the world," he said, spreading his arms wide and grinning. "You must know that."

"No, signor, you see a boy who eats because he is, as you say, skilled with a brush. The woman you want does not exist." She wound the amulet's leather cord around her wrist. "What is this place?"

"It belongs to a kinsman of my nurse. He's gone from Siena for several months. I thought you could come here to work."

Sofia said nothing as she watched the amulet dangle.

"You can work here undisturbed," he said. "I'll find you materials. I think a *Maestà* would serve the purpose. What do you think?"

She'd like to try her hand at another *Maestà*. The one she had painted for Salvini's kinsman had included a clutch of fawning nobles representing key members of the family dressed as saints. She wanted to do something more intimate. Mother and child only.

"You like the idea."

"Maestro Manzini has the keeping of me. He determines what I paint."

"I'll ask his permission."

"He won't give it."

"How do you know he's not already given it?"

Her chin flew up. "Has he?"

"I, ah, well, no. But it doesn't matter. I can pay you. Surely that's enough."

"And what use have I for money?"

He widened his eyes in surprise. "You could, ah . . ."

"Exactly," she said. "What would I do with it?"

"You could return to your home."

"I have no home."

"I don't understand anything about you," he said, sighing as he stepped forward, his arms outstretched. "I don't even know your name."

"You're a foolish boy. You think you can have everything you want because you're rich." She gasped as he drew her close and put one hand behind her cropped head.

"I don't care what you were."

"The maestro will never allow it."

"I'll deal with the maestro."

"He'll need to be paid well." Sofia did not believe the words coming from her mouth. She should pull away and run. But she did not move. She could not move.

"You're far too beautiful to have such a head for business matters." He laughed, pulling her even closer. "But I would have you."

"No, signor. Please, I must return to the workshop before I'm missed."

"Stay with me."

"I . . . no." Sofia closed her eyes. Perhaps if she wasn't able to see him, she wouldn't be so tempted. But the darkness made matters worse. As she melted into his arms, she allowed her soul to drift. He drew her closer.

"I can't call you Sandro anymore. Tell me your name." One hand slid down her back and wrapped around her waist. The other hand reached into her smock. His fingers grazed the rough linen binding her breasts.

The jolt of pleasure was an agony she could not afford. With a gasp, she opened her eyes and pushed him away. "No! You're betrothed to another. I'm not your whore and you *won't* hear my name."

"You forget yourself." His voice hardened as he reached for her again.

"You can't treat me like I'm put here to do your bidding." A white-hot rage replaced the passion that had almost robbed her of her wits. She may not be of noble birth, but her father had not raised a harlot.

He held out his hands, palms up. "Come, Sandro. I won't hurt you. If you do this panel, we can see each other often." He smiled as he moved closer. "Manzini won't object. I'll pay him double."

Sofia crossed her arms across her breasts. "You wish me to do a panel for your betrothed."

"Well, yes. Is that so strange? My father must promise me to someone."

"Who is she?"

"Why does it matter?"

"I want to know."

Salvini shook his head, smiling. "But I don't want to tell you. Now stop this foolishness. Agree to do the panel for me and let us be friends."

"You wish to be my *friend?*" Sofia infused the word with such scorn that Salvini took a step backward and had the grace to look abashed.

"I'm sorry," he said stiffly. "I've forgotten myself."

"Yes, you have. As a poor apprentice, I can't be your friend, and as a woman, I won't be your whore."

"More of your logic?"

"Perhaps."

"So you won't do the panel for me?"

"I didn't say that." In spite of everything, she wasn't quite ready to give up the chance to create another *Maestà*.

"So what *do* you say?"

"I'll make the painting," she said, then held up her hand when he eagerly stepped toward her. "But I have a condition."

"You can't give me conditions."

"Then you don't get a *Maestà* for your betrothed."

He regarded her with such an expression of mingled confusion and desire that she almost went back into his arms. But she kept her expression somber, her eyes downcast. She was playing a game that would destroy her, and yet she couldn't make herself fear him.

"I could have you turned into the streets."

"Will you?"

"You know I will not. What's this condition you speak of?"

"I must work on the panel in the maestro's workshop."

"But then we cannot be alone while you work."

"Yes, signor. That's exactly the point."

"You don't want to be with me?"

"I told you already. I'm a painter, not your whore."

"I wouldn't have you think that."

"And yet that's how you treat me."

Sofia stepped out of range of his arms. "Go to the maestro and ask him for my services, and forget about me working here." She looked around the shop. "Besides, this place lacks sufficient light. And I need Francesco to help me."

He moved behind her and placed his hands upon her shoulders. His breath was hot on her cheek. "*I* could help you."

For a moment she allowed her body to melt into his, to imagine how it would feel to give herself to him. Then she stiffened her spine and turned to face him. Her chest rose and she saw the desire in his eyes. Hastily, she hunched her shoulders. "I must leave now."

"Sandro."

"No, signor. This can't be." She pushed open the door. He could take hold of her smock and drag her back if he chose. She tensed, waiting. But he made no move. The searing heat of the summer day inflamed cheeks burning from his touch as she emerged into the street.

She could never let him know how much she desired him.

"You've made an impression on young Salvini." Maestro Manzini did not turn around as he daubed at the fresco. "He came to me this morning."

Sofia held up a dish of white lead tinted with red. So Salvini had spoken to the maestro. Several weeks had passed since her visit to the apothecary shop. She had seen Salvini just once, at the entrance to his father's palazzo, but he had been talking with a kinsman and had ignored her. She handed the dish to Manzini and waited.

"Do you want to know what he said?"

"Yes, maestro."

"He's quite the admirer of your work."

"It's your work that he admires, maestro."

"Aye, well, we both know that's not true." Manzini added a few rough strokes to the wings of an angel, then clambered down from the scaffolding. "Messer Salvini wants you to create a panel for him."

"I'd be honored, maestro."

Manzini waved one paint-smudged hand. "Yes, yes, of course. And I'd be glad enough to oblige him. But he asks that you work on this panel at a place in his kinsman's *contrada*. Do you know why?"

"No, maestro."

"You're sure? I've seen him speaking with you in the workshop. He's never said anything?"

Sofia shook her head. It was easier to lie if she did not speak. What had happened to her condition? She'd told Salvini she would only consider completing the panel if she could work at Manzini's workshop. But if she said as much to Manzini, he'd know she'd spoken with Salvini. A fine mess. What would her father have thought?

"I should never have allowed him to come to the workshop so often," Manzini was saying. "But he's brought me so many new patrons. How can I refuse?" Manzini looked at her sharply. "He doesn't know, does he?"

Sofia could not lie but she could deflect. "If you don't object, maestro, I'd be happy to work for Messer Salvini." Would she really? Alone? Surely Manzini would never agree to it.

"Yes, yes, I don't doubt it. He's a great admirer. But his request is so strange."

"He's paying well?"

"Very well. I don't dare offend him." Manzini chuckled. "Imagine what my sainted wife would say if I refused such a commission? She's bought two new tippets this past month and is making noises about pearls. Perhaps I should speak with young Salvini's father."

Sofia busied herself with stacking the paint dishes, carefully keeping her face averted to hide her red cheeks. The elder Salvini probably knew nothing about the arrangements that his son was making with Manzini for the services of young Sandro.

"I think, maestro, that Messer Salvini might want me to work in secret to produce a panel to surprise his father. Do you think it likely?" Was she mad? Could she really consider going to work in the apothecary shop with Salvini as her only companion?

"Possibly, possibly." Manzini shook his head. "I've never heard of such a thing. And yet . . ." Sofia could almost see the numbers swirling beneath the cowl he wore wrapped around his head. "I suppose you could be spared for a few hours in the mornings. But take care you work quickly and don't betray yourself. Salvini speaks too freely with you."

"He likes to watch me paint, maestro."

"Hmm. I still don't like it. Monna Giuliana will have my skin if she finds out I've let you out of my sight."

"Messer Salvini has brought us many new commissions." Sofia kept her voice neutral. She should refuse the commission and stay safely in the workshop. Why was her heart beating so quickly? Did she not realize the risk?

"He certainly has brought in a great deal of new work. You're sure you can do this commission of his?"

"I can, maestro. And I won't tell Monna Giuliana."

"See as you don't. Now, finish cleaning up here and let's go home. I'll tell young Salvini you may complete his panel."

"Thank you, maestro."

She would soon see Salvini! Alone! She resolved to keep him at a distance. If she held firm, there would be no risk. He could watch her paint—how could she stop him? But he would *not* take her.

"Did I bring up a fool?"

"No, Papa." She stood in front of him and gulped back the tears. The scorn in his eyes was worse than any reprimand. For as long as she could remember—even in the few years when her mother still lived— Sofia had always been first with him. He had taught her and cared for her, was both father and mother to her, loved her. And now he was calling her a fool. She didn't deserve it.

"He's a good man, Papa. And I love him."

"Love? I'd not set eyes on your mother until the day I married her. What can you know of love? No, Sofia, I won't give my consent for you to marry Giorgio Carelli."

"But, Papa, his father is one of the richest merchants in San Gimi-gnano. Their new tower is almost as tall as the one belonging to Messer Salvucci."

"These are hardly matters for you to think about. Gather up your colors and finish the robes of Saint Christopher before Emilia brings supper."

When finally her father gave his consent for her to marry Giorgio, Sofia had thought herself the happiest creature on God's earth. She would not make the same mistake twice.

◌◌

"You can't expect me to use the likeness of your betrothed for the Madonna if I've never seen her." Sofia laid her brush down and crossed her arms across her chest. She had loosened her bindings slightly. Salvini had left her strictly alone since she began work, and she saw no need to suffer in the summer heat.

"Well, she's beautiful," Salvini began. "And, ah, she has white skin. Black hair. And black eyes."

"How singular."

"I've only seen her a couple of times. And she was veiled."

"So you won't know if I catch her likeness." Sofia picked up her brush. "I'll paint a white-faced, black-haired, black-eyed Madonna with a serene expression and plump cheeks. Will that do?"

"I don't think her cheeks were plump."

"No? Perhaps she's unwell. Are you sure you want a sickly wife?"

"You take too many liberties." But Salvini was smiling as he sat next to her and looked at the figures taking shape on the panel. "You're improving."

"What does that say about the first panel I did for your family? If my work's improved, is it not logical to presume that the work I did before was somehow lacking?"

"You delight in correcting me."

"That's because you so often need correcting." Sofia smiled to soften the words as she shifted her gaze from her work and looked at Salvini. He held her gaze for several moments and then, before Sofia could stop him, lifted one hand and smoothed a few strands of hair from her forehead.

"No!" Her hand grasped his, pulling it away from her skin to erase the feel of him. "Remember what I am, signor. You must not."

Salvini's face inched closer while his other hand snaked around her waist. "I remember exactly what you are."

"You can't think of me that way." She heard the panic in her own voice. He could not break their agreement now, not after so many weeks. "Please! You promised."

"I know," he said, pulling back his arm. "Coming here to watch you paint is becoming unbearable."

"So don't come so often." The figure of the blessed Child still needed work. She should concentrate on that and leave the face of the Madonna for another day. "I have the materials I need. I don't need your help." That much was true. Sofia could not deny that she enjoyed Salvini's company. He had so much to share with her about the world and she loved to tell him about painting and the great works she had seen while traveling with her father. But as an assistant, Salvini was hopeless. If she asked him to grind a pigment, he grew bored after a few minutes. And he complained constantly about the smells.

"Come, Sandro, you know that can't be true. Use the logic you love to throw at me. You know why you agreed to do this panel for me."

"The maestro asked me."

"I could ask any number of painters in this city."

Sofia filled her brush with red lac mixed with white. "Then you should commission one of them. I won't be able to finish your panel in time for your wedding if you insist on coming here to distract me."

"I'll wager you don't object to the distraction."

"I object to anything that takes me away from my work." Sofia leaned forward and added light strokes of palest pink to the cheeks of the Child. He looked too much like an old man. And yet she had not deviated from the practice her father taught her. Every painting Sofia had copied over the years of her apprenticeship in Barducci's workshop showed the Child sitting or sometimes standing on the Madonna's knee, staring solemnly out with the eyes of a man. She had no right to make changes to what was proper. And yet, the miniature man had no life.

"You wish me to leave?"

"Hmm?" A dab or two more white under the chin. And maybe the hand should rest upon the Virgin's knee. Yes. She touched her brush to the dish of white and leaned forward.

"I said, do you want me to leave?"

"If you wish." As she picked up another brush, he moved toward the door and opened it, letting in a shout of laughter from the street. Once he was gone, she would really be able to concentrate. The light from the window Salvini had cleaned for her was perfect. She smiled at the memory of him on his knees with a cloth in his hand. It must have been the first work he'd ever done in his life.

"May I attend you tomorrow?"

Sofia set aside her brush and sighed. She had offended him again. This arrangement was insane. She would complete the face of the Child today and take the panel back to the workshop to finish it.

"Messer Salvini," she began. "I . . ."

He stepped forward, dropped to one knee, and took her hands between his. "You're torturing me."

A sharp stab of pleasure and then a flush of shame. How could she rejoice in his longing? And yet she couldn't suppress a warm nugget of gratitude. That a man like Salvini, with his fine wit and finer beauty, should want her. It was too much. God must be testing her. Sofia kept silent, her head turned away. She had used silence as a weapon against Giorgio many times, and she used it now against Salvini because she didn't know what else to do.

"Sandro. Please, look at me."

"Sofia," she whispered. She had not spoken her own name for more than a year and a half. She wasn't even sure if such a woman had ever existed—or could exist again. She stared into the eyes of the Child taking shape on her panel. God forgive her.

"What did you say?" He stroked her hands. Another spasm passed through her—as sharp as a dagger's point but with an agony that was exquisite.

"You heard me, signor." She could barely gasp out the words.

"Sofia. That is your name?"

"Yes." Sofia heard the rough desire in her voice and wondered if he heard it too. She should pull away now before he went further, but she knew she could not move. He slid one arm around her waist and drew her up from the chair. His arms enfolded her so her cheek nestled into his chest.

Where was the logic in this?

Salvini would take her and then throw her away. She knew it. She believed it. And she didn't want to stop it.

He drew back a moment. "Sofia. It's a good name for you. Greek for wisdom. It's not a common name, but then you're not a common woman."

"My father was a learned man, despite his profession. He always told me I must live up to my name."

"And have you?"

She shook her head. "I don't think I'm being very wise now." But she didn't move away from his grasp. When his lips covered her mouth, gently, tentatively at first, and then more insistently, she felt her body soften into his.

"Stay here with me, Sofia," he murmured. His hands found the binding around her breasts. He began to pull at Monna Giuliana's knot, sighing as it gave way and the rolls of linen fell to the floor, spilling her breasts into the thick summer air. His hands closed around them, holding them with a tenderness that shocked her. "I promise I won't let harm come to you."

She knew he would not—could not—keep his promise. She knew that God would punish her. She'd be found out and dragged through the streets, her lips and nose cut off, her body left at the gates of the city to starve. She'd seen it happen to others. And what of Giorgio? In the eyes of God, she was a married woman. The jaws of hell would open for her, dragging her into endless torment. But the heat of flames imagined held no sway over the heat coursing through her blood as he kissed her, lightly at first, then when her lips yielded to his, with more insistence. She raised one hand to his clean-shaven chin and brushed it with her fingertips. Such a fine, strong jawline. She moved her hand up and stroked his forehead, admiring his clear skin, the depths of his eyes. She pulled back to see him more clearly.

He groaned. "Dear God, Sofia!"

"Shh, let me look at you," she whispered as her fingers brushed his cheek, then cupped the base of his neck below hair as thick and silky as a woman's. "I would paint you."

"Not today." She felt his smile as he brought his lips to hers again. "Leave off your looking, *amore mio*," he murmured. "I would have you all for myself."

She thought of Giorgio and shuddered. Would it be the same? Were all men the same? For a moment she wanted to pull back, to escape from the hot room into the bustle of the city where she would be safe from the eyes and probing hands of men. He took her shiver for desire and gathered her into his arms. She let her hand drop from his face and rested it on his shoulder. Under the fine velvet, his muscles bunched and moved.

A wave of hot passion suddenly took her in a grip she had no will to break. She must see beneath the velvet, must take all of him.

"Come," he whispered, leading her to a cot in the corner of the apothecary shop. "I'll go slowly. You are a maid."

For one wild moment, Sofia considered telling him the truth. If he loved her, perhaps he would forgive her. But no, the risk was too great. She lowered her eyes. He would take her silence for modesty and God would decide her fate.

He folded her in his arms again, sat her on the cot, then kneeled before her. He kissed her lips, then trailed his tongue down her neck to her bared breast. He teased at one nipple. She gasped and cried out. She had never known such a white-hot jolt of pleasure. With Giorgio, even when they were first married, the taking had always been fast and always for his pleasure alone. She never dreamed her body could feel like this. How could God make such sensations a sin?

His lips closed over her nipple and nothing but the point where her flesh met his mouth existed on God's earth. She let him push her back onto the cot, let him peel off the rough leggings, let him turn her from lad to woman. And when he finally opened her and thrust with gentle strength, she was beyond caring for anything except him.

"Will you take your cap off for me today?"

"I'll stay as you see me."

"You're safe here."

"So you often say." Sofia tilted her head to one side and stared at the shape of the Madonna. The angle of the head was wrong. She needed to paint over it with white lead and start again. Another day lost.

"You don't trust me?"

"I trust you well enough, Matteo, but it's not you who will be whipped through the streets. Now, do you want me to complete this panel or not?"

"You forget yourself." His voice took on an edge that caused Sofia to look up. She had already discovered that he did not like her to talk with him too freely. He tolerated a measure of familiarity, at least when they were together on hot afternoons with their skins fused and their breaths mingled, but he never wanted her to forget her position.

"I'm sorry, but when I encounter a difficulty with my work, I need to be silent." She smiled and held out a hand. "If you wish, I can leave off for today. Give me time to cover this area with white lead so I can make corrections tomorrow, and then I'm yours until the light fails."

Salvini's frown relaxed as he returned her smile. Sofia had also learned that he never remained angry for long and that his anger was like a puff of smoke on a wet day. It billowed up and was just as rapidly extinguished.

"When will you finish the panel?"

"When you stop asking me."

"That's no answer." He sat next to her worktable and rolled a lump of yellow pigment between his palms.

"Matteo!" She lunged at him and batted his hand. "That pigment is poison. Never touch it!"

He dropped the nugget and stared at the yellow smears on his fingers. "What's this? You paint with poison?"

"Many of the pigments we use have noxious qualities," she explained as she picked up the lump of realgar with her pincers and placed it on a shelf. "We learn what we can handle safely and what requires care."

"This is no profession for a woman," he said, shaking his head. "You shouldn't allow yourself to be so exposed."

"And what choice do I have?" she asked, looking at him in surprise. "I've told you before, Matteo. I am no longer a woman. Why do you persist in treating me like one?"

"You don't object to me treating you like a woman when we are together."

"Don't talk such wickedness," she scolded, but she smiled while she mixed crushed white lead with tempera, then added clear water and brushed it over the head of her Mary. The *Maestà* panel was not progressing as swiftly as she would like, but Sofia suspected that part of the reason was her reluctance to end her time with Matteo. "You must have patience."

"When it comes to waiting for you, Sofia, I can have no patience."

"When I was a girl, Fra Angelo often chided me for my restlessness. He said patience is one of the great virtues."

"For a woman, perhaps. But for me? I don't think so."

"I'm done," Sofia said, laying down her brush. "Now, did you wish to speak with me? Or perhaps you didn't have speaking in mind?" She pulled off her cap. Sometimes, she longed to present herself to him dressed in a fine gown, with her hair properly dressed and perfumed, a jewel at her throat, and rings upon her fingers. He sat next to her so their knees touched. Sofia's coarse linen smock with its daubs of paint and frayed hem looked ridiculous next to the rich burgundy velvet of his tunic. They had no business being together.

He ran his fingers through the short ragged ends of her hair, grimacing. "You are far too beautiful to go around like this."

"That's a fine way to begin," Sofia said with a laugh. "Close your eyes if my hair offends you."

"But then I can't look into your eyes."

She stood up and slowly lifted her smock, revealing bound breasts damp and straining. "Will you take me now, my lord? Or must I wait until you've finished cataloguing my shortcomings?"

"You delight in teasing me."

"And you delight in the teasing."

He lunged for her, caught her, and pulled her against his chest. She felt that delicious shiver deep in her belly. Her breath quickened, grew ragged. If only she could live forever in Matteo's arms, safe from the world, safe from all pain. Her bones turned to liquid as he laid her on the cot, then tenderly kissed her lips, her breasts, her thighs. In the August heat, their skins joined into one flesh and one soul that ascended together to heaven.

"Matteo!" she gasped as his hands and lips obliterated reason. She had no words to ask him for what she wanted, but he knew. Oh yes, he knew.

CHAPTER TWELVE

A color known as lac is red, and it is an artificial
color . . . I advise you, for the sake of your works,
to get the color ready-made for your money.
—Cennini, *Il Libro dell'Arte*, Chapter LXVII

Where have *you* been?" Pietro loomed over Sofia, blotting out the sunlight filtering between the densely packed buildings.

"None of your business. The master knows and that should be enough for you." Sofia quickened her pace, unnerved by Pietro's size and the rank stench of his breath.

"You think a great deal of yourself."

"Aren't you wanted in the workshop?" She glanced up at him, scowling to hide the bloom of her cheek. Her whole body still trembled with the memory of Salvini's caresses. She wanted to get home as quickly as possible, to hold on to the feeling as the night came on and she could be alone to smile and remember.

"We've done for the day," Pietro said with a shrug. "As you'd know if you were there. Where do you go every day?"

"Ask the master."

"I'm asking *you*." A meaty hand shot out and closed over her arm. "Slow down, Sandro. I won't hurt you." His voice was low, almost gentle.

Sofia was so surprised that she stopped dead in the middle of the street and turned to stare up at Pietro. He gazed down at her with a curiously sentimental expression. Sofia realized with a start that he looked at her like a man looks at a maid. He'd found her out! He'd go to the authorities and have her arrested. The lash would shred her back to bleeding ribbons. She'd be cast off, shunned. Even Maestro Manzini would not be able to help her. And as for Matteo. Would he step forward? She wanted to believe that he would, but was terrified he could not.

"What do you want?" She tried to make her voice as gruff as possible. Perhaps he'd realize he was mistaken and let her go. But his grip on her arm tightened as he drew her to him. She wasn't strong enough to wrench herself away. His fingers were talons.

"Sandro!" He prodded her into the shadows of an alleyway. The stench of rotting waste stung the back of her throat. She thought of crying out, but to what purpose? No one would come to her aid. As a young lad in the coarse dress of a worker, she was almost invisible in the teeming streets of Siena. His grip slackened and his lips edged toward hers. "You're like me," he breathed. "I know it."

"What?"

His hand was on her buttocks now, stroking and squeezing with the same vigor she used to knead the cakes of sizing in the workshop. He was pulling her against him. The bulge in his crotch pressed into her thigh and his breathing roughened. He moved his hand up her back, groaning now with desire. She realized with horror that he was perfectly capable of taking her in the stinking alleyway, of thrusting into her, of killing the joy of Salvini's touch. She was spun around and slammed back against him. She felt a rod of iron pushing against her as he fumbled with her smock, lifting it, then thrusting his hand between her legs.

He clutched at her warmth, fingers digging into the softness, sending waves of agony into her belly. The hard fingers scrabbled and prodded, then froze. An oath echoed in the dank passageway. He dragged his hand back, then dug a sharp elbow between her shoulders. She stumbled, fell into the muck, cracked her head against the bricks. As the world swirled around her, she scrambled to her hands and knees and swung around to face him. He was staring at her, his face a mask of fear and confusion. "You're a maid! How . . . ?"

Sofia scrabbled backward to brace herself against the alley wall, too stunned to know what to say. He loomed above her, blocking out the light. "I thought . . ." he stammered. "You looked at me sometimes and I was so sure . . ." The naked misery on his face confused Sofia. She wanted to despise him and felt only pity.

"Go!" she whispered. "Go now or I tell the maestro what you are, what you tried to do."

Pietro said nothing more. He ran back into the street, leaving Sofia so weak from relief and shock that she could barely stand. Pietro had longed for her all these months—and not as a maid but as a boy. Impossible!

Slowly she swayed to her feet, then edged out of the alleyway, keeping close to the buildings as she limped past the stalls of merchants too absorbed in their commerce to notice her. She passed a barrel of eels outside a fishmonger. Their sinuous, twining shapes made her skin crawl at the same time as they reminded her of how she and Salvini melted together, their arms and legs twisting around each other to merge into sweet oblivion.

She turned from the eels and limped back to the workshop, her throbbing head hunched into her shoulders. She wondered if she should tell Francesco, but then thought better of it. Francesco would fight Pietro and be hurt. No. Pietro's secret was safe and she would pray to the Virgin that he never found a way to get his revenge on her without exposing himself.

∽

"Sofia."

She smiled to hear her name spoken. No one ever used it in Siena and at times she missed its sound.

"Yes, Matteo? You are looking thoughtful. Did my work today not please you?"

"Of course it pleased me." He came up behind her and she let her head fall back against the velvet of his gown. He stroked her hair, then kissed the top of her head.

"You distract me."

"That's my intention." He took the brush from her hand and laid it on the table. "Today, we are going out."

Sofia smiled up at him. "You're not serious, Matteo. You can't be seen walking the streets with a poor painter."

"I'll risk it. Come. Put on your cap. I wish to show you something." He pulled her to her feet and kissed her, then helped arrange her cap so none of her hair showed. "You'll have to do," he said with a grin. "Walk next to me and keep your head down."

"I'm well used to *that*," Sofia said as she followed him out the door. The morning air was pleasantly cool after several weeks of stifling summer heat. She smelled a hint of autumn—a subtle sharpness that reminded her she had been in Siena for almost two years. She barely thought of San Gimignano now, only occasionally feeling a twinge of guilt about Giorgio. Most of the time she convinced herself that Marcello had exaggerated her husband's grief. Giorgio never loved her—not like Matteo did, with such deep and languid care. The memory of Matteo's caresses sent a delightful shiver through her body. Thanks to him and the panel she worked on now and those she had yet to paint, her life was as complete as God intended. No creature deserved to be happier then she was at that moment as she walked with Matteo past shops teeming with goods and life.

They stopped at a gate set into a stone wall. Matteo took out a key, unlocked the gate, pushed it open, and ushered her through, then locked the gate behind them. Sofia took a few paces, then stopped and inhaled deeply. Verbena and roses, mint and lavender, peaches warm and fragrant in the late summer sun.

"Matteo! What is this place?"

"My father's garden. He has great plans to make it one of the finest in all of Siena." He gestured toward a raked path enclosed on each side with hedges of red and white roses. "Come."

Sofia followed him through an arbor clad in vines heavy with clusters of ripe grapes to a clearing where a profusion of sweet herbs surrounded a large hole. Blocks of sliced marble were scattered nearby.

"For the fountain," Matteo said. "My father wants it finished in time for my wedding."

Sofia froze. The sky was clear and deep blue, and yet she felt like a thundercloud had passed before the sun. She looked at Matteo and saw him smiling complacently as he surveyed the garden that would one day be his.

"It is a beautiful place, Matteo, but I must return to my work. If you need the panel in time for the wedding, I can't spare time for walking in gardens. The varnishing requires months to dry and I've not yet finished the figures. Your wedding is when?" She kept her voice steady, as if she was asking him directions to the market.

"We plan for the spring," he said. "But, Sofia, what's wrong? Your face is white."

"I spend my time indoors," she said. "Thank you for bringing me here, Matteo, but please take me back."

"But I mean for us to spend the day here," he said, coming toward her and trying to take her hands. She kept them firmly at her sides, her entire body rigid.

He stroked her shoulder, then sought her lips with his. "Sofia," he murmured. "Stop this foolishness. We're together now." He wrapped his arms around her, pulling her close. Her treacherous body melted under his touch.

"We must stop, Matteo," she whispered. "You will be married and then what will become of me?"

"Hush. We'll not think of it today. God has brought us the beauty we see around us and that I see before me." He smiled, then pulled off her cap and kissed her black curls. "I promise I will not let harm come to you."

His hands stroked the place where her waist flowed into the curve of her buttocks. He was so gentle, so attentive. She must make him stop. It was wrong—in the eyes of God and of man.

"*Amore mio,*" he whispered. "*Tesoro mio.*" My love. My treasure.

"Matteo." She wanted to say no, had to say no. He was betrothed to another. She could never have him fully.

He slid one arm under her legs, lifted her easily. She looked up at vines blocking the sun while he carried her to a white pavilion completely screened in roses. Inside, a finely woven rug had been placed upon a bed of fresh rushes that rustled under her body when he set her down.

"Sofia," he said. "Beautiful Sofia."

Sofia wondered if Matteo would one day whisper such endearments to his wife. She didn't even know her name. She tried to hang on to her logic, to remind herself that she was a painter set on earth to glorify God, not a whore at the mercy of brute passion. But she had no voice. Instead, she moaned softly as his hands drifted down her body, wiping out all logic, replacing it with a savage, sudden arousal as he coaxed her to the brink of sanity. When finally he stripped off her leggings, leaving her open to the warm September breezes and his heat, she dropped over the edge.

Afterward, they stayed entwined for hours, laughing softly, talking, exploring. Matteo asked about her life before Siena, but Sofia still had enough wit to dissemble. She talked only of her father, of the places she had traveled, of the frescoes she'd seen and the panels she'd worked on.

"But how did you come to be in Siena in the first place—and in such a disguise?"

Sofia answered with a kiss and a hand that strayed below his waist. He gasped as she stroked him deliberately, using light and hard pressure in slow sequence, laughing softly when he responded. By the time they were done, he'd forgotten his question.

⁓

"Come, Sofia! On our way to the garden, I want to show you something."

She looked up from her work and smiled. Matteo was such a delicious mix of man and boy—strong, decisive, abrupt at times, but also playful and teasing. Every day she loved him more. He took her hand and pulled her up, kissed the top of her head, then led her into the street. Instead of turning left toward the garden at the edge of the city walls, they turned right, in the direction of the *campo*. She almost hugged herself as she anticipated the time they would spend that afternoon in the garden.

Matteo led her across the *campo* in the direction of the Palazzo Pubblico. They ducked into the Via di Malcucinato, a side street that led alongside the new prison. Sofia shuddered at the plight of the poor wretches inside. If she were caught, would the whipping be followed by containment in a foul cell within hearing of the *campo* bells?

"Now that's what I call a fitting punishment." Matteo had stopped and was gesturing toward the prison wall. She stepped closer to see what he was pointing at and grimaced.

"Oh, Matteo. How awful!"

"What's that? The man was an enemy of my father."

"Yes, but did he deserve such humiliation?" Sofia could barely look at the crude painting of a man hanging head-down from a gallows. Just one scrawny foot tethered him to the crossbar. On the ground, a pig snuffled to the left of his head and a coiled basilisk appeared to the right.

"*Pittura infamante*," Sofia said, turning away and walking rapidly back in the direction they had come, hoping to erase the tormented image from her mind.

"Sandro! Ho! Slow down. My father was much abused by this man. He had this public shaming ordered to bring him down a peg or two."

Sofia stopped walking but did not turn around. "I've no quarrel with him."

"What does that matter? You share my opinion."

He said it with such conviction that Sofia wondered if she was being unreasonable—ungrateful even—to disagree. She could feel him behind her, his breath ruffling the hair on her neck as his hands on her shoulders slowly turned her to face him. When they were together, naked in each other's arms, Sofia sometimes forgot their differences. But when he stood before her, the midnight blue of his gown shot through with gold thread and his waist cinched with a belt made from links of burnished copper studded with amethysts, Sofia realized only too well the gap that separated them.

"Forgive me," she said quietly, "but I hate the practice."

"Of shaming our enemies? Why should you? Such pictures appear on walls all over Siena and can be quite effective in bringing about repentance."

"I should imagine they're more likely to bring about resentment. What did this man do?"

"Swindled my father," Matteo said vaguely. "I don't have all the details."

"And what's to stop him from having a similar picture painted of your father?"

"He wouldn't dare!"

"Why not?"

"Because he would not. You dishonor my father to even think such a thing."

"Oh, Matteo, let's not quarrel about something we cannot change." She smiled up at him, reached for his hand. He snatched it away.

"We're in the street!"

"I know, but no one is about. I'm sorry if I offended you, Matteo. It's just that my father taught me to hate such harsh treatment of enemies."

"Then your father was a fool."

"Matteo!"

He flushed, and for a moment the boy took over. "I thought you'd be pleased." The bewildered hurt in his voice reminded Sofia of Francesco and she softened. How could she blame him for wishing to uphold his father's honor?

"Please, let's go to the garden, Matteo."

"No." Matteo turned on one heel and, before she could say another word, stalked past the offending picture and rounded the corner back into the *campo*.

Sofia wanted to run after him, to fling herself at him, not caring what people thought if only he would return to her, take her back into his arms. What if she had offended him so much that he never came back? He could turn her in to the authorities without a backward glance.

"I won't have tears in my workshop."

Sofia bit her lip to stop the trembling and kept her teeth clamped together. Barducci strode around the table to peer over her shoulder. "Rubbish!" He ripped the panel off the table and flung it into the corner.

"Papa! The patron."

"He'll have to wait until I have time to do a panel myself. You've disappointed me, daughter. I told you to make sure the surface was perfectly smooth before you started drawing."

"I thought it was."

"And you were wrong. Go back to your needle. I'll not have you here today."

"But may I return tomorrow?" Sofia stood up, her knees trembling as she faced her father. "I promise I'll check more carefully. Please, Papa."

But Barducci was already stalking back to his bench. Sofia peeled off the rough apron she used to cover her gown and quietly let herself out of the workshop. The sky had clouded over and the air was thick with heat and smoke from the midday fires. Disappointed! The many parts of the word rolled around her head like a swirl of lutes on a feast day. Her father was disappointed in her. She let the tears come, heedless as they slid down her hot cheeks, splashing into the dust at her feet. It was some minutes before she realized that the black spots speckling the dust were not only tears.

The sky opened and she felt as if God was emptying a bucket of cold water over her head. Wildly she looked around but could see nothing through the sheets of rain. She ran as fast as her heavy gown would let her back in the direction of the workshop. One foot slipped. A hand gripped her arm and she heard a mocking laugh.

"Take care, bella."

Sofia reared back, surprised by the familiar tone. A young man not much taller than she was regarding her with such frank admiration that she blushed. "Thank you, signor," she stammered. "The rain . . ."

"Is making the way treacherous. Hold my arm and I'll get you to shelter."

*She thought about pulling away. To be seen walking in the street
with a young man she had never met would bring scandal to her father's
door. He was angry enough already. But the man was already leading
her to an archway cut into the town wall. Once under it, the pounding
of the rain was muted and she could look at him more closely. He was
perhaps ten years older than she and had an appealing softness that she
had never seen before in a man. But then, she reflected, in the fifteen
years of her life, she had rarely been in the company of any man except
her father and the men in the workshop who always gave the daughter
of the master a very wide berth. She felt a strange fluttering in her heart
as she smiled shyly, then stared at the rivulets of water slicing through
the dust between their feet.*

"I mustn't stay," she said. "My father . . ."

"Your father is Maestro Barducci, is he not?"

"How do you know?"

*"My father has used his services on occasion—standards and
armor mostly. He speaks well of him, but I never heard mention of a
daughter."*

*Sofia said nothing. She had already spoken too freely to this stranger.
She knew it was very wrong and that her father would be furious if he
found out. "The rain is stopping. I must return to my father's." She
stepped into the moist air.*

*As she hurried away, she heard him laugh and call out, "Giorgio
Carelli, bella! And I never forget a debt."*

Sofia walked slowly back to the apothecary shop. For the first
time in her life, she had no appetite for working. What was the
point? Without Matteo, her life stretched before her with such
insipid dullness that her belly twisted with panic. She could not live
without him! Why had she not realized it? And now it was too late.
The next day, she would ask Francesco to come with her to clean up
and move the panel and her materials back to Manzini's workshop.
She should never have left it in the first place.

◌

"What are you doing?" Matteo stood in the doorway to the apothecary shop, his hands on his hips, the gold ring on the index finger of his left hand just catching the light from the street.

Sofia looked up, startled. She truly had not expected to see him again. "Francesco and I are packing up."

Matteo nodded at Francesco, who stared at him open-mouthed. That morning, Francesco had leaped at the chance to help her move her materials from the apothecary shop back to Manzini's. She'd never seen him work so hard.

"You can send your man away, Sofia," Matteo said. "There's no need for any packing."

"Francesco is not my man."

"As you wish." He inclined his head in a mock bow. "But I would have you send him back to Manzini's. I'm here now and we've no need of his services."

"Sandro?"

Sofia silenced Francesco with a twitch of her hand. She heard him breathing behind her, sensed his hurt. "You wish me to stay, Messer Salvini? I thought you were angry."

Matteo waved away the suggestion as if it was a stray fly. "Send your man away," he said again. "I will speak with you."

Sofia stood a moment longer—frozen between Matteo, who filled the shop like light fills the day, and Francesco, as tall as Matteo but where Matteo glowed with wealth and privilege, Francesco was the trunk of a large tree, solid and steadfast. Sofia knew which one she should choose, which one deserved to be chosen. But then she looked at Matteo's hand resting casually on his hip and remembered.

"Thank you, Francesco," she said. "You can return to the workshop now. I'll be along by sundown."

"But, Sandro . . ."

She shook her head, not able to look at him. "Please, Francesco."

"Good lad!" Matteo said as Francesco brushed by him on his way out of the workshop. Sofia wanted to follow him at the same time as she wanted to stay. Matteo crossed to her in two easy strides and gathered her into his arms.

"*Mio tesoro!*" he crooned. "You are forgiven." He stepped back, tipped up her chin with one elegant finger. "I forget sometimes that for all your skill, you are still only a woman."

A chill settled into her bones when she looked up at him. *Only a woman.* Monna Giuliana was right. In a few years, her disguise would not be enough to combat aging skin and a thickening waist. And in Manzini's workshop, she often caught Pietro staring at her, resentment making his surliness even more poisonous. How much longer could she depend upon his silence? He could expose her and step back to enjoy the spectacle. Nothing she said about him would matter once the whipping began.

"Don't look so downcast, *mio amore.* I've said you're forgiven. We can continue as before." He stroked her cheek, kissed the top of her nose, smiled. She wanted to pull away, to tell him to leave and take his nobility and empty promises with him, but she could not.

When she was with Matteo, it was so easy to pretend that everything was well.

CHAPTER THIRTEEN

. . . be guided by judgment; and if you are so
guided, you will arrive at the truth.
—Cennini, *Il Libro dell'Arte*, Chapter XXX

S andro." Francesco paused, breathed deeply, then placed his large
hands on either side of the panel she was painting. "Sofia."

"What do you want, Francesco?" she said, looking up impatiently. If she finished the gilding before the light faded, she could
spend the next day with Matteo. The commissions were coming
in so rapidly that she and the other apprentices and assistants were
barely able to keep up.

"You can finish it tomorrow."

"Tomorrow I will be with Messer Salvini."

Francesco frowned. "You're not yet done with his panel?"

"No." Sofia felt a blush warm her cheeks. She'd lain with Matteo just four days ago, and her thighs still quivered at the memory.
He had taken her again to the pavilion in his father's garden.

"Sofia," he said again.

"Why do you call me that?"

"It's what *he* calls you."

"You mean Messer Salvini?"

"It's not right what you're doing," Francesco said. "You know it's not, Sofia."

"Stop calling me that. And what am I doing that's so wrong?" Guilt was making her voice sharp. She hated seeing the hurt look on Francesco's face, and hated even more that she'd put it there. "I'm sorry, Francesco. Perhaps I've been overtaxing myself. The maestro has so many commissions." She looked around the workshop, aware suddenly that it was empty. "Why aren't you with the others? Didn't Manzini give everyone leave to attend the procession?"

"You're still here," he pointed out.

"Yes, but I never join the others if I can help it. But you should go and enjoy yourself. The procession celebrates Siena's four patron saints and goes to the cathedral. There will be food." She smiled, hoping to be forgiven as she always was. Dear Francesco. He deserved a better friend than she.

"I'd rather stay with you."

For the first time, Sofia noticed that his voice had lost its adolescent squeak and now vibrated through the air of the empty workshop as richly and fully as Matteo's. His face was taking on definition, the cheekbones sharp beneath black eyes. Despite the differences in their ages, he was no more her little brother than Pietro.

"Francesco—" she began.

"No!" Clumsily, he leaned forward. She turned her head, but his lips grazed her cheek. "Please don't go to him anymore."

"Francesco!"

"I can take care of you. The maestro will help. He thinks I'm a good worker and Pietro's teaching me carpentry."

"What?"

"I can take care of you," he said again. "I'll never let harm come to you, Sofia."

"I know you won't, Francesco," she said gently. "But I can't be with you."

"Why not? You love me."

"Of course I love you."

"Then we can be together." He grinned, looking again like a boy. "Is that not a good example of your logic?"

Sofia reached up and stroked his cheek. It would be so easy to be with Francesco. He would never use her and then marry another woman, never grow coarse, never strike her or leave or despise her. And he was so very dear. But to her, he was her little brother, no matter how tall he grew or how deep his voice or thick his arms.

"I'm sorry, Francesco," she said again. "But I love Messer Salvini." And as she said it for the first time out loud, even to herself, she knew it was true. She loved him and would give up everything for him.

Francesco's face crumpled. For a moment, Sofia was afraid he would cry. She wanted to gather him into her arms the way she had done when she found him next to the charred remains of his family. Then he sucked in air, straightened to his full height, and looked down at her like she was the boy and he the man.

"I can't keep you safe if you stay with him."

"I don't need protection."

"Dear Sofia," he said, imitating her. "How has God made you so stubborn?"

"I don't think God had anything to do with it, Francesco."

"I must say something to you, and it needs to be said quickly."

Sofia twisted around to look up at Matteo, her mouth closed but her eyes dancing. She wanted to fall into the depths of his eyes and be lost forever, to stay in the squalid apothecary shop with him until God saw fit to take them to heaven . . . or hell.

He drew away from her and paced around the room, his footsteps kicking up dust.

"Be careful, Matteo. The dust will settle into the paint and I'll need to sand it again." She moved her body closer to the panel, shielding it with her arms. "Stop pacing and tell me what you want to say."

He paused a few feet from her and drew a deep breath.

"Dear God, Matteo. What is it?"

"I wish to marry you."

"*Marry* me?" Sofia stared at him for several seconds, then burst out laughing. He reared back as if she had struck him, but she was laughing too hard to notice. "You wish to amuse me, Matteo, but I can't say it's a good joke."

"I don't jest."

"You must be jesting because you can't seriously mean you'll go to your father and tell him you want to marry the painter's apprentice. And what of your betrothed?" Sofia gestured to the panel that showed the head of the Madonna as a white smudge. She had tried three times to catch the likeness of Salvini's betrothed and each time he had told her to try again.

"My betrothed is dead."

"What? Oh, Matteo. I'm so sorry. You should have told me."

"I *am* telling you."

"But how? When?"

"A few days ago. She took ill and died not long after Fra Bernardo arrived. I never met her more than three times. She was my father's choice."

"But just because she's dead doesn't mean you're free to marry me. What of your father? He decides who you marry."

"Marrying you is God's answer to my prayers," he said as he came to her and knelt at her feet.

"That's a wicked thing to say."

"God forgive me, but, Sofia, you've bewitched me. I think of you every moment of the day and at night . . ."

"So you'll go to your father and tell him you wish to marry Manzini's apprentice, who dresses in a smock and has hair cropped shorter than most boys?" Sofia felt the dimple pop into her cheek when she smiled. He looked so earnest kneeling before her.

"Of course we must make you back into a woman," he said, sitting back on his heels and then with one fluid movement rising to his feet to resume his pacing.

"I see no need to change. The maestro has commissions enough to occupy me day and night and, God willing, I'll work again on a fresco. And sometimes I have you. I am content, Matteo."

"I offer you a home and riches beyond any you have known."

"And what will your father think of you marrying a woman who has spent two years living as a boy?"

"I have a plan. You're to be a relation of my mother's from Venice. My mother has been dead for three years, and I know a notary who will forge a letter from one of her kinsmen."

"Your father would never allow you to marry a woman with no money."

"I didn't say you had no money," he said with a smile. "It's all been arranged. But these aren't matters for you to concern yourself with. We'll be married and you will give me sons. That's all you need to know."

"Can I believe you?"

"You must know by now that I never say what I don't mean. And I say that you'll be my wife. You'll be presented to my father by a kinsman who is in my confidence and we will be married."

"As simple as that?"

"Yes, Sofia," he said, gathering her into his arms. "You will be mine."

"And I have nothing to say in the matter?"

"What could you have to say?"

Sofia almost felt like laughing at the genuine look of puzzlement on his face, but instead she felt a fist close around her heart. He was right. She had no words. She let herself be taken into his arms, let him cover her mouth with kisses and whisper her name over and over. A twinge of fear, so slight as to be scarcely discernible, quivered down her spine. But no, she was safe. Salvini would keep her safe. No one would ever believe that the new wife of a Sienese nobleman could have any relation to a saffron merchant from San Gimignano.

She wrapped her slim arms around Salvini's neck and moaned with pleasure as his lips brushed her throat and his hands removed her bindings with practiced care. God could not mean to punish her for such happiness.

~⁓

"I can't imagine what to do with your hair." Monna Giuliana ran one hand through the jagged tufts sprouting from Sofia's head. As a girl, Sofia had been many times obliged to include vanity about her hair as one of her sins in confession to Fra Angelo. And in the early months of her marriage, Giorgio had loved to stroke her hair and wrap thick hanks of it around his wrists, admiring its sheen and thickness. Salvini would one day do the same, she thought with a smile.

"I don't know how you can smile," Monna Giuliana said. "We've so much to do to get you ready. When are you to be presented?"

"Messer Salvini has decided on next Sunday after service."

243

"Five days? You give me five days to turn you back into a woman?"

"Yes, Monna Giuliana. It's a great deal to ask after what you've done for me."

"It is." Giuliana shook her head. "Why did I ever allow Luca to talk me into taking you?"

"I hope my work has pleased the master."

"Your *work* has certainly pleased him."

"And you, Monna Giuliana? The new commissions have made a difference?"

"You'll not find me ungrateful, which is why I'm helping you in this scheme." Monna Giuliana sighed dramatically, her large bosom heaving. "But I imperil my own immortal soul. What about the husband you already have?"

"My husband is dead, Monna Giuliana," Sofia said quietly.

"What? You never said." Giuliana peered into Sofia's eyes. "How could you know?" Sofia lowered her eyes. "Well? How came you by this news? When did he die? How?"

"I, ah . . ." Monna Giuliana stood squarely in front of her, her mouth set in a grim line. "I mean to say," Sofia began again, "that my husband . . . Giorgio, he, ah . . ." She paused and then finally shook her head. It was no use. She could not abuse Monna Giuliana with a lie, even if she could think of one.

"It's as I suspected. Well, let's just hope that Siena is far enough from San Gimignano and that God smiles upon you. I'll not be the one to prevent this union."

"Thank you."

"Yes, yes, you're a great one for thanking," Giuliana said briskly as she dabbed her eyes with one corner of her wimple, "but save your thanks for God. Now about your hair. I'll need to fashion some sort of covering."

"Yes, Monna Giuliana," Sofia said as she submitted again to Giuliana's hands upon her head. She thought of Matteo. Their stolen days in the apothecary shop were soon to end.

And what was to come would be even better.

CHAPTER FOURTEEN

. . . grind [red lac] with urine; but it becomes
unpleasant, for it promptly goes bad.
—Cennini, *Il Libro dell'Arte*, Chapter LXVII

Y ou're sure your father will accept me?" In just three days, she
would be presented to Salvini's father. Despite Giuliana's pro-
tests, Sofia had returned to the apothecary shop to continue her
work. While she talked, she was taking down the stretched parchment from the room's only window.

"I already told you that everything's arranged."

"I know you have, Matteo, but I'm worried. You weren't permitted to choose your own bride the first time, how can you now?"
Sunlight flooded the workshop.

"My father was much grieved when my betrothed died so
unexpectedly. He spent so many months arranging the match that
I think he's lost the taste for more such work." Matteo was standing
in the middle of the room, not moving to help. "Acceptable brides
aren't as thick upon the ground as he would wish."

"But given time, he'll arrange another marriage." She looked
critically at the table. The sun wasn't quite at the right angle. She
grasped one end. "Here, Matteo, help me shift the table."

Matteo still didn't move. "In normal circumstances, yes, I believe my father would find someone suitable, but he's much occupied with the council. He was recently appointed to the Nine."

Sofia dropped her hands from the table and clapped them. "That's wonderful news, Matteo! I've heard of the Nine from my father. But you're of the nobility. My father told me the Nine was made up only of merchants."

"Politics is none of your concern, Sofia. My father may be of noble birth, but he's no stranger to the concerns of merchants. They accept him as one of their own. His election to the Nine comes as no surprise."

"But can you really be sure your scheme will work, Matteo? Your father's service with the Nine won't make him blind." She positioned herself at the table again, nodded at Matteo to pick up the other end.

"As I've told you before, you don't need to concern yourself with how I've imposed upon my father. He'll be content with my choice, and I know that when he finally looks upon you, he'll love you as I do."

He took her hands from the table and folded her in his arms. Sofia wanted with all her heart to believe him. One hand slowly stroked her short hair, sending a delicious shudder through her body. The next time she saw her Matteo, she would be dressed as a woman in the gown Giuliana had made for her, with her cropped hair hidden beneath a veil and the stains on her fingers scrubbed clean. She felt as if her heart would break with happiness. She would have her own dear Matteo and her work. He enjoyed Sandro's growing fame as much as she did. With his heart beating next to her cheek, Sofia let herself imagine the days to come. Matteo would need to acquire one or two loyal servants to help her slip away from the Salvini palazzo to go to the workshop, and she would likely not be able to keep up the pace of commissions she'd grown accustomed to, but arrangements could be made to allow her to continue painting. And Maestro Manzini certainly expected it. He wouldn't want to forgo the extra income that her work brought in.

She remained a few moments longer in Matteo's arms, savoring the comfortable smell of him, then stepped back and looked up into his face. "As usual, you are distracting me. We need to get this table moved, and then will you stay and help me with the colors?"

"I thought we came here today to gather your materials and return them to Manzini. Another painter can complete the panel."

"Another painter? The maestro has no other painter equal to this work."

"Then Manzini himself can finish it. I don't much care."

Sofia felt like her feet had grown thick roots into the dirt floor. She could not move. She could barely even breathe. "What do you mean?" she asked, careful to keep her voice flat.

He surveyed the mess of painting dishes and nuggets of pigment on the table. "I'll help you clear up. And then you can ask your man to carry everything back to Manzini's workshop. Francesco, isn't it? Such a strong lad should be able to accomplish the task in one trip. If you wish, you may bring him with you when we marry. I'm sure a good position can be found for him in the household. Would that please you?" He smiled indulgently as, with one finger, he prodded a lump of red lac.

Suddenly, Sofia saw herself as a girl of eight squirming next to her father's workbench, anxious to attract his notice, hoping he would favor her with a few moments of his time.

"I think Francesco is of more use to me if he stays with the maestro," Sofia said. "He can continue to assist me."

"You'll have maids enough to assist you. What could a young man such as Francesco have to do with you?"

"I mean with my work, Matteo. Francesco knows how to prepare the panels and grind the colors and—"

Salvini dropped the lump of red lac and stepped forward, stopping her mouth with a kiss. "Shh, Sofia," he whispered. "Enough. Forget your pigments and grinding and all the mess of this profession. When you are my wife, you won't need to do anything."

"But, Matteo." She pushed herself away from him. "I *want* to continue painting. The maestro expects it."

"The maestro can find someone else."

"You've said yourself that I'm one of the best painters in all of Siena."

"No, Sofia, I've said that *Sandro* is one of the best painters in Siena. But within the week, you will no longer be Sandro." He tried to take her again into his arms, but she dodged his grasp and stood with her hands crossed over her chest, staring at him as if he was the first man she had ever seen.

"Matteo." She said his name quietly, rolling the consonants over her tongue, savoring the feel, wondering if it would be the last time she would say them. Suddenly, she knew that God had no intention of seeing her happy.

"Yes, my love?"

"Are you telling me that I won't paint after we marry?"

"Of course you won't paint. The notion's absurd. You'll be a Salvini. My wife can't be painting pictures."

"Then I won't be your wife." The words tore from her throat, almost against her will, but as soon as they were in the air, she knew she could never take them back.

"Don't be ridiculous. You certainly will be my wife. I offer you the world."

"Not all of it, Matteo."

He stared at her, his face blank except for two bright spots on his cheeks. Sofia knew from experience that he was angry—terribly angry. Perhaps it wasn't too late. Perhaps she could take back her words. Matteo knew how she sometimes teased him.

"I can expose you," he said, his voice low. The venom in the words hit Sofia with such force that she reached out one hand and steadied herself against the table.

"Matteo!"

He wasn't listening. Slowly, he stepped toward her, his hands at his side. Sofia saw the fists clenching. "One word from me and you'll be caught and whipped through the streets like a dog." He spat the words.

"You'd betray me?" Sofia lifted her chin defiantly. Her life was in his hands. The fear rose in her breast like a living thing that threatened to consume her. The breath stalled in her throat as she imagined the lash cutting into her back, the noise of the crowd, the humiliation.

"I . . ." He stopped, flushed, turned away.

"I'm sorry, Matteo," she whispered. "But I can't marry you."

Salvini turned. "You dare reject me? But you don't need to live like this. As my wife you will have everything."

"Except the one thing that is even more important to me than you."

"Sofia." He held out one hand, opened the fingers. She wanted to take his hand, kiss his warm palm, let him take her to a new life. It would be so easy. Her father would say she was a fool to turn him down. What could painting give her that Matteo could not?

She lowered her gaze to the panel on the table. The head of the Madonna was still shrouded in white lead, but the rest of the panel—the colors and lines were clean, wholesome. She thought of how she felt when she bent over her work, lost to all the world when she mixed and applied the pigments. When she painted, she was with God.

"Sofia," he said again, all trace of anger gone from his voice. "Stop this foolishness. Be my wife." His hand still extended, he stepped closer. "This is God's will."

"No."

Matteo lowered his arm slowly, gave her one last agonized look, then turned and walked to the door. Without saying a word or looking back over his shoulder, he wrenched it open. The clamor of the street filled the room.

"Matteo!" She felt as if her body would collapse in on itself, squeezing her heart like a lump of ocher beneath her grinding stone.

Salvini paused for a second, framed in the doorway. Sofia was sure he could not leave her. He loved her. And then he shook his head and stepped forward into the street. With one arm, he swept aside a beggar who fell back against a wall, then shook a blackened fist at Salvini's retreating back. Sofia ran to the door and watched as Salvini's tall, strong figure pushed through the crowd. Her beautiful Matteo. She should run after him and catch his hand, then lead him back to the shop, where he could take her forever. He loved her. She would make him understand that she could not deny her work, even for him.

But he did not turn around and soon he was lost in the gloom. With a low moan, Sofia returned to her table and looked through eyes dim with tears at the white lead covering the head of the Madonna. She picked up the panel and flung it across the room. What use was painting to her now? She would return the panel to Manzini and then get word to Salvini that she had changed her mind. He would forgive her. Of course he would forgive her. He loved her and he would care for her. That was all that mattered.

The panel hit the wall with a dull thud, then clattered to the ground. Some paint flaked off the cheeks of the blessed Child and a dent distorted the Madonna's gown. The maestro would be furious.

How could she treat her work with such disdain? The panel depicted the blessed Virgin and Child. She had no right flinging it away from her as if it was no better than an old boot. She picked up the panel and cradled it. The blank space where the Madonna's head should be mocked her. Sofia tasted salt on lips that had lately tasted Salvini.

"Tears are for children," her father said sternly as Sofia's lips quivered and her eyes filled. "If you must cry, you have no place in my workshop."

Sofia stared at the panel depicting Saint Sofia. She had done everything her father had asked her to do, drawn the saint with her three children—Faith, Hope, and Charity—clustered at her feet exactly as he directed. And now he was telling her that the saint looked as graceful as a common washerwoman.

"Look at her arm, daughter. I'd be ashamed to show such an arm to my patron. Do it again."

"Yes, Papa. I'm sorry."

"Sorry? That won't bring me commissions. Wipe your tears and show me that you can follow my directions. Or be off with you. I've no time for a blubbering female in my workshop. Go to Emilia and get her to give you some useless scrap of needlework."

How could her father talk to her so? She worked tirelessly to do his bidding. For a few moments, Sofia was tempted to throw down her brush and flounce out of the workshop, back into the main part of the house to sit at the window and perhaps glimpse Giorgio Carelli when he rode by.

"Are you going to work or just sit there mooning?"

The saint's arm really was crooked and her gown draped in stiff folds. Her father deserved better.

And so did she.

Sofia placed the *Maestà* panel gently upon the table and picked up a brush. She would finish the panel and present it to Manzini. Thanks to Sandro's growing fame, Sofia was sure that plenty of patrons would be glad to take it. She would keep coming to the apothecary shop every day until the panel was finished. And perhaps, if she took long enough, Salvini would come back to her. He had to come back to her.

She thought of the times when her teasing had angered him so much that she'd glimpsed a hardness. But it had been a hardness that she had always been able to soften. It would be the same this time. He'd forgive her. He'd come back. And she would let him take her and love her. She was at fault for rushing him. She should have gone slower—let him get used to the idea of her continuing to paint. What a fool she'd been. Of course a man of Matteo Salvini's rank could not have a wife painting. But he was a reasonable man under the sometimes haughty air he affected—and he loved her. He could no more leave her than she could leave her painting. He just needed time.

Feeling less desperate, Sofia shifted her angle to allow more light to illuminate her workspace. As she dabbed with whisper-thin strokes at the face of the Child, she was soon flying with the angels.

"Sandro!"

Sofia's head snapped up. Francesco stood in the doorway of the apothecary shop, the late afternoon sun turning his unruly thatch of hair to fire. In the two weeks since Salvini had left her, Sofia had finally roughed in the features of the Madonna. Francesco should know better than to disturb her when she still had two hours of daylight left. Had something happened to Monna Giuliana or the master? Francesco's face was red and his cap askew. He looked like he had been chased by all the hounds of hell.

"Francesco!" she cried. "What's wrong? Is it Monna Giuliana?"

"No!" Francesco panted for breath. "No . . . it's Pietro."

"What of him?" Relief made her sharp. Whatever the loutish Pietro had done or not done was of no interest to her. He had stayed well out of her way since their encounter in the alleyway and she had wiped the memory of his grasping hands from her mind.

"I saw him talking with a man in the street."

"That's hardly a crime, Francesco."

"Sandro! Listen to me." Francesco could barely get the words out. Despite the brisk October day, his face was bright with sweat. "The man—he was giving him money."

"Who?"

"Pietro! I heard him."

"Heard Pietro?"

"No! Please, Sandro, listen! The man was giving Pietro money, and he said your name." Francesco lowered his voice and leaned forward. "He said Sofia Carelli."

"What did this man look like?" The beating of her heart was the pounding of drums before an execution.

"Not tall, somewhat stout. Dark curly hair, red face, a tunic much stained with travel."

When she was alone, her eyes burning after a long day of painting, Sofia sometimes wondered how she would feel if Giorgio found her. She expected despair to squeeze the life from her. But all she felt was a profound numbness, like she was a deaf woman standing alone in a field while thunder crashed overhead. She looked back at the panel on the worktable, the paint of the Madonna's cheeks still glistening with damp.

Manzini had lost his most promising apprentice after all.

"Sandro!" Francesco's voice cracked. "Do you know the man?"

"He is my husband. I'm sorry, Francesco, but I must leave you."

"But he can't just take you!" Francesco exclaimed with all the blind vigor of youth. "The master won't allow it."

"The master won't dare object. I can only hope that Giorgio doesn't have the master charged."

"*I* won't let you go!"

"You must, Francesco."

"Can I go with you?"

"Your life is in Siena. I can offer you nothing in San Gimignano, and my husband would never permit me to bring you." Sofia stepped forward and touched his broad forearm. Her heart squeezed with love for her adopted little brother. "The master values the work you do for him in the workshop, Francesco. And think of poor Monna Giuliana. Who would appreciate her cooking as much as you do?" Impatiently, she blinked the tears from her eyes. In the weeks and months and years ahead, she would have plenty of time for tears.

"We can run away."

"No, Francesco." She held up her hand. "I know you'd do anything for me, and I love you for it, but you'll serve me best by staying here in Siena and making something of yourself." She breathed deeply and forced a smile. "And you can do one thing for me right now."

"Anything, Sandro."

"Take this to the master." She picked up the panel of the *Maestà* and thrust it into his hands. "He'll find someone to finish it. I won't have him losing money on my account."

"What will you do?"

"I will wait. Pietro will lead my husband to me, and I'd rather he finds me here than at the workshop. Tell the master"—her voice caught—"and Monna Giuliana that I am grateful for all they have done for me." She shook her head at Francesco's anguished cry. "You must not." She pushed him out to the street, then followed him and rose on her tiptoes to kiss him on the cheek.

A matron bustling by clucked her displeasure. "Goodbye, Francesco. Go with God."

She heard the clank of metal and an oath. "Run!" she cried. "For me!"

The torment on Francesco's face tore at her. She turned away from him and stood in the middle of the street, her arms crossed as two men dressed as soldiers came toward her. She smelled hot metal mixed with sweat. The shorter man grabbed her arm with his gloved hand. He couldn't have been much older than Francesco, but he looked undernourished and filthy—a thug hired by the city to keep watch over the populace. The two soldiers pushed against her, urging her forward. Neither said a word. She thought of struggling, of crying out even, but knew she could not give Francesco any excuse to rush to her aid. She chanced one glance over her shoulder. He was holding the panel in one hand while the other hand smeared the tears from his cheeks. But he made no move to follow her. Even to the last, he obeyed her.

"Face forward," growled the older of the two soldiers. The hand gripping her upper arm squeezed and she felt her muscles grind against the bone. He could probably snap her arm in two. The hand she used to paint with went numb.

"Where are you taking me?" Fear made her forget to keep her voice low. The younger soldier peered at her curiously. She realized he had not been told she was a woman. For that mercy at least she could thank the Virgin. If they knew what they held between them, her path to Giorgio would doubtless include a detour.

"You'll see soon enough," the older one said.

The soldiers hustled her along the street and into Il Campo. The bright afternoon sun flooded the space with a light so painful that Sofia could barely keep her eyes open. She looked across the piazza to the Salvini palazzo, imagined Matteo striding out of the entranceway, his face suffused with fury as he scattered the soldiers and swept her into his arms. He would have taken care of her and kept her safe. Why had she refused him?

The soldiers hustled her across the *campo* and toward one of the dark streets leading into an area of the city Sofia did not know. Sofia closed her mind to everything but the dirt under her feet, feeling the ground dip and then begin to rise as they crossed the center of the *campo*. She stared at the scuffed toe of her shoe. A single drop of red paint had fallen onto the brown leather. Would Giorgio expose her to the authorities? Stand by and watch while she was whipped through the streets?

Another step forward and then another. How long would she be safe, suspended like she weighed no more than an empty sack between the two soldiers? In their impatience, they almost lifted her from her feet, then swung her through a doorway into what Sofia thought must be a rough tavern. How fitting. Giorgio was probably already drunk with the day not yet half over. The soldiers let go of her arms and she fell forward in an untidy heap. She kept still, her face pressed into the filthy straw covering the floor. The only sound was the rustling of the soldiers moving restlessly behind her.

And then new sounds—brisk footsteps and the clink of a sword.

"Sandro? What ho, you there! What are you doing? He has done nothing to warrant such treatment.

Sofia felt Salvini's strong arms lift her up and steady her. He stared first at her and then at the two soldiers. "What are you doing? You must have the wrong boy. This is Maestro Manzini's best apprentice."

"I believe you are mistaken."

Salvini kept hold of her arm as he slowly turned to face the man who had spoken. "Pardon me?"

A chair scraped. Giorgio rose to his feet and faced Salvini. He did not spare a glance for Sofia.

"I don't know who *you* are, signor," Giorgio said, "but I would thank you to let go of my wife's arm."

"Your *wife?*" Salvini stared first at Giorgio, and then down at Sofia. She let his eyes hold hers for a few seconds, let herself drink in the look of him, and then she nodded.

"I'm sorry, Matteo," she whispered.

"What's this?" Giorgio grabbed Sofia's other arm. She wondered if they would pull her apart like the child before King Solomon. It would be a fitting end. But Salvini dropped her arm like it was a piece of flaming kindling. She kept her eyes upon him, pleading silently for him to help her.

"Are you acquainted with my wife?" Giorgio asked.

"Forgive me, signor. I've mistaken this wretch for someone who once worked for me. You say she's your wife?" He let out a short, sharp bark of a laugh. "I imagine you've not authorized such a getup. Do you wish to have her up on charges? May I be of assistance?" Salvini affected to look around the dingy tavern as if he could summon a magistrate from the shadows.

"Thank you, signor, but that won't be necessary. I'll see to her." Giorgio bowed to Salvini with all the deference due his superior dress and air. He then threw a few coins in the direction of the soldiers, who caught them up and hustled out of the tavern, leaving Sofia alone with her husband and the man who wanted to be her husband.

Had wanted.

Salvini returned Giorgio's bow. Surely Matteo would not forsake her. He could not. They had loved with a blinding white passion. No man could forget so quickly. She stared up at him, willing him to look at her, to tell her with his eyes that he still loved her.

She would speak now. Matteo would take her back. He had to take her back.

"Matteo. Please." She felt Giorgio's eyes on her, but she did not care. Every ounce of her being was directed at Matteo—praying for him to look into her eyes, to love her again, to remember their afternoons in the apothecary's shop, the wild desire in the garden, his love like an elixir that had filled her up with such impossible happiness.

And then he swung around on one elegant heel and strode into the clattering noise of the street, not even glancing in her direction, his fine gown swaying at his knees. She slumped to the floor, rested her head against a splintered table leg. God had thrown her into the desert with no drop of water to relieve the torture. Desolate sand stretched in all directions; a sluicing wind froze her skin.

"*Will it always hurt, Papa?*"

"*Yes, cara mia. But in time the pain will become duller and you will smile again.*"

"*No, Papa. I can never smile again.*"

"*I know, daughter.*" *He drew Sofia to his chest and held her as her sobs filled the bedchamber where just days before her mother had brushed Sofia's hair and scrubbed the paint from her hands.*

"Get up."

Sofia struggled to her knees and then finally to her feet. As her eyes came level with Giorgio's, her tears dried in an instant. Never again would she let him see her cry.

"How did you find me?" she asked.

"Is that all you have to say to me? How did I *find* you?" Giorgio raised his arm and Sofia braced herself for the blow. There was no one to see him, or to care even if they did. As far as anyone knew, she was nothing more than a servant who had displeased his master. She would not look away or cower in fear. She would not even look at the hand he raised.

"Go ahead. You have the right."

Giorgio's arm began its descent and then, just inches from Sofia's head, it stopped. He lowered it slowly. The lines etched deep into his face made him look far older than his thirty-four years. What was left of his once-thick hair was gray, and Sofia saw him as he would become—a brick-faced, stupid old man. He did not deserve her pity and he would not get it. But with a start, Sofia realized that she could not hate him. She could not even hate Matteo. After all, what choice had she given him? Every law—civic and Church—was against her. And as for Giorgio, how could she blame him for doing what any man would?

Sofia touched Giorgio's cheek. He shivered and tried to push her away. But she held her hand against him and felt his jaw soften beneath her touch. "I'm sorry I caused you pain," she said. "I did not mean to."

"You said you were with child." He sounded bewildered and hurt, like a child himself.

"I was not."

"So it was all a lie? From the beginning?" His eyes, usually dull with drink and ignorance, glittered with tears. Sofia remembered his happiness when he believed himself about to become a father. Marcello had not lied. Giorgio had suffered cruelly when that joy was taken from him, not by sickness or by accident, but by the deliberate actions of his wife.

"I had no choice, Giorgio," she said. "My father . . ."

With one swift movement, he gripped her wrist and twisted. She cried out as he spun her around and then pulled her against his chest, his forearm like a thick branch of fire-hardened oak across her bound breasts. Giorgio's other hand covered her mouth. She wondered if he would squeeze the breath from her and leave her for dead on the crawling floor of a Sienese tavern.

"Always your father," he hissed. "Never me." He increased the pressure against her chest until Sofia was sure she would faint. She was a fool to take pity on him. He was a monster and deserved every pain she could inflict. She felt herself falling and imagined sliding right through Giorgio's arms to the floor and then out to the street. Death in one of Siena's foul alleys was preferable to a return to San Gimignano. If only she didn't feel so weary. The darkness pressed in on her and she struggled to gulp air into her lungs. She could smell Giorgio but she couldn't see him. Perhaps he was already gone. Perhaps she was already free.

PART THREE

San Gimignano, Tuscany
October 1340

CHAPTER FIFTEEN

And so it is a good plan to wait as long as you
can before varnishing . . . then [the colors]
become very fresh and beautiful,
and remain in pristine state forever.
—Cennini, *Il Libro dell'Arte*

For many weeks, each day in the tower was very much like the day before and the day after. Sofia spent most of her waking hours lying on a straw pallet in the corner farthest from the ladder. Giorgio had allowed her to change back into a gown, but even the fur lining could not keep the chill from penetrating her bones. Her only companion was Brida, a raw-boned blonde woman from the north who barely spoke Tuscan. Each morning at terce, Brida brought a single tray of food up the ladders. The few times Sofia tried to eat, a terrible nausea gripped her stomach, forcing her to the stinking pot in the corner, making her long for the release of death.

"Fra Angelo says that killing yourself is the very worst crime before God. Why is that, Papa? Why wouldn't killing someone else be worse?"

"A good question. Did you ask Fra Angelo?"

"Yes, and he made me sit on a stool and told everyone I was not to be talked to for the rest of the day."

"Ah. Well, I'm not sure that Fra Angelo would agree with my opinion."

"Fra Angelo says there can be no room for opinions in such matters. It's God's law. But doesn't God wish us to think?"

"Now there's a question you most definitely do not want to ask Fra Angelo," Barducci said with a chuckle. "Leave off this talk about killing and help me paint the wings of this angel."

He stood her in front of him and placed a brush into her hand.

"Take this red color, mix it with a touch of brown, and add some strokes just here. Yes. That's it."

As she worked, his solid chest rose and fell behind her head. Nothing could ever harm her.

Brida was the first to see the truth.

"With child." She pointed to Sofia's stomach and held her hands far in front of her own belly, her mouth stretched in the first smile Sofia had seen on her face. "Master happy. You move now."

Sofia wanted to tell Brida that the only movement she wished to make was flinging herself from the tower. But the window slit was too narrow and the child she carried was innocent, even if she was not. Her mind sorted through possibilities. Her best option was to keep her condition a secret until the baby was born and then direct Brida to find a woman in the town to take it.

"Brida! The master must not be told."

"What?" Sofia saw Brida struggle to form the Tuscan words to describe her joy. When no words came, Brida contented herself with rubbing one hand across Sofia's belly and smiling even more broadly.

Sofia grabbed Brida's wrist. "I said no!" She spoke very slowly. "No master." She shook her head vigorously. "He must not know."

Brida's pale blue eyes filled with tears as she pulled her wrist from Sofia's grasp. "Child. Good."

"No." She released Brida's arm and almost pushed her toward the ladder, then seated herself at the window, oblivious to the chill wind. She stared at a landscape of brown and barren fields, her head aching from the incessant sounds of building. Would San Gimignano never rest? Its towers were beyond counting. A new one had gone up so close to her own that she could have spoken with someone sitting in the top room without needing to raise her voice.

She stroked her belly. How had she not noticed it growing hard and round? In the month since Giorgio brought her home to San Gimignano, she had not been allowed to wash herself or even been given new linens. Most nights, she did not even bother to remove her gown to sleep.

Matteo's child. If Brida helped her escape the tower, Marcello must take her back to Siena. Surely he owed her that much. And Matteo would *have* to marry her if he knew she carried his child.

"Such weakness," her father snorted as he watched a woman being led into the piazza and punished for adultery. He looked on impassively while her head was shaved, then the lash snapped across her back. "A woman has only herself, daughter. Remember that. She must not give it to any man who asks."

Would the same thing happen to her? She would not be harmed while she carried the child, but after? She had to keep it a secret. Sofia sat at the window until the sun slipped below the far horizon. Finally, she tacked up a piece of ragged cloth and lowered herself to her pallet. She felt a slight rolling in her belly, like the lurching of the cart that had returned her to San Gimignano. The sensation startled her and then, to her surprise, a peculiar warmth spread upward from deep inside her. She thought of Caterina—how she looked each time she was with child—like she knew something too precious and joyous to share.

And for the first time in her life, Sofia knew she was not alone.

○∽ᗡ

"The child is mine."

Sofia opened her mouth to speak, but Giorgio silenced her with an impatient wave of his hand. "He will be my son. I'll tell Brida to move you below." Giorgio began pacing back and forth across the room, his face flushed bright red like it always did when he tried to think.

"Below?"

"Quiet." As he continued pacing, Sofia's fear began to fade. When he had first squeezed himself into the tower room, she had been gripped with a terrible certainty that what little she had left to live for was to be taken from her. But the Giorgio before her was not angry. A smile curved his fleshy lips and his brisk movements were those of a man with a purpose.

"My lord?"

"I said, be quiet." He stepped forward, his hand open. She flinched back against the stone wall, her eyes wide. Without realizing it, she clasped her belly with both hands. Giorgio saw the movement and stopped so abruptly he almost stumbled forward. He lowered his arm and continued to pace.

Many minutes later, he stood directly in front of her. "You carry my son and I thank God for it."

Sofia nodded, too shocked to speak. Giorgio seemed to be waiting for her to say something. He stared at her, his expression expectant, almost hopeful. "Of course, my lord," she said finally. "God has blessed us."

"He has." He turned from her and lowered himself down the ladders. His boots smacked the floor below, then the floor below that. Some minutes later, a laugh rose faintly from the street.

An hour later Brida moved Sofia to her old bedchamber, then bathed and dressed her in fresh linens and the deep blue gown she'd worn when she watched her father die. Giorgio summoned Sofia to the dining area and motioned for her to sit opposite him at the heavy table. When Brida entered with a steaming platter of wild boar, Sofia's stomach heaved and her body felt dipped in an icy stream. She swallowed bile and gagged. It was no use. She pushed her chair back so quickly it banged to the ground and only just made it out to the loggia before her scant breakfast of hard bread splashed onto the stone tiles. Behind her, Giorgio roared with laughter.

"See to your mistress," he called, and laughed some more when Brida hurried outside and led Sofia to the edge of the loggia. A cool wind brought color back to her cheeks. Brida clucked as she wiped Sofia's mouth and straightened her headdress.

"Shh," she whispered, then spoke in her strange, guttural language. Sofia did not understand the words, but she sensed their gentleness. In her heart, she knew she should be grateful to Brida for telling Giorgio about the child because at least she was free of the tower. But the certainty of Brida's betrayal made her wary. She gathered her skirts and pushed Brida away, then swept back into the hall, where Giorgio was elbow-deep in grease, his lips purple with wine. Her stomach rose again, but this time she was prepared. She closed her mouth firmly and bit the inside of her cheek until she tasted blood.

"What? You leave my table and now you wish to return?"

"I'm sorry, my lord. I felt unwell."

"So I see. Get off to bed. I won't waste good meat on you." He stared up at Sofia. "You carry my son now. Remember that."

Sofia inclined her head enough to let him see she understood and then walked quickly to the bedchamber. Brida trailed along behind her, anxiously babbling, eager to please the master by helping the mistress. Sofia suffered Brida to unlace her gown, then dismissed her and reclined, uncovered, upon the bed. Her belly was growing. Already she could look down the length of her body and not see her thighs. She rubbed her belly and smiled at the fluttering beneath her fingers. God and the Virgin had blessed her this day. She would be sure to do extra penance the next time Giorgio allowed her to see Fra Angelo. She wondered if the wily old hypocrite would suspect anything when he heard of her condition. But even if he did suspect, she doubted he would raise any alarms.

Sofia was surprised to discover that, in her absence, Giorgio's status in the commune had improved markedly. She knew few details, since Brida could tell her nothing and she had seen Fra Angelo only once, but she gathered that her husband's grief had finally been tempered by a return to commerce and a renewal of friendly relations with his brother, Ruberto. With Giorgio's fortunes on the rise, Fra Angelo knew the wisdom of keeping his own counsel. As her father had often maintained, good Fra Angelo had his eyes on Avignon, where it was said the Pope was building a new palace at the same time as he was attempting to curb the extravagances enjoyed by some of the richer monastic orders. Fra Angelo affected a pious devotion to poverty and railed against the worldly concerns of the great families of San Gimignano with their lavish towers and expensive feuds, but Sofia knew about the fresco her father had painted for Fra Angelo's private quarters.

For the first time since she was taken from Siena, Sofia felt a stirring of contentment. The child's safety was assured so long as she did nothing to antagonize Giorgio. She would never again enjoy the freedom she had in Siena, but perhaps it would be possible to one day reclaim her place in the tower and take up the brush. With that, her first cheerful thought in many weeks, Sofia drifted off to sleep, exhausted by her good fortune.

❦

"Who you think you are? The mistress not see you." Brida's voice carried across the loggia. Sofia struggled out of sleep. In the hot, dark room, she couldn't be sure if it was morning or night. Why was Brida shouting? Sofia closed her eyes, tried to gather back the ragged ends of her dream. She had been in the garden with Matteo. Cool, delicious air was flowing across her body at the same time as Matteo was inflaming it.

"No! You not go in!"

"I'll only be a few moments."

Sofia's eyes popped open and she bolted upright. He could not see her like this. She swung her feet to the ground and stood shakily, her legs like limp pasta after the long weeks in bed. Messer Donato, the cursed physician Giorgio had secured to wait upon her, was insisting that she be kept quiet, alone, and in the dark until the child was born. She detested the little man, who stank of the urine he carried around in large glass beakers and held up to the light.

"Sofia." He crossed the room in two strides, took her hand, and raised it to his lips. "Dear sister. My mistress told me you'd come back."

Sofia snatched back her hand. "Marcello! How dare you come here to gloat at my misery?"

"Sofia . . ."

"Don't call me that."

"Monna Carelli. Please. I am not your enemy."

"No? How else did my husband find me?"

Marcello shook his head miserably. "I swear, madonna, I didn't tell him. I wouldn't."

"You thought I should return to San Gimignano," she said accusingly, wrapping her arms around her stomach. "I hope you're satisfied now. I'm back and good for nothing more than to stay in bed and wait for Giorgio's son to be born."

Marcello raised one eyebrow but wisely said nothing. Instead, he bowed stiffly. "I came to see for myself that you are well."

"I'm as you see me."

"You must believe that I had nothing to do with your return. When my mistress said you were back, I was as surprised as anyone." Marcello looked stricken, and for the first time Sofia noticed the parts of him that were not like her father.

"You should never have left me." Sofia knew she sounded peevish and hated her own weakness, but ever since Giorgio had taken her from Siena, she'd wondered how he had found her. When she'd asked, he'd dismissed her with a cuff to the side of her head, and once he learned about the child, he acted as if she had never left San Gimignano at all. Marcello *must* have told him that she lived at Manzini's workshop. How else could Giorgio have known?

"You must believe me, madonna. I did not tell your husband. It was Delgrasso."

"From my father's workshop? How?"

"I overheard my mistress telling the master that Delgrasso had been to Siena, seen one of your panels, and suspected you had painted it. He told your husband."

"Delgrasso?" She should have realized. Delgrasso was the only person who knew of the work she'd done for her father. If he'd seen one of her panels in Siena, he would easily recognize the style. She almost smiled. To have been undone by her own work was somehow fitting.

"Madonna?" Marcello was gesturing toward a slight figure framed in the open door by the sunlight bouncing off the loggia.

"Paulina!"

Her maid had become a woman with round cheeks and shining eyes. She came into the room and clasped Sofia's outstretched hands. "I am happy to see you, mistress. When Marcello said you were back, I had to come, to see for myself that you lived."

Sofia pulled Paulina into her arms and looked over her shoulder at Marcello. "What is this?"

"The reason I couldn't stay with you in Siena," Marcello said. "Paulina and I . . . My mistress kindly allowed us to marry."

Sofia's heart swelled with a gladness she hadn't known since her months with Matteo in Siena. "God bless you," she murmured into Paulina's hair, then stepped back and looked over at Marcello. "You're a lucky man. God has sent you a brave wife."

"I know it, madonna."

"Your mistress was kind to let you marry," Sofia said. "Tell Caterina that I am well enough. She'll be worried. Now leave me before my husband returns. He doesn't allow me to have visitors."

Marcello and Paulina both bowed, and then Marcello took his wife's hand and led her from the room.

Sofia collapsed onto the bed, her gladness wiped out by a desolation even more severe. Her only consolation now was that at least one of her father's children had found happiness.

"Soon," Brida said, fussing around Sofia's bed, plumping a pillow, smoothing the checked bedspread. She stopped and laid her large hand on Sofia's belly. Her touch was calming. Using a combination of sign language and her few words of Tuscan, Brida had already told Sofia that she had once been a midwife.

"Visitor. Monna Caterina."

"Caterina comes to see me?" Sofia struggled up to her elbows. "My husband . . ."

Caterina pushed the door wide open, letting in a stream of light alive with dust. "Sister! Your time grows close." She settled herself onto the bed and gazed around the dim room. "This darkness is too confining. Your physician insists on it?"

"As you see."

"Such nonsense." She patted Sofia's hand. "But it will all be over very soon. And then you'll know my joy." She rubbed her own stomach. "I'm just a few months behind you."

"This makes five?"

"Six. You missed a great deal while you were away. But now you're back and will be made a mother. God is merciful. I wish Giorgio had allowed me to see you sooner."

"Why has he allowed it now?"

"He doesn't know, of course. He's gone with Ruberto to Florence. Didn't you know?"

"Florence! What could Giorgio possibly have to do there?"

"You don't know?"

"Stop asking me if I don't know. I obviously don't. Pray tell me what you're speaking of."

"I don't pretend to understand what's happened. Ruberto tells me nothing, but these past months have seen much strife in the streets of our city."

"Strife in the streets of San Gimignano is hardly news. Which side is it this time? Salvucci? Ardinghelli?"

Something gripped her deep in her belly.

"I thank God that my Ruberto and your husband have escaped the stain of either house and were elected to speak with the Florentines."

Sofia felt a heavy pressing and then gasped when a dull pain ripped through her. What was this about the Florentines? Their involvement in the affairs of San Gimignano could not be to its benefit. Her father had never trusted the Florentines. He preferred to accept commissions from other city-states such as Pisa or Bologna.

"Dogs," Maestro Barducci spat. "The Florentines care only for one thing."

"What's that, Papa?"

"Themselves."

"But isn't that what everyone cares most about?"

"Ha! As always you are right, cara mia. But I think you may care about yourself and still notice the plight of others."

"You can notice, Papa. But does that mean you help? Every day we see the effects of famine in our city, but we do nothing to help."

Maestro Barducci scowled, then shifted in his seat next to Sofia. He was working on a sketch for a new fresco. The subject was the raising of Lazarus from the dead, but Barducci was having difficulty deciding on a suitable background.

"We can't do something for everyone we see," he muttered. "Now peace. We both have our work to attend to. What progress have you made on the panel for Messer Rinaldi?"

Sofia took up her brush and held it above the panel. The patron had ordered a depiction of the death of Saint Justina, who was martyred because she would not give up her chastity even on pain of death. He wanted to display the panel in his young wife's chamber and had been very specific that the message of fidelity be made crystal clear. Sofia wondered if Messer Rinaldi's lady would need such a reminder if Messer Rinaldi himself were not so fat and old. She thought dreamily of her Giorgio. He was certainly neither fat nor old. She would not need a painting to remind her to stay true to Giorgio.

Another rolling pain gripped the base of her belly. Sofia cried out. Immediately, Caterina was at her side, her face a flutter of concern and excitement.

"The pains begin?"

Sofia bent forward in the bed, her hands clutching her belly, her teeth grinding. The fear that gripped her overpowered even the pain. She clasped Caterina by the arm. "Sister! How can I bear it?"

"Oh, you've just begun," Caterina said cheerfully as she disengaged her arm. "The pains will come on much harder. But you're strong enough. You'll not die."

Minutes later another pain—much sharper and deeper than the first pains—tore through her. Sofia did not believe for a moment that she wouldn't die and wondered if she should have Fra Angelo sent for. She loathed the pompous cleric, but she didn't want to add to her sins by dying without confession.

Brida hurried into the room, her arms full of clean towels and her mouth open in a broad smile. Sofia knew how Brida had been looking forward to this moment, and she hated her for it. That Brida should smile when her belly was being cleaved in two! It was too much.

"How long?" Sofia gasped when the pain subsided and she slumped back against the pillows. Brida flung off the cover and massaged Sofia's belly, then coaxed her legs open and, to Sofia's horror, plunged one hand inside her. Brida's face screwed up in concentration, the smile now gone. Moments later she removed her hand and nodded at Caterina.

"Long time yet. You stay?"

Long time? What was this? Sofia struggled up against the pillows and looked wildly around the room. Why weren't they bringing in the birthing chair? Giorgio had boasted to her that it was brand-new. Nothing but the best for his son.

"Shh," Caterina said as she smoothed the hair off Sofia's forehead. "It's often like this with a first child. You'll need to be very strong, but Brida and I are here to attend you. Brida doesn't think anything is amiss."

"You good," she said, nodding vigorously. "But long time. Child come maybe tomorrow."

Tomorrow? The long black shadows falling across the bed told her the sun was still up, that nightfall was many hours away. Surely,

Brida did not mean she would suffer until the new day? Another pain gripped, pulled, coiled in on itself, and then when she could stand it no longer, ebbed into a dull ache. This was intolerable. No woman was capable of enduring such pain. Hadn't her father reminded her often enough of a woman's weakness?

"*You have a good mind, daughter," he said, "but don't think yourself the equal of a man. You're by nature a frail thing who must be guided.*"

"*Yes, Papa. I am aware.*"

"*See as you are, particularly if you marry this Giorgio fellow.*"

"*If?*" She smiled impishly. "*You mean you'll change your mind?*"

"*I've not made up my mind. I speak only of the hypothetical. Whatever man takes you for a wife must know he's the master.*"

"*Yes, Papa.*"

"*I won't have it said that my daughter doesn't recognize what's due first to me and then to her husband. You must obey him in all things. I suffer you to speak your mind here in my household, but it won't do outside.*"

She screamed as a knife plunged deep into her belly and twisted. The pain went on and on. Dimly, she felt a cool cloth upon her forehead and through glazed eyes saw Brida light more candles. She stared at the flames and prayed. The pain subsided and she panted with relief. The time *must* be growing near. Another pain, another scream. And again and then again and again. On and on into the night the pains took possession of her. She heard the bells for compline, matins, and prime, and still Brida shook her head and told her not to push. As light began to creep back into the room, Sofia became aware of a shift in how both Brida and Caterina attended her. Their tone was no longer cheerful, the expressions on their faces increasingly grim. Sofia suspected they were not telling her something, but she was past caring. All she longed for now was the release of death and the arms of the Madonna. Perhaps she would even see her father again. And her mother. Surely her mother had not suffered like this.

As she panted between the pains, she thought of Matteo's strong hands and soft mouth. Would he care that she was about to give birth to his son? Another pain, worse even than all that had come before, threatened to rip her apart. She screamed so long that her throat was laced with needles. Brida examined her again, and then Caterina came forward to help move Sofia from the bed to the birthing chair. She eased onto the wooden slats and leaned back. Sofia wanted more than anything in the world to push the child from her body, to release it into the world and deliver herself from such torment.

Brida shook her head. "No push. Not yet. Soon."

Sofia wailed with frustration and pain. She would die. The light was strengthening. The new day had come to send her into the arms of her Savior.

And then Caterina was standing behind her, bearing down on her shoulders.

"Push, sister! The child comes."

Another scream, so loud and long that Sofia knew for certain it would be her last. Caterina was shouting and Sofia felt her muscles stiffen to the task, but nothing happened. The pain just grew and grew and took her over.

There would be no child.

"Push!"

"No!" The wail tore from her throat. A giant fist dug into her stomach, crushing, squeezing, curling her insides into a tight spiral of agony. Oh God, if only she could die!

And then she felt a release so complete and so wonderful that she must have finally left the earth to join the blessed Virgin. She heard a shout of triumph from Brida and then, moments later, a sputtering, gurgling cry.

"A daughter!" Caterina cried. "God has blessed you with a beautiful daughter."

Sofia opened her eyes to look while Brida washed and wrapped the child carefully, then placed the bundle in her arms. A pair of very dark eyes opened and stared into her own. For a fleeting moment, Sofia saw Matteo. Then the child's eyes closed and the tiny mouth snuffled in sleep. One fist slipped from its swaddling and latched on to her finger. Sofia felt the entire room shining with the pure light of heaven.

And then her own eyes closed and the child was taken from her.

CHAPTER SIXTEEN

And if ever you make a slip . . . take a bit of the
crumb of some bread, and rub it over the paper,
and you will remove whatever you wish.
—Cennini, *Il Libro dell'Arte*, Chapter XII

Sofia felt the quickening in her breasts, the swollen tenderness. She called for Brida to bring the child. Brida and Caterina had both been shocked that Sofia had not immediately handed the child over to the solid young woman they had procured as a wet nurse. But with Giorgio thankfully still away from home, Sofia asserted herself. She wanted to keep the child as close to her as possible for as long as possible. She decided to name her Antonia, after her father, Antonio. Brida smiled as she placed little Antonia into Sofia's arms. "Good girl. Sleeps."

As Sofia guided the tiny mouth to her breast, Antonia's eyes fluttered open and looked up with solemn concentration. Sofia studied the smooth pink skin, the curled fingers, the chubby elbow. A delicate blending of white with just a touch of vermilion and a grounding of lightened *terre-verte* would be perfect for the rounded planes of the face. And the eyes would need highlighting with flecks of gold. Sofia closed her eyes as her baby suckled and remembered the *Maestà* she'd painted for Matteo's betrothed. She hoped Francesco had taken it back to Manzini to sell it to a patron who didn't want to wait for a new commission. Sofia bent forward and kissed the head of soft curls. If only she could paint again. She would produce a *Maestà* with a real baby—show Our Lady as a real mother who would have held her child with the same reverence Sofia felt for her own Antonia.

◦⌇◦

Sofia never could have imagined the depths of her love for little Antonia. Every day, the baby's cries teased her gently awake. She lifted her from the cradle and brought her into the bed with her, delighting in the tiny mouth closing over her breast, sighing with pleasure as the milk flowed. Sometimes she thought about the child's father and their long, hot afternoons twined together in sin and passion. Would he have loved their child as much as she did? She saw his eyes, warm with desire when he looked at her. She imagined him sitting on the edge of the bed, stroking the child's head and smiling. She should have accepted him. Matteo was not an unreasonable man. He would have relented in time. Surely a way could have been found for her to paint again.

And then she remembered the look that had twisted his handsome face that day in the tavern when he had denied knowing her. She gathered the child closer to her breast and kissed her silky head.

"Mistress?"

Sofia tightened her hold on Antonia. "What is it? She's not done."

But Brida was tugging at one corner of the cloth binding the baby's legs. "Please, mistress. The master." Brida pulled the baby from her breast and hurried from the room. At the same time, Sofia heard the heavy tread of boots on the stairwell.

"Wife! The babe is come? Where is he?"

Sofia had at least hoped he would have learned from Ruberto through Caterina that she had not produced a son. She'd even indulged herself by hoping Giorgio would be so angry he would refuse to see her—that he would leave her and Antonia in peace.

A vain hope, indeed.

She quickly covered her breasts and sat up, her hands folded in her lap, her back straight.

"Where is he?" Giorgio stamped into the room, bringing with him the smell of horse dung and the grime of long hours on the road. Sofia shuddered as he drew close to her, grateful now that Brida had taken Antonia. She did not want her child anywhere near this brute of a man who would care nothing for her.

"You've not been told," Sofia said flatly. She kept her hands firmly clasped to stop them trembling. She didn't really think even Giorgio would harm an innocent child, but she wasn't confident he might not harm her. Another man's son was one thing. But a daughter?

"Told what?" Giorgio asked absently as he looked around the bedchamber. He strode toward the fireplace. "Where have you put him? I don't see the cradle. Did it not arrive? I had one commissioned from the finest woodworker in San Gimignano. He promised to have it delivered in time. Did it not come? I don't understand. I've been told the babe was born weeks ago."

"Yes, my lord. The cradle was delivered as you ordered. It's very fine." She must speak now. The longer she waited with this talk of cradles and woodworkers, the worse it would get.

"It should be by the fire, should it not? I want my son kept warm."

"The cradle is well placed, my lord," she said. "Please don't trouble yourself." She cleared her throat. "My lord."

"Where is he? I want to see my son, not waste time talking with you. Where is he?"

"She, my lord."

Giorgio stopped his pacing so abruptly that Sofia almost laughed. He teetered forward on one mud-crusted boot and then fell back. He flung one arm out to steady himself but only succeeded in grazing his knuckles against the thick walnut of the bedpost. He cursed loudly.

"You have a daughter," she said quietly when the air went silent and he stood with his knuckles in his mouth, sucking while his eyes bulged. "I named her Antonia. After my father. Fra Angelo has been to see her already."

Giorgio still did not move. He continued to suck his knuckles and stare. Then, slowly, his eyes widened and his fist fell to his side. Sofia saw dirt glistening with his saliva.

"A daughter?"

"Yes, my lord. A fine, strong child. Caterina says she is sure to live."

"Caterina? That cursed mare who pops out sons to my cursed brother? How many is it now?"

"I believe Caterina has two sons and three daughters."

"Yes, and another to come any week now. Two sons! And you give me nothing."

"Antonia is not nothing!" She swung her legs to the floor and rose unsteadily to her feet.

"You defend yourself?"

"I am sorry that you didn't get the son you wanted, but I won't curse God for sending me my Antonia."

"*Your* Antonia? You dare make a claim?"

"I bore her, my lord. She's mine." Sofia breathed in and thrust her shoulders back, meaning to make herself look taller and succeeding only in pushing forward breasts swollen with milk. Too late she saw a gleam of lust in Giorgio's eyes. Surely he wouldn't dare? It was too soon—barely a month. She stepped back and felt the side of the bed.

"I won't have the bastard in my house."

"What? No, Giorgio! Husband! She's beautiful. You must see her!" Giorgio's solid form filled her vision. Hot breath stained her cheek. He reached for her with both hands and, before she found breath to scream, crushed her against his chest, then lifted her off her feet and forced her backward onto the bed.

"You'll not have her! Now keep still. I'll have a son from you yet."

He thrust one hand up under her shift and clawed her legs open. She was still raw and sore. "No, Giorgio! I'm not yet healed."

He clamped one hand over her mouth and held her down. Her stomach heaved. The weight of his chest, still encased in a plate of rough armor, crushed her tender breasts and sent waves of ragged agony through her that were soon eclipsed by the searing pain between her legs. She had no breath to scream. She shut her eyes tight and searched her mind for an image to give her comfort. The serene face of Martini's Madonna from his *Maestà* in the Palazzo Pubblico—she focused all her will upon the blessed Mother as she breathed in the stench of Giorgio and felt her insides burst into flame. The Madonna's eyes locked onto her own and held her. She heard her own voice inside her head begin to repeat the rosary.

Ave Maria, gratia plena, Dominus tecum.

As her flesh tore, Sofia imagined the blood that would stain the cover. Brida would say nothing. Sofia hated that her servant would see the depths of her humiliation.

Benedicta tu in mulieribus, et benedictus fructus ventris tui, Iesus.

Giorgio's grip on her mouth slackened as he neared his time. She could scream now, but what good would it do? She would alert the whole household. It was enough that Brida would know.

Sancta Maria, Mater Dei, ora pro nobis peccatoribus nunc, et in hora mortis nostrae.

Giorgio groaned aloud, shuddered, and then collapsed on top of her.

Amen.

She began again. *Ave Maria, gratia plena, Dominus tecum.* Slowly, he withdrew himself and rolled away from her. She closed her legs and gathered her shift, huddling into its soft folds. *Benedicta tu in mulieribus, et benedictus fructus ventris tui, Iesus.* She reached up, coiled a lank of short hair around her finger, and tugged just enough to feel her scalp burn. *Sancta Maria, Mater Dei, ora pro nobis peccatoribus nunc, et in hora mortis nostrae.*

The pain comforted her, told her she still lived. Dimly, she heard Giorgio leave the bedchamber. After his exertions, he would be shouting at the servants for food. She only hoped he would stop to eat before going in search of Antonia. *Amen.*

She stared up at the heavy beams bisecting the ceiling high above her head. Despair flooded her mind and grasped hold of her heart. Giorgio would abandon Antonia at a convent and she'd be lost to her forever. If she fought, she'd be locked again at the top of the tower.

"That line's not straight. Your building will fall down."

"It's not a real building, Papa."

"The people who fill your picture are also not real, but you give them sufficient arms and legs to look real."

"Yes, Papa."

"You must give the same thought to the structures that lend substance to your story. That balcony should look like it can be stood upon and that staircase should have steps that can be climbed. Go outside and look at the houses around you."

"But, Papa, it grows late and I want to finish this portion of the panel before we lose the light. You said yourself that the patron is anxious to receive it."

"I'd rather you gave him a panel we are proud to charge a good price for than to rush, daughter. Put down your brush and do as I ask. You must learn to look."

"I know how to look, Papa," Sofia muttered but not loud enough for her father to hear. She did not want to leave the cool workshop to go outside into the blazing afternoon. The glare of the sun against the sand-colored bricks would hurt her eyes and make her cross. Her father was always nagging her to look. Why couldn't he just leave her in peace?

Sofia forced herself to sit up. Every muscle ached in protest, but she pushed herself onto her elbows and lifted her knees. She paused for a few moments to let the fiery jolts of pain pound through her body and then slowly lifted her legs off the bed and set her feet firmly on the floor. When she stood up, a gush of blood slicked the inside of one thigh. She shuffled across the floor to the door leading to the interior room where Brida kept Antonia in her cradle. A soft gurgling coming from the cradle reassured her.

She still had time.

⁐

"Don't worry about Ruberto."

Sofia looked with amazement at her sister-in-law. Caterina's full lips were set in a line and her pale eyes flashed with a determination that Sofia had never seen before. Since the birth of Antonia, Sofia had new respect for Caterina. Five times had Caterina's body been ripped apart with the pains and she would soon experience a sixth. And yet she remained cheerful and generous.

"You're sure?" Sofia held Antonia close, heard her quiet breathing, felt the warmth of her tiny body as an extension of her own. How could she just hand her child over?

"Please, sister. I won't let our Antonia come to harm."

Already she referred to Antonia as her own. A lump rose in Sofia's throat. God asked too much. "Why would Ruberto agree?"

Caterina shook her head, smiling the quiet, secret smile of a woman who knew what it was to love and be loved. "Ruberto will do as I ask."

"Antonia is nothing to him."

"Ah, sister, that's not what Ruberto will think."

"I don't understand." Sofia tightened her hold on Antonia.

"I know you don't. But my Ruberto is not like his brother." Caterina put her hand to her mouth and blushed. "Forgive me. I promise I'll take care of Antonia and bring her up as my own. Ruberto will agree because I ask him to."

Caterina's quiet confidence in her husband made Sofia's eyes grow hot with tears. Why had Caterina been blessed with a man who loved her and even bowed to her judgment?

"He's a fool for that silly woman," Giorgio scoffed. "She crooks her finger and he comes running."

"Your brother is a good husband."

"He's good reason to be. His wife gives him sons."

She could *not* give Antonia away, even to Caterina. What if Ruberto changed his mind? What if he refused to keep his brother's bastard child? He'd every right. Sofia bent low over the warm bundle as her whole body convulsed with grief. God could not ask this of her. She would run away—take Antonia and beg to be taken into a convent. And with no dowry and no means to support herself once she'd taken the veil, she would be lucky to be given a job scouring the convent kitchens.

"Please, sister. You must give her to me now. Giorgio will return soon."

"Will I see her?"

"I don't know. But she'll be safe."

Sofia was hurtling into the pit of hell. She kissed the top of Antonia's head, now wet with her tears, and then with one swift movement passed the child into Caterina's waiting arms. She fixed her gaze upon the empty cradle at her feet, still dazed by the speed with which Caterina had convinced her to give up Antonia. It was a simple plan that depended completely on Caterina's assurance that she could bend the will of her husband. It didn't seem credible, yet anything was better than what Giorgio had threatened to do with the child.

"I'll send her to the country. Some peasant will take her for a price."

"No! How can you be so cruel? She's an innocent child."

"Cruel? You call me cruel? You who left me to suffer the scorn of all San Gimignano?" His cheeks quivered as spittle flew. "I've redeemed myself, thanks be to God—and no thanks to you."

"You'd keep her if she was a boy."

"Yes, but she's not. I'll make the arrangements. Your bastard will go to the country this very afternoon and may God damn her soul."

Sofia returned to her bedchamber and sat upon the bed to wait for Giorgio. The aching between her legs had eased. She would ask Brida to bathe her with warm water and sweet herbs. Darkness fell, but she didn't move or call for candles. Instead she eased back against the pillows and let her eyes close. Never again would she hold her child in her arms or look upon that perfect skin and imagine how to mix colors and then mold them into the planes and curves of that perfect face.

She didn't know what God wanted from her now and she no longer cared.

☙

"Don't give up hope, my son. She's strong. You'll soon be delivered of a son."

Sofia heard the voice of Fra Angelo just outside the door. She shuddered as she imagined him holding out his ring for Giorgio to kiss. And then another pain took hold—longer than the last and more urgent. The time was close. This child was coming more quickly than Antonia had, and for that she was grateful. She wanted the ordeal to be over so she could be left in peace.

Almost two years had passed between the birth of her Antonia and the day when Brida told Sofia she was finally with child again. The years had been filled with such black despair that Sofia often wondered how she survived them. She'd seen Antonia just once. Ruberto and Giorgio had been called back to Florence, so Caterina brought the child. But the visit had not been a success. Antonia was already walking—a fine, sturdy girl with a strong will that set her apart from Caterina's docile brood. Antonia didn't care to be fondled by the strange woman with the intense eyes. She squirmed out of Sofia's grasp and charged across the floor toward the fire, almost succeeding in pitching herself into the flames before Brida grabbed her. After that, such wails of rage filled the room that Sofia had no choice but to allow Caterina to take her daughter away.

Giorgio had kept surprisingly quiet when he found out that Caterina had taken Antonia into her husband's household. Perhaps he'd decided that keeping peace with his brother was preferable to causing a scandal. Whatever his reasons, Sofia was grateful. All that remained for her to do was submit to him every night and pray to the Holy Mother for patience.

Brida helped her from the bed and onto the birthing chair. Again the slats dug into her back. The air was cold on her bare skin when she opened her legs and bore down. The babe would be born into the end of a bitter winter. The frosts had started in November and continued without relief into March. Each morning the fields groaned under a thick crust of white that had delayed planting. Even the great Arno River in Florence had frozen solid.

"Push, mistress," Brida commanded, then pressed down upon Sofia's shoulders. A final pain ripped through her belly, and then Sofia felt the great release and moments later heard crying. Brida let out a whoop of joy. Sofia slumped forward in the chair, heedless of the ministrations of the other midwife fussing over the afterbirth, then pressing towels warmed against the fire between Sofia's legs. She must have produced a son. Why else would Brida make such a noise? But she couldn't even bring herself to raise her eyes to look.

"No, master!" Brida's shocked voice rang out above the crying. "You can't come in!"

But Giorgio was already inside the bedchamber, heedless of the other midwife's shriek of protest when he lunged toward the basin into which Brida was just lowering the squalling bundle of arms and legs.

"I must see him!" He squatted on his heels and stared with wonder at the child. He reached out one hand and gently touched one glistening shoulder as it rose from the water. "I have a son!" He looked up anxiously. "Why does he cry? Is he healthy?"

"The babe will live," said the midwife attending to Sofia. "Now leave the chamber. Your wife must have privacy."

"My wife?" Giorgio said it with such venom that even Sofia, in her stupor, noticed. She lifted her head and stared dully across the room at him. Her skin was as white as the bleached bones poking from the frozen carcasses littering the streets of the city.

Brida hastily arranged Sofia's skirts and, turning her back on Giorgio, pulled Sofia from the chair and helped her cross the room to the bed. "There now, you rest," she whispered. "I will bring the babe when he is washed. Be still now."

"The child can go to the wet nurse."

"But, mistress!"

"You have me settled now. Take out the child and my husband will follow." Sofia closed her eyes. She wanted more than anything to have the chamber to herself, to breathe without Giorgio looming over her, to think without the sound of the child wailing. Where was the joy she had known at Antonia's birth? All she felt this time was a terrible, aching loneliness. She wanted to love the new child. It was only right. He was innocent of the sins of his father. She was wicked and unnatural—a travesty of womanhood, a disgrace. Her mind drifted from the cold, damp room. She was tired—too tired. The years to come stretched before her with tedious predictability. Fra Angelo told her often enough that she needed to learn patience. Patience for what? She could be as patient as Fra Angelo demanded and still she would never again hold a brush.

Sofia heard Giorgio shouting in the street. "I have a son!"

"Yes, Giorgio, you have a son at last," she whispered. "And I have nothing."

CHAPTER SEVENTEEN

And do not apply any pink at all,
because a dead person has no color . . .
—Cennini, *Il Libro dell'Arte*

"Mama, that girl's staring at me and I don't like it."

Sofia's stomach tightened as she followed her son's pointing finger. Antonia stood across the piazza, her eyes like two black coals. Caterina had kept her promise so well that Matteo did not know the girl as his cousin. And Giorgio, also, had been content to keep the families apart. But if anyone other than Sofia's four-year-old son were to look closely, they couldn't fail to see how the eyes of the girl were the eyes of the woman. The resemblance was so obvious that Sofia wondered why people didn't stop to comment on it. But of course no one noticed. No one ever does notice the lives of others unless they affect their own lives, Sofia reflected.

She caught up Matteo's hand. "Don't stare."

"I'm not the one staring. *She* is." Matteo planted his two chubby legs and tried to pull his hand from his mother's grasp. "Tell her to stop."

Sofia tightened her grip and then, with more force than she intended, tugged at her son's arm. He stumbled forward, tripped over a pig that darted between them, and then landed hard on his backside. For a moment he sat in silence, his eyes wide with surprise. And then he opened his mouth and let forth a scream of rage and pain that filled the piazza and caused everyone to stop what they were doing and stare. Sofia looked around for Brida, but she had gone off to the market stalls. She should never have insisted on coming out with Brida. She should have stayed home and attended to the panel that she'd been working on for Messer Delgrasso. Spring was upon them already and she had much to do. But the soft air of the first warm day in March after another cold winter had been too much for Sofia to resist. When Brida prepared to take Matteo with her to the market in the Piazza della Cisterna, Sofia, on an impulse, had decided to accompany them. Giorgio had gone away again, this time to Pisa to sell his crocus bulbs, and she was determined to enjoy the limited extra freedom his absence gave her. Perhaps she'd even find an opportunity to slip over to Messer Delgrasso's workshop and replenish her supplies.

In the four years since Matteo's birth, Sofia's life had improved more than she could have dreamed. She and Giorgio still maintained a loathing distance, and thankfully Giorgio rarely bothered to come to her bed now. He also no longer threatened to lock her up or insist she spend all her days indoors. She had been quick to take advantage of his indifference. Each time he left the city to assist with the tedious negotiations that would ensure his standing with the Florentines who sought to limit the power of San Gimignano's increasingly fractious municipal government, Sofia made her way to her father's old workshop. She had long forgiven Messer Delgrasso for telling Giorgio that she was in Siena. He was not clever enough to have done it out of malice, and Sofia was more interested in painting again than indulging a personal *vendetta*. In the years since Barducci's death, Messer Delgrasso had built a respectable business painting the coats of arms of San Gimignano's *contrade* on shields and banners. Fortunately, Messer Delgrasso recognized the profits to be made by renewing relations with the skilled daughter of his former master. *He* could not manage panels, but she could, and there was a market waiting to be exploited. She'd approached Delgrasso one hot summer afternoon about two years after the birth of Matteo.

"Your husband won't find out?" *Delgrasso stroked his bare chin.*

"I'll make sure of it. Have your assistants prepare the panels and I'll fill them with the subjects your patrons request."

"Can you do buildings?"

"Yes, and mountains and trees and beasts. Whatever is needed for the story."

"What of payment?"

"I ask only a portion of what you charge your patron."

"What portion?"

"One-half."

Delgrasso clutched at his chest and cast his eyes heavenward. Sofia watched the performance impassively while inwardly her heart beat faster. This charade about the money was tiresome but necessary.

"With the paintings that I can do for you, you will attract more and better commissions."

"Yes, but if I'm found to be selling work done by a woman, I'll be ruined."

She could not dispute that, so she remained silent. What she was proposing was dangerous, but she would be careful. Brida would help her and say nothing.

"One-quarter?"

Sofia pretended to look affronted, then let several seconds elapse before nodding curtly. "Agreed."

In the two years since making the agreement with Delgrasso, Sofia had completed just two panels. The work went slowly because Giorgio had been called only three times to Florence, and then for only a handful of weeks each time. But with Brida's help, Sofia mounted the ladders to the top of the tower and spent many long afternoons with her head bent low over her work and her heart soaring as she again mixed colors and felt the paint flow from her brushes. To her surprise, Sofia even began to grow fond of Messer Delgrasso. He lavished praise upon her work and likened it to the work of Martini, even Giotto. When no one was nearby, he declared her a finer painter even than her father. He just wasn't too interested in paying for the honor of having her hand complete the panels.

"Mama!" Sofia snapped her attention back to her son, who still sat on the ground, his face almost purple from crying. Sighing, Sofia patted his hand in a vain attempt to soothe him. He dripped with filth, which meant no visit to Messer Delgrasso's workshop that day.

"Come, Matteo. Dry your tears. It was just a little fall. We'll return home."

That didn't suit Matteo at all. He gathered his breath for another assault on the ears of the local populace, but before he got out more than a strangled squawk, Sofia picked him up bodily and started back across the piazza to the street leading to the Porta San Giovanni. She passed the solemn girl who stood apart from her brothers and sisters and continued to stare—first at Sofia and then at the struggling child in her arms. Antonia was a good head taller than Caterina's daughter Fillipa, born just a few months after her. Sofia thought of Salvini's strong legs and wide-spaced brow, his prominent nose that, in profile, made him look haughty and unapproachable. His daughter had the same look, but she also had Sofia's eyes and the intensity of her stare. Sofia knew she was foolish to indulge such thoughts, but what joy she could have had teaching the child to paint. Would she have the skill of her mother and her grandfather?

It was an idle thought, unworthy of her.

The girl's eyes flickered to a point over Sofia's right shoulder, then widened. At the same time, Sofia saw people all around the piazza drop what they were doing and rush forward.

"Hush, boy," she said to Matteo. "Something's happened."

In the middle of the square, a woman appeared with her arms raised half over her head. Her hair had come loose and hung in heavy black hanks all over her head, half obscuring her face. Her gown was ripped from one arm. Even from where Sofia stood, some two dozen paces away, she could see a large patch of blackened skin extending from the woman's bare shoulder to under her arm. At the armpit grew a lump the size of a duck's egg. It had split open and was oozing thick yellow pus. With a voice raspy with disease, she pleaded with the crowd for help.

Someone over by the large well in the center of the piazza screamed.

"What is it, Mama?" Matteo's voice sounded frightened as more people started shouting until soon the entire piazza heaved with panic. A young man rushed at the woman, a splintered length of wood held between his two hands. He shouted at her to go back to her home. Several men joined him, and together they slowly pushed the woman out of the piazza and down a side street.

"They'll force her back into her home and board it up," one man near Sofia said.

"Quite right too," said another voice nearby, an older, severe-looking woman. "The contagion must be contained."

"What of her children? I know her. She has three."

"It's God's will," someone else said. "A punishment for our sins."

Sofia moved quickly in the opposite direction. She didn't recognize the woman, but she saw by the clothes she wore that she was the wife of a prosperous merchant, much like herself. The woman was not the first victim of the pestilence in San Gimignano, but so far as Sofia knew, she was the first to show herself so brazenly in public. Sofia had heard whisperings of other families that had been stricken. The day before she saw three funeral processions pass by her door.

"Mama! You're hurting me!"

Sofia loosened her grip on Matteo but did not let him down to walk on his own. A choking fear gripped her throat. For weeks now they had heard news of the pestilence claiming hundreds of lives in Pisa. God help her, she had even hoped it might afflict Giorgio before he could return to San Gimignano. And now God was punishing her. She must get Matteo safely home and then see to her household. Had they sufficient food? What of wood for the fire? It was still only March and they must be kept warm. She clutched Matteo closer to her breast and quickened her pace. Her son had not filled the hole in her heart that Antonia had left. He was too much like his father—in looks and in temperament. But he was hers and she would protect him. She kissed his forehead and he looked up at her, his eyes wide with surprise.

"Mama! What's wrong?"

Her heart ached at the look on his face. She had not cared for him as a mother should, and here was her reward. He'd found more love from Brida than he had from her. "Nothing's wrong, *caro*. Hold tight to Mama. We'll be home soon."

A man came out of a nearby house and staggered into her path. His clothes were ripped and the stench that came from his burst bubocs made her want to retch. He looked at her with sunken, frantic eyes. "Madonna! My wife. She's dead. Please. Help!"

Sofia covered Matteo's eyes with her hand as, God forgive her, she sidestepped the man and hurried to her own front door. She heard him moaning behind her. But even if she stopped, what help could she give? No, she had no choice but to leave the man in the street, wailing now as his own sickness brought him closer to death. His fate was in God's hands.

Giorgio's man Niccolò met Sofia in the passageway. She stared at him with surprise. He should be in Pisa with his master, not blocking her way. His eyes were purple hollows, his customary sneer marred by a sore on his lip.

"Where's the master?"

Listlessly, Niccolò stood aside. She caught a whiff of contagion.

"Papa!"

Sofia felt her heart growing too big for her chest. Surely she would faint. She took a deep breath through clenched teeth and followed Matteo into the workroom, jumping forward just in time to catch him.

"No, Matteo! Leave Papa."

Giorgio stared up at her from a litter on the floor. His lips were cracked and red, stretched back over his teeth so he looked already like the skull he would soon become. "Let the boy see his father."

"He will be infected."

Giorgio still had strength to struggle to his elbows. Sofia saw the buboes beneath his arms. They had not yet burst, but she doubted it would be long before they did.

"Come closer, boy."

"No!" Sofia cried, but Matteo squirmed from her grasp and squatted next to Giorgio. He reached out one plump hand to touch his forehead.

"Papa?"

Giorgio stared into his son's young face and began to cry. The tears made two troughs through the grime on his face. Some landed on his cracked lips and he winced. For the first time in many years, Sofia felt a stirring of pity. In a voice she barely recognized as her own, she called for towels and water to bathe the master's sores, then gently lifted Matteo away and carried him into the passageway. "Go to the kitchen. Brida will find you something to eat," she whispered. "Papa must rest now."

Sofia directed Niccolò and another of the manservants to carry Giorgio upstairs to bed. "Don't speak of this outside the house," she warned. "With God's help, he will be well again. No one needs to know." She didn't believe her own words and she wasn't sure the servants did either. Niccolò scowled and the other servant looked at her rebelliously. She lifted her chin and stared at them, and after a few seconds' pause, they hoisted Giorgio to their shoulders and carried him up the stairs. She considered calling for the physician and then decided against it. The sight of him coming to the house would alert the neighbors. The pestilence was still new to San Gimignano, but as she had seen in the piazza, the people of the city were already terrified. They would know Giorgio had just arrived from Pisa. She thought of the mob that had chased the woman from the piazza to her home. They would nail boards across her front door, condemning everyone inside to death. If the pestilence did not take them, starvation would.

Sofia would not let that happen to her household. She would bathe Giorgio's wounds and put cool cloths upon his head and burn sweet-smelling herbs. Her husband of twelve years and the man she loathed above all men could not die and leave her and Matteo alone and unprotected.

The pounding on the door woke Sofia from a deep sleep. She had been dreaming she was back in Siena and in Salvini's arms. For a moment, she let herself drift on a wave of memory—Salvini's hand stroking her breast, his lips fixed to her own, the way he laughed gently when she talked to him of painting. She sat up quickly, angry with herself for letting Matteo Salvini back into her dreams. He had no business there. For all she knew, he was dead already. The news was that the pestilence had already been raging for a full month in Siena.

The pounding increased. Where were the servants? Niccolò should have been at the door long since. But the pounding did not stop, so finally Sofia eased herself up from the straw pallet Brida had made for her on the floor next to the bed. The room was thick with the scent of burning herbs, but nothing could hide the stench that rose from the bed.

"Brida!" Her voice cracked. She stood in the middle of the room and listened. The pounding continued. She pulled on a heavy dressing gown and opened the door into the corridor that led along the outside loggia to the stairwell. She peered over the edge to the street below but saw only shadows in the early morning gloom. Whoever was at the door was alone. No mob had come to barricade her door. But who was making such a noise—and where in God's name were the servants?

Sofia ran lightly down the stairs in her bare feet and into the workroom. She saw no sign of Niccolò or any other member of her household. It wasn't like Brida to sleep through such a racket. When finally she pulled open the front door, a figure almost completely obscured by a black cloak pushed past her.

"Caterina?" Sofia closed the door and rushed over to catch her sister-in-law's arm as she swayed. "What is it?"

"Sister!" Caterina threw off her hood, clasped Sofia in her arms, and began to sob loudly. "Oh sister!"

Sofia patted Caterina's broad back and waited while the sobs grew to wails and then, after many minutes, choked into silence.

"Is Ruberto . . . ?"

Caterina nodded. "And Giorgio?"

Sofia shook her head. "I don't know. Niccolò brought him back last night and I tended to him, but . . ." She paused, struggling for composure. "I've just awakened and none of the servants are here." She looked around the empty passageway. "I think I have been left alone to fend for myself."

"What of Brida?"

"She must be gone. What about your servants?"

"Ruberto's body didn't enter the house. Marcello took him straight to the church. Oh sister, so many were there before him. Fra Angelo's half out of his mind."

"The children?" Sofia asked the question casually, as any woman would of another woman.

"They seem well, although one has a slight headache and complains of chills. I think it's just an ague."

"Which one?"

Even in her grief, Caterina heard the panic in Sofia's voice. She shook her head. "Antonia continues well, sister. I speak of my Margherita."

"God will be with her. Now, we must decide what to do."

"Do? What do you mean?"

"Your Ruberto is gone," Sofia said matter-of-factly, ignoring the fresh stream of tears from Caterina. "I don't know if Giorgio still lives. I'll go check on him now. If he recovers, I'll see to it that he takes care of you and your children."

"And if he doesn't?"

"God cannot be so cruel."

Sofia turned, mounted the staircase to the loggia, then crossed to the bedchamber. The stench was doubly powerful after her respite in the workroom. Giorgio had vomited onto the floor—a pool of black blood was seeping into the wooden floorboards, staining them forever. She held her arm over her nose as she approached the bed. Giorgio was encased in a miasma so thick, so revolting, that Sofia needed every ounce of courage not to turn and flee.

"Giorgio? Husband?"

A low groan cut the thick air. Sofia felt her heart pounding with relief. He still lived. She stretched out her hand to touch his burning forehead, then drew it back in horror. An enormous bubo under his arm had burst in the night, sending a stream of blood striped with green pus across the sheets. Some of the mess had dripped upon the floor. Her stomach heaved. Even Giorgio did not deserve such an end.

"Sofia." The whisper was so low, so racked with pain that at first Sofia was not sure she heard it. He was staring up at her—his eyes rimmed with yellow pus, the whites streaked with livid bands of red. "Sofia," he said again, his voice slightly stronger. Then a spasm ripped through his body and he groaned. One of the sores at his groin burst open, soiling the gown he wore beneath his heavy traveling cloak. Sofia had not been able to strip him the night before and had left him to sleep in the dirt- and blood-soaked clothes he had worn from Pisa.

"What is it, husband?" She could not remember the last time she had used such a gentle tone with Giorgio. When they spoke at all, it was in clipped phrases that didn't even pretend affection. As she looked at him now, she could not feel affection, but she did feel pity.

"I am sorry for it," he whispered. Then another spasm took him and it was many minutes before he ceased his groaning and thrashing. When finally he was quiet again, he was beyond any attempt at talking or even listening. Sorry for what? The pestilence? The coldness of their lives together? His own death?

She dampened a cloth and placed it carefully over his forehead. The coolness seemed to soothe him. He moaned and closed his eyes. Sofia waited and watched. She could perhaps leave him now and go find Fra Angelo. Even Giorgio did not deserve to die unconfessed. She heard the rustle of a gown behind her. Caterina stood at the entrance to the bedchamber.

Another groan came from the bed—weaker than before but still so full of pain that Sofia shivered. She must get to the Duomo.

"Sister! Help me into my gown and then stay with Giorgio and Matteo until I return."

"I can't!"

"What is it you cannot do, Caterina? Help me dress or stay with your nephew who has done you no harm and needs your help? I promise to be quick."

Caterina glanced fearfully at the bed. "I must return to my children."

"Your children can wait a little longer. You still have servants to attend them." Sofia opened the large chest under the window and began rummaging through it. She stripped off her dressing gown, slipped a black gown over her head, and turned to let Caterina secure it around her waist with a silk tie. Her hair hung loose but without Brida, she had no way to dress it. With clumsy fingers, she tried making a thick braid but succeeded only in filling her hands with a tangled mass of black curls.

"Put on your cloak and draw the hood up," Caterina said. "I don't think you'll be noticed."

"You'll stay?"

Caterina nodded, her face averted from the mound of flesh on the bed, her sleeve covering her nose. "With Matteo."

Outside, the city was coming to life. As Sofia hurried up the street toward the Piazza della Cisterna and from there into the Piazza del Duomo, she could almost think it was a normal spring day. She smelled bread baking and several merchants were already opening their shops. And then she heard a wail coming from one of the houses just ahead. Two men emerged into the street carrying what looked like a black sack between them. A woman followed.

"My son! My child! Where are you taking him?"

Neither man replied as they turned in the direction of the Porta San Giovanni. People in the street quickly backed against the houses as the men passed. Sofia heard mutterings about what to do with the woman. Someone stepped forward and caught the woman by the arm, then dragged her back into the house. Another man called for help. Within minutes three large men, muscles bulging as they wielded their hammers, were nailing thick planks across the front door. The woman's screams echoed down the street. Merchants who just minutes before had been preparing for another day of commerce began packing up their wares and moving back inside. Fear contorted the face of every man and woman hurrying along the street, some already with bundles upon their backs, fleeing the city for the cleaner air of the country. Sofia was just a few paces from the Piazza della Cisterna. The morning sun blazed off the tops of towers that pierced a clear blue sky. She stopped, looked up, made her decision. Salvation was with God and God had forsaken the city. Abruptly, she turned on her heel and pushed her way through the crowds back to her home.

Caterina was just leading Matteo out the door. She looked up at Sofia and shook her head. "I'll send help," she said and then, without waiting for an answer, stepped into the street, slamming the door behind her. It cut off the clamor of the street and left Sofia in total silence and almost complete darkness.

She ran up the stairs. At the last moments before his death, Giorgio had rolled off the bed and smashed the back of his head against a corner of the bed frame. His eyes remained open and staring. In the dim light Sofia fancied they followed her as she set to work gathering what she needed for her flight into the country. She had no idea how she would escape alone, but she knew she must get herself and Matteo out of the city before the pestilence claimed them.

She pulled down the window covering to let in fresh air and light and then opened the chest at the end of the bed and extracted a casket containing her brushes, the lumps of pigment she mixed into colors, and the real prize: two panels already smooth and white with gessoes, ready for her brush. The deaths couldn't go on for much longer. When the pace slowed, she could return to her work.

With both Giorgio and Ruberto dead, she would need the meager sums Messer Delgrasso paid her.

Another long wail of despair reached Sofia's ears through the open window. She looked over at Giorgio's body one last time and tried to summon back the pity she had felt earlier. But all she felt was a deep, burning rage for their years together and an even deeper rage that he was leaving her alone at such a time. She wondered if she should move the body. It wasn't right to leave it in the bedchamber to rot. When the danger passed, she would be bringing Matteo back to his home. Sofia clutched her bundle of clothes and the casket to her breast. She didn't have the strength to move Giorgio to the ground floor and out into the street. And what if she was caught? Barricaded in her house? Left to starve?

Sofia bent down, untied Giorgio's purse—still gratifyingly heavy with coins—then rose, turned her back on her dead husband, and ran down the stairs to the street. She would fetch Marcello from Caterina's house. He would know what to do. As she hurried up the Via San Giovanni, she passed a cart filled with what looked like a heap of brown logs. A bare foot stuck out at an odd angle, the skin black and peeling. She looked away and quickened her pace. By the time she reached the Piazza della Cisterna, she was gasping for breath. She crossed it into the Piazza del Duomo and from there entered the Via San Matteo and the house lately owned by Messer Ruberto Carelli.

Paulina opened the door.

"Dear God. Paulina!"

"The mistress is with the children," Paulina said with a limp gesture in the direction of the stairs. "She'll be glad of your company."

"But you are ill!" Paulina barely had the strength to nod. Her nose dripped, and as Sofia moved forward into the house, she smelled the same peculiar, richly putrid odor she had left behind with Giorgio. Sofia put her arm around Paulina's thin shoulders. "You should rest. Is Marcello near? I can fetch him for you."

A fit of coughing overtook Paulina. Sofia held her tightly until the spasms subsided, then led her to a bench and coaxed her to sit down.

"I can't," Paulina gasped. "The mistress needs me to help with the children."

"Hush. I'll find her myself and then I'll send Marcello to you. You should be in bed."

"You are kind, mistress," Paulina said as she leaned her head back against the rough stone wall. Her eyes closed and the harsh lines of pain etched into her face relaxed. Sofia held her hand against Paulina's burning forehead and whispered a prayer. How could God take Paulina, who had never harmed anyone in her life?

Sofia found Caterina leaning over her seventh and youngest child—a boy not yet two years old named Bartolomeo. The child was sobbing with pain. On the bed next to him slept nine-year-old Paolo and next to him was Caterina's eldest, a sturdy boy of thirteen named Ruberto after his father. On another, smaller bed close to the floor, six-year-old Fillipa—the child born not long after her own Antonia—tossed fitfully next to her three sisters, seven-year-old Margherita, eleven-year-old Isabetta, and Paolo's twin sister, Appolonia. Sofia dropped to her knees next to Fillipa and placed a hand on her forehead. Like Paulina, the child was burning up.

Sofia looked around at the crying children and felt a chill go through her. Where was Matteo? And Antonia? Surely they had not been taken so quickly. People infected with the pestilence generally died within three days. Just hours earlier, Caterina had told her that Antonia was fine—that only Margherita had a headache. And now all seven of Caterina's children were stretched out upon their beds and her own two children were gone.

Caterina knelt next to Sofia and soothed Fillipa with a light touch and a few murmured words. "Matteo remains well, sister. He's in the kitchen. But my babies." Her voice choked. "What have I done to make God so angry with me? They're just innocent children, and see how they suffer."

"And Antonia?"

"What?" Caterina looked around vaguely. "I don't know where she's taken herself off to. Perhaps the kitchen or up to the tower. She knows it's forbidden, but Antonia is willful. She won't be led."

The relief that flooded through Sofia was so profound that she needed to grasp on to the side of the fireplace for support as she rose. "I'll go look for them. They will be frightened."

Caterina waved her hand. "As you wish, but as soon as you've found them, come back and pray with me."

Sofia escaped the oppressively hot room with its roaring fire and the ripe smell of sickness. A piercing cry from one of the children—she thought it might be Margherita—followed her into the corridor.

"Does God hear us when we pray, Papa?"

"That's what they tell us."

"They?"

"Our holy men, in the Church."

"Yes, Papa, but what do you believe?"

Maestro Barducci laughed at the earnest child who sat next to him and watched while he gently placed layers of gold leaf to create a halo for Our Lady. "I believe what I'm told, as you should. Now watch carefully."

Surrounded by the stink of dying bodies and a fear so thick as to be almost visible, Sofia desperately hoped the father of her childhood had been telling the truth.

"Matteo!" she called. She mounted another set of stairs to the kitchen. Ruberto had built his kitchen in the new fashion—at the top of the house. From there, a low door led to the tower. The thought occurred to her that, with both Ruberto and Giorgio gone, all the Carelli holdings, which included the homes and towers of both brothers and some land in the country, now belonged to her Matteo. She would need to visit the notary very soon.

Paulina stood in the middle of the kitchen, her arms full of fresh white towels, still warm from their airing in front of the fire. The flesh on her sunken cheeks looked gray and a steady stream of mucus ran from her nose. She had long since given up wiping it away.

"Have you seen my son?"

"No, mistress. Try the warehouse. He may have decided to explore."

Sofia didn't say that Matteo was unlikely to do anything so adventurous as explore. He was a timid child who rarely strayed from Brida's side. Sofia left the kitchen and walked back down the stairs to the loggia overlooking the street. She finally found Matteo huddled against the wall, his feet pulled up under him. He was sobbing.

"Matteo! Mama has been looking everywhere for you. I need you to stay with the other children. They are your cousins and will be kind to you."

Matteo raised his tearstained face. The black spot upon one cheek, red-rimmed eyes, and runny nose told her all she needed to know. She stumbled backward and felt the stone rim of the balcony dig into the small of her back. Overhead, a clear blue sky arched above her with all the purity and promise of a spring day. She should have been a mother to her son instead of plotting to steal time to work on Delgrasso's panels. All the love she had suppressed for the child spilled forth. She fell to her knees and gathered him into her arms. His skin felt like melting wax. She almost drew her hand back from his flesh, then forced herself to hold him, to caress him, to form her voice into the murmuring words of comfort she'd heard Caterina lavish on her own children. His head lolled back and he looked up at her, his eyes wide with fear.

"Why do I feel like this?"

"Hush now. You'll be well soon. Let Mama hold you." Sofia felt her heart break—a clean, sharp severing. She deserved no better, but perhaps if God spared her son, she would be more of a mother to him. Death had taken her own mother when she was just a few years older than Matteo. With almost no memory of her mother's caresses, she had known only the stern expectations of her father—expectations Sofia had tried without success to impose upon Matteo. But he cared nothing for her words. He wanted only her arms around him at night.

Only now, as she clasped his burning body to her breast, did she finally understand. She had attributed her lack of feeling for Matteo to the man who had fathered him, but the truth was she didn't know how to love him like a mother should. She would make amends. Now, before it was too late. She would gather up her son and escape from the city. With the money in Giorgio's purse, she could buy provisions and find a place in the country to hide. She would pray for patience and nurse her Matteo back to health. It had to be possible.

And then she remembered Antonia.

Sofia tried picking up Matteo, but he was a heavy child—as solid as one of the stone columns holding up the loggia. Vile-smelling mucus streamed around and over his cracked lips. She felt her knees give way.

"Shall I take him?"

For just a moment, Sofia was sure her father had returned. Or perhaps she, too, had the sickness and had joined him. A hand touched her shoulder. If only she could sink back into his arms and let him carry her off. And then she shook herself out of such foolishness and turned to face Marcello. As he gently took the child from her arms, Sofia's hand brushed a swelling under Matteo's left arm. It was about the size of an egg, but hard—like a lump of marble.

"He is infected," she whispered.

"I'll take him to join his cousins."

"And Paulina? I told her I'd find you. She has the sickness, I think."

Marcello nodded miserably. "I've been with her. She's lying down now, but . . ." His voice broke.

Sofia reached her arms around Marcello, encircling her son in his arms. "I'm sorry, Marcello." They stood together—a family that was not a family—for several minutes until finally Sofia stepped away. "I'll be back as soon as I can." She turned in the opposite direction, her whole being on fire to find Antonia. Ruberto's house was not so large as her own, and his tower was one of San Gimignano's shortest—rising just two levels above the roof of his house. Antonia could not have gone far. She passed through the kitchen, where only one servant was still up and working, then pushed through a small door that she knew must lead to the towers.

"Antonia!" She called up the ladder through the open trapdoor to an expanse of stale, dusty air. A slight rustling told her something was up there, but when she placed one foot on the first rung of the ladder, she heard a squeak and saw a blur of black fur shoot past the opening.

"You're Matteo's mother."

Sofia stepped down from the ladder so quickly that she felt the wooden floorboards shudder beneath her weight. In the gloom, she had failed to notice the small body wedged between two barrels in one corner of the square room. "Yes. And you are Antonia. You shouldn't be here. Your mother is worried."

"My mother is busy with the others," came the indifferent reply. "She will not miss me."

"She's sent me to find you."

Antonia stepped into the middle of the room and stood an arm's length from Sofia. She looked up at her, squinting slightly in the dim light from the open door. "I don't think so."

Sofia resisted the impulse to bend to the child's level. Somehow she knew that this child would see it as weakness. Antonia was such a strange mixture of Salvini's openness and an aloofness she recognized as her own that Sofia felt quite at a loss.

"I think you're afraid," Antonia said.

"Of course I'm afraid."

The child clearly had not expected Sofia to agree so readily. Her large black eyes stared defiantly up at Sofia for a few more seconds, then filled with tears that spilled across her pink cheeks. Sofia wanted to scoop her up in her arms and hold her, lavishing all the affection she never had for Matteo on a child she barely knew.

"They say my father's dead," Antonia said.

"Yes. I'm sorry." Sofia wondered if indeed the child's father was dead. Or was Salvini at that moment in his rich palazzo with his wife and children, awaiting God's judgment? Antonia continued to stare up at her, but the tears had stopped and her expression was more quizzical than sad. Sofia held out her hand. "Come. We must return to the kitchen." The child allowed her hand to be taken and together they ducked through the door.

The kitchen servant plucked at Sofia's sleeve. "Mistress, what will happen to us? Will we all die?"

"Only God knows that." Her words were no comfort to the poor girl, who was probably no more than eleven, just five years older than her Antonia. Sofia led Antonia over to the spindle and loom by the window. A linen shirt intended for little Bartolomeo needed hemming. "Do you know how to use a needle?"

Without replying, Antonia picked up a needle and carefully threaded it by the light of the window. She then took up the shirt and set to work. As Sofia descended the staircase that led from the kitchen to the bedchambers on the second floor, she wondered if Antonia had any idea that the owner of the shirt would never wear it.

The moans of the children and Caterina's voice raised in prayer filled the passageway. Sofia lifted her sleeve to her nose and entered the room. All of Caterina's children and her own Matteo were lying upon thin mattresses on the floor. She doubted any of them would live to see the next day. She should be like Caterina—bowed with grief and calling on Our Lady for mercy. Sofia forced her legs to move forward into the room, to sink to the floor beside her son, to place her smooth hand upon his forehead, and to curve her lips into a smile. "Hush, boy," she whispered. "Try to sleep and God will make you well."

Matteo's eyes clouded over. He stared up into her face, but she knew he couldn't see her, that he would never see her again.

"Brida," he croaked. "I want Brida."

Sofia knew she deserved no better, but something thick and putrid twisted within her. Brida—who at the first sign of disease left the family she served for seven years. Had Brida seen the great pestilence as her one opportunity to escape San Gimignano and find her way back to her own country and her own children? The thought gave Sofia some comfort. Perhaps she was not the only woman in San Gimignano who sought freedom in the midst of so much death.

And surely God did not mean to kill *all* His children.

Matteo's eyes closed and he seemed to be sleeping. Sofia leaned over and kissed his burning forehead. She remembered the numbness she had felt at her father's death and prayed she'd feel it again.

This sharp agony—like a thousand spear points—was a pain without end. She dared not go, yet if she stayed she might miss her only chance of getting Antonia to safety. Caterina was kneeling on the floor in one corner clutching her rosary beads, her face streaked with tears. Her murmured prayers cast a soothing pall over the room. All of the children had stopped crying and several had fallen asleep. The rosemary and lavender sprinkled over the embers of the fire could not mask the appalling stench of sickness. The very discharges from the children's noses and mouths and open sores smelled of all the foulness of the earth. Sofia stood up and backed toward the door.

"Sofia."

Caterina crossed the room to stand in front of Sofia. Her hands hung limply at her sides. Her face—usually so plump and cheerful—was gray with despair. "You must take Antonia. Now, before the contagion spreads."

"What of the others?" Sofia reached out and took one of Caterina's hands between her own. "I can't leave Matteo—or you."

"You must." Caterina's voice was flat, expressionless—the voice of a woman who was about to lose everything.

"What about you?"

"I must stay with them." She gestured vaguely to the room full of dying children. "But you can still save Antonia. Take her, Sofia. She is yours. Marcello and Paulina can go with you."

"Paulina has the sickness."

Caterina bowed her head. "Poor Marcello," she whispered. Then she looked up, her eyes wide with grief. "I loved your Antonia like she was my own." She withdrew her hand from Sofia's grasp and looked straight into her eyes. "She is very like you."

"Thank you, Caterina," she said simply. "God bless you."

Caterina nodded and turned to kneel by one of the children who had woken up and was whimpering. She soothed the child with a cool hand to his forehead, then looked back at Sofia, who still stood at the door. "Go from this cursed place and take your daughter and your brother with you." A small smile played across Caterina's face in response to Sofia's gasp. "You may think me stupid, sister, but I am not blind."

Caterina turned away and with her broad back dismissed Sofia from her home and from what was left of her life. Sofia took one last look at her son—asleep or dead, she could not tell—then asked for God's forgiveness as she closed the door and went in search of Antonia.

CHAPTER EIGHTEEN

The most perfect steersman that you can have,
and the best helm, lie in the triumphal gateway
of copying from nature.
—Cennini, *Il Libro dell'Arte*, Chapter XXVIII

Outside the Porta San Matteo on the northwest side of San Gimignano, the view of fields and forests spreading to the horizon was of such unsurpassed loveliness that Sofia could not believe it could exist alongside the despair that bled from every house they had passed on their way out of the city. San Gimignano was dying, and the earth was coming alive after a long winter. She grasped Antonia's hand more firmly and followed Marcello down a steep path that veered away from the main road. They passed a few mean-looking huts. No smoke rose from the chimneys and only a few half-starved sows wandered the barren yards looking for food scraps.

"Where are the people?" Antonia asked. It was the first thing she'd said since leaving the city.

"I think they may be dead. Come, we have a good distance yet to walk."

Antonia wrenched her hand free and, before Sofia caught her, ran into one of the huts.

"Antonia!" Sofia started forward but found her way blocked by Marcello.

"Wait. She comes back."

Antonia emerged from the hut holding a filthy bundle. Her eyes were wide with the horror of what she'd seen inside the hut, but her mouth was set in a thin, determined line.

"Put that down, Antonia! You'll be infected."

Antonia shook her head. "I can't. It still lives."

"What?"

A faint mewling sound came from the bundle. Antonia shushed it and gently rocked it in her arms. She looked up at Sofia. "I promise to care for it. Mama often let me help with Bartolomeo. I know what to do." She tightened her grip on the bundle. "You have to let me." Defiance shone from her eyes.

"*This isn't work for children.*"

"*You let the son of Messer Benozzi come to the studio every day. I've seen him. He helps crush the colors.*"

"*Pigments, cara mia.*"

"*He's just a few years older than I am.*" Sofia glared up her father. "*And he's stupid. He didn't know the name of the city where Our Lord was born.*"

"*And you do?*"

"*Of course! If I tell you, will you teach me to paint?*"

"*I already know where Our Lord was born.*"

"*Oh!*" Sofia's face fell. She had been so sure her father would relent when she proved how smart she was. Even at eight years old, she knew her father admired men of great mind, as he called them. He often told her stories of meeting the poet Dante Alighieri when he came to San Gimignano many years before.

"*Now there was a man with God's grace upon him. He wrote poetry like an angel.*"

"*Papa! Can you say such things?*"

"I can say what I wish in my own home, cara mia. Now be off with you. Emilia has sewing for you."

"I hate sewing!"

"We're wasting time," Marcello said. "The child cannot be left and we must get on before the sun sets." Without waiting for Sofia to say anything, he lifted Antonia and the child into his arms and continued down the path.

Marcello moved so quickly that Sofia had to run to keep up, the bundle she'd tied around her shoulders bouncing painfully against her back, her heavy skirts a constant hazard. The bundle held food from Caterina's kitchen, a change of linen, a spare gown for herself and one for Antonia, and her precious casket containing the two prepared panels, some brushes, a few nuggets of pigment, and Giorgio's purse. Marcello, his voice cracking with grief when he rose from the side of his dead wife, had told her he knew where to take them. It was a place outside the city walls but still quite close. The fine spring day began to fade and the shadows descended, a nipping cold reminding her that the season was not yet far advanced. They could not sleep outside. As they walked, the number of huts dwindled to none. The only human habitation Sofia saw in front of her was a squat stone tower barely as high as the one adjoining her house in San Gimignano. With its position on a hill, it would have a commanding view south to San Gimignano as well as a panoramic view to the north. Surely Marcello did not mean to take them there. The soldiers who inhabited it would not welcome a woman and a child.

Two children.

"Stay here." Marcello put Antonia down, then nodded toward the tower. It was now close enough for Sofia to see smoke rising from a fire at its base. "I'll warn them."

"What is this place?" Antonia looked around curiously, her arms still holding the bundle tightly to her narrow chest. "Will we stay here? Will Mama and my brothers and sisters come here too?"

Sofia noticed that Antonia did not ask the question with any trace of fear or whining. She simply wanted to know the sequence of events. That her mother and her brothers and sisters would not soon follow did not occur to her.

"Marcello will keep us safe," Sofia said with more conviction than she felt. "And your mama will come when she can." That much was not a lie, at least. Caterina certainly would come from the city if she could.

If she lived.

Sofia shivered as the biting wind swirled her cloak around her. She longed to warm her hands against a fire and eat a few bites of bread.

"They are not welcome here!" A rough, angry voice rose above the wind. A few moments later, Sofia heard the sound of metal clashing and the grunts of men fighting. She grabbed Antonia's hand and pulled her behind a thicket. If Marcello were to be killed, her only hope would be to run back to the city. She saw the towers of San Gimignano bristling upon the hill across the valley—black teeth against a deep blue sky. Could she make it that far? Or could they stay the night in one of the huts full of death and contagion? Sleeping out of doors was preferable. Sofia gathered Antonia to her. The child Antonia carried woke and started to whimper.

"Keep it quiet," Sofia whispered. "It will give us away."

Like a little mother, Antonia bounced the child against her chest and made cooing noises. Sofia remembered how Brida had done the same with Matteo.

"Monna Sofia!" Marcello's voice was so close that Sofia jumped. She heard him stifle a groan as in the dim light he hurried toward them. He was limping.

"What is it? Marcello! Are you hurt?"

He waved away her question, then lifted Antonia and the baby and carried them up a steep rise. Sofia stumbled on the hem of her gown as she tried to follow. She stopped, took a deep breath, and willed her heart to calm its frantic beating. Whatever was lying in store for them at the top of the hill had to be better than cowering in the bushes in the cold spring night. Marcello led her through a door into the ground floor of the tower. She smelled moldy grain and horse dung but, thankfully, not the foul stink of pestilence. The evening light from the open door was not enough for her to see much beyond some shadowy forms that she took to be barrels and sacks.

"What is this place?" Antonia's young voice sounded too loud in the silent room. She looked up at Sofia. "I don't like it here."

"It's dry enough and will soon be warm when I build up the fire," Marcello said. "Antonia, give the child to Monna Sofia and come help me. Here are sticks that you can stack for the fire."

Without another word, Antonia held up her arms to Sofia, who had no choice but to take the child. It was so light she almost dropped it. Through the cloth she felt bones barely covered with flesh. Two eyes like flecks of black mud stared out from a wizened face. The creature was so weak it could not even cry. A glimmer of pity stirred in her heart. Gently, she pressed the child to her heart and surveyed her surroundings. Antonia was already opening the bundle of food and clothes and Marcello was dragging barrels in front of the door.

"Leave that!"

Antonia looked up, startled, her hands clasping the fine wooden casket containing the materials for Sofia's work. For a moment, Sofia was afraid she would drop it. "Please," she said, holding out one hand. "I didn't mean to be sharp. Put down the casket and help me find something to feed the child." She looked up at Marcello. "Have we water?"

"There's a full bucket in the corner. It should be enough to last until morning." He stepped toward the fire and, for the first time,

Sofia saw the long red gash across his thigh. The blood had stopped flowing, but she saw that the wound was deep.

"You *are* hurt."

Marcello's mouth curved into a smile. "So you see. The occupant of this place did not want to give it up easily."

"Was he a soldier? Will there be others?"

"He was nothing—a vagrant who was taking refuge here. He had no claim to it."

"What is this place?"

"It was a watchtower."

"Was?"

"I passed it coming back from Pisa with my master and saw it had been abandoned. The soldiers must have fled to avoid the pestilence. We should be safe enough here for a while."

"What if more soldiers come?"

"That is in God's hands, Monna Sofia. But I doubt He'll send any soldiers tonight." Marcello nodded at Antonia, who was attempting to soften a nub of bread with water to feed to the baby. "We have more pressing matters."

By the light of the flames filling the rough fire pit in the center of the room, Sofia set about making a space for them to sleep. She looked over at Antonia, who was sitting next to the fire, the child in her lap. She must be frightened, yet she did not appear so. She glanced up at Sofia and smiled shyly, but with a touch of pride. With the determination of a child, she had managed to feed the baby a few bites of soggy bread. Some of it had come back up and onto Antonia's shoulder, but she didn't appear to mind. She bounced and soothed the child until its eyes closed and it slept. Sofia realized she had not even asked if the child was a boy or a girl, and then realized that it didn't matter.

Antonia had done her best, but Sofia did not believe the child would see the morning.

❧

"The towers don't look like that!" The childish scorn in Antonia's voice caused Sofia to look up from her work.

"I'm not finished."

"They look like you're above them, but that can't be right." Antonia pointed across the valley to where the towers of the city shimmered in the late summer heat. "We are below them."

"I don't paint exactly what I see."

"Can you teach me?"

Sofia put down her brush and looked into the eyes of the determined child next to her. Antonia sat with the baby upon her lap. Thanks to Antonia's care, the baby was thriving. She was a girl whom Antonia insisted they call Caterina, after her mother. Sofia knew she could not object, but her heart pricked all the same at being so supplanted.

"I want to learn!" Antonia said again as she hoisted baby Caterina over her shoulder with practiced ease and rubbed her back while she continued to stare at Sofia.

"Put the baby to bed and then bring me a square of parchment from my casket. You'll start with drawing."

"I want to work with the colors, like you do."

"No, Antonia. You start with drawing or I don't teach you."

Antonia frowned and bit her lip, a gesture of defiance that Sofia had become accustomed to in the months they had spent at the tower. Sofia smiled to herself as she thought of the trouble poor Caterina must have had with Antonia. She was a headstrong child who resisted all attempts to tame her.

"I don't like that."

"I can see that you don't, Antonia, but still I am resolved. You must start with this piece of charcoal and learn to draw the rocks

321

and trees and beasts you see around you. As you get better, you can try drawing Marcello and Caterina and even me."

Antonia shook her head. "I don't want to draw *you*."

Sofia picked up her brush again. "You may suit yourself, *cara mia*. I have a great deal of work still to do on this panel and my colors are drying. Go and find Marcello and ask him to give you a chore. When you are ready to do what I ask, you may return."

Antonia glared at Sofia. "You're not kind to me. My mother always gave me what I wanted."

"I should imagine she did," Sofia said mildly.

Antonia stared across the valley at the towers of the city. "I wish I was with her."

"No, Antonia, you don't," Sofia said. "Your mother and your brothers and sisters are with God now. I told you that."

"*I* want to be with God."

"Not yet, *cara mia*. God wants you to stay with me a little longer. Your mother would want the same thing."

"How do *you* know what my mother would want? She's dead." Antonia's voice did not tremble and her large eyes remained dry.

"Take Caterina inside, and then you can help me with the green in this tree."

"Really?" Antonia jumped to her feet. "Thank you, Monna Sofia! I will be a great painter!" She adjusted the baby's weight in her arms. "Just like you."

"I thought you said my towers looked wrong," Sofia called as Antonia disappeared into the watchtower. She chuckled to herself and added some highlights to the tallest tower—the *torre grosso*. She wondered if the *podestà* who lived in the tower had survived the pestilence. Marcello sometimes went into the city at night to find food, and he came back with terrible stories of the death that stalked every street and every house. He learned that Caterina had followed Matteo and Paulina and all seven of her children to the grave. Even pompous Fra Angelo had died. The dead were stacked up in the piazzas, rotting in the hot sun. Even worse were Marcello's stories of how the living comported themselves. People copulated in the streets and raucous parties tore apart the long nights so the sick could not even die in peace.

"It is the end of the world," Marcello said one evening a few weeks after Sofia's first painting lesson with Antonia. He sat with Sofia at the base of the watchtower and watched the sunset cast long shadows over the towers of San Gimignano. "God has forsaken us."

"God and you have kept us safe, Marcello. Our father would have been proud."

"He was a great man."

"He was a man," Sofia said. She let the silence between them extend for many minutes before speaking again. "I believe he loved your mother."

"Yes."

"I am sorry, Marcello." A month ago, Marcello had returned from one of his forays into the city with the news that his mother, Emilia, Sofia's old nurse, had succumbed to the pestilence.

"My mother will be content enough in heaven," he said quietly. "This life wasn't kind to her. But I would have liked to see her one last time."

"I loved your mother too. When my own mother died, it was Emilia who cared for me."

Marcello said nothing for a long while. The towers were only just visible as ragged teeth against an indigo sky. "Did you know? Back then?"

Sofia shook her head. "I'm afraid not, Marcello. I was a selfish girl and never paid much attention to anything except my father's good opinion and the work he let me do. But even when I was small, I knew he did not love my mother. And then as I grew older, it never occurred to me to ask why."

"My mother wanted him to train me in his workshop."

"Really? And why weren't you?"

"Your father refused." Marcello managed a small smile. "I think he decided that one prodigy was more than enough."

"Ah! And yet I know he wished I had been a son."

"I should think he did, but that didn't mean he'd elevate the child of the nurse."

"Perhaps not."

They lapsed into silence, each lost in thought about a past they could not change. When darkness finally swallowed San Gimignano, Sofia and Marcello returned to the tower, where they found Antonia and Caterina already sleeping. Sofia lit the stub of a candle and held it over her child.

"The light may attract intruders," Marcello said.

"Just a moment longer. She is so beautiful."

"And as like her mother as any child I've ever seen."

Sofia laughed as she blew out the candle. "Have you known long?"

"Only a blind man would not know, and even then, your voices are very like. Forgive me, Sofia, but I cannot believe her father was your husband."

Sofia smiled into the darkness. "You're right, Marcello. Your sister is a sinner."

"We are all sinners. That's why God has brought this pestilence upon us."

Sofia did not reply as she folded her body around Antonia and the baby. God forgive her, but she no longer believed that God had forsaken her. Instead, she took great strength in the quiet joy that wrapped itself around her as she closed her eyes and listened to the sweet sound of her child breathing.

"That's my mother! You're painting my mother."

"Yes, Antonia. Your mother was a very brave woman." Sofia's throat constricted with the memory of Caterina praying next to her dying children. "Do you think it's like her?"

Antonia stood solemnly before the panel and gave it all her attention. Her brow furrowed and she bit her lip. She stared at the panel for so long that Sofia wondered if the likeness to Caterina upset her. The child had suffered so much. Placing her mother before her was perhaps more an act of cruelty than the kindness Sofia had intended. She picked up her brush and leaned forward.

"I'll change it."

"No!" The word rang out in the clear morning air—too sharp for such a young child. Antonia looked directly into Sofia's eyes. Tears glistened at the corner of each eye, but her mouth was set in a line of acceptance that kept grief in check.

"You have caught her, Monna Sofia." And then the baby cried and Antonia hurried off to tend her.

When Antonia was out of sight, Sofia let her own tears splash unheeded down her cheeks. She rarely indulged them. Each time he went into the city, Marcello brought back a report of another friend or acquaintance who had died of the pestilence. Sofia could not spare tears for them all. Fortunately, Delgrasso lived still and occasionally even sent pigments and other materials with Marcello. Many of the patrons fortunate enough to survive the pestilence were commissioning *Maestà* panels to aid with their devotions. Sofia was gratified with how Caterina's broad forehead and serene eyes lent a comforting stability to the little panel. She imagined it mounted on a private altar, candles flickering over the smooth features as the lady of the house whispered her Ave Marias.

Sofia packed away her materials in the casket. Tomorrow, she would teach Antonia how to apply a light wash to the folds of the Madonna's gown. The girl was showing a remarkable aptitude for the work—and she was younger by at least two years than Sofia had been when her father had first let her into his workshop. Already Antonia drew strong, clean lines that were far better than those drawn by many apprentices twice her age. Sofia looked forward to the day when she could take her daughter back to San Gimignano and start training her just as her father had trained her. With the work Delgrasso found for her, she would surely make enough to feed Antonia and the baby. Marcello would help her put the house to rights and he would likely be much in demand to help rebuild the town after so many deaths. When she was not painting, Sofia would devote herself to teaching Antonia. With proper training, the child had the potential to surpass her grandfather and, Sofia thought with a smile, even her mother.

Sofia shivered as she left the tower and stood quietly under the dawn sky, her gaze steady upon the opposite hill where the towers of San Gimignano rose against the horizon. The smothering heat of summer was finally loosening its grip on the parched country-side. Vivid red and black clouds arced high across a clear sky like silk ropes inset with beads of onyx. Against such a vast and fiery backdrop, the dozens of towers looked almost insignificant. Their number and size were nothing next to the glory of God's creation. To the east, the first rays of the rising sun faded the night sky to lemon and all around Sofia the trees and fields rose from the dawn mist.

Then the sun was up and the world washed in the golden light of a new day. Although already October, the sun promised a clear and steady light that would be perfect for painting. Her panel of the *Maestà* was coming along nicely. The face of the Madonna was complete, and now Sofia was ready to start upon the Child. Perhaps

Antonia would hold the baby so she could sketch her. Antonia rarely liked to stay still for more than a few moments, but perhaps she would be enticed by promises of more painting lessons later in the afternoon and maybe some reading. Her daughter was proving herself to be an eager student. She knew all the letters and spelled many simple words.

Marcello came out of the tower, his hair still tousled from sleep and stood beside her. She was about to say something about the beauty spread in front of them when he leaned forward, his hand shading his eyes against the sun. His muscles tensed.

"Get inside!"

"What for? The day is fair and I think will be warm. I see no need to spend it indoors."

With one swift movement, Marcello pushed her back into the tower and slammed the door. "Hide yourselves!"

Sofia stumbled into the room, cursing Marcello. She turned to open the door but found it barred from the outside. A knot of panic rose in her throat. For almost seven months they had continued at the tower unmolested, save for the occasional vagrant fleeing the pestilence in San Gimignano. Marcello usually fed them and directed them on their way. Once only was he obliged to add another body next to the shallow grave dug for the wretch who was occupying the tower when they'd arrived.

Antonia was starting to stir and Caterina was already up and lurching about the room in search of food. Sofia lifted her up and rested her on her hip. The baby tried to wriggle free, protesting loudly for Antonia, but Sofia held on to her. The noises she heard coming from outside the tower were enough to convince her that she had no time to lose.

"I hear horses!" Antonia sat up straight and looked around the room. "What's happening?"

"Get up and take Caterina."

Antonia scrambled quickly from the pallet she shared with Sofia and the baby and took Caterina from Sofia's arms. "Where can we go?"

Sofia could not help but feel a swell of pride as she looked at the determined face of her daughter. "Up," she said, pointing to the ladder that led from the ground floor to the next level. The tower consisted of just four levels. If Antonia made it to the top with the child, she would be safe, at least for a while. Sofia had complete confidence in Marcello. He was a fierce fighter and he would protect them.

"What about you?" Antonia asked.

"Leave the ladders and I will follow. Go!"

Sofia snatched up her painting of the towers and looked wildly around for the *Maestà*. She must have dropped it in the dirt when Marcello had forced her back into the tower. Outside, barely muffled by the thick walls, she heard Marcello's voice raised in a battle cry. She could not climb the ladder while holding the panel, but she could not bear to see it destroyed. A large square of leather that Marcello had used to carry provisions caught her eye. She seized it and hastily wrapped her panel, thanking God that she had managed to finish and varnish it just the month before. Her foot nudged a loose brick in the floor. She fell to her knees and used her hands to widen the hole enough to insert the panel. It only just fit. She replaced the brick and tamped it firmly with one foot. Above her, she heard Antonia cry out. She must have looked out the tiny window at the top of the tower and seen the fighting. Sofia lunged for the ladder. If she was to die, she would die with Antonia in her arms.

Rough voices were growing closer to the barred door. She paused, one foot on the lowest rung of the ladder, and listened intently. Surely Marcello would have drawn his sword by now. Few men could best him in close combat. She peered through the gloom. Something shone dully just near the door.

Her heart turned to stone as she recognized Marcello's sword.

When moments later two men burst through the door, they found a slim, beautiful woman standing in the middle of the room, her hands streaked with dust, her face impassive.

Sofia whispered to God to save her child just as one of the men struck her full in the face.

"No!"

For a moment, Sofia wondered if perhaps Marcello had survived after all. Perhaps he was rushing in to throw her attacker to the ground. She struggled to one elbow but saw only a tangle of legs and arms. She heard an oath, a grunt, and then stillness.

"Leave her!"

She blinked against the dust billowing up from the floor. A large hand closed around her wrist and pulled. She struggled, crying out. But the pressure increased and she let herself be dragged to her feet rather than risk snapping her wrist. And then another hand was behind her back, steadying her. She sensed a large man. She was helpless in his grip, like a child as young and weak as Antonia.

A wail, unmistakably that of a baby, cut through the sudden silence. Sofia closed her eyes and prayed. God could not take Antonia and Caterina. But then God had taken so many. What mattered a handful more? The hand that held her arm slackened its grip. Sofia slipped away and flung herself onto the ladder. Her skirts tangled around her legs, but she kicked them away. Behind her she heard a voice cry out, and she had the strange feeling she recognized it. Then, shaking her head, she concentrated all her will on pulling her hands and her feet up the ladder as quickly as God and her skirts would allow. She had just about reached the landing of the first level, had even placed one palm onto the wooden floor, when a large hand closed around her ankle.

"Sandro! Please!"

CHAPTER NINETEEN

. . . by their labors they may live in peace
and keep their families in this world, through grace,
and at the end, on high, through glory,
per infinita secula seculorum, AMEN.
—Cennini, *Il Libro dell'Arte*, Chapter XXXIII

Sofia could not stop shaking. She drew a rough blanket around her shoulders and pulled Antonia against her skirts. Night had fallen, and a fire crackled and danced before her. She had hit her head when he dragged her from the ladder and she was just waking up, her heart ready to burst.

"Is your head better?"

Sofia nodded as tears filled her eyes. He seemed to take up most of the space in the tower. Dirt caked his face and his hair was snarled and filthy. His huge hands cradled the sleeping Caterina. Sofia did not trust herself to speak. All she wanted to do was sit still and drink in the look of him, tracing through the grime the lines of the boy she loved.

"Where is Marcello?" she asked, although she knew the answer.

"I'm so sorry, Sandro." Francesco shook his head miserably. "He attacked us and . . . well . . ."

God had taken her father's son and given her back Francesco. The sparring of grief and joy threatened to wrench her in two.

"Is Marcello dead?" Antonia's clear young voice should not have to say such words.

"Yes, Antonia." Sofia stroked her daughter's head. "He died defending us."

"Against *him*?" Antonia thrust her chin at Francesco. "So why does he sit with us and hold Caterina?"

"Will you take her now?" Francesco held out the sleeping baby. "I can see you're a good sister and will care for her well while your mother and I talk."

"She is *not* my sister!" Antonia stood up and pushed herself away from Sofia's knee. "And *she* is not my mother. My mother's dead."

Francesco's eyes widened as he looked from Antonia to Sofia. He raised one eyebrow and Sofia nodded, then shook her head. She tried to struggle to her feet, her gown twisting around her, imprisoning her. "I must see to Marcello. He should be buried." She choked on her words.

Francesco laid a hand on her arm. "We've already done it, Sandro. Please. You can see for yourself in the morning, but for now, stay quiet and warm. The children need you."

"We?" For the first time, Sofia realized that the room held another body. She sat heavily, her heart sinking even lower when the flickering firelight brought into focus the coarse features of Pietro. He was lying faceup in the corner, snoring. Of all the people Francesco could have brought with him! Why hadn't Pietro died instead of Marcello? Which one had wielded the blow that had killed him? She knew she could never ask.

"How did you find me?"

"I'm not even sure I was looking for you. When we left Siena, I wanted only to escape the pestilence." He kissed the top of Caterina's head before handing her to Antonia. "So many bodies." When he looked up, Sofia saw tears slicing white lines through the dirt on his cheeks. She longed to ask him what had happened to Maestro Manzini and Monna Giuliana, but she didn't have the courage.

"Forgive me," he said, his voice catching and then growing stronger again. "I went back to my father's farm, but a family I didn't know was living there. They chased us away. Pietro and I slept rough for a few weeks and then found two horses and rode on to San Gimignano. I asked for you in the town, but no one remembered you—or at least no one would say."

"My head whirls to think of what you must have suffered, Francesco. Antonia and I came away from San Gimignano in the spring and, with Marcello's help, took refuge here. We found the baby abandoned after the pestilence had taken her family."

"Marcello? He was your man?"

"My half brother," Sofia said quietly. Antonia stared at her as she gathered Caterina into her arms, but Sofia kept her eyes on Francesco. What did it matter now?

"I am sorry, Sandro."

"You couldn't have known."

"Monna Sofia, why does he call you Sandro?" Antonia frowned at Francesco. "Her name's Monna Sofia. Sandro is a *boy's* name."

"And what is your name?"

"Antonia."

"That is a beautiful name for a beautiful girl."

Antonia peered up at Francesco in the firelight. "Did you kill Marcello?"

Francesco shook his head sadly. "I don't know. There was so much confusion. If I killed him, I did not mean to."

Antonia considered his answer for a few moments and then made up her mind. "I'm not afraid of you."

"I hope not. I'm very sorry about Marcello, but I'd like to be your friend."

"I don't know about that. Marcello was my friend and he's dead."

"Hush, Antonia!" Sofia said. "Take the baby and yourself to bed. You can talk more with Francesco in the morning. He'll be just as much our friend as Marcello was." Sofia stood. "Will you see to the fire?"

Francesco rose too, towering over Sofia. "I thank God to see you again."

"As do I, dear Francesco." She reached out one hand and placed it against his cheek. He shivered beneath her touch. "You will be surprised to know I have been painting again."

Francesco shook his head, grinning. "I'm not surprised to hear you are painting again, Sandro. I think I'd be more surprised if you were not."

"What will become of us, Francesco?"

The fire fizzled as his strong hand clasped her shoulder and he exhaled softly. "I don't know. What does your logic tell you? Can we live when so many have perished?"

"I hope so." She thought of the painting depicting the towers that she'd buried under the brick floor. If Francesco was able to get the panel to Delgrasso, some rich merchant who'd survived the pestilence might be willing to pay a few florins for it, even if it wasn't much good for prayers. And with Francesco's help, she could set herself up in San Gimignano with the children. Delgrasso would find her commissions, and Francesco had the skills to prepare the grounds and grind the colors.

She gathered the sleeping children close. God had sent her Francesco, and Francesco would keep them safe.

❧

The next morning the towers across the valley rose as gray fingers from a mist that wiped out the horizon. Sofia stood in the open doorway cut into the base of the tower. She was floating in a bottomless sea. She stepped forward and saw that her panel of the *Maestà* had been shattered in the fighting. One shard showed Caterina's round face staring serenely. She picked it up, fingering the rough edge, then followed a path to where a mound of freshly dug earth marked Marcello's grave. Francesco had fashioned a rough cross from two sticks. She knelt and placed her open palm on the earth. The grief was something separate from her—an entity that drifted off to the side—as shapeless and transparent as the angel that Marcello would become in heaven. She wanted to reach out and gather his spirit to her, weep for the fine man who had been her brother. But she felt only emptiness and the certainty that her heart would never again be whole.

And then her very soul leaped into her throat, threatening to choke her. She closed her eyes, then opened them again. A dull ache took hold of her right shoulder as her nostrils filled and her throat crawled with spikes. She held her hand up to the dawn light, opened and closed the fingers, stretching them and watching with wonder as they bent and moved with ease.

A spot not much larger than the halo encircling the head of one of her painted saints blackened the back of her hand. She knew what was next—racking pains and burst sores and odors that nauseated all who came near her. Sofia closed her eyes and saw her death in the bright points of light behind her eyelids.

Antonia!

Sofia's eyes flew open. She could not risk infecting Antonia. She would leave the tower now, before the child was awake, before Francesco could wake up and stop her. At the thought of Francesco, her resolve weakened. She had been so happy to see him again, so sure he would make everything right. Sofia rose to her feet and crept back into the tower. For a moment, she wondered about taking the panel of the towers from its hiding place and slipping into San

THE TOWERS OF TUSCANY

Gimignano to hand it over to Delgrasso. If he found a buyer, he could give her share to Francesco to help with the children. But no, she would make too much noise prying up the bricks.

In the dim light, she could just make out the two large humps that were Francesco and Pietro. Francesco was still snoring, but Pietro's open eyes gleamed in the half-light. She wanted to drive Marcello's sword through his eyes, but she merely shook her head and motioned for him to go back to sleep. She picked up a cloak and wrapped it around herself, then removed Giorgio's purse from a chink in the wall. She knelt next to Francesco and placed the purse near his hand. She wanted to reach out and touch him, but she knew she dared not risk waking him.

Antonia mumbled something in her sleep. How could she leave Antonia? Perhaps the sickness that was taking over her body would not kill her. Marcello had told her that some people in the town were surviving. The first signs of the scourge did not always mean death. Sofia reached out to stroke Antonia's forehead. But before she touched her, a hand gripped her wrist and wrenched her to her feet.

"Keep silent," Pietro hissed, then pushed her to the door.

Sofia wanted to cry out. Francesco would come to her aid in an instant, killing Pietro if he had to. Then a vision of Antonia covered in sores, moaning with fever and pain, her eyes clouded with fear, flashed before her. She had brought Antonia into the world. She could not be the one to take her from it. She let Pietro push her out into the morning air. He smelled vile—like he had rolled himself in a pile of fresh dung. "You don't need to push me. I will be gone."

Pietro said nothing as he walked behind her toward a steep path leading into the forest. "Go," he said when they were far enough along the pathway so the tower was no longer visible. "I will tell Francesco that you've run away."

"He won't believe you."

"I'll make him."

"What of the children? Will you make sure they're cared for?"

"Francesco will."

"And you?"

For a moment, Sofia glimpsed anguish in Pietro's eyes. Did he regret his betrayal? Had the florins Giorgio paid him been enough to soothe his own hurt?

"Sandro," he began, then stopped, corrected himself. "Monna Sofia."

"Yes?" Sofia did not want to believe Pietro was the last person she would see on God's earth.

"I, ah, I . . ." He shook his head.

If it hadn't been for Pietro, she might still be in Siena, under Manzini's protection and free to paint. She let her anger well up inside, brought it forward to smolder and spark. Pietro had ruined her life, condemned her to obscurity. Under Manzini, her reputation would have grown until she got her own workshop, been her own man. She could have kept her disguise forever, taken back her father's name. Sandro Barducci.

It could have been.

And if it hadn't been for Pietro, she would never have given birth to Antonia or Matteo or seen Marcello again. Sofia stretched out her arm, almost touched him.

"No!" he cried. He shoved her hard enough to send her sprawling into a pile of autumn leaves. But just as he turned away, his rough voice cut the morning air.

"Forgive me."

And then he was striding back along the pathway to the tower.

"Go with God, Pietro," she whispered. And as she said it, a peace floated down and swathed her burning flesh in folds of cool air. She kept still for a time, inhaling the sweet decay. Already the fever was crawling through her body. She hoped she'd be one of the lucky ones who went quickly. Some of them needed days to scream their way to death.

Through the trees she could see the towers of her city rising from the mist. Sofia thought of her hidden panel and of the solemn face of her Antonia, of little Matteo, who did not deserve the father she gave him, of her own father and of Marcello, and finally of Francesco, who must now be father to Antonia.

With a gasp of pain, she struggled to her knees, her hands thrust deep into the crackling leaves. She must rise, must make her way into the forest to die under the trees. She must . . .

The warmth of Matteo's hand on her cropped head brought a smile to Sofia's face. She had not thought of him for so many years. Why was that? He was drawing her close, whispering something in her ear, tickling her skin with his breath. She smelled egg yolks and the dense earthiness of her pigments—the tools of her trade, her life-blood. In a moment, he would coax her around to face him, gather her to his chest like he always did when he wanted to distract her from her work. The velvet of his tunic reminded her of a perfect *gesso sottile*, smooth as warm honey from hours of mixing. What was he saying to her? His voice was different—deeper, younger. And why was her skin burning, no longer cool against the velvet? She was one of Marcello's rabbits caught for supper and stretched across an open fire to cook.

A bolt of pain opened her mouth in a scream.

"She's waking up. Hand me that cloth, Pietro."

"Leave her."

"No."

More than anything in the world, Sofia wanted to open her eyes, to look into Francesco's face one more time. How could she have mistaken him for Matteo? No man had loved her more than Francesco. But darkness sealed her eyes as she breathed only for the pain coursing through her blood in streams of fire.

"Sandro." Francesco's voice faltered.

When had his voice become the voice of a man? Where was the boy she'd taken from the ashes of his dead family? She must open her eyes, show him she knew him at the last. She felt a hand on her forehead; something wet dropped onto her hot cheek. Was Antonia near? She should not see her mother like this. Sofia wanted to tell Francesco to take care of Antonia, to keep her safe, and little Caterina too. And the painting. Yes, the one with the towers wrapped in leather. He must take that to Siena.

"She's gone, Francesco. Leave her. We must be off."

If only her eyes would open so she could tell him. Another wave of agony, this one fiercer than any that had gone before, forced another scream to pierce the air. She felt Francesco's lips on her cheek, smelled the dirt on his face. As her scream faded, she heard his sobs. She should comfort him. She tried lifting her arm, but it lay useless at her side, a separate, lifeless thing.

Slivers of gold, like the tiny leaves she layered onto her panels to create haloes, danced in the darkness behind her closed eyes. She should like to paint haloes again.

And then, with one last, blessed sigh, Sofia let go of the earth with its sweet-smelling leaves and its bright skies, and soared to the towers rising from the city of her birth.

❧

The girl with the eyes of the woman stared across the valley at the towers. There was so much she did not understand. Francesco was kind to her; Pietro frightened her; little Caterina needed her. And what of Monna Sofia? She had promised to teach her how to paint, had already let her use a tiny brush to add flecks of red to a tree in the little painting of the towers.

And now she was dead, just like her mother and her father, her brothers and sisters.

Behind her, she heard Pietro talking. She hated him. He stank and looked at her and the baby as if they were as much use as two worms wriggling in the black earth.

"What are we to do with the daughter and the babe?"

Antonia sat down hard in the dirt and bowed her head. Daughter. What did he mean? Antonia's mother was dead. That's what Monna Sofia had told her months and months ago when they first came to the tower. She didn't understand. Everything was wrong. She wanted her mother, her *real* mother, to fold her into her soft arms and sing to her. Monna Sofia was *not* her mother. Horrible Pietro was wrong.

"We will take them with us to Siena," Francesco was saying. "Maestro Manzini was alive when we left. If Monna Giuliana also survived, she'll be glad to take in Sandro's daughter. This pestilence can't last through the winter."

"It's as good an idea as any," Pietro grunted. "And I'll be glad of Manzini's warm workshop. But I will not trouble myself with the brats."

"You won't have to."

Siena. Monna Sofia had told her about Siena. She'd made it sound like the most wonderful place on earth, with more towers even than San Gimignano. Antonia raised her eyes to look again upon the towers of the only home she had ever known. Why couldn't everything stay the same? Caterina started to cry. She was sitting on her bottom in the dirt, her tiny fist clenched, her face red. Antonia scrambled to her feet and gathered the child to her thin chest.

Francesco was coming toward her, his arms outstretched to take Caterina, his mouth smiling although his eyes were sad.

"Are you ready, Antonia? Do you want me to carry you too?"

Antonia stared up at Francesco towering above her and shook her head. She looked back at the squat tower, its gray stone glowing in the afternoon sun. Antonia had been almost happy there with only the baby to care for and Marcello to play with her and talk to her and all of Monna Sofia's attention when she wanted it—so different from being one of eight in her mother's house. She didn't want to leave.

"We must go now, Francesco, get into the forest before the light fades."

Antonia was being hoisted into Francesco's arms. His jaw was rigid, his eyes narrowed as he gazed across the valley. He tightened his grip on her, holding her close to his chest next to Caterina.

"I can walk," Antonia said.

"Perhaps later," Francesco said. "You must be brave now. Like Monna Sofia." His voice broke and Antonia felt his shoulders heave.

"Did you love Monna Sofia?" she asked.

"Very much. Now hush. We must start on the road to Siena."

Antonia laid her head against Francesco's broad shoulder and closed her eyes. There was so much she did not understand, but at least, for now, she knew she was safe.

EPILOGUE

New York City, May 2014

LOT 54

Workshop of Antonio Barducci
(active San Gimignano c. 1320–1340)
Cityscape (possibly San Gimignano)
tempera on panel
8½ x 12¼ in. (21.6 x 31 cm.)
CIRCA: 1345–1350 San Gimignano, Tuscany
ESTIMATE: 40,000 to 50,000 USD

Marla Ashland-Willoughby knew she had to have the little panel of impossibly slender towers painted in bright pinks and greens and contrasting grays. She would place it in the sunny front room overlooking the valley and enjoy it every morning while she sipped her cappuccino. Signor Carelli, the art dealer in Florence who was helping her build Matt's collection of fourteenth-century Tuscan art, agreed that the panel would be a good buy. He even thought it might have been done by the same person who had painted the lovely Nativity panel that Matt had given Marla on their last anniversary. That panel had been passed down through the centuries from the Ardinghelli clan, one of the two principal families warring for supremacy over the Tuscan town of San Gimi-gnano in the fourteenth century. Marla particularly loved the tower painted in one corner of that panel. This new panel of the city from a distance would make the perfect complement.

Matt would love it. No. Matt would have loved it. Sometimes Marla wondered if she would ever stop forgetting.

The two curators in charge of Early Renaissance acquisitions for the auction house could not agree on an attribution. One of the experts had dated the panel to around 1340, from the workshop of Antonio Barducci of San Gimignano; the other attributed the panel to Luca Manzini, a mediocre painter from Siena who had produced only a handful of really competent works, mostly from the early 1340s. Fortunately, the lack of a firm attribution would keep the price low. Marla could go as high as $150,000, but with an estimate of $40,000 to $50,000, she was confident the panel would be hers.

While she waited for the auction to start, Marla flipped through the glossy catalogue supplied by the New York auction house to find information about what she already considered *her* panel. It had been discovered in 1850 when a wealthy family from Florence built a villa over the ruins of a thirteenth-century watchtower across the valley from the Tuscan town of San Gimignano.

Her villa. She smiled and then sighed as the familiar sadness enveloped her, cutting her off from the world that Matt had left with such brutal speed. The counselors and well-wishers and even strangers all said that time would dull the sadness. They were right, but time couldn't take it away. She and Matt had bought the villa together, not two months before the stench of unspeakable grief had wiped out the tang of autumn leaves crunching underfoot along the campus pathways.

The wooden panel had been wrapped in leather when it was found and was remarkably well preserved. It had remained in the family's collection until just before World War I, when a Mr.

Samuelson from Chicago acquired it. In the 1960s, his heirs donated the panel to a museum in New York. Forty years later, in 2008, the museum responded to cutbacks to its curatorial program by selling off most of its collection of Early Renaissance and Late Medieval Italian art. When the private collector who acquired the panel died, his heirs put the panel up for auction. Marla wondered if any of that long string of collectors had actually loved the panel. She would give it the home it deserved.

The silver-haired auctioneer with a British voice that could melt steel announced Lot 54. Marla gripped her paddle. Auctions made her nervous. Matt had loved them. Even in the early days, when he barely had enough money for coffee, he would slip into the back row to watch. When finally the money flooded into their lives, bringing with it such joy at first and then such burdens, he acquired several good pieces, many of which he featured on the television show that popularized art history and had made him famous. Marla hated that show. She blamed it for taking Matt away from her. If it hadn't been for the millions of fans all demanding a piece of the handsome Matthew Ashland, she would still have him.

Signor Carelli had offered to bid on her behalf over the phone, but Marla knew Matt would think her a coward. She was in New York tidying up the last strands of the estate and had no real excuse to keep her from attending the auction.

"We'll start the bidding at forty-five thousand dollars." The auctioneer nodded at someone to Marla's right. "Thank you, sir." He lifted an elegant eyebrow. "Fifty thousand?"

Marla flipped up her paddle.

"Thank you, madam. May we go to fifty-five thousand? Yes? We have fifty-five on the phone. Sixty thousand?"

Marla raised her paddle again. Her heart raced. Who were the other people bidding? She swiveled her eyes in the direction the auctioneer was looking, but saw no hand rise from the crowd.

"We have sixty thousand on the phone. May we go to eighty thousand? Yes?" He looked at Marla, but she wasn't fast enough. His eyes flicked across the room. "Not yours, madam. Thank you, sir. I have eighty. May we have one hundred? Yes? Thank you. We have one hundred thousand dollars on the phone. How about one hundred and ten? Do I hear one hundred and ten thousand dollars?"

Marla wished she'd gone for $100,000, but it was too late. She raised her paddle quickly and had the satisfaction of seeing the auctioneer incline his head toward her and nod.

"Thank you, madam."

The three-way bidding continued, spiraling the cost of the panel up and up until Marla's limit of $150,000 was reached and then quickly exceeded. Neither of the other bidders showed any signs of backing down. To continue bidding, she would have to postpone the renovations to the villa. But what did it matter now? Matt wouldn't have cared about new plumbing and granite countertops. He loved the villa the way it was—on the verge of crumbling back to the Middle Ages. What she would never do, even if the money ran out, was sell any of Matt's art collection, especially not the lovely panel of the Annunciation attributed to Luca Manzini from the Sienese school. She and Matt had bought that one together from his first big check.

Marla *needed* the panel of the towers. She couldn't say how she knew, but she was convinced that the same hand that had infused the Annunciation with such life had also painted the towers. And Matt would certainly approve. Such a secular work was very rare from a period when almost every piece of art depicted a religious subject.

"We're at two hundred thousand dollars. It is with you, madam." The auctioneer looked over at her opponent and waited. Two hundred and ten, sir? No?" He glanced over at the bank of phones. "Do I hear two hundred and ten?" He waited. A few nervous coughs broke the silence in the room. The price was high for a small panel with no firm attribution.

"Going once at two hundred thousand dollars." Pause. "Going twice." Pause. Then the sweet sound of the gavel hitting the auctioneer's desk. "Sold, for two hundred thousand dollars." He nodded to Marla and allowed a smile to play across his normally impassive features. "Well done, madam."

Marla felt as if she had just run a marathon. How could Matt have possibly enjoyed this? She waited quietly through another few lots and then edged her way out of the room into the empty lobby.

Jet lag awakened Marla very early on her first morning back at the villa. She padded across the cool tile floor of her bedroom and retrieved the panel from her suitcase. She stripped away the auction house's careful packaging and held the panel at arm's length. The painted city floated above a dull brown clearing broken by just five trees. The trees in the distance were almost the same size as the trees in the foreground. Perspective barely existed. The city was a fantasy city with no signs of human habitation. It was almost as if the unknown painter meant to show a dead city.

Marla moved to the window and gazed across the valley to the towers of San Gimignano on the opposite hill. Slashes of light the color of fresh blood pierced the roiling black clouds. Matt's blood had been a very dark red—like claret. Even the emergency room nurse had noticed and commented. Marla remembered the surprise in the nurse's voice—as if she didn't see blood every day. She also remembered how her own anger had sliced through her shock with such power that she still felt the primal urge to lash out and kill. The Italians called it *vendetta*. The grief counselor told her she must find forgiveness in her heart if she was to get beyond the grief. Marla shook her head at the thought. The anger still kept her warm at night, kept Matt close to her. If she lost the anger, she would be admitting that the disturbed young man who had sprayed bullets around the lecture hall like so much spittle that autumn morning deserved redemption.

The clouds swirled and parted in the dawn wind. The red faded to orange and then to purest lemon yellow. For a moment, the whole world stopped and waited. The anguish she kept at bay with relentless activity edged into the silence. The familiar nausea swelled, receded, swelled again. The ancient wood of the panel was alive in her hands. She looked at the towers and saw Matt's face on that last morning. Why had he thrown himself in front of her when the boy had opened fire? Why had he loved her so much? She didn't deserve it.

Then, with an almost obscene abruptness, the sun burst above the horizon. It glinted off the towers, almost blinded her with its brilliance. She closed her eyes against the glare and fire burst beneath her eyelids.

She heard a whisper, felt a light touch on the hand that gripped the panel.

Grazie mille.

A thousand thanks.

Her eyes popped open and the sunlight streamed in. Who had spoken? Matt? No! A woman's voice—low and urgent. What did she want?

Marla carefully set the panel on the wide windowsill and folded her hands over her stomach. She smiled at the heel pushing against her hand. Matt had been so excited when they heard the news— just days before the gunman took him. Four months ago now. She looked from the panel to the towers across the valley. Did her heart have room to forgive?

And then, for the first time since Matt had left her alone, a peace descended, as profound as the dawn. She fought against it for a moment. She didn't want it, didn't deserve it. She wanted the anger, needed the anger. And yet slowly, with the heat of the new day's sun, the peace penetrated her bones to temper the sadness with a quiet joy. She had survived. Her child would live and be loved.

And then she knew without knowing how she knew that the voice belonged to the painter who had left her own soul upon the panel for Marla to find.

And that Matt would always love her.

AUTHOR'S NOTE

The hill town of San Gimignano is justifiably famous for its thirteen towers that still march dramatically across the Tuscan skyline. But in its heyday in the fourteenth century, the skyline bristled with more than seventy towers. The idea for *The Towers of Tuscany* grew from my musings about what such a small town must have looked like with so many towers. I couldn't even imagine it! I began the novel with the idea that the main character, Sofia, would paint a landscape featuring the towers of San Gimignano, even though I was well aware that painters during the fourteenth century almost never depicted secular subjects. But as Sofia began to come alive for me, the idea of her painting the towers just wouldn't go away. I had to find some way to make the story plausible. Fortunately, help arrived.

Not long after I started the novel, I discovered that two amazing artists in San Gimignano had created a scale model of the town as it existed in the year 1300. Imagine my delight! Now it was possible for me to see what the city might have looked like in the 1340s. I had my flight booked to Italy before I'd even closed the webpage for San Gimignano 1300 (see www.sangimignano1300.com). The morning I spent at the San Gimignano 1300 museum with the very well-informed young guide was pure bliss. A few days later, I took a bus to Siena and visited the lovely Pinacoteca Nazionale, an art museum that features room after room after room of paintings from the fourteenth century. Almost every painting is a *Maestà*—a Madonna and Child. In the fourteenth century, the Madonna was a popular subject, more popular, by far, than Christ. The Madonna's popularity waned in the fifteenth and later centuries, possibly as a result of Church fears that she was becoming a bit too influential. In a dimly lit corner of the Pinacoteca, almost lost among all those staring Madonna eyes, I found a tiny panel depicting a town of towers on the shores of the sea. Called *City by the Sea (Città sul mare)*, the panel is attributed to Sassetta and dates to the fifteenth century. Later, I read that some experts dispute this attribution and believe the panel was painted by Ambrogio Lorenzetti in 1340. Lorenzetti also painted the magnificent fresco *Effects of Good and Bad Government on the Town and Country* that Sofia sees on a visit to Siena with her father and that I had seen the day before in Siena's beautiful Palazzo Pubblico. For the purposes of my novel, I decided to go with an attribution of 1340 for the little panel of the towers, with apologies to Sassetta. As far as I was concerned, Lorenzetti was not going to be the only fourteenth-century Tuscan artist to depict towers in a landscape.

I hope readers of *The Towers of Tuscany* decide to learn more about the art of fourteenth-century Tuscany. Figures and buildings are flattened and stylized, perspective is only hinted at, and the warm colors are redolent of the Tuscan sun. Check out the work of Giotto, Duccio, Martini, Lorenzetti, and Lippo Memmi. In my opinion, the more florid realism of paintings done a century later in the Renaissance lacks the intense, naive, and yet wonderfully sophisticated soul of paintings created in the decades before plague bisected the fourteenth century and changed Europe forever.

In the course of my research, I visited both San Gimignano and Siena and consulted many books. I owe a great debt to the seminal work of Cennino d'Andrea Cennini. Quotes from his work *Il Libro dell'Arte* (the edition I reference was translated by Daniel V. Thompson) begin every chapter in the novel and provide a wonderful glimpse into the workshops of Late Medieval and Early Renaissance painters. Other very useful books include:

Boccaccio, Giovanni. *The Decameron*. Oxford: Oxford University Press, 1351?, 1993. Translation by Guido Waldman.

Cole, Bruce. *The Renaissance Artist at Work: From Pisano to Titian*. London: John Murray, 1983.

Dean, Trevor. *The Towns of Italy in the Later Middle Ages*. New York: Manchester University Press, 2000.

Frugoni, Chiara. *A Day in a Medieval City*. Chicago: University of Chicago Press, 2005.

Jansen, Katherine L., Joanna Drell, and Frances Andrews, eds. *Medieval Italy: Texts in Translation*. Philadelphia: University of Pennsylvania Press, 2009.

Kelly, John. *The Great Mortality: An Intimate History of the Black Death, the Most Devastating Plague of All Time*. New York: Harper Perennial, 2005.

Maginnis, Hayden B.J. *The World of the Early Sienese Painter*. Philadelphia: University of Pennsylvania Press, 2001.

Norman, Diana. *Painting in Late Medieval and Renaissance Siena*. New Haven and London: Yale University Press, 2003.

Ward, Jennifer. *Women in Medieval Europe 1200–1500*. London: Pearson Education, 2002.

Wiesner-Hanks, Merry E. *Women and Gender in Early Modern Europe*. New York: Cambridge University Press, 2008.

QUESTIONS FOR DISCUSSION

1. How does Sofia change and develop over the course of the novel?

2. How do Sofia's interactions with the principal men in her life—Giorgio, her father, Francesco, and Salvini—reveal her character?

3. Manzini quotes a real law to Sofia after seeing a young woman whipped in the streets. What does this law tell us about gender-bending in medieval Italy?

4. Salvini is already half in love with Sofia before he discovers she is a woman. Would his love for her have been as intense if he'd never had the chance to know her first as a boy?

5. Did Sofia make the right choice when she refused to marry Salvini? Why or why not?

6. So far as we know, the only women who painted in fourteenth-century Italy were nuns who illuminated manuscripts in isolated convents. There is no documented evidence of women painting alongside men in artists' workshops. However, is it plausible that women could have painted and participated in other professions ostensibly closed to them? Why or why not?

7. Like many artists of the period, Sofia's father traveled extensively to fulfill commissions. He took his precocious daughter

with him on many of these trips. What are some ways in which Sofia's travel experience (unusual for a woman at the time) might have colored her worldview?

8. During the time period in the novel, humanist thinkers such as Petrarch were starting to question established orders. Sofia's father was both a thinker and a painter. He taught his daughter about logic and about thinking for herself. How do her father's attitudes about the Church, beauty, logic, and the role of women influence the choices Sofia makes?

9. Although Sofia learned about logic from her father, she lived in an intensely religious time where angels and demons were considered real, not imagined. How do Sofia's beliefs influence the choices she makes?

10. Although Sofia and Caterina represent opposites—the rebel and the conformer—both women find fulfillment. How are they ultimately very similar?

11. The theme of the novel is the triumph of the creative spirit. How is this theme realized for Sofia and her daughter, Antonia, in the fourteenth century, and for Marla in the twenty-first century?

12. What is the significance of the painting of the towers of San Gimignano that Sofia hides at the end of the novel and that is purchased by Marla in the Epilogue? Consider that secular art was almost unknown during this period. The vast majority of all art produced depicted religious subjects. Sofia had seen some secular-themed works in the Palazzo Pubblico in Siena. How might her viewing of these works have influenced her choice of subject when she took refuge at the tower outside San Gimignano during the plague?

13. At the beginning of 1348, more than thirteen thousand people lived in San Gimignano. Six months later, only four thousand people remained. Other communities in Europe lost up to 90

THE TOWERS OF TUSCANY

percent of their inhabitants. As far as many people were con-cerned, the plague was the end of the world. Of course, the world survived. How is the journey of Sofia's final painting of the towers a metaphor for survival and the healing power of art?

14. Antonia goes with Francesco to Siena. What do we hope might happen to her?

15. In the Epilogue, Sofia's painting of the towers is described as having no firm attribution but is presumed to be a particularly fine example of the work of Manzini or Barducci. How might the value of the painting change if it could be proved that it was the work of a woman? Would it matter?

16. Bruce Cole, in *The Renaissance Artist at Work*, writes, "Our notion of a work of art would have been unintelligible to some-one living in the Renaissance [or the Middle Ages]" (35). Cole states that "art was created for practical purposes" and had to be "well-conceived, well-wrought, and long lasting. [The art-ist's] creation was perceived not only as a *Virgin and Child* or a *Resurrection of Christ* but as an object with a function, a thing made by a skilled craftsman for a specific commission" (32). How does this attitude toward art differ from our twenty-first-century notion of art as intensely individual and "original"?

ACKNOWLEDGMENTS

Writing a novel is a leap of faith—a very long leap of faith in my case. Fortunately for me, many wonderful people propelled my leap and ensured a soft landing. Thanks first to my intrepid group of women friends (whom I've known since childhood) for being the first people to listen to me read excerpts from early drafts of *The Towers of Tuscany*: Cathy Hamre, Selinde Krayenhoff, Jean Leckie, and Elizabeth Wilson. Your encouragement means more to me than I can say. Thanks also to the many other good friends and family members who have patiently listened to me ramble on about the novel in its various iterations, particularly Pam Conrad, Paul Cram, Carol Grieves, Katharine Vingoe-Cram, and Stephanie Williams.

And now to the pros who helped me whip *The Towers of Tuscany* into shape. First up is Cathleen With, my mentor in Betsy Warland's Vancouver Manuscript Intensive program. Cathleen's good humor and encouragement were golden. Thanks also to Betsy Warland for getting the ball rolling with her insightful line editing. What a gift she gave me! A huge thank you to Dr. Efrat El-Hanany, who generously shared her expertise about fourteenth-century Italian art and read the manuscript twice to ferret out historical errors. If any remain, they are my fault. Thank you also to Mark MacDonnell of the Dorotheum auction house in Vienna for answering my questions about valuing a painting from fourteenth-century Siena, and to the wonderful staff at San Gimignano 1300, a museum containing an amazing scale model of the town of San Gimignano as it looked in 1300. Production of the first edition of the novel involved the talents of cover designer John Dowler on Bowen Island, gorgeous photographer Heather Pennell, awesome proofreader Davina Haisell, and most especially the eagle eye of copy editor extraordinaire Heather Sangster of Strong Finish in Toronto. Thank you! Thank you! I'd also like to thank Danielle Marshall and the dream team at Lake Union Publishing for all their hard work in bringing the new edition of *The Towers of Tuscany* to the world.

And finally, I would not be able to write a word if it wasn't for the constant, ongoing, and unconditional support of my beautiful daughter, Julia Simpson; my incredible mom, Ruby Cram, who also read many drafts of the novel and provided invaluable critiques; and my soul mate, partner, and best friend, Gregg Simpson. Love you!

ABOUT THE AUTHOR

Before her debut as a critically acclaimed author of historical fiction, Carol M. Cram wrote dozens of bestselling college textbooks for courses in computer applications and communications. She served on the faculty at Capilano University in North Vancouver, Canada, for over two decades, and also facilitated numerous workshops for corporate and government clients in her role as vice president of Clear Communications Consultants. Carol holds an MA in drama from the University of Toronto and an MBA from Heriot Watt University in Edinburgh. She lives on Bowen Island near Vancouver, British Columbia, with her husband, painter Gregg Simpson, where she is very active in the local arts community.